McAlistair's Fortune

Alissa Johnson

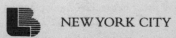

LEISURE BOOKS   NEW YORK CITY

*For Jo, Sondi, and Tracey, because you always stand beside me,
even when you're not quite sure where I am.*

A LEISURE BOOK®

June 2009

Published by

Dorchester Publishing Co., Inc.
200 Madison Avenue
New York, NY 10016

ISBN 10: 0-8439-6251-8
ISBN 13: 978-0-8439-6251-2
E-ISBN: 978-1-4285-0680-0

The name "Leisure Books" and the stylized "L" with design are
trademarks of Dorchester Publishing Co., Inc.

Printed in the United States of America.

10 9 8 7 6 5 4 3 2 1

Visit us on the web at www.dorchesterpub.com.

"You don't understand men."

Evie spluttered a bit before responding. "I've no trouble at all understanding Whit and Alex."

"They're family."

She crossed her arms over her chest, a defensive posture that pressed the soft mounds of her breasts up another tantalizing inch. McAlistair dragged his eyes to her face, watched as she caught her plump bottom lip with her small, white teeth. It was too much. The need that had been clawing painfully under his skin like a wild animal, tore free. He took a step toward her and gained a wicked satisfaction at the way her eyes widened and her breath hitched. "They don't want to kiss you," he growled.

Her arms fell to her sides. "Well, no, not—"

He took another step and had her retreating. Oh, he liked that. He liked the unfamiliar power in having the upper hand. For once, *for once*, she could be the one to back away. "They don't think about it, every bloody second of the day."

"I…I should hope not."

He stalked her mercilessly. "They don't imagine what it would be like to have you alone, like this. Like the night in the woods. At the inn."

She stopped backing away and swallowed hard. "Why should you only imagine it?" she whispered unsteadily. "You know I want to kiss you."

He swallowed a groan and reached up slowly to rub the pad of his thumb across her bottom lip. "A man's imagination extends beyond kissing."

Other *Leisure* books by Alissa Johnson:

TEMPTING FATE
AS LUCK WOULD HAVE IT

McAlistair's Fortune

❊ One ❊

*M*iss Evie Cole had long ago come to the conclusion that, contrary to popular opinion, ignorance was not bliss.

There were, after all, a great many miserable fools in the world.

Furthermore, *she* was a perfectly happy young woman, and no one who knew her well would ever accuse her of ignorance. She was always in the know.

She made absolutely certain of it.

Just as she was making certain of it now, crouched outside the thick burl wood doors to the Haldon Hall library, her weight shifted to her stronger leg and one dark brown eye peering through the keyhole. Probably she should feel a bit guilty at eavesdropping on a private conversation. But having found herself the subject of that conversation, she experienced not so much guilt as fascination, amusement, and no small amount of annoyance at having stumbled across the scene too late to ascertain all the details.

What she understood well enough, however, was that her aunt, the dowager Lady Thurston, and two family friends, Mr. William Fletcher and Mrs. Mary Summers, were currently sequestered on the other side of those lovely old doors, arguing over how best to go about finding the stubborn Evie Cole a husband.

It was nearly as amusing as it was insulting. Nearly.

Mr. Fletcher, seated on the small settee in the center of

the room, leaned forward and spoke with some excitement. "What better way to win a lady's heart than to rescue her from certain danger? I can have a threatening letter drawn up and sent to Evie from London next week. Have her young man here the following day to protect her. It's fast, simple, and effective."

Clearly impressed with neither Mr. Fletcher's scheme nor his enthusiasm, Lady Thurston added a deliberate dollop of milk to a cup of tea and calmly handed it to Mrs. Summers. "It will never work, William."

He settled his stout frame back against the cushions. "Have you a better plan?"

"The plan, though I do not approve of it, is not the problem." She poured her own cup. "The problem is the objective itself—it simply cannot be done."

"You cannot make someone fall in love," Mrs. Summers pointed out, straightening her rail-thin shoulders.

"Least of all those two," Lady Thurston added. "I am not at all certain they're well suited. What's more, Evie has categorically refused to marry."

"I refuse to accept that." Mr. Fletcher ran a hand through what remained of his hair. "I made a promise to a man on his deathbed."

Mrs. Summers sent him a pitying glance. "You were tricked into a promise by a man who would—were he still alive—be the first to admonish you for taking this match-making business quite so seriously. The late Duke of Rock-eforte was a reasonable sort, despite his penchant for jests. I very much doubt he expected you to succeed in marrying off five children."

"You weren't so dismissive when it was your Sophie we set out to match. Nor you," he added, turning to Lady Thurston, "when it was Whit and Mirabelle."

"Yes, but that was Sophie, Whit, and Mirabelle," Lady Thurston returned evenly. "Not Evie."

"Nevertheless, the promise was made, and I intend to keep it." Mr. Fletcher held out against the ensuing silence for a solid thirty seconds—an impressive show of fortitude to Evie's mind. She'd been subjected to that knowing silence from the inestimable Lady Thurston. It was daunting.

"I intend to at least try," Mr. Fletcher finally added.

Lady Thurston gave a delicate shrug of her shoulders. "If you feel you must."

"I do. I'll begin by—"

Evie would never be entirely certain of how, exactly, Mr. Fletcher intended to begin, because the sound of laughter and approaching footsteps necessitated her immediate retreat to the small parlor across the hall. It was doubtful that the intruding staff would tattle, but it was best to not take chances.

No matter, she'd been privy to the most important bits of the conversation, or at least enough of them to be quite confident that she was, once again, very much in the know.

As Evie slipped out the side door of the parlor, Lady Thurston and Mrs. Summers patiently listened as William Fletcher finished outlining his plan, again.

Lady Thurston smoothed the pale green silk of her gown. A diminutive woman with a soft voice and round, rosy cheeks, she was sometimes taken, by those who didn't know her well, for a kindly sort who perhaps needed a bit of looking after.

A mistaken impression invariably short-lived.

"Your plan is certainly . . . detailed," she allowed when William finished. "Unfortunately, it is also poorly conceived. Such a scheme would only serve to frighten Evie. I will not allow it. And I will not agree to using her work with mistreated women as the source of your faux threat. It touches too close to the truth."

"But—"

"She is quite right," Mrs. Summers cut in. "Evie faces very real danger as a result of her work. Adding a contrived threat would be unconscionable."

William blanched. "Unconscionable seems a bit—"

"Did I tell you what happened to Mrs. Kirkland last summer?" Lady Thurston asked, turning to Mrs. Summers.

Mrs. Summers nodded sadly. "Exposed by the very woman she sought to help."

"And her home burned to the ground the very next day. She was lucky to have escaped."

Mrs. Summers took a sip of her tea. "The authorities ruled it an accident."

Lady Thurston gave a most genteel sniff. "Shameful."

"That *is* most unfortunate." William tried again. "But I hardly intend to start fires or—"

Mrs. Summers shook her head. "It is no good, William. Not only does your plan go too far, the strategy itself is flawed. In order for the ruse to work, Evie would need to believe in the threat. If she believes in the threat, she will be too preoccupied to notice the attentions of a young man. No sensible young woman would be thinking of love whilst her life was in jeopardy."

"Sophie did," he pointed out quickly, rather surprised he was able to get a word in edgewise.

Mrs. Summers pursed her lips thoughtfully. "True, but Sophie, though I adore her, is not always the most sensible of women."

Lady Thurston nodded in pleasant agreement.

William scowled. "And you're absolutely certain Evie is a sensible young woman?"

"Yes," both women answered simultaneously.

"Blast." He frowned a moment longer before sighing and finally reaching for his own cup. "Well, I still say it was a clever idea."

Mrs. Summers smiled at her old friend fondly, if a bit condescendingly. "Exceedingly. But you shall have to think of something else."

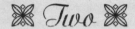

Two

Two Weeks Later

It was conceivable that ten years ago, Mr. James McAlistair would have laughed out loud at the notion that he might one day fall in love. It was easier to imagine, however, that he would have simply hooked up one corner of his mouth in the sort of cool and unfathomable expression that can really only be successfully affected by either a profound poet or a talented assassin.

Anyone looking at him now—standing on the grounds of Haldon Hall, his dark gaze unreadable, and his tall frame honed to the muscled leanness of a panther—would have a difficult time mistaking him for the former.

Pity, that.

Because despite what his reaction may, or may not, have been ten years ago, McAlistair had indeed fallen in love. And a man in love could always use the gifts of a poet.

Particularly when burdened with the sins of an assassin.

Reflecting on those sins now, he rolled his shoulders in a rare, albeit barely perceptible, show of nerves.

He shouldn't be there.

With Evie Cole in danger, though, he couldn't possibly be anywhere else. He scanned the lawn before him, mapping out his path before taking a step. "Act in haste, repent in leisure," his dear, departed, and no doubt often repentant mother had been fond of saying. An interesting bit of advice from a woman who'd birthed six bastards.

He moved forward silently, keeping to the long shadows in the late evening light. It was a precaution taken out of habit more than necessity. He'd already checked the grounds and woods immediately surrounding the house for signs of an intruder. All was as it should be. And he knew, down to a branch, *exactly* how it should be. Those woods had, after all, been his humble home for years. Long years of hardship and solitude—of trying to atone for, or perhaps just forget, the heavy burden of his memories.

The forest would be his home still if he'd had his say in the matter, but William Fletcher, his one-time employer and current thorn in his side, had been steadily pushing him back into the world over the past few months.

McAlistair had capitulated to a point—walking away from the old forgotten hunting cabin he used during inclement weather and buying an equally old, but slightly less secluded cabin just outside the Haldon estate. He was making use of the money he'd earned from the War Department. Money he'd thought he would never touch. He had an armoire filled with the clothing of a gentleman. He owned the fine gray mare he'd just slipped into the Haldon stables. But those trappings were as far into the realm of society as he was willing to venture. He wanted to be left alone, to live as he pleased. And he would . . . as soon as this business with Evie was sorted out.

To avoid the irritating custom of being announced, and to skip the pesky formality of knocking, he let himself in through a rarely used side door of Haldon Hall. He had to pick the lock, of course, but that was a minor detail, and not unexpected given the nature of his visit. Whittaker Cole, Earl of Thurston, was no fool, and when it came to the safety of his family, took no chances.

Once inside, he shot a brief glance at the ceiling, where Whit's muffled voice filtered down from the study above. The sound drifted softer and louder as McAlistair navigated the twisting halls and stairways of Haldon, taking a side trip here and there to avoid the staff. He moved with silent efficiency, a vital talent in his former career.

He arrived at the open doors of the study without being detected—a matter he intended to discuss with Whit later—and quietly slipped inside, taking up a position in the dark shadow of a bookcase.

An argument was in progress, with Whit and Lady Thurston of the mind to keep Evie at Haldon, while William Fletcher, Mrs. Summers, and Evie were of the opinion that a trip to the shore would be in her best interest. He said nothing, simply kept to his corner and watched.

He was accustomed to watching and waiting. And, in recent years, to wanting.

He was not, however, accustomed to being indoors, boxed in by walls and surrounded by noise and movement. The mix of voices, the shuffle of feet, and the random creaks and bangs of a busy household scraped at his nerves.

But that was nothing, *nothing*, compared to the torture of standing so near Evie Cole. She was little more than three feet away, her back turned to him, and he could make out each soft brown curl on her head, take in the clean lingering scent of her soap, and hear every breath as it left her lips. He remembered, quite clearly, what it was like to caress that hair with his fingertips and feel that breath against his mouth.

He recalled vividly—and with far more frequency than was comfortable—that she'd tasted of lemons and mint.

He wanted to roll his shoulders again.

He really shouldn't be there.

Dragging his gaze away from Evie, he looked to the rest of the group. The argument appeared to be at a stalemate, neither side able to claim victory or willing to accept defeat. The futility of it annoyed him, trying his already strained patience. They were wasting time. His hands itched to scoop Evie up, toss her over his shoulder, and carry her off into the woods—*his* woods, where he knew every trail, every noise, every hidden place. His woods, where he knew he could keep her safe . . . from everyone but himself.

Of its own accord, his gaze tracked back to Evie and trailed up the stiff line of her back, the creamy skin of her narrow shoulders, the delicate arch of her neck. She was such a small thing, barely reaching his shoulders. Too small to defend herself against the violence of a madman. And certainly sensible enough to realize as much.

Bloody hell, she must be terrified.

Evie was having a splendid time of it.

She surveyed the scene before her and decided that it was, without question, the single most absurd bit of artifice she'd ever had occasion to witness. What a superb lot of liars they all were, she thought with affection. Who would have imagined her friends and family held such an affinity for theatrics?

And who would have guessed they'd be so proficient?

Lady Thurston was actually pale. *Pale.* How did one manage that sort of thing? Mrs. Summers was sitting tight-lipped and straight-backed, her hands gripped in her lap. Whit, pacing back and forth in front of his desk, looked half ready to pull out his hair. And Mr. Fletcher, with his brow furrowed and his cravat coming undone, made the perfect picture of the concerned family friend.

She, of course, was every inch the brave little soldier, keeping her chin up and her shoulders square despite the *tremendously* dire state of her circumstances. Upon receiving the threatening letter, she had briefly considered trying something even more dramatic—a touch of panic, perhaps even a swoon—but the notion of carrying on in such a fashion for more than a minute or two held little appeal. Besides, she had never swooned in her life and wasn't entirely certain how to go about it. It seemed the sort of thing one ought to practice a time or two in private first.

She had selected stoicism instead and, at the risk of becoming smug, rather thought she was making a respectable go of it. They were all making a good show of their respective roles—standing-ovation and encore-worthy performances.

They should take to the stage, each and every one of them.

She could admit to some initial surprise at Mr. Fletcher's suggestion that she leave for the coast with a small group of armed guards. But, confident they couldn't possibly mean to send her where she would be out of their interfering reach, she chose to argue in favor of the trip. For no other reason, really, than to cause a bit of trouble. She might be willing to play along in the interest of getting the silly matchmaking business over and done with, but there was no point in making it easy on the meddling schemers.

"I'll not send her half a country away," Whit snapped. Tall, fit, and gifted with a deep voice suited for authority, her cousin had always struck Evie as very much the quintessential lord of the manner. Not that she was in the habit of ceding to that authority; she merely appreciated the image.

Mr. Fletcher pinched the bridge of his bulbous nose.

"Norfolk is hardly half a country. It is a mere two days' journey."

"Two days too far from her family," Lady Thurston replied.

"It's for the best," Evie argued, and my, didn't she sound noble? "My presence here puts everyone else in danger. And with Mirabelle and Kate returning next week from the Rockefortes', things will only—"

At the mention of his wife, who was currently expecting their first child, and his younger sister, Whit cut her off with a curt wave of his hand. "I can easily extend their visit."

"They would be more than happy to stay, I'm sure," Evie agreed. She'd been truly disappointed when a head cold had kept her from making the trip to see Alex and Sophie, the Duke and Duchess of Rockeforte, and their three-month-old son, Henry. "At least until word of this reaches them—and it will most certainly reach them—then they'll *insist* on returning."

Either to enjoy the scheme or to stand beside her in a perceived time of need, Kate, Mirabelle, and Sophie would most certainly come. As her cousin, Kate was the only one of the three considered family by blood, but in their hearts, all of them were sisters. They would never allow themselves to be kept removed from such a situation.

"I've already sent word to Alex," Mr. Fletcher said. "I suspect he'll be here before morning."

Evie nodded. "You can be sure Sophie will be, as well, and with Kate and Mirabelle in tow."

Whit swore softly but emphatically. Evie supposed it was a testament to how important their ruse was to Lady Thurston that she did little more than sniff disapprovingly at her son's language.

"This conversation is going nowhere," Lady Thurston pronounced.

"We need an objective opinion," Mr. Fletcher agreed with a nod before turning in Evie's general direction. "What do you think, McAlistair?"

That simple question, obviously addressed to someone directly behind her, instantly dashed Evie's enjoyment of the scene. Her heart stopped beating in her chest—an uncomfortable feeling, to say the least—and she turned around slowly, certain she'd misheard. And uncertain whether she hoped or feared she had not.

She hadn't.

The man in question was standing in the shadow of a bookcase not three feet away from her—a fact that had her heart starting again with one great, painful thud.

Dear Lord, there he was . . . McAlistair, the Hermit of Haldon Hall.

Only he didn't much look like a hermit at present, she noted as he stepped into the light. She narrowed her eyes, suspicious of the transformation. The last time she had seen McAlistair had been in the Haldon woods. He'd been wearing the serviceable garments of a peasant. His hair had been long and wild, almost as wild as his dark eyes. And he'd been carrying a rather large knife.

Now he was dressed in gentleman's attire—a well-tailored green waistcoat, tan breeches, a pair of Hessians, and a perfectly knotted cravat. He'd trimmed his thick brown hair and pulled it back into a neat, if unfashionable, tail at the nape of his neck. His jaw was clean shaven, his hands scrubbed free of dirt, and there was nary a weapon in sight. He looked utterly respectable.

And somehow twice as dangerous.

Evie took in the sharp arch of brows, the square cut of jaw, and the nose that had obviously been broken more than once. She noticed—and blushed upon noticing—the bulge of muscle in his legs, the broad width of his shoulders, and the wiry strength of his arms. McAlistair was no London dandy come to call. A wolf in sheep's clothing, she thought, that's what he was, or possibly a big cat with a collar about its neck. He might look harmless, or tamed, but one need only peer closer at his eyes to see the lie. They were still just as wild.

She had stared into those eyes once—lost herself in them—right before she'd lost herself in his kiss one fantastical evening in the woods. And she had thought of him, as she had promised to think of him, every day since.

For five bloody months.

She narrowed her eyes further, the flush of heat giving way to the burn of anger. He had told her he'd be away and had made no promises to return, but *really*, would it have been so terribly difficult for the man to have sent one blasted letter? Even *she* could have managed as much—if she'd known where to find him—and she was a dismal correspondent.

She watched as Whit stepped around her to deliver a bolstering pat on McAlistair's shoulder and draw him farther into the room. "McAlistair, good to see you. We could use another voice of reason. I believe you're acquainted with everyone here but our Evie."

McAlistair turned his dark eyes on her, and for one terrible moment she feared he might give away their secret. When he did nothing more than stare, unblinking, as if drinking her in with his eyes, her fear turned to embarrassment.

Uncertain how one was expected to react to a long, knowing look from a man one was not *supposed* to know, she dropped into a quick and awkward curtsy. "M-M-" She bit the end of her tongue in an effort to regain control. She *detested* that she stammered when nervous. "Mr. McAlistair."

"Miss Cole." He bowed, an eloquent bend at the waist

perfectly in tune with his attire and so very incongruent with the picture of the wild hermit she still held in her head. He turned to Lady Thurston next and bowed even lower in a sign of deep respect. "Lady Thurston. It is an honor."

His voice was still rough, Evie noticed, still gravelly, as if he weren't accustomed to using it. She wished she didn't find the sound quite so appealing.

Lady Thurston dipped her head in acknowledgment. "It was good of you to come. I assume Mr. Fletcher advised you of the contents of the letter Evie received?"

"Some." McAlistair looked to Whit before jerking his chin at a side table holding a sheet of paper and envelope. "That it?"

"It is." Whit gestured at the table in invitation.

With her mind still reeling—what on earth was the man doing here?—and her heart still racing—*heavens*, he was handsome—Evie watched him cross the room and pick up the paper. He wasn't illiterate then, she thought somewhat ruefully. That had really been her last hope of an excuse for his silence.

She managed, barely, to refrain from making an unpleasant face at him as he unfolded the letter and began to read. He showed no reaction to the message it contained. Bit disturbing, that. Even she had cringed at the contents, and she'd known them to be a lie.

It was a filthy string of insults and threats—considerably more filthy and threatening than she personally felt was necessary, but it did get the point across. It promised, in no uncertain terms, retribution for her sins.

McAlistair looked to her. "What sins?"

Which sins would likely be more accurate, but she rather doubted he was interested in a list. It hardly mattered, at any rate. She assumed the author of the letter had very specific sins in mind. At least, she certainly hoped so. She didn't care for the idea that Mr. Fletcher was apprised of all her misdeeds, including the fact that she had kissed a strange hermit in the woods.

Lady Thurston answered for her. "Evie has, with my permission, been quietly active in several women's charities—organizations with missions some might consider radical, and therefore sinful. We assume that is the author's point of contention, given the nature of his insults . . . and the fact that Evie is otherwise quite exemplary in her conduct."

Evie smiled at her aunt and concentrated on looking suitably innocent—and not looking at McAlistair at all. Exemplary, indeed.

McAlistair set the letter down. "Suspects?"

"None that stand out," Mr. Fletcher answered.

Whit pulled at his cravat. "We're working under the assumption the threat comes from a family member or employer of one of the women Evie sought to help."

Mrs. Summers sent her an approving smile. "Over the years, she has assisted in arranging secret passage out of the country for a number of mistreated women. Wives who suffered violence from their husbands. Women of ill-repute who sought to escape their abusive employers."

"Those women left a fair number of angry husbands and bawds behind," Mr. Fletcher added. "Although how they detected Evie's involvement, we've yet to determine. And until we do, I feel it would be best if she is hidden away elsewhere. Somewhere safer."

"Absolutely," Mrs. Summers chimed in.

"Absolutely not," Lady Thurston snapped at the same time.

"He's right," McAlistair said, earning a hard glare from Whit and Lady Thurston. "Too many doors here. Too many places to hide."

"The staff has been instructed to—" Whit broke off with a scowl. "Who let you in?"

McAlistair shook his head.

"Damn it. Did anyone see you?"

Another head shake from McAlistair and a soft stream of expletives from Whit.

He turned to Evie. "Pack your things. You're leaving in the morning."

She was? "I am?"

"It's what you want, isn't it?"

Not particularly. "Yes. Yes, of course."

Whit gave a very decisive, very unhappy nod. "Be ready by first light."

First light? They really meant to send her away? How the devil had that happened?

"Tonight would be better," Mr. Fletcher argued.

"I'll not have her on the road at night." And with that final pronouncement, Whit excused himself from the room.

Looking somewhat preoccupied, Mr. Fletcher gave Evie what he apparently thought was an encouraging smile and followed Whit. Lady Thurston and Mrs. Summers, exchanging heated whispers, rose from their respective seats, stopped to place reassuring kisses on Evie's cheek, and made their exits as well.

Evie was so taken aback by the news she'd actually be leaving Haldon, it took a minute to realize she'd been left in the room with only McAlistair for company.

And he was staring at her again.

She scrambled for something to say. Preferably something that would, at the very least, induce him to blink. It was unnerving the way his dark eyes focused on her—almost as unnerving as her reaction. She swore she could actually feel her heart trying to beat its way out of her chest.

"I . . . You . . ." She swallowed hard. "You've b-been well, I hope?"

He gave one small nod and did not, she couldn't help noticing, inquire after her own well-being. The blighter.

"Well, I am delighted to hear it," she ground out, and moved to walk around him.

He caught her arm as she passed. "You're angry."

Furious, actually, but still sensible enough to realize some of that anger might be unwarranted. She opened her mouth, but before she could attempt to explain, or try to reach some sort of understanding between them, he let go of her arm and gave that small nod again.

"Good."

She blinked at him, utterly astounded. "Good?" That was his response when faced with the possibility of her ire? Good? "You *want* me t-to be angry with you?"

"For the best."

"Well, far be it from me to disappoint a guest," she snapped, and brushed past him out the door.

❊ *Three* ❊

The trouble with having a limp was that it was nearly impossible to execute a proper stomping. That wasn't the *only* trouble, of course, but it was the inconvenience that most vexed Evie at present.

Gritting her teeth, she continued down the hall in the slow, short steps required to maintain an even gait. After severely injuring her leg in a carriage accident, her stride would never be perfectly smooth. But unless one was actively looking for the slight dip of her frame or listening for the brief drag of her foot, one wasn't likely to notice her limp. That was all well and good, but slow, short steps and an even slightly dragging foot made it exceedingly difficult for her to storm off with the sort of haughty disdain the situation clearly warranted.

Good, indeed.

She threw open the door to her room, stepped inside, and slammed the door behind her. The resulting noise provided a small amount of satisfaction.

Glaring in the general direction of the study, she tried desperately to sort out her fractured feelings. She was livid, which went without saying, but not all that anger was directed at McAlistair. A fair amount of it was reserved for her own foolish behavior.

What the devil had she been thinking all these months, that McAlistair would return to Haldon with a fistful of flowers and a book of poetry to recite? Had she expected words of love, public courtship, perhaps an offer of marriage? She turned her glare to the back of the door and briefly wondered how much it might hurt if she kicked it. Too much, she decided, and crossed the room to drop down in an overstuffed chair.

She didn't want to marry, she reminded herself. And it had only been a kiss. A single kiss from a man she barely knew. Obviously he understood as much and likely recognized that she had mistakenly built it into something more. So he sought her anger rather than face her infatuation.

How utterly mortifying.

He might have attempted some diplomacy, she thought

glumly, but then he was a hermit, not a barrister. And it was hardly McAlistair's fault she'd turned their brief encounter in the woods into a fairy tale. He certainly wasn't to blame for the fascination she'd had since the day she first spotted him, years ago, sitting on an outcropping of rock, quietly skinning a rabbit. He'd been little more than a myth to her until that moment—a story Whit had concocted to scare and entertain the young ladies of Haldon. A mysterious former soldier haunting the woods of Haldon. A wild man, dark and dangerous, hiding away from the world. They weren't to fear him, they'd been told, but they were to keep a respectable distance should they cross his path.

As she was the only one of the girls who enjoyed walking the woods at odd hours and eschewing the trails when there was still light, Whit had made certain to repeat his warning to her at regular intervals.

She hadn't believed a word of it . . . until she'd seen McAlistair that day on the rocks, with the dying light of the sun outlining his taut frame in gold. It had only taken a heartbeat for him to catch her eye, and then he was gone, into the woods. She'd stared after him for a long time, feeling as if she'd caught a glimpse of something unworldly, something magical. Something wonderful. Every time she'd stepped into the trees after that, it had been with the hope she would glimpse that magic again.

Which was, she thought now, a perfectly ridiculous reaction—golden light and magical sightings. Honestly. When had she become so fanciful? And why the devil had she not realized it before now? She should have told her friends about seeing him, rather than keeping it to herself all these years. They would have laughed and gossiped and speculated, and otherwise turned the whole business into what it truly was—silly and insignificant.

It *wasn't* particularly important, Evie assured herself. His hadn't even been her first kiss. She wondered what McAlistair would say to that. Not a thing, she decided with an annoyed puff of breath. Likely as not, he'd simply gift her with that disconcerting stare he had—the one that made her heart race and her skin tingle.

She caught sight of her exasperated expression in the vanity mirror and groaned. Then groaned again when she noticed her plain ivory gown. If she'd known McAlistair was to come, she would have changed—worn something perhaps a bit less comfortable and a bit more flattering. Not that the dress wasn't lovely; it was, but Lady Thurston had taught her that there was lovely, and then there was *lovely*. And while she may have blown the kiss out of proportion, it hardly followed that she couldn't do her very best to remind McAlistair of *why* he'd kissed her. As she had noticed that men had a tendency to allow their eyes to drift downward from her face when in her company for more than a few moments, she rather thought one of the reasons might be her generous bosom.

Rising, she stepped closer to the mirror to study her face. It was nice enough, she thought without vanity—heart-shaped with wide brown eyes, a thin nose, and full lips—but it wasn't beautiful. She would never be beautiful. Her finger traced the long thin scar that ran from her temple to her jaw, another result of the carriage accident in her childhood.

She'd been terribly self-conscious of the flaw as a child, perhaps because the injury had taken so long to heal. Even months after the wound had closed, the skin around it had remained red and swollen. And between her marred countenance and noticeable limp, she'd been certain she appeared a veritable monster.

It hadn't helped, particularly, to have her own mother pale at the mere sight of her.

Evie had taken to hiding herself away from the gaze of others and to stammering when their gazes couldn't be avoided. It wasn't until Lady Thurston had brought her to live at Haldon (an offer Mrs. Cole had accepted with great relief) that the worst of her shyness had begun to ease. She'd been so quickly accepted, so openly loved by her aunt and cousins that, over time, she regained some of the confidence she had lost. Now she only grew nervous and stammered when faced with the staring eyes of someone she didn't know well . . . someone like McAlistair.

"You're going in circles, girl," she berated herself.

And because she was, it was probably best that her musings were interrupted by the crash of the connecting door to her room. Lizzy, the lady's maid she and Kate shared, rushed in, looking breathless and excited.

"Is it true, miss? Is he really here?"

Evie turned from the mirror and resumed her seat in the chair. "I assume you're referring to Mr. McAlistair?"

Lizzy rolled her eyes. "No, the smithy. I'm always such aflutter when he arrives. Yes, of course McAlistair."

Evie laughed despite her foul mood. She rather thought Lizzy had to be the cheekiest lady's maid in all of England— a distinction Evie appreciated and encouraged.

"Mr. McAlistair has indeed graced us with his presence."

"Mister, now, is it?" Lizzy raised her eyebrows comically. Of average height and build, with a long nose and round face, she was a woman some might consider plain. But Evie had always been of the opinion that Lizzy's dramatically expressive face made her uniquely attractive. It was impossible not to smile while in her company. "Is he a gentleman, all of a sudden?"

"He was dressed as one."

"Oh." Lizzy's face fell. "I'd rather hoped to see him in all his hermit glory."

"Life is rife with disappointment."

"Apparently." Lizzy took the seat across from her. "What's he like as a gentleman, then? Is he handsome? Or have years of living as a savage taken their toll?"

"He's handsome enough." Enough to steal the air from her lungs.

"But what does he look like? Is he tall, short, blue-eyed, or—?"

"Tall, dark-haired, and dark-eyed. You'll see him for yourself soon enough, I imagine."

"Yes, but I'd like to know what to expect." Lizzy leaned forward in her chair. "Is he terribly frightening? Does he growl and snarl if one attempts conversation?"

"No, he's simply . . . reticent."

Lizzy pursed her lips and stood. "He's not the only one."

"Well, I do have other things on my mind at present."

"The letter, do you mean?" Lizzy frowned. "Too much fuss over one little missive, I should think. Lord Thurston won't allow for any harm to come to you."

Evie pressed her lips together. "He means to send me to Norfolk to make certain of it. I'm to leave first thing in the morning, under armed guard."

Lizzy visibly started. "To Norfolk?"

"Under armed guard," she repeated.

"You can't be serious."

"Whit certainly is." She blew out a long breath. "I need to pack."

Packing was accomplished with little speed and even less enthusiasm. It didn't help matters to have Lizzy running off downstairs every ten minutes with excuses that ranged from the practical, "Lady Thurston might have some idea how many days you'll be gone," to the absurd, "I wonder if Cook remembered to slice the onions thin, the way Mrs. Summers prefers."

"Caught sight of him yet?" Evie inquired after Lizzy returned from her seventh trip.

"I've no idea what you mean." Lizzy pasted on an innocent expression and began folding the last of the chosen gowns into a trunk.

Evie smirked and carefully wrapped a bonnet in tissue. "All this running up and down the steps hasn't been an attempt to catch sight of Mr. McAlistair, then?"

Lizzy scowled. "The man's frightfully elusive."

"He's had considerable practice, you'll recall," Evie said with a laugh.

"And puts it to good use. I asked John Herbert if he'd managed a peek. He hasn't, and John always knows what's afoot in Haldon."

"John Herbert? The new footman?"

"He's been here near seven months, miss. I don't know as I would qualify him as new."

"That's because you qualify him as dreadfully handsome," Evie teased.

"He is that." Lizzy sighed dramatically.

Eager to avoid a discussion on John Herbert's tremendous handsomeness, which would inevitably be followed by a monologue on Robert Klein's immense physical strength, which was guaranteed to precede a lengthy discourse on Calvin Bradley's devilish charm, Evie asked, "Has anyone else arrived?"

"Mr. Hunter," Lizzy replied, reaching for another gown, "an hour ago. And word just came from Lord Rockeforte by way of special courier. He's been delayed, something about having to slip out of the house under the cover of night."

Evie grinned at the idea of the proud and powerful Duke of Rockeforte finding it necessary to sneak out of his own home to avoid his wife and her friends. "How is it you're aware of what the duke had to say? Eavesdropping, were you?"

"Not this time," Lizzy answered without the slightest hint of shame. "Mr. Fletcher read the missive aloud for the benefit of Mr. Hunter. I happened to be in the parlor at the time."

"Very convenient."

"It was, rather." Lizzy frowned absently at the contents of the trunk. "Does he seem at all familiar to you?"

"Mr. Hunter?" Evie set down her work. "Kate asks me that every time we see the man."

Lizzy nodded. "There's something about him, something that niggles at my memory. And he seems to always have this look about him, as if he knows exactly why that might be, and won't tell."

"Has he been unkind to you? Has he—"

"Oh, no, miss. Nothing of the sort." Lizzy shook her head. "He's very much a gentleman to the staff—more so, in my opinion, than some who've been born to the position. I think he has a secret, that's all."

"Perhaps I can ferret it out at dinner for you."

Lizzy winced. "Dinner. Oh dear, I'd forgotten. Lady Thurston says you're to take dinner in your room tonight."

Evie blinked at that news. "Did she say why?"

"Not to me, but I overheard her informing Mrs. Summers she was uncomfortable with the idea of you being downstairs late at night."

"Conveniently in the parlor again?"

"No, I was eavesdropping."

Evie snorted out a laugh. "Well, it's an absurd idea. She can't possibly mean it."

A knock on the door and the arrival of a maid carrying a tray of food told Evie that Lady Thurston was very much in earnest. Uncertain whether to be amused or annoyed at being banished to her room for dinner, Evie directed that the tray be set on the bed. After seeing the maid out, she sat down and reached for a roll.

"I repeat, this is absurd."

"There are an awful number of doors and windows in this house," Lizzy pointed out.

"I thought you said there was too much bother being made of all this."

"I'm not sure I'd consider being served dinner in bed such a bother."

Evie stopped with the roll halfway to her mouth. "You have a point."

An excellent one, Evie admitted silently. And now that she thought on it, she didn't particularly care for the idea of going downstairs for dinner. She never did when there were guests in the house. Guests at the table meant stares and a pressure to speak. With McAlistair as one of those guests, the staring and the pressure would be infinitely worse. Well, the staring would be.

She wondered if being relieved by the knowledge she wouldn't have to face him across the dinner table made her a coward. She bit into her roll, thought about it, and decided she didn't much care. She was who she was. Perhaps she was less than courageous in some areas, but she made up for it with bravery in others.

"All done here, I think."

Evie swallowed, mentally shook herself from her wool-gathering, and looked up to find Lizzy standing over a pair of closed trunks. "Beg your pardon?"

"You're all packed," Lizzy repeated. "Unless we forgot something."

Evie took mental inventory of everything they'd fit into the trunks. "I've enough, I think. I'll not be gone for more than a fortnight."

Lizzy nodded in approval. "That's the spirit. Lord Thurston will take care of this business before you're halfway to Norfolk."

Evie muttered a noncommittal, nonsensical reply. Whether the ridiculous business was done or not, she was returning to Haldon at the end of the fortnight.

Her agenda was clear for now, but in two weeks' time, Mrs. Nancy Yard from London would be expecting someone to meet her behind Maver's tavern in the nearby village of Benton. It was Evie's job to be that someone—to see that the woman received instructions and funds for the next leg of her trip. If all went well, Mrs. Yard would have a new life in Ireland, free from the violent whims of her husband.

William Fletcher had a fortnight to set his conscience at ease, and not a day more.

Lizzy glanced about the tidied room. "Well, if there's nothing else, miss, I'm going for my own dinner and an early bed."

Evie nodded and tried to generate some interest in her meal as Lizzy closed the connecting doors between their rooms. She wasn't particularly hungry, but the food was there and she had little else to occupy her time. She managed another bite of her roll, picked at the chicken, poked at the carrots, and otherwise turned her plate of food into a wholly unappetizing mess. Giving up, she set the tray on the vanity and, deciding not to bother Lizzy again, managed to change into her night rail on her own.

If she couldn't eat, she'd sleep. Granted, it was barely after nine, but after a long day, and with a painfully early morning looming before her, going to bed early seemed wise. Anything and everything that would turn her mind from a particular houseguest seemed wise.

She crawled under the covers and willed her mind to clear. She wouldn't think of him. She wouldn't. Not a single thought would be given to the handsome and mysterious Mr. McAlistair. She wouldn't think of the kiss, of the way he'd held himself perfectly still as his mouth gently took hers. She wouldn't think of how her heart raced and her breath caught when he looked at her with those dark, intense eyes. She wouldn't think on where he might be sleeping tonight, or what he might be doing now, or . . .

"Oh, bloody, bloody hell."

She rolled over, sat up, pounded her fist into the pillow a few times, and then finally flopped back down with a frustrated groan.

It was going to be a painfully long night.

Evie managed, somehow, to fall asleep—for all of two hours. She might have made it through the whole night, but for the second time that day, Lizzy stumbled in through the connecting door. She looked just as wide-eyed as she had the first time, but now she wore a night rail and clasped a pile of bedding to her chest.

Evie shot up in bed, instantly awake, if not entirely coherent. "What is it? What's the matter?"

"He's in my room. He booted me from my own room."

Evie bounded out of bed. "He? He who?"

"The hermit," Lizzy breathed. "McAlistair."

"In your room?" Evie grabbed a wrap to throw over her night rail.

Lizzy nodded and swallowed. "Came right in, pretty as you please—well, he did knock first," she allowed. "But *then* he came right in and told me to take my things and sleep in here."

"I can't believe it. I cannot *believe* he'd barge into your room." Did the man really think he could treat Lizzy however he pleased merely because she was employed as a servant?

"*I* still can't believe he's real," Lizzy breathed. "All that time I spent looking for him and suddenly he—"

"Barges into your room," Evie finished for her. She cinched her wrap shut with a decisive yank. "We'll see about this."

"Shouldn't we send for Lord Thurston, or—"

"I can handle the likes of Mr. McAlistair." She headed toward the door, intent on doing just that.

❈ *Four* ❈

*E*vie had never considered herself a prude. Quite the contrary, in fact. At fourteen, she'd been the first of her friends to experience a kiss. At nineteen, she'd met her first prostitute, and by twenty she'd been propositioned by a bawd, a pimp, and a handful of drunken sailors. Such was the enlightenment of a woman who occasionally spent time in some of London's seedier neighborhoods.

According to the standards set by her peers, she was a scandalously forward young woman—or would be, if any of those standard setters ever became apprised of her transgressions. But despite her broader than average education, she wasn't quite prepared for the sight that greeted her on the other side of the connecting door.

Not when that sight was McAlistair, half undressed. Well, more like a quarter undressed, if one wished to be overly precise about it. The salient point was that it was McAlistair, in the room directly connected to her own chambers, and he was in a state of undress. He was down to shirtsleeves, and *that* had been unbuttoned down to his waist, exposing a smooth expanse of skin and muscle. Good Lord, the muscle. The man was as toned and sculpted as the wild cat she'd thought him earlier.

"W-W-" Oh, blast. She bit the tip of her tongue, then averted her gaze, pushed aside the sudden heat she felt *everywhere*, and tried again. "What d-do you think you're doing?"

He said nothing, which was understandable given that what he was doing was fairly obvious. She felt her cheeks turn to fire. Why the devil hadn't she thought to knock?

"You had no right to remove Lizzy from her own r-room."

Out of the corner of her eye, she watched him rebutton his shirt. "For her own safety."

Utter bafflement momentarily replaced embarrassment. "Her own safety?"

He pointed at the large windows. "If I were coming for you, I'd use those."

She looked at the windows in Lizzy's room, then stepped back to peer through the connecting door at the more expansive windows in her own room. "Why not use my own?"

"Too well guarded."

"Well, why not come in d-downstairs or through the windows of an unoccupied room?" Lord knew there were plenty of them at Haldon.

"These are closer."

There was something rather odd about his argument—above and beyond the fact there was slight chance of an intruder climbing through any of the windows in Haldon—but she couldn't put her finger on just what.

Since she couldn't, she looked directly at him—a task much more easily accomplished now that he'd finished buttoning his shirt—and asked, "Are you an expert on such matters?"

There was a long, long pause before he nodded.

"I . . . oh." How would a soldier-turned-hermit know of such things? For that matter, why would a regular, literate, possibly well-bred soldier choose to turn hermit? She tilted her head to study him. "Who are you?"

Surely, kiss or no kiss, he would afford her the courtesy of answering that much.

An extended silence informed her that, no, in fact, he would not.

She fought against the lump of disappointment and hurt that formed in her throat. It was ridiculous. The kiss, the scheme, his reticence—all of it was absurd and therefore no reason for her to suddenly begin leaking like a sieve. She was an experienced woman of six and twenty, she reminded herself, not a silly miss fresh from the nursery to be undone by one man's disinterest.

"Keep your secrets, then," she muttered and turned for the door.

"Evie."

She shouldn't stop. She knew she shouldn't. But she did.

He waited until he caught her eye. "I meant no insult," he said softly. "To either of you."

She hesitated. She knew she shouldn't ask. Knew she shouldn't bring it up. But she couldn't seem to stop herself. "Why . . . that night in the woods . . . why—" She cut off at the shake of his head.

"I shouldn't have. You're not meant for me."

Suspicion, ugly and as painful as his earlier silence, seeped in. "And who am I m-meant for, Mr. McAlistair?"

"Someone . . . other," he answered softly. "Just other."

Suspicion left as quickly as it had arrived. He wasn't speaking of a specific man for her, only a man who wasn't him. He didn't know of the ruse, then. Presumably.

"I am meant for whomever it is I am meant for," she returned. "My fortune isn't for you to tell."

Pleased with her response and relieved she'd managed to deliver it without a single stammer, she turned and walked through the doorway, shutting the door behind her.

She found Lizzy still standing in the center of the room, clutching her bedding to her chest.

"Well, what did he say?" Lizzy demanded.

"That he expects your windows would prove too much a temptation for any murderers creeping about the grounds."

Lizzy's mouth fell open. "They'd come through my windows? Through me?"

Guilt stabbed at Evie. It was possible Lizzy knew nothing of the scheme, though unlikely, as a matchmaking ruse was something Lizzy would find very irresistible.

"Of course not. He's overreacting, that's all. Didn't you say Lord Thurston wouldn't allow for any harm to come to us?"

"To you," Lizzy corrected and earned herself a hard glare from Evie. "Yes, all right, to any of us. Am I to sleep on the floor, then, miss?"

"Don't be silly. There are a dozen other beds in the house. What of your old room next to Kate's?"

"I couldn't." Lizzy shuddered dramatically. "Those rooms are enormous. I'd be too nervous to sleep with Lady Kate gone."

Evie wanted to laugh. Kate's nocturnal composing had been the very reason Lizzy had recently chosen to take up residence in the room next door. It was difficult to sleep when your mistress left candles burning half the night, hummed to herself, and had a tendency to trip over furniture.

Laughter, unfortunately, was not an appropriate response under the current circumstances. She wasn't supposed to be amused, she reminded herself. She was supposed to be frightened. Terribly frightened—and terribly brave about it.

"Sleep here, then. The bed is large enough for the both of us."

Lizzy didn't need a second invitation. She tossed her bundle on a chair and scrambled onto the four-poster. "Thank you, miss. I'll sleep a world better with someone else in the room."

As Lizzy had a tendency to snore, Evie doubted she could say the same.

She wasn't given the chance to complain. A soft knock on the door to the hall heralded the arrival of Mrs. Summers, wearing a frilly night rail and frillier cap.

Evie blinked at her, absolutely baffled. "Mrs. Summers?"

"Good evening, Evie." She swept past her to the bed. "Wiggle aside a bit, Lizzy dear. I prefer the outside."

Evie gaped at her. "The out—"

"Mr. McAlistair has taken up residence in Lizzy's quarters, has he not?" Mrs. Summers sent her a questioning glance as she removed her wrap.

"Well, yes, but—"

"Then I insist on taking up residence here. Threat or not, you have a reputation to consider." And with that pronouncement, she slipped under the covers next to Lizzy.

Evie threw up her hands. "I can't see how anyone else would know. We haven't any visitors who are likely to betray a confidence, and the staff would never gossip."

"Most of the staff, certainly," Mrs. Summers agreed as she adjusted a pillow to her liking. "But your aunt informs me you have several relatively new maids and grooms on hand."

As Lizzy had pointed out earlier, the most recent additions to the household had arrived more than seven months ago, but it hardly seemed worth the energy to argue. Besides, it would probably be best to drop the topic of

McAlistair's presence in the next room before Lizzy let slip that he hadn't been in there alone. Given her current company, the slip wouldn't ruin her, but it would certainly elicit a very lengthy, and therefore very tiresome, lecture from Mrs. Summers.

"Well, push over then, Lizzy. I don't care for the middle, either."

"And I do?" Lizzy grumbled, but nonetheless shifted to the center of the bed.

Absolutely the cheekiest maid in England. "You're welcome to sleep elsewhere," Evie reminded her and climbed under the covers.

Lizzy sniffed once. "The middle will be fine."

Sleep hadn't been McAlistair's reason for undressing. He had no intention of closing his eyes for anything more than a light doze. Comfort had been foremost on his mind when he'd begun stripping off his clothes. One of the many benefits of being a hermit had been the freedom to wear what he liked, and stiff waistcoats and even stiffer shirts were decidedly not among the list of things he liked.

He eyed the feather bed dubiously. Also on the list of things he disliked was sleeping indoors. He preferred the soft whisper of the wind through the leaves over the murmur of voices to lull him to sleep. He certainly preferred listening for the crunch of sticks and underbrush rather than the subtle creak of floorboards to tell him someone was approaching. And he was definitely more comfortable in the open woodland than with the limited options afforded by a room with only two exits.

As a hermit, he'd often slept in the old cabin in the Haldon woods, but being the lone occupant of a one-room shelter was considerably different from being one of many residents in an enormous manor. Everywhere he turned here, there were more people, more rooms, and more walls. There seemed an endless number of barriers between him and the woods.

Even now, when he had a larger home of his own, he took a blanket outside at night and made his bed under the stars whenever the weather allowed.

And he didn't sleep in that bed wearing a damn nightgown.

He finished unbuttoning his shirt, pulled it off and tossed it over the back of a chair. Remembering how Evie had floundered at the sight of his bare chest, his mouth hooked up in a half smile. She was lovely when she blushed. She was always lovely to his mind—those enormous brown eyes, the soft curve of her cheek, the tempting figure that was somehow both slight and generous. How many nights had he lain awake, imagining that figure beneath him, over him, around . . . ?

He uttered a single succinct curse and stalked to the windows to throw them wide, knowing full well no self-respecting villain would be so foolish as to climb through them. One more reason he wasn't fit for Evie's company, let alone her favor. He'd lied to her, smoothly and without remorse.

But he'd be damned if he would take up a room at the other end of the hall for propriety's sake. The difference between life and death was often the matter of a few precious seconds. What if she had need of him? What if she screamed?

He made a conscious effort to relax. She was just a few feet away from where he stood. She was fine. She was safe.

He was bloody well going to make sure she stayed that way.

❋ Five ❋

Evie made her way downstairs with her mouth stretched open in an enormous yawn and—because it was difficult to see properly whilst yawning—with one hand gripped firmly on the banister. She'd been woken before first light by Mrs. Summers and practically shoved out of bed by Lizzy. She'd been fed, clothed, and left to arrange the business of seeing her things downstairs before her eyes had fully opened. She had managed, eventually, to see to the task, but rather feared she had groused unfairly at one of the footmen in the process. Mornings, as any of her family could attest, did not show Evie to advantage.

Now she was tired, feeling guilty, and giving serious consideration to the idea that the whole charade wasn't worth the bother. First light, for pity's sake. Was there anyone in full possession of his faculties who *preferred* to start the day at first light?

"Looks as if you could use this."

Evie stopped at the foot of the stairs and blinked, first at the realization that Whit was standing before her and then at the steaming cup he held out for her.

"Hot chocolate." She sighed with delight and took the drink to draw in the heady aroma. "Bless you, cousin mine. All I've had this morning is an undercooked egg and a cup of weak tea."

"The staff's a bit preoccupied, I'm afraid."

He stepped back, affording her a view through the open

front doors. The drive was a hive of activity—footmen loading the carriage, grooms checking the horses, maids running about doing . . . she had no idea what. Lady Thurston, Mrs. Summers, and Mr. Fletcher stood on the front steps, overseeing it all. Somewhere in all the mess was very likely the man they meant as a match for her. He'd have arrived last night, surely. Or before she'd risen, the poor soul. Likely he was on the other side of the carriage, she mused, or off doing whatever it was Mr. Hunter and McAlistair were doing.

She gestured to the open doors. "Isn't this rather obvious? If anyone were watching the house—"

"McAlistair and Mr. Hunter are checking the grounds now. There's no one about who shouldn't be."

"It's a large area to go over. What if they're mistaken?"

"They're not."

She eyed him speculatively. "You're very sure of them."

"I have my reasons."

How very interesting. She dearly wished she were awake enough to devise a clever plan to find out those reasons. If she tried now, with her head still foggy, she'd only embarrass herself and possibly make Whit suspicious.

She took another sip of hot chocolate and said, half to herself, "I suppose it doesn't matter, as you'll be along to—" She broke off, realizing for the first time that he wasn't dressed to travel. "Aren't you coming along?"

His mouth compressed into a thin line. "No. It was agreed I should stay here and search for the bastard with Alex and William. Begging your pardon."

She rolled her eyes. "I don't know why you insist on apologizing when you know I'm not offended."

"Habit," Whit answered with a shrug.

"Well, it's damned annoying," she teased and leaned up to

kiss his cheek when he scowled. "I suppose it's best that you remain here. Sophie, Mirabelle, and Kate will be returning eventually. Alex might be able to convince Sophie not to interfere, but Mirabelle and Kate are another matter."

"I can handle my wife and sister."

"Delighted to hear it. May I inform them you said so, upon my return?"

"Absolutely not."

She laughed softly as Whit gave her a one-armed hug about the shoulders.

He stepped back and searched her face. "You're taking this very well."

Not too well, she hoped, and contrived to affect a more suitably worried expression. "I'm not certain how else to take it."

He considered that, and her, for a moment before nodding. "You should be going. The others are waiting to say good-bye."

He led her to the front stairs, where Lady Thurston took her performance to new heights, fussing over Evie extensively before bravely sniffing back tears and exiting quickly into the house. The woman was astonishing.

Lizzy sidled up next, just in time for them both to watch McAlistair and Mr. Hunter ride up the drive.

"He's a wild one, isn't he, miss?" Lizzy whispered with a subtle—thankfully—jerk of her chin toward McAlistair. "He has a pistol on him and a knife in his boot."

Evie eyed the tall form on the gray mare and positively refused to acknowledge the heat that crept into her chest. "How could you possibly know that?"

Lizzy shrugged. "Don't know why I notice these things. But the gun shows through his coat—see there? And he adjusted the knife before he and Mr. Hunter rode off this morning. I'll wager you it's not the only one."

"I'd be a fool to take that bet."

"You would, at that." Lizzy shifted her weight from one foot to the other. "I suppose you should be off."

Mrs. Summers stepped up to join them. "She certainly should."

Evie took in her demurely cut peach traveling gown. "Are you leaving today as well, Mrs. Summers?"

"I am." She picked up a small valise and headed for the carriage. "I am to be your chaperone."

Evie gave Lizzy a quick kiss and followed, fighting a smile. Her chaperone. Of course. A well-bred young lady wouldn't think of making an escape from a life-threatening situation without a proper chaperone.

"Are you certain of this, Mrs. Summers?" Evie asked, picking up the blue skirts of her own gown—a smart and flattering piece she'd chosen with great care. "You're putting yourself in grave danger. Terribly, terribly grave danger."

Mrs. Summers came to a stop at the carriage door and turned to face her. "Terribly and grave are rather redundant, dear."

"Yes, well." Oh, blast, she was having too much fun, and it was beginning to show. "I only wish to be certain you fully understood the . . . the . . . er . . ."

"Danger?"

"Rather."

Mrs. Summers gave a quick nod. "I do. You should know that Lady Thurston wished to come in my stead, but Whittaker put his foot down on the matter."

Mr. Fletcher strode up to stand beside them. "As well he should have," he snapped with surprising force. "As well should I where you're concerned."

"You did," Mrs. Summers calmly reminded him as she stowed her valise inside the carriage. "But you are neither an earl, nor my son. I chose to ignore you." She turned to Evie. "In you go, dear."

Evie climbed into the carriage, settled herself in a seat, and turned around in time to witness Mr. Fletcher press a kiss to the back of Mrs. Summers' hand.

"You will take care, Mary," he ordered rather than asked. When she nodded silently, he lowered her hand and assisted her into the carriage, closing the door behind her. Then opened it again.

"And you as well, Evie."

She smiled at him, touched by his concern for Mrs. Summers and amused that she should be an afterthought. "We'll be fine, Mr. Fletcher."

She'd wager every penny she had on it.

He nodded and shut the door.

"Close the curtains, dear," Mrs. Summers advised when the carriage started forward with a soft lurch.

Evie reached over to pull at the material. "Do you mean to nap? You couldn't have slept well last night." *She* certainly hadn't.

"A short nap sounds lovely, but we shall keep them shut for the duration of the trip."

Evie felt her eyes widen. "The entire trip?"

"Better no one should see you."

Oh, for heaven's sake. She gritted her teeth to keep from arguing. It was such a lovely day, sunny and warm, and she found the idea of sitting in the dark for the whole of it distinctly unappetizing. But if she argued, she'd appear unconcerned for her own safety.

"May I at least peek?"

Mrs. Summers appeared to give the matter some thought. "Only when you're certain there's no one else on the road."

Well there wasn't anyone on it now. They hadn't yet

reached the end of the drive. She pushed the curtains back an inch and found McAlistair riding along on her side of the carriage. Determined not to think about him—again— she scooted across the cushions and looked out the other window, where she found Mr. Hunter riding alongside the carriage.

A furrow worked into her brow. She knew Christian, a very old friend of Mirabelle and Mr. Fletcher's, was driving the carriage, and she'd noticed before climbing in that he sat alone up top. A middle-aged man with a soft brogue, dancing green eyes, and a weak arm and leg, Christian had sparked an immediate, if not yet deep, feeling of kinship in Evie.

But kinship or not, she wasn't about to marry a man twenty years her senior. Surely there was someone else about. She checked both windows again, craning her neck to look to the front and back of the carriage. There was no one else.

She sat back, feeling a bit stunned. These were her guards? Christian the driver, Mr. Hunter the businessman, and McAlistair the hermit? They were fine men, all, and quite probably capable of protecting a lady from harm. But surely none of them had been chosen as her intended rescuer?

"Are we to meet anyone else along the way?"

Mrs. Summers took her own turn peeking out the window. "We are all here."

"At the cottage, then?" Evie tried. "Are there others waiting for us there?"

"No, this is the entire party. Christian shall drive, and Mr. McAlistair and Mr. Hunter shall ride alongside the carriage."

"Oh."

Mrs. Summers retrieved a small traveling pillow from her valise. "Are you worried, dear? Because I assure you, these gentlemen—"

"No, I'm not worried." What she was, was puzzled. Who among the three men was meant to be her knight-errant?

It must be Mr. Hunter, she decided, pulling back the curtain again to take another look at him. Not a bad choice, really, though it was surprising. She could have sworn Lady Thurston knew his interests lay elsewhere.

Still, the man was devilishly handsome. Not in the traditional sense—he was too large, as tall as Alex and even wider across the chest and arms. And his features were too dark to appeal to the current taste for pale hair and eyes. But he had very nice deep-set brown eyes, a strong, wide jaw, and a wickedly charming smile.

Rumor had it, he also had one of the largest fortunes in the country. On the marriage mart, he would be considered by some to be a fine catch. True, his parentage was suspect, but many among the *ton* were willing to forgive— or at least conveniently overlook—such matters when there was vast wealth and the recommendation of an earl involved.

Pity they would never suit, Evie mused. He needed someone . . . softer. Someone a bit more like Kate.

"Mrs. Summers, do you think—"

She broke off when she noticed Mrs. Summers was fast asleep and therefore in no position to offer an opinion.

A short nap turned out to be more of a second night's sleep for Mrs. Summers. Evie passed the time reading until the fine print and jostling of the carriage threatened to give her a headache. She put her book aside and occupied herself by making a mental list of the work she intended to see to at the cottage, taking in the occasional glimpse of passing landscape, and trying her utmost not to dwell on the fact that, for her, McAlistair comprised the most interesting part of that scenery.

Her success was limited. Enough so that she was more than a little relieved when Mrs. Summers woke and dug out a late lunch for them to share. She desperately needed the distraction of conversation. If only Mrs. Summers would cooperate, but the woman still seemed half asleep, and clearly unenthusiastic about carrying on an extended chat. Under other circumstances, Evie would have been sympathetic to her plight. After hours of only her own thoughts for company, however, sympathy was in short supply.

"Will we be stopping to change the horses soon?" Evie bit into a thick slice of bread.

"Soon enough, I imagine."

She swallowed and tried again. "Have you been to this cottage before? It belongs to Mr. Hunter, doesn't it?"

"It does, and I haven't. I am not particularly familiar with Mr. Hunter."

The familiarity comment reminded Evie of the sweet scene she'd witnessed that morning.

"I don't mean to pry." She thought about that. "Well, yes, I suppose I do. I can't help myself. Have you and Mr. Fletcher formed an attachment?"

The slightest hint of rose tinted the older woman's sharp cheekbones. "It is possible we have."

"Oh, that's lovely, Mrs. Summers." Evie grinned, genuinely happy for her friend. "Absolutely lovely. When did this happen?"

"I'm not entirely—"

The remainder of that sentence came out in a gasp as the carriage jerked and tilted sharply to the side. Evie felt herself being thrown across the interior.

A crash. They were crashing.

An image flashed across her mind, a memory of screams and pain, and the sharp smell of burning wood.

Panic swelled in an instant, wiping out all thought, all sense of her surroundings.

The next thing she knew for certain, she was on the floor of the carriage, her head against the wood frame of the front bench and something round and hard digging uncomfortably into her back.

She took several deep breaths, willing away horrific images and managing her fear. She wasn't trapped, she wasn't in pain, and nothing was burning. This was not the carriage accident of her youth. She was fine. A trifle muddled, and certainly uncomfortable, she amended as she shifted and felt that large something dig into her back again, but otherwise fine.

The last vestiges of panic faded just as the door flew open, blinding her with a wash of bright sunlight.

"Evie!" Strong hands lifted her to a sitting position.

McAlistair.

He ran his hands over her, searching for injuries. "Are you hurt?"

Disoriented, she reached behind her to brush at her back. Her hand returned sticky with the mashed remains of an apple. "So *that's* what—"

McAlistair caught her face in his rough hands. "Look at me. Are you hurt anywhere?"

She blinked, coming back to herself. "I . . . no. I'm fine." When he continued to search her face with his dark gaze, she reached up to pull at his hands. "I'm fine. I . . . Mrs. Summers!"

Evie whipped her head around to find Mrs. Summers sitting upright on the floor, brushing at a smear of butter on her skirts. "I'm perfectly well, dear, if a bit messy."

"Is Christian . . . ?" Evie demanded.

Christian stuck his head in the open door. "Nary a scratch,

miss. But the linchpin worked its way out, and the thill looks to have been cut near through—only a matter of time before it snapped."

Mrs. Summers stilled and whispered in a tersely controlled voice. "Sabotage?"

McAlistair and Christian shared a look and spoke at the same time. "Ambush."

Mrs. Summers gave Evie a none-too-gentle nudge toward the door. "Take her. Go."

Take her? What the blazes was she talking about?

Evie tried to ask just that, even as she was hauled out of the damaged carriage and set rather unceremoniously on her feet, but McAlistair spoke before she could so much as take a breath.

"Can you ride?"

"Ride?" She shook her head to clear it. "Yes, yes, of course."

"Astride," he clarified.

"Oh." She glanced nervously at Mrs. Summers. Riding astride was not a gentlewoman's talent. "I can, actually. I taught my—"

"Get on the horse."

"But—" He cut off any further discussion by simply grasping her around the waist, lifting her off her feet, and dropping her into the gray mare's saddle.

"Good Lord, what do you think you're doing?"

McAlistair didn't answer. Instead, he turned to take a bundle from Christian and tied it behind the saddle of the other horse. Baffled, Evie looked to Mrs. Summers, but found her placing the remains of their lunch in the gray mare's saddlebags. Everyone seemed to be doing something, and doing that something with remarkable haste. Christian and Mr. Hunter were struggling to unhitch the horses. McAlistair and Mrs. Summers continued to pack supplies on the two free mounts.

Not one of them appeared the least bit concerned that she was currently sitting astride a horse with her skirts hiked almost to her knees. Considering, she looked to Mr. Hunter. No, not so much as a glance in her direction. That couldn't possibly bode well for the would-be matchmakers.

Shifting and squirming, she pulled the material down as best she could before returning her attention to the group. She watched, bemused, as they hustled about, speaking among themselves in clipped voices and short sentences.

"Team's stuck tight."

"Head north first. Avoid the east road."

"Send word to William."

They were so efficient, Evie mused, so coordinated, so . . . She narrowed her eyes.

Good Lord, had they *rehearsed?*

"Rehearsed what, dear?"

She blinked at Mrs. Summers. Had she said that aloud? "I . . . nothing. I'm a bit muddled, is all."

Mrs. Summers trained worried eyes on her brow. "You're quite sure you didn't hit your head?"

"Yes. Mrs. Summers, what is all this?"

"The men suspect an ambush may be forthcoming. It is not safe for you to be stranded here in the open." She reached through the crumpled carriage door, dug about a bit, and returned with a pistol, which she calmly handed to Evie. "Keep it close, dear."

Oh, for pity's sake.

She bit the inside of her cheek to keep from giggling, and, with a studiously serious expression, stowed the pistol away.

"I'll be careful." She very much doubted the thing was even loaded. "Thank you."

Mr. Hunter stopped in his task to frown at them. "I'm not certain arming Miss Cole is a wise choice."

"Miss Cole is a fine shot," Mrs. Summers informed him.

"Shooting a target is not—"

"Leave it." McAlistair swung up on the dark chestnut gelding. "We'll meet up with you at the cottage. Day after next."

"Meet them . . . *in two days?*" Evie felt the first wave of true unease. "You don't mean—"

He did, apparently. He reached over and swatted the mare's rump.

And they were off.

❈ *Six* ❈

$\mathcal{I}$t was all she could do to keep up with the man.

Evie considered herself a fine horsewoman, and there were few activities she enjoyed more than a breakneck race across an open field, but the rugged path chosen by McAlistair was nothing like the wide pastures in which she was accustomed to riding.

They wove through trees, up and down steep hillsides, following no discernible trail at all. The man was pushing them as if he thought the devil himself were behind them.

It was a dangerous way to ride and, to Evie, that in itself was sufficient evidence that McAlistair had no knowledge of the ruse. He wouldn't be taking such chances unless he believed them absolutely necessary.

The absurdity of it was that she knew it was completely *unnecessary*. Enough was enough, she decided. She'd been insulted in a letter, removed from her home, bruised in a carriage accident, and was now riding hell for leather over unfamiliar terrain, all because a few misguided meddlers thought she'd be better off with a husband. Their little scheme had ceased to amuse her.

She'd been willing to play along to a point, but that point did not extend to breaking her neck. Or McAlistair's.

It was time to tell him the truth.

She called out to him: "Mr. McAlistair! Mr. McAlistair!"

Either he didn't hear her, or he chose to ignore her. She finally gave up and simply pulled her horse to a stop. He'd figure out she wasn't following him, eventually.

She didn't have to wait long. McAlistair spun his mount around and brought it to a halt facing hers.

"Are you tired?"

She blew an errant lock out of her eyes—one of many at this point, she was sure.

"No, I'm not tired." They'd only been riding for a quarter hour, for heaven's sake. "I wished to s-speak to you. I . . ." Oh, dear, this was going to be very awkward. "The thing is, Mr. McAlistair . . ." She shifted in her saddle. "The thing is, this is entirely unnecessary. All this f-fuss and bother, it's just . . . unnecessary," she finished lamely.

He didn't speak, or move, or give any indication that he'd heard her. If he hadn't been staring directly at her, she'd have thought he wasn't listening at all.

"It's a ruse," she continued with a bit more force. "A very silly ruse that's gotten entirely out of hand." She twisted her lips in disapproval. "A carriage accident, honestly. Someone could have been injured."

He remained still, but unless she was mistaken, his eyes narrowed a bit. "Explain."

"Right. Well. It's nothing more than an absurd attempt

at matchmaking, you see. The note, this trip, all of it was set up with the hope I would fall madly in love with my rescuer."

"Who?"

She tried not to smile at the sign of jealousy. How lovely.

"I'm not entirely certain, but I suspect it's Mr. Hunter. Odd choice for a white knight though, isn't he? Gray perhaps—"

"No. Who's responsible?"

"Who's . . . ? Oh." *Oh.* "Mr. Fletcher, with Lady Thurston and Mrs. Summers. It has something to do with a deathbed promise Mr. Fletcher made to the late Duke of Rockeforte."

He seemed to consider that for a moment. "No."

"No?" She blinked at him. "What do you mean, no?"

"You're mistaken."

"I'm not. I overheard their conversation on the matter . . . most of it," she amended. "Enough of it," she added when he sent her a dubious look. "Enough to know the threatening letter was sent by Mr. Fletcher."

"No."

Irritation bit at her. "Yes. No. Who. Tell me, Mr. McAlistair, do you ever speak in whole, multiple-word sentences?"

"Occasionally." He took hold of her horse's bridle and tugged gently to start them moving again. "Ride."

She leaned forward and slapped his hand away. "*No.*"

For the first time since meeting him, Evie had the occasion to see McAlistair look surprised. It was only a slight widening of his eyes, but she noticed it, just as she noticed when his brow furrowed by the smallest fraction of an inch.

"You're not stammering."

How thoughtful of him to point it out. "I stammer when

I'm nervous, and I'm not nervous at the moment. I'm annoyed. I don't care to be treated like some helpless idiot you can order and drag about."

"You're not an idiot."

"Then why—"

"But you are mistaken."

If she thought he'd give her the time, she would have squeezed her eyes shut and counted to ten, slowly. She squeezed the reins instead, hard. "How can you be so . . ." *Damnably bloody-minded.* ". . . So certain this isn't all a preposterous attempt to see me maneuvered into matrimony with the right gentleman?"

"Because," he said with a wry hook of his lips, "she sent you with me."

McAlistair started them forward again, and this time Evie let him.

She considered resisting further, but since he didn't seem inclined to be reasonable, and because the pace he set was hard, but no longer dangerous, she decided against it.

Besides, he had a point.

She sent you with me.

Why the devil had Mrs. Summers sent her off with McAlistair?

Why had Mrs. Summers sent her off at all? There were a thousand different ways that could have been contrived to put her together with her intended rescuer. Most of them, she was sure, did not require a carriage accident, a dangerous ride through the woods, and two days alone with a man who was not an immediate member of her family. If anyone were to discover she'd gone off alone with McAlistair, she'd be ruined.

If it weren't for the fact that a scandal for her meant a scandal for her entire family, Evie rather thought she wouldn't mind being a ruined woman. Surely there was great freedom in no longer being subjected to the stringent rules of the *ton*. But there *was* her family to consider, and if anyone caught wind of her ride today . . .

She threw a glance over her shoulder and wondered if she could find her way back to the carriage without McAlistair's guidance. Likely not, she decided, which left her no choice but to continue on and hope that when they finally stopped, she could convince him of the ruse, persuade him to return to the others, and pray no one outside their little group would ever be the wiser.

And then what? Did she want to go back to the others and tell them she knew the truth? The scheme would be called off—which seemed a fine idea at the moment—but Mr. Fletcher would only try again at a later date, and with more care taken to assure she didn't discover the ploy in advance. That prospect seemed considerably less fine.

And the possibility of scandal was fairly low, she admitted. The secretiveness of the whole ridiculous endeavor made certain of that.

Though she didn't much care for the idea, it seemed following McAlistair was her best option at present.

So follow him she did, up and down more hills, fording streams, keeping primarily to the woods and entirely off the roads. They slowed to a walk from time to time, giving the horses a chance to rest, but for the most part they pushed their mounts, and themselves, as hard and as fast as the terrain would safely allow.

There wasn't a cloud in the sky, and the sun beat relentlessly on Evie's head and shoulders. Under other circumstances, she would have relished the feel of it. Sunny days were not so common that she was in the habit of taking them for granted. Just now, however, she didn't feel grateful so much as hot and increasingly sticky. The watered beer she drank offered little relief, and it didn't help matters that she'd neglected to take her bonnet from the carriage.

To top off what she was beginning to think of as the most disagreeable excursion of her life, her leg was beginning to give her pain. In the past, Evie had found that her weak leg always began to stiffen and ache after she'd been in a saddle for more than an hour. She could go a bit longer if she made regular stops to walk about and stretch, but even with that, two hours was really her limit.

At a guess, she and McAlistair had been riding nonstop for well over four hours. The muscles in her leg had begun to protest mildly after the first hour; after the third they'd been screaming. Now, however, they'd become disconcertingly silent. She made an attempt to flex her toes and found she couldn't feel them. She was dead numb from the top of her right hip all the way down.

Dismounting, she realized grimly, was going to be a problem. Then again, that particular worry operated under the assumption that dismounting would, at some point, be on the itinerary. Given the way McAlistair was driving them, she wondered if he meant to ride straight through to Norfolk.

More than once she opened her mouth to demand a break, and more than once pride held her back. She hated being seen as weak or fragile. She detested the looks of pity she received from others when her leg grew tired and her limp became apparent. And she despised the whispered comments she sometimes caught as she passed through crowded ballrooms: "Poor dear. Quite badly damaged in the accident, you know."

Damaged. She loathed that word above all others. She most certainly was not damaged, and if need be, she could stay on a horse as long as any man.

Most men, she qualified after a time.

This man, she qualified again after another hour. She could, and would, stay on a horse as long as McAlistair. Even if it meant she couldn't move afterward, which was, unfortunately, becoming a more likely outcome with every passing minute.

On the next occasion of McAlistair slowing the horses to a walk, Evie took the chance of awkwardly pulling her foot from the stirrup in the vain hope that even a slight change of position would help. It was a struggle to balance and to fit her foot back into the stirrup when they began a faster pace, but there was nothing else for it. She had to do something.

Unfortunately, the somethings she tried appeared to be of little use, and by the time McAlistair brought the horses to a stop in a small clearing, she was nearly at her wit's end. She was exhausted, annoyed, sore in all the places she could still feel, and rather disappointed with herself. It shouldn't be so damnably hard to sit in a saddle for a mere half-day's ride.

She watched as McAlistair scanned their surroundings.

"Are we done running away, then?" she groused, fully expecting her angry words of exhaustion to be met with angry words of pride. Gentlemen never ran away.

His pride, however, seemed sturdy enough to weather her peevishness. He swung off his horse in a fluid movement she envied. "For now. The horses need to rest."

They weren't the only ones, she thought. What she wouldn't give for a hot bath, a change of clothes, a soft bed, and a few minutes of privacy just then could be counted on one hand.

McAlistair glanced up at her briefly before setting to work untying one of the bundles from his saddle. "Get down. Stretch your legs."

Oh, how she'd love to. "No, thank you."

He stopped and looked at her. "Get down."

She straightened in the saddle, trying for a regal appearance, and suspected she failed utterly. "I'm perfectly comfortable, thank—Don't!" She threw a hand up as he came toward her.

A small line formed between his brows. "What is it?"

"It's nothing. It's . . . I'm a bit stiff, that's all."

"Then let me help you down."

She shook her head, a small clutch of panic and embarrassment blooming in her chest. If he tried setting her on her feet now, she'd only topple onto her face. "I . . . I'd rather you didn't."

"Why?"

She began rubbing her hip discreetly in the hopes of bringing it back to life. "Because I'm not fond of being tossed on and off my horse like a sack of flour. An odd sentiment, I'm sure, but—"

"It's your leg."

Her hand stilled. Blast, the man had eyes like a hawk. "As I said, I'm a bit stiff. I'll be perfectly fine in a—"

She cut off when he simply reached up and wrapped his large hands about her waist. There was nothing for her to do but grasp his shoulders when he swung her off the horse.

He set her on her feet, but much to either her relief or horror—she'd decide that later—he didn't let her topple. He slid a strong arm around her back, the other around her shoulder, and took the majority of her weight.

"Does it hurt?" he asked softly over her head.

She couldn't bring herself to look up. They were pressed together as if in an embrace. The soft wool of his coat tickled her nose and carried the alluring scent of soap and leather and man. She could feel the muscles of his legs against hers—one of hers, anyway—and the hard expanse of his chest pressed against her breasts, which seemed to have inherited all the feeling lost from her leg. They felt heavy all of a sudden and acutely sensitive. She heard him murmur something over her head, but it was impossible to decipher the words over the roar of blood in her ears.

She wanted him to let go and step away. She was terrified he would.

A strong hand stroked down her back and she struggled not to shiver.

"Evie, does it hurt?"

Her eyes fixed on a small white button of his shirt and stayed there. "No . . . not yet. It's numb."

She thought perhaps he nodded. She felt the movement in his broad shoulders, but she hadn't long to consider it before he shifted, slipped an arm around the backs of her knees, and lifted her.

She gasped and wrapped her arms around his neck without thinking. It was the oddest sensation, being carried as if she weighed nothing. Once again she found herself torn between delight and discomfort. But before she had time to think on that or dwell upon how much she wanted to lay her head against his shoulder and close her eyes, he was kneeling down to gently place her on a soft patch of grass.

"You should have said something earlier."

"I did," she responded, reluctantly letting her arms slide from his neck. "I said this was all a ruse and we should go back." Strictly speaking, she hadn't said that last bit, but it certainly could have been inferred.

Without responding, he reached to pull her skirts up to her knees. Stunned, she instinctively swatted his hand away and yanked them back down.

He raised his dark head to catch her eye and ran his tongue across his teeth. "I've been looking at your knees all day."

"I know." Or, at least, she'd known he *could* have, and if she weren't feeling so wretched at the moment, she probably would have been gratified to learn he had. "I'm sorry. It's a spontaneous response to having a man push my skirts up." Oh damn, that sounded dreadful. "That is . . . I've never been in the position before, but—"

"It's all right."

He gathered up the material again, and this time lifted it gently and slowly. Still, she had to fist her hands to keep from shoving it back down again. How ridiculous. She had been riding about all day with her dress caught up above her knees. Why should it bother her now?

Because she'd been on a horse, riding a comfortable distance from McAlistair, she realized, not on the ground with him only inches away—certainly not with his bare hands on her bare leg. Never mind that she couldn't feel his hands at present; she could see them—the way he carefully danced his fingers along her ankle, her calf, her knee.

"Nothing at all?" he asked.

She shook her head, unable to speak. She was mesmerized by his hands—the size of them, the elegant fingers with blunt tips, the way the tanned skin stood out so starkly against her pale leg. She imagined how they would feel—rough and strong and—

"How far up?" he asked.

"What?" She blinked rapidly for a second. "Oh. Er . . ." She hesitated, then touched her hip. "All the way, I'm afraid."

He moved to push her dress up farther, and she slapped his hand again. "I'll not apologize for that. You haven't been looking at . . . at that all day."

She would have sworn, absolutely sworn, she heard him mutter something that sounded suspiciously like, "Pity."

"Did you just—"

"We need to get the blood flowing," he said, effectively cutting her off.

"By looking and prodding?"

"By massaging."

"Oh." She used her hands to keep her skirts pinned above her knee. "Right. I can do that."

He shook his head. "Lie back."

Lie back? In the middle of the woods with a strange—or very nearly strange—man, whilst her skirts were gathered about her waist? "You can't possibly be serious."

He was, apparently. He pried her hands free, and took her by the shoulders to gently, but insistently, push her down. "Stay."

"I'm not a dog, Mr. McAlistair."

"Stay," he repeated, keeping his hands on her shoulders. "Or I'll tie you down."

Such a threat would normally have elicited a furious response from Evie, even if only on principle's sake, but the urge to fight back eluded her at the moment. She found it comforting to have his warm hands on her arm and his broad form looming over hers. Though his face remained hard and set, she could see the concern in his eyes.

"I'll stay," she muttered. Then, because her pride wouldn't allow for complete submission, she added, "But should you ever attempt to tie me down, *I'll* attempt to break every bone in your body, and after they heal, break them all again."

The faintest smile touched his lips. "Fair enough."

He drew back and she felt, through her strong leg, her skirts being drawn up. Uncomfortable with the spark that shot through her at the sight and feel of McAlistair's dark head bent over her legs, she shut her eyes and concentrated on what was happening to her numb appendage.

There were movement and pressure first, odd sensations that seemed to originate above her hip. After a time, the first signs of life began to return. Her toes started to tingle, little pricks and stings she found more relieving than uncomfortable. Though she'd tried to block it out, she'd been harboring the small and irrational fear that feeling would never return—that her leg had gone from troublesome to completely useless.

Her relief at having that disturbing possibility removed was short-lived. The tingle traveled up to her ankle, her knee, her thigh. She knew what it meant. She'd woken in the small hours of the morning with a numb arm or foot often enough to know the innocuous pins and needles would soon be replaced by knives and daggers.

That too started in her toes, the horrible burning and cramping that made even the thought of being touched nearly unbearable. It worked its way through her foot to her ankle. She gritted her teeth and squeezed her eyelids tighter, determined not to cry out.

She could feel McAlistair's hands now, but she was no longer fascinated by the idea of his touch. His fingers felt like hot coals pressing into her skin. In an effort to keep her hands from slapping his away, she grasped at the dirt and grass beneath her. Please stop, was all she could think. *Please stop.*

His voice floated over the pain. "Move your leg."

She knew he was right. Knew that movement would help the pain pass more quickly.

The very idea of moving made her want to weep.

She managed a very muffled "no" through compressed lips.

The burn spread past her calf.

"Move your leg, Evie."

She shook her head and bit the inside of her cheek. The cramping reached her knee, her thigh, her hip. She was in agony.

"Evie—"

"Oh, sod off!"

She bolted upright, gripped her leg at her thigh, and began to swear.

❋ *Seven* ❋

For a time, Evie had been in the habit of collecting swear words. It had begun as a sort of academic study—an attempt to understand the colorful language that was sometimes tossed about in the less respectable neighborhoods she visited. But it had quickly grown into a hobby. One she'd enjoyed immensely. She'd badgered anyone who had been willing to aid her in her quest and, over time, had managed to amass a truly impressive arsenal of curses.

She used each and every one of them now.

The most vulgar came first, spat out between gritted teeth and a jaw locked tight with pain. A small part of her cringed at what she was saying and hoped desperately that it was unintelligible. But as that small part of her was also insisting she stop talking, it went largely ignored.

As the burn began to ease, so did the intensity of her curses. The merely moderately offensive were brought out as the daggers retracted, and when the last cramped muscle relaxed, she ended her symphony of profanity with the phrase, "Oh, bloody, bloody, *bloody* hell," and fell back onto the grass with a long exhale.

Utterly exhausted, she remained there with her eyes closed and her breath coming in pants. She was aware of McAlistair moving around her, even going off into the trees for a bit, and wondered what he was doing. But it was several more minutes before she mustered the energy to open her eyes and assuage her curiosity.

She found him standing over her with what looked to be a damp cloth in his hand. Kneeling, he pressed the cloth to her forehead. "Better?"

She nearly whimpered with pleasure at the feel of the cool water against her brow. Another layer of misery slid away. "Much, thank you."

He turned the cloth over. "You swear."

There was no censure in his voice, no shock or disappointment, just a hint of surprise. It was such a mild response to the horrid words she'd spoken. If the air was actually capable of turning blue, Evie imagined the space between them would be darker than the deepest part of the ocean, at night.

She felt heat rise to her cheeks. "I beg your pardon."

"No need."

She remembered suddenly that at least one of those swears had been specifically addressed to him. She grimaced. "There is. I told you to . . . that is, I said—"

"You were in pain. It's understandable."

"Thank you." She waited for him to say more, then realized that waiting for McAlistair to elaborate on something was rather like waiting for ice to thaw in January. A singularly pointless pursuit. She searched for something else to say, instead. "Aren't you going to ask how I learned them?"

"Same as everyone else. From others."

"I . . ." She pursed her lips. "I could have read them in a book."

"All of them?" He cocked his head. "May I borrow it?"

She felt a smile form slowly. "Was that a joke, Mr. McAlistair?"

He withdrew the cloth from her forehead. "Of a sort."

Of a sort counted, she decided. "Not half bad for a man who appears to be out of the habit."

"I wanted to see you smile."

Her heart warmed. "And a kind word to boot. I should make myself uncomfortable more often. It's made you positively charming."

"Uncomfortable? Is that how you'd describe it?"

She was surprised to see a muscle work in his jaw, more surprised to be the one responsible for putting it there. Studying him, she kept her smile in place and her voice light. "Well, I could use a few more fitting adjectives, but I do hate repeating myself."

His face visibly relaxed at her small jest. "Certain you're all right?

He leaned in farther, his eyes searching her face, and suddenly, she was all too aware of how close they were. He was so near, so very near, that she could make out the smallest details of his face. He had wonderfully long lashes, endearing lines at the corners of his eyes, and the single most enthralling mouth she'd ever seen. She wanted to brush her finger along the full bottom lip. She wanted to reach up and spear her fingers into his hair—hair, she noticed for the first time, that was not just brown, but a luscious blend of browns and blacks and even reds where the sun hit it. A few strands had fallen from their tie to frame his face.

She imagined pulling him down for another kiss.

What would he do? she wondered. Pull away? Push her away? Or kiss her back, cede to her demands and lie down where she could feel the weight of him, taste him, breathe in that aroma that only came in tantalizing wisps now.

"Evie?"

"Hmm." He'd hold her this time, not stand aloof as he had before.

"Evie."

"Hmm?" She blinked, snapping herself back. "What? What?" She focused her eyes and noticed that the tic in his jaw had returned. "I'm sorry?"

"I asked if you were feeling better."

"Yes. No." She grimaced. "Yes, I feel better. I'm sorry, I'm rather tired." *Deliriously* tired seemed more fitting, given that she was daydreaming about ravishing Mr. McAlistair in the woods. How extraordinarily absurd.

Well, perhaps the woods bit wasn't entirely absurd, but the rest was several degrees, several *dozen* degrees, beyond ridiculous.

"I'd like to get up." She didn't wait for his agreement, and he didn't argue, but when she moved to stand, he put a restraining hand on her shoulder.

"Sit. Rest."

"I'd like to, but . . . that is, I've need . . ." She waggled her finger at a thick clutch of trees.

"To take a walk?"

"What? No." She dropped her hand. "Well, in a way. I've been on a horse for hours, Mr. McAlistair. I require a moment of privacy."

"Ah." He straightened. "Do you need help?"

Help? "With what?"

"Standing. Walking."

"Oh." Oh, she dearly hoped not. She wiggled her toes experimentally, pushed her heel down and felt the pull up to her hip. "No, thank you. I believe I can manage."

Please, *please*, let her manage.

She accepted his offered hand, but let go with a great rush of relief when she found she could stand on her own without difficulty. Her leg was still tender and likely would ache for days. But she could *feel* her leg, put weight on it, and place one foot in front of the other, all of which meant she could take her moment of privacy without assistance.

Thank heavens.

"Don't go far," McAlistair advised.

"I rather doubt I could."

She hobbled into the woods and muddled through the process of seeing to her needs out-of-doors. There were times, she groused to herself as she righted her skirts, that a woman should be allowed to wear breeches, or at least fewer, and preferably shorter, layers of fabric.

When she returned, several minutes later, she found McAlistair lifting a satchel from the back of his horse.

Curious, she wandered closer. "What are you doing?"

He spared her a single assessing glance. "Unpacking. You're well?"

"Yes, of course." She waved the question away, more than ready to be done with the subject of her health. "Why are you unpacking?"

"We'll camp here."

"Here? In the woods?" Evie looked around. Why she bothered, she didn't know.

"You like the woods," he pointed out, reminding her that he knew a great deal more about her than she did of him.

"I like walking in the woods, not sleeping in them."

"Have you ever tried?"

"I have, actually. I snuck out of Haldon when I was fifteen and made a camp in the woods for a night."

He stopped what he was doing to look at her. "You didn't care for it?"

She'd loved it, and not only because it was forbidden and therefore appealing. She'd lain under an old Scots pine and listened to the trees creaking in the wind while the smell of the outdoors filled her lungs. Her last thought as she'd drifted off had been that sneaking out to sleep in the woods was quite the finest idea she'd ever had.

Her next had been that it was the worst. She'd woken

midway through the night in terrible pain, her leg cramping mercilessly in protest of the hard ground.

She could only imagine how she would fare after a ride like the one she'd just endured.

"Evie?"

"I . . . couldn't we press on? There's light left yet."

"You need rest."

So very true, and so very irritating. "I'm not one of the horses. And I thought you were worried someone was chasing us."

"Good a time as any to make a stand."

She felt her lips twitch. "I'll assume that's another joke, though it marks you as a man who prefers quantity over quality."

"Out of practice," he reminded her. "Answer my question."

She bit her lip—more in an effort to stop herself from commenting on his high-handed order than an act of nerves—and shifted her feet, which was, she was forced to admit, very much an act of nerves. How many times would they both have to be reminded of her infirmity in one day?

"Evie."

She shifted again, then capitulated. What was a little more lost pride? "Yes, I enjoyed sleeping in the woods . . . but my leg did not. May we move on now? I—"

"Did you take care where you placed your bedding?"

"Well, of course. I brought a blanket and cleared a space of rocks. I'm not a fool."

He shook his head. "There are ways to make a spot more comfortable for sleeping. Pine boughs, grass, even leaves can soften the ground."

"Oh." She frowned a little. "No, I didn't think of that. I didn't know."

"How would you?"

Common sense came to mind. She very much hoped it didn't come to his. His opinion of her was apt to be depressingly low as it was. She wasn't so swamped in her own discomfort that she couldn't see how that very discomfort was making her unpleasant.

She made herself smile a little. "Perhaps you're right. And it won't hurt me—" Then again, it might. "That is, I am willing to try." Particularly since it meant she wouldn't have to crawl back onto a horse for the remainder of the day. "Thank you for the suggestion."

Evie chose the soft, grassy spot where McAlistair had set her down earlier, and when she had finished tossing aside a few hidden pebbles, she made her way to the edge of the woods to find branches for her makeshift mattress.

She was so tired, she thought she could probably sleep standing up, but she made several trips before standing back, hands on hips, to survey her work. It looked, in her estimation, like a very small, very leafy nest. "This can't possibly work."

"It will work."

She glanced over at McAlistair, and noticed for the first time that he was stacking wood on a small space of cleared ground.

"You're building a fire?" she asked. "Aren't you worried it will give away our position? Not that anyone is looking for said position, but if someone were, a fire would be rather like sending him a map, wouldn't it?"

"We passed dozens of houses, all—"

"We did?" She couldn't recall seeing a single one.

"Skirted the properties," he amended. "Lots of chimneys."

"And a great number of fires for our mythical foe to investigate," she finished for him with a nod.

He broke a branch in half and laid the pieces crossing each other. "It'll be dark soon, besides."

She watched him haul a large log over to the pile.

"You're stronger than you look." As he looked rather strong to start, she felt that was saying something.

His only reaction was a raised brow.

"It looks heavy," she explained, gesturing at the log. "And you've picked me up." Which wasn't something she needed to feel embarrassment over, she told herself sternly. "More than once now."

He tossed the log down. "You're small."

Her eyes narrowed. Was he making sport of her? She wasn't small, or even petite, as her family and friends generously referred to her. What she *was*, was short and decidedly curvy. But she couldn't detect any sign of humor in McAlistair's voice or face.

Then again, it was McAlistair; detecting a sign of anything bordered on the miraculous.

"Well . . ." How was she to respond to that? Because she had absolutely no idea, she said, "Is there something I could do to help?"

"Fetch the food."

Certain—or relatively so—that he didn't intend offense at the short command, she shrugged and walked to the saddles to unpack the remainder of the lunch she and Mrs. Summers had shared. There was a very sad-looking ham sandwich, a bit of bread and cheese that looked the worse for wear, and what appeared to still be a fair amount of watered beer.

They weren't to die of thirst, but there wasn't enough food to satisfy even one of them.

She glanced at McAlistair, who was busy hauling logs for the fire. He was bigger, he was working harder, and she had amends to make for her peevish behavior.

"I'm afraid our rations are rather slim." She waited until he set down the last log to hand him the sandwich and the lion's share of the bread and cheese. "But I'm not particularly hungry, anyway."

He broke the sandwich in half and handed her a section. "Eat."

She stepped back without taking the food. "I will eat. I've enough of the bread and cheese to—"

"Take it, Evie."

Realizing they were perilously close to another argument, she stepped forward and took the half he offered. "Bit silly, really, for me to choke it down when you haven't enough. Are you certain—?"

"I've plenty." He jerked his chin at his pile of bread and cheese. "Take more of that, as well."

"Perhaps," she evaded. "If I'm still hungry after the sandwich."

Rather than press the issue, he knelt to light the fire and with a skill clearly born of extensive practice, created a cheerful little blaze in a matter of minutes. Evie settled across from him, polished off the last of her food, and made a point not to glance wistfully at McAlistair's bread and cheese.

For a long while, the pair of them sat in comfortable silence—the sort that comes less from familiarity and more from both parties being weary to their very bones. Evie stared into the flames, letting her mind wander as darkness fell around them.

"Why would they do it?" McAlistair asked suddenly.

Her gaze shot up. "I beg your pardon?"

"Why would the others conspire to find you a husband?"

"Oh." She blinked away her stupor and smiled at him. "You believe me, then?"

"No. It's a hypothetical question."

She felt herself slump. It was a little disheartening, really, that he should so easily dismiss what she'd told him. "Well, whether you believe it or not, it is a ruse. It has something to do with a deathbed promise Mr. Fletcher made to the late Lord Rockeforte—Alex's father. Can't imagine what sort of promise it was that required matchmaking or why he thought to include me. I barely knew the man."

"Can't you find a husband on your own?"

"Certainly, I can," she answered quickly, and hoped he couldn't see her flush in the dying light. *Probably*, she could find a husband on her own. She'd never actually received an offer of marriage, but then, she'd been careful not to lead any gentlemen in that direction. "I've simply no interest in the endeavor."

"Why not?"

She picked up a small twig and tossed it into the fire. "One could just as easily ask why one should."

"Children and a home of your own."

"Haldon is my home, Mr. McAlistair, for as long as my family resides there. Beyond that, not every woman relishes the idea of planning her life around marriage, birth, and running a house."

"Many do," he pointed out. Then he added, "McAlistair."

She blinked at him. "I'm sorry?"

"It's McAlistair, not Mr. McAlistair."

"Oh." Goodness, the man really was odd. "McAlistair is your first name?"

He shook his head.

"*Have* you a first name?" she inquired.

"Yes."

She waited a beat. Then another. Then laughed and rolled her eyes. "La, how you do go on."

"Mr. McAlistair was my father."

"Generally, that is how it works."

"I don't care for the reminder."

"I see." She plucked at a blade of grass, torn between doing what was polite and letting the matter drop, and doing what she wanted, which was to satisfy her insatiable curiosity. "Was he unkind?"

"I don't know," McAlistair answered without a hint of emotion. "He left when I was four."

"I'm very sorry." She plucked at the grass again. "I suppose you haven't any siblings, then?"

"I've six younger brothers." He handed her some of the remaining bread.

"Younger? . . . Ah." She bobbed her head and, because she was starving, and he was holding it out so insistently, and it was such a small portion, really, and . . . oh, very well, because she was weak, she accepted the food. "That makes sense."

It wasn't until she'd taken a bite that she realized he was staring at her again. She chewed and swallowed. "What?"

"Makes sense?"

She cocked her head at him. "Did you expect me to condemn your mother?"

"Yes."

"Oh. Well." He certainly was blunt. "I don't see why. Most members of the demimonde consider extramarital affairs to be fashionable—provided the lady has produced at least one male heir, of course."

"Are you a member of the demimonde?"

"No, but I'll not judge an abandoned woman for seeking comfort. She wasn't left a choice, was she? Pity she couldn't have obtained a divorce."

"You approve of divorce?"

Heavens, were they having an actual conversation? "Under

certain circumstances, yes. I don't think people should go about changing spouses willy-nilly, but neither should it be so difficult for a woman to free herself from an injurious union."

"Like the women you help?"

She took another bite of bread. "Exactly."

He stared at her, unblinking, for a full five seconds, as if considering her very carefully. "My brothers have different fathers."

She stopped midchew. "What, *all* of them?"

He nodded once.

"Well. I see." She swallowed and thought this new bit of information through. "Perhaps she required a great deal of comfort."

It was hard to tell in the encroaching darkness and with the way the fire cast light and shadows across his chiseled features, but she rather thought he might have smiled.

Then she was absolutely certain he was scowling. Not at her, mind you, he was staring at something off to her left, but still, he was scowling.

Confused, she followed his line of sight. "What is it?"

"Don't move."

"What? What is it?"

She saw it then, the brown snake with black jagged marks along its back, slithering not two feet away from her side. Though it wasn't the first adder she'd come across, it was certainly the first she'd encountered while sitting on the ground. She felt an involuntary shiver run over her skin.

"Oh, hell."

"Stay still," McAlistair repeated sternly. Crouching, he pulled his knife from its sheath. Before she had the chance to even wonder what he meant to do, he lunged forward in a fluid movement, grabbed the snake with his free hand, and neatly sliced off its head.

Even as her heart fluttered at the danger and her mind reeled with the sheer speed at which McAlistair had acted, Evie's stomach turned over at the woeful sight of the be-headed snake. "Was that *really* necessary?"

"Yes." He stood to toss the carcass into the woods. "Or I wouldn't have done it."

"It wasn't hurting anything."

"Yet."

"You could have—" She broke off and, for once, was grateful he wasn't inclined to fill the silence. Her arguments were foolish. There wasn't anything else he could have done, short of catching the snake, saddling one of the horses, and riding—in almost darkness—deep into the woods to release it far enough from camp that it wouldn't be inclined to return.

She frowned sadly in the direction of the dead snake. "It's a great pity."

He resumed his seat. "You've a fondness for snakes?"

"I don't know if it could be termed a fondness," she said, thinking of the cold shiver she'd felt. "But I have a respect for them and an aversion to killing a living thing that's not intended for food."

Unless she was much mistaken—and she rather thought she must be—a hint of devilish humor crept into his voice. "Should I fetch it back and cook it?"

"I . . ." Her gaze jumped back to him. "*Can* one eat an adder?"

"Yes."

"You're certain? You've had them before?"

"Number of times."

She bit her lip and considered. "What do they taste like?"

"Mild."

Mild, she thought, could mean a great many things. It could, for all she knew, mean mildly disgusting.

"Wouldn't you like to soothe your conscience?" McAlistair inquired.

She would, but not at the expense of her stomach. She peered at him over the flames.

"Are you goading me?"

"Challenging you."

"A dare, is it?" She couldn't resist a dare any better than she could resist curiosity. "What would the terms of the challenge be?"

"You eat four bites, and you get your choice of blankets for the night."

She snorted. "You'd have given me that choice, at any rate."

"Not without the four bites," he replied, and this time she was quite sure she could hear a bit of the devil in his voice. "Not now."

"I see." She laughed. "And what do you get, should I fail? Aside from a more comfortable night's sleep?"

He said nothing for a long, weighted moment. When he finally spoke, his voice was soft as velvet. "A kiss."

Her mouth opened but no sound emerged. A kiss?

A kiss in the woods? Was he mocking her? She narrowed her eyes at him, but found she couldn't see his face well enough to tell. Surely he would never be so cruel.

"A kiss," she finally repeated hoarsely. She cleared her throat and attempted to instill a touch of sophistication in her tone. "Just a simple kiss, nothing more?"

"A kiss on my terms."

A log crackled in the fire, sending a shower of sparks into the air. The reflection of the bright shards danced in his eyes, and briefly illuminated his face. There was no humor to be found in his expression, not a hint of amusement softening his hard features. If anything, he looked rather . . . determined.

"You said . . ." She licked lips gone dry. "You said I wasn't meant for you."

"You're not."

"Then why . . . ?"

He shook his head. "Those are the terms. Do you accept?"

"It . . ." She cleared her throat again. "It seems a skewed bargain. Winning only gains me something you've decided to take away. I want the boon of my choice."

"Such as?"

She wracked her brain for something, *anything*, she wanted more than another chance to kiss McAlistair. "I want . . . I want . . ." She hit on just the thing. "I want you to take seriously and be open to discussing that this whole business is a matchmaking ruse."

"I'll take your concerns seriously," he countered. "More would be a lie."

She considered that and decided she appreciated the honesty. "Very well. We have a deal."

❈ *Eight* ❈

The sky had lost its last vestiges of gray by the time McAlistair finished skinning, cleaning, and cooking the snake.

It didn't look altogether terrible, Evie mused after he'd handed her a portion. It didn't smell altogether terrible either. She broke off a small piece, squared her shoulders, and popped it into her mouth.

"What do you think?"

It *was* mild. In fact, it was rather bland. Had she not been all too aware of the fact that it was snake, she might have assumed it was some kind of tastelessly prepared fowl. "It's not altogether terrible."

"Can you eat the whole of it?"

"Certainly." And to prove it, she took another bite and chewed around a smug smile.

He was sitting closer to the fire, and to her, than he had been earlier, and the flickering light allowed her to make out the lines and angles of his face. He offered her a half smile as he tore off a chunk of meat and bit in. Her eyes lingered on his mouth.

The memory of how that mouth had felt as it moved over hers—warm, gentle, and with the faintest hint of demand—flashed into her mind, and a nearly overpowering longing swept over her.

She could have that again. All she had to do was lose the dare. Her pride winced at the thought, but she slowed her chewing nonetheless. What could it hurt—aside from the obvious answer of her pride? She could make do with a thinner blanket, and McAlistair struck her as being too sensible to ignore the reality of a matchmaking scheme for very long. And even if he were convinced of the ruse this very moment, it was too late now to turn back and find the others. No matter how it had come to be, they were stuck together for the remainder of the trip.

She slowed her chewing further, and poked a bit at the remainder of the meat.

"Problem?" McAlistair asked.

She made a show of choking down the food in her mouth. "Not at all."

She picked at the meat, tore off a small piece, and stared at it. Making sure he was watching her, she tore the piece in half, then in half again, then—

"That's not a bite, Evie."

"It is." She put the now miniscule piece in her mouth and made a show of chewing once. "You see? I bit." She might have swallowed as well; the piece had been too small to say.

"Doesn't count." He gestured at the remainders of the piece. "All of it."

"That's more than four bites."

"Can't you do it?"

"Of course I can." She really could. Bland or not, her belly would be more than happy to have the meal. The rest of her, however, wanted something else. She pushed the pieces with the tip of her finger. "It's a bit bland, that's all."

"Should make it easy to swallow."

"You'd think," she agreed in an absent tone. "But the idea of it . . ." She poked a bit more.

"Think of something else."

She shot a glance at him. He was awfully encouraging. Did he want to lose the wager? She wasn't in a position to judge, mind you, but *her* losing on purpose meant she would be kissed. *His* losing on purpose meant he didn't want to kiss her— bit insulting, that. And odd, as it had been his idea.

"What if I were to eat the remaining two bites at once?" she inquired. "Would that count?"

"I'll accept it."

She hid a scowl at his quick agreement. He *did* want to lose. "Well, how much would that be?"

He reached over and tore off a piece—a gargantuan piece that equaled nearly double her original portion.

Very well, he didn't want to lose.

"I can't fit the whole of that in my mouth at once," she told him with a laugh.

The corner of his mouth hooked up. "Then don't."

"That's not two bites, which is what I owe you. It's not even four bites. It's a six-course meal and after-dinner snack."

He jerked his chin at the tiny bits of meat she'd torn a moment ago. "The penalty for cheating."

"I don't cheat." Some might argue she was cheating right now, but she wasn't one of them. "I'm simply not hungry."

"You've had little to eat today."

"I had lunch with Mrs. Summers, or part of a lunch at any rate, and the remainder of it only a few hours ago."

And she was still hungry, but a few hours' fast would be more than worth the chance to kiss McAlistair again.

He flicked her a cool glance. "You made the bargain, Evie."

She certainly had. And she wouldn't have been arguing except that it would be expected of her, were she trying to win that bargain.

She played with the meat while McAlistair ate.

"I can't do it," she lied when he had finished. "I just can't."

He was silent and still for a long moment. And then, to her complete astonishment, he said, "You tried. We'll call it a wash."

"What?" She wasn't certain if she should laugh, cry, or throw her food at him. "You can't do that."

"You want to lose?"

"That would be silly of me, wouldn't it?" she asked, by way of avoiding the question. "But you said it yourself. We made a bargain, a wager, and—"

He reached for the watered beer. "I'm releasing you from it," he said after a long drink.

"That is insulting to both of us."

His brows rose at her cool tone. "Care to explain?"

She opened her mouth, intent on delivering a scathing

lecture, but in the end decided on a simple, "You wouldn't offer to release me of the wager if I were a man."

His lips twitched. "Wouldn't have made the wager if you were a man."

"That is not the point." She turned to scowl into the fire. McAlistair's decision to release her from the bargain disappointed her for more reasons than the lost kiss. "You imply I am not to be held to the same standards. That leniency is required, as if I were incapable of fully understanding the bargain, or that my word is of less value than a man's. I find that attitude insufferable." Very well, she was going to lecture. "Furthermore, it shows you to be a small-minded individual who places little worth in—"

"Don't move."

"What?" Her heart leapt to her throat and her eyes darted about, searching for another snake. Was she sitting on a bloody nest of them?

"My way," McAlistair said. With his dark gazed fixed on hers, he closed the distance between them.

"Your—?" Her eyes widened as she realized his intent. The kiss. He was going to kiss her. On his terms.

Her heart, already in her throat, began to beat wildly.

Taking her hands gently, he placed them on the ground and held them there. He leaned forward, close, closer, then stopped, just a breath away. "Don't move," he repeated in a rough whisper.

She nodded, or thought she did.

And then he was kissing her, and all thought was lost. She didn't mean for that to happen—for her mind to go so utterly blank. She'd wanted to concentrate, to remember, to file away every minute, every second, every heartbeat of the kiss. It had seemed vital to do so only a moment ago. But now that his mouth was on hers, sensation pushed aside thought—his smell, his taste, the heat in her belly as he tasted her in return—and it only seemed vital that she kiss him back.

Her hands fisted under his. She wanted to touch, to pull him closer, to insist, but he held her still and moved his mouth over hers gently.

"My way," he whispered.

He brought his lips back to hers and kissed her with exquisite tenderness, rubbing his mouth across hers in the lightest of brushes before retreating, shifting, and brushing again. He kissed her as if he were testing, as if she were fragile . . . or dangerous.

Without the strength to move there was nothing she could do but let him continue his delicate exploration, until she thought she might go mad for wanting more.

He meant to sample, nothing more.

That was what McAlistair had told himself when he'd made the bet and what he swore even as he'd taken Evie's hands in his and bent his head to find her mouth. But after that first taste, that first intoxicating taste that was uniquely Evie, he was forced to admit what part of him had known all along: it was a promise he might not be able to keep.

Just the hint of her, that slightest meeting of lips, had the blood pounding in his veins and need clawing at his skin. Erotic images whirled dangerously through his mind: his hands in her hair, on her waist, under her skirt. Evie's hands on his face, on his back, on his skin.

Restraining her hadn't been the act of a man intent on lording power over a woman. It had been the act of a man who feared the power that woman had over him. A single brush of her fingers would be enough, more than enough, to snap his control. And he was furiously determined to retain what small amount he could still claim.

Just one more taste, one more sample, and he would force himself to stop.

Her tongue brushed his. It was just the tip, darting out in a gesture both hesitant and bold, but it was sufficient to make his blood boil and his need roar until he heard nothing else.

Chasing the need was fear.

He snapped himself back, gripping her shoulders as if he could hold or perhaps push her away. Later, he would realize it was a senseless gesture, as she was not only sitting, but sitting perfectly still. For now, however, it seemed absolutely necessary to keep her at arm's length.

"Enough." Even to his own ears, his voice sounded strained.

Evie blinked her eyes open slowly.

Enough? How could it possibly be enough?

There was more, wasn't there? she wondered, as her mind floated several inches above her head. Yes, of course there was more. She'd heard prostitutes speak of that more in very explicit terms. Those terms had sounded a little unreasonable to her at the time, but just now, she thought they sounded rather . . . interesting.

"Don't you want more?"

The moment the words were out of her mouth, her mind came crashing back to leave her stunned and reeling. "I don't . . . I c-can't . . ." She bit the end of her tongue. "I can't believe I said that." Even if she was terribly keen to hear his answer. It simply wasn't something a lady said. Worse, it came perilously close to begging.

McAlistair released her arms and stood, and the sudden distance left her feeling cold despite the warm night air. She searched for something to say, anything to break a silence she felt becoming increasingly awkward, but he turned away and walked a few feet to their supplies before anything appropriate came to mind.

Evie stood to watch him. She could have watched just as easily while sitting, but it added another layer of discomfort, to be on the ground like something discarded whilst he was up and about.

McAlistair grabbed the thicker blanket and brought it to her.

Instinctively, she stretched out her hand to take it. "I thought I'd lost the better blanket," she said softly.

"No, you lost the chance to choose. Go to sleep."

Just like that? After what they'd done, what she'd felt? Have a blanket and go to sleep? She swallowed past a lump in her throat. "If you're angry—"

"I'm not angry," he said in a gruff voice.

"Well then, if you're—"

"I'm not."

The lump turned into one of annoyance. "How can—"

"Let it alone, Evie."

She blew out an irritated breath. "For a man who speaks little, you interrupt a great deal."

"For an intelligent woman, you require a great deal of interrupting."

She gaped at him. "Are you . . . are you being *snippy?*"

His only response was a growl before he turned and stalked off into the woods.

It was a simple matter for McAlistair to move through the dark. It was his element, his milieu, and he'd had years to hone his skills. He could move easily and silently through the trees and underbrush without disturbing a single twig.

He just wasn't doing it right now.

In fact, he was, he could admit, stomping just a little. It

couldn't be helped. Speed was of the essence. There was a stream nearby, and with any luck, it would be frigid. He planned on dunking his head in it.

What the devil was *wrong* with him? What the hell had he been thinking, kissing Evie Cole *again?*

That was the crux of the problem, of course—he hadn't been thinking.

He scowled at his faulty reasoning. No, he had been thinking plenty—of holding her, tasting her, loving her. He'd thought of little else for years. The trouble was, imagining what it would be like to make love to Evie Cole while he'd been in the woods, alone, was very different from imagining what it would be like while they were in the woods, alone together. Now the temptation was very real.

He'd known it would be. The moment he'd led her into the woods without the others, he knew they'd be spending days with only each other for company, but he'd been sure he could resist. He'd had confidence in his self-control.

Bloody fool.

He hadn't been able to resist her for more than ten seconds the first time she'd been within grabbing distance. What had made him think he could manage it after a full day of trying, and failing, not to look at the pale skin of her bare legs, the way her body moved with the rhythm of her horse, and the way her light brown hair slipped from its pins to be tousled by the breeze? Why the devil had he thought he could resist her while they sat alone under the moonlight, her face kissed by the glow of the fire and her warm laughter floating on the dark air?

It was the laughter that did it. That low, almost husky sound of pleasure had been his initial introduction to Miss Evie Cole. He'd heard it his first week as the Hermit of Haldon Hall, drifting up through the trees from the back lawn. It had had the strangest effect on him. He'd been sitting there, staring at the small stream that ran through the woods, alternating somewhere between blissfully numb and dangerously on edge. Without a mission to accomplish, with nothing else to occupy his mind, his thoughts had turned to the life he'd waited too long to leave behind and the bleak future that lay ahead.

He had felt hollowed out, burned to his very core.

And then he'd heard her.

He would never be able to say why it was her laugh and no one else's that affected him so strongly. Why her voice had felt like a balm against his wounds, cooling the worst of the burn, softening the hardest edges of his memories. Perhaps because it was such a genuine sound—after years of dealing in lies, in the false, it was the sheer honesty of her delight that had moved him.

There had been nothing artificial in it, nothing that spoke of the phony or the designed.

There was still truth in the world, he'd realized, and it could be found in one woman's laughter.

He'd fallen in love with her that very day. Without seeing her, without even knowing for certain who she was, he'd fallen in love. It had been an innocent sort of love initially, the sort a lost and hungry man might develop for a woman who takes him in and enchants him with food and kindness.

But it had been love nonetheless.

For a time, he'd been content with that level of affection, to simply listen for and appreciate the sound of her laughter. But he was only a man, and eventually his desire to know more had led him to seek her out. Drawn by the sound of her voice, he'd made his way to the edge of the woods by the lawn one evening and caught his first glimpse of the woman who'd brought him some measure of peace.

He knew who she was the minute he laid eyes on her.

Before he'd taken up residence in the Haldon woods, Whit had given him a description of every member of the house. Small, curvy, and with a scar running the length of her cheek, the object of his adoration could be none other than eighteen-year-old Miss Evie Cole.

He'd watched her and a younger, taller girl who could only be Lady Kate Cole as they played with a pair of lop-eared puppies in the grass. He stayed no more than a quarter hour, just long enough to witness the gentle way she tussled with the pups, the affectionate way she teased her friend . . . and the disturbing way his body tightened when she stood up and bent over to pick up one of the puppies, showing him a clear outline of her backside.

He'd walked back to his camp that afternoon with a love very different from the sort with which he'd walked out.

Pity, he thought now, that it hadn't been the fleeting sort.

He found the stream and knelt to cool his face. It wasn't frigid as he had hoped, but it did the job. Calmer, if not exactly comfortable, he sat back on his heels and took stock of the situation.

He'd kissed Evie—again—and that couldn't be undone. He doubted he would take it back even if he could. It had been heaven, and no man gave up paradise willingly, even when it was undeserved.

A man could, however, make a better effort not to steal it.

He'd keep his distance from her. He would remember who she was—a lady, an innocent, cousin and niece to the people he owed more than he could hope to repay. More importantly, he would remember who he was, and what he had been.

Feeling considerably more resolute, McAlistair stood and began a walk around the perimeter of the camp. He hadn't the least expectation of finding anything. He wouldn't have indulged in the kiss or gone stomping through the woods if he had believed, for a moment, that anyone could have followed them without his notice.

It wouldn't matter if a pursuer had taken every precaution to go undetected; McAlistair would have known of the danger. He had, after all, made a fine living from ferreting out men who had done their very best to hide.

Still, he wouldn't be comfortable forgoing the patrol.

Evie would no doubt consider the precaution pointless. Scowling again, McAlistair carefully pushed his way through a cluster of low-hanging branches. This notion she had of a matchmaking ruse troubled him. Not because he thought there was any truth to her theory, but because a woman certain of her safety was far more likely to take chances with her person.

It irritated him as well that she hadn't accepted his rejection of the theory. She had an unexpected stubborn streak.

Bullheadedness, however, could not stand forever against reason and reality. She'd come around eventually. And likely it was best she do so in stages. It would be less traumatic for her to grow accustomed to the idea gradually, rather than to be hit over the head with it all at once. He rather doubted she was inclined toward hysterics, but one never knew.

And he could keep her safe in the meantime.

With that settled and his patrol completed, he turned his steps toward camp . . . and his mind back to the kiss.

It occurred to him suddenly that apologizing to Evie might be the proper thing to do.

To hell with that.

It was enough that he had pulled away before things had gotten out of hand. He'd let the matter drop—simply pretend it hadn't happened. It had been some time since he had been subject to the rules of gentlemanly behavior, but he was certain—well, *relatively* certain—that pretending the kiss had never occurred was the next best thing to apologizing for it.

It would have to be. He wouldn't steal paradise, but damned if he'd apologize for sneaking a glimpse.

Left alone after McAlistair stormed off into the woods, Evie had considered staying up simply because he had ordered her to go to sleep, but in the end, she'd decided that pretending to sleep was a sight less humiliating than standing about, waiting for him to return.

Staring up now into the thin sliver of night sky afforded in the clearing, she might have taken some pleasure in the realization that her pile of leaves, branches, and a layer of thick blanket made for a surprisingly soft bed—might have, if she hadn't been so damnably uncomfortable.

Her body still hummed from McAlistair's kiss, making her hot and restless, and her mind still reeled from his sudden withdrawal.

Why had he turned away? Why had he tossed her the blanket, then *run* away? She wondered where he'd gone and when he would come back.

Perhaps she should have gone after him. Perhaps she should go after him now.

She wondered how mortifying it would be if she tried it, slipped and fell in the dark, and had to call out for his help.

She was weighing the benefits of getting up and pacing off her agitation around the glowing remains of the fire, when she heard the rustle of branches. Slowly (she was attempting to feign sleep, after all) she turned her head to the side. Squinting into the dark, she was able to discern the outline of McAlistair's form as he gathered branches at the edge of the clearing.

She turned her head back, rolled over, and shut her eyes as he made his way toward her. She wanted to ask if he was quite done being snippy, but thought better of it—particularly after he settled down behind her. He was so close she could hear his every breath. If she were to roll over, she could reach out and touch him. The urge to do just that was nearly overpowering. But even stronger was the desire for it to be him who reached.

"Evie?" he called softly, and nearly had her jumping off the blanket.

"Yes?" She winced at the wealth of hope in that one word.

"It's James. My first name is James."

"Oh." Heavens, the man really *was* odd. "Shall I . . . shall I call you James?"

"No. My father was James, as well."

"McAlistair, it is, then."

He wouldn't reach, she realized, but at least he wasn't angry or cold. Willing to accept that for now, she closed her eyes and let exhaustion drag her into sleep.

❈ *Nine* ❈

*T*he sun had yet to break over the tops of the trees when Evie next woke. It filtered through branches and leaves to shoot long beams onto the forest floor and softly light the clearing. She blinked blurry eyes at McAlistair's blanket, only to find him gone.

She sat up slowly, wincing at the stiffness of her leg and . . . well, the stiffness of everything, really. "McAlistair?"

She was answered by the soft crunch of leaves behind

her. Turning, she saw McAlistair stride out from the trees into the clearing, two fish dangling lifelessly from one hand.

She made a futile attempt to rub the sleep out of her eyes. "Where did you get those?"

"Stream. Caught them."

She saw no sign of a fishing pole or net. "With what?"

He held up his free hand, wiggled his fingers.

"Oh, you did not." She laughed. He couldn't possibly have. She watched him set his catch down next to the fire and stir the embers. "Did you?"

A corner of his mouth hooked up. "I could show you."

"What, *now?*"

He shook his head. "At the cottage. There's a stream."

"You've been there?"

"No. I asked Mr. Hunter to draw a map at Haldon."

"Oh." She yawned hugely. "Is it nice?"

He glanced up. "Wasn't a portrait. Just a sketch of surrounding towns, landmarks, buildings."

Of course it was. What else would it be—a rendition of every room, brick, and tree in watercolor? She grimaced. "I'm not at my best in the morning. I much prefer evenings and nights. In London—"

She broke off, suddenly remembering last night in particular.

That she could have forgotten, even for a moment, was a testament to just how muddled she was in the mornings.

Good heavens, he'd kissed her. She'd kissed him back. Rich delight warred with a sudden wash of nerves. Should she say something—somehow acknowledge what had happened? Would he?

He slapped a fish down on a large flat rock and pulled out his knife. "In London, what?"

Apparently, he would not. "I—Nothing."

Disappointment neatly wedged out delight. Had it been so mundane to him, that he could so easily dismiss what had passed between them? Or was it simply that what she had felt—that wonderful, nearly overpowering thrill, had not touched him as well? It was a humiliating thought, and because she didn't care for humiliation as a rule, she pushed it aside.

He was being a gentleman, that was all. A man of breeding would never remind a lady of what some might consider a moral lapse. Never mind the fact that a gentleman would not have kissed her to begin with; he was being one now. She should be grateful, really. It would save her from a considerable amount of awkwardness, not to mention another round of fanciful daydreams.

He'd told her she was meant for someone else, hadn't he? To her mind, that excuse was tantamount to a "no, thank you." That, along with his sudden forgetfulness, told her that a few stolen kisses were all he was interested in. She would be wise to remember it.

Pasting on an indifferent expression, she wandered forward and eyed the fish on the rock. "Whit and Alex would be monstrously impressed—"

She broke off again and made a face as he began the cleaning process.

He glanced up. "Haven't you seen a fish gutted before?"

"Oh, yes. Many times." She kept her eyes studiously away from him and his work. "Whit and Alex often fish. Have since they were young boys." She made another face. "Boys have a tendency to play with the bits and pieces."

"Left them in your bed, did they?"

"And face the housekeeper's wrath?" She laughed and shook her head. "They preferred chasing us about the yard with the head and . . . whatnot, stuck to the end of a stick."

"Nasty lot, little boys." He smiled and reached for a fish. "Did you enact retribution?"

"Tied their lines into hopeless knots," she confirmed. She tilted her head to study him. He was practically chatty all of a sudden—asking about her family, offering to teach her to fish, initiating conversation. He was bright-eyed, alert, almost cheerful, or as cheerful as she'd ever seen him.

"You're a morning person." She hadn't meant for it to come out sounding quite so much like an accusation, but well, she had a long-standing, deep-rooted suspicion of morning people. It was so unnatural.

"I like the light," he replied—cryptically, in her opinion.

"I like it too," she mumbled. "At noon."

"You sleep until noon?"

"Not unless I want a lecture from Lady Thurston on the pitfalls of sloth. I'm just not fully awake until midday." She rubbed a hand down her face. "What do you mean, you like the light?"

"It's softer."

"Is it?" She glanced to the east and winced. "Seems uncommonly bright to me."

"Depends on one's viewpoint."

"I suppose." Forgetting to be disgusted, she watched him set aside the first fish and reach for the second. "Something I can do to help?" she asked.

"Build up the fire."

Evie questioned the wisdom of having her play with fire first thing in the morning, but did as he asked all the same. And in the end, she was able to produce a nice flame from last night's coals with only a singed bit of sleeve for her trouble. She sighed at the damage to her gown. Her blue travel ensemble had gone from smart and stylish to hopelessly wrinkled, stained, and now burnt. She expected the rest of her looked nearly as frightful, but aside from twisting her hair into a braid she tossed over her shoulder, there was very little she could do about it until they reached someplace where she could make use of some soap and a mirror.

To her disappointment, McAlistair quickly dispelled the idea of stopping at an inn.

"We stay off the road," he informed her after he'd cooked the fish, handed her half of one, and packed the other away for lunch.

"Couldn't we stop *somewhere?*" Evie asked as she ate her miserly portion.

He doused the fire with handfuls of dirt and a few judicious applications of his boots. "Where?"

"A tavern? A farmer's? A—?"

"No."

As she had rather suspected that would be his answer, she didn't bother grousing.

She did, however, indulge in a fair amount of grumbling when she climbed into her saddle to leave. Yesterday's ride had turned her entire body into an aching mass of muscle and bone, and it had been a mere half-day's journey. How much worse would a full day in the saddle be?

It wasn't nearly as awful as Evie had feared. In deference to her comfort, McAlistair made regular stops for her to dismount and stretch. It bruised her pride a little, and her leg continued to ache, but it was far better than the numbness she'd experienced the day before. In turn, she resolved to set aside her discomfort and make the best of the trip. It was an adventure, after all, and not one she'd likely repeat.

Meaningful conversation with McAlistair was out of the

question, as he seemed always to be riding ahead, or behind, or off to the side, or . . . well, just away from her. She preferred to think he was trying to discern if they were being followed, and not just avoiding her, but in either case, she was left to entertain herself.

And that entertainment was *not* to include lingering over the sight of him galloping along on his horse . . . even if he did look rather dashing, with his dark locks slipping from their tie to blow across his restless eyes, and the hard muscles of his legs rippling under the fabric of his breeches, and—

She jerked her gaze away from him and pointedly turned her mind to safer subjects, like the study of an unusually large shrub. Mirabelle, she told herself, would want to know all about that shrub. In fact, Whit's wife, who had a hobbyist's fascination with plants, would probably enjoy hearing a detailed description of every flower, tree and bush Evie came across.

And considering what she could share or bring her friends from her journey was certainly a happier thought than dwelling on her jumbled emotions. Thinking of them, instead of herself, she began to look around with renewed interest.

It was lovely countryside, she decided. Though she'd been to Cambridgeshire before, she'd never traveled far outside the major towns, and she'd never gone so far off the road. It was a whole different world, and a new experience to watch the familiar soft hills and patches of forest slowly give way to the low-lying fenlands. If she'd been in a carriage, she likely would have occupied her time with reading or conversation, only bothering with the occasional glance out the window. She wouldn't have appreciated the gradual changes, the soft shading of color, or the airy charm of a distant windmill.

She reached out and pulled a few leaves from a tall plant, noting the light sage fragrance, and tucked them into her pocket for Mirabelle. Perhaps she could find a wildflower to press for Kate. Sophie would like nothing better than a fine story or two, and Evie was certain she'd have plenty before the trip was out.

Preoccupied with her surroundings and thoughts of her friends, Evie barely noticed the morning passing until McAlistair rode up beside her, declared it time for lunch, and brought the horses to a stop. They settled on one of the blankets—at Evie's insistence, for he would have been content to stand and eat—and quickly consumed the fish McAlistair had saved from breakfast. Generally, Evie preferred her fish warm and with seasoning, but having had so little to eat in the last twenty-four hours, the meal tasted like ambrosia—a sadly inadequate portion of ambrosia.

Evie gave a passing thought to offering a portion of her share to McAlistair. Then she ate her meal in four greedy bites. She wasn't quite that noble.

To distract herself from the fact that the fish had done so little to assuage her hunger, she once more turned her attention to the scenery. It occurred to her that if someone had been out for her head, she'd be ill at ease riding, not to mention sitting, in such open land. "What convenient targets we make," she commented absently.

McAlistair finished the last of his fish and looked to her. "Sorry?"

She waved her hand at the open landscape. "There's no place for us to hide here. Not that we need it," she was quick to add, "but if we did, we wouldn't have it."

"No place for anyone else to hide either."

"You have a point." Anyone who might like to take aim at them would need to make himself a target as well. "What would happen then, if a man on a horse came charging toward us all of a sudden? Would we simply begin firing at each other and hope we have the better aim, or would we run and hope our horses could outlast his, or—"

"I won't let anything happen to you."

His earnest tone had her turning to him. The intensity of his gaze had her turning away again, her breath caught in her lungs. A discomforting combination of heat and guilt settled in her chest.

That had been thoughtless of her.

McAlistair believed the ruse to be real. He shouldn't, of course—she had told him the truth—but the fact remained that he *believed* her to be in danger. And that belief made his willingness to see her safely across several counties an act of genuine selflessness. She had no reservations about arguing with him about the necessity of his concern, but she should take more care not to poke fun at him for it.

"I know you won't," she said quietly.

"Because you don't think yourself in danger," McAlistair guessed.

"Well, yes," she admitted, still unable to meet his eyes. "But only in part."

"You think you're capable of seeing to your own safety."

"Well, yes," she said again. "But if I *were* in danger and incapable of taking care of myself, I would certainly trust you to see to the job."

"You're too kind," he said in a dry tone.

It sparked a laugh from Evie, and laughing helped the tense moment to pass. "It's true, I am a bottomless well of generosity." She blew out a long breath and rubbed her hands against her blue skirts. "And now that we've agreed upon it, I suppose we should be moving."

"In a hurry to ride?"

She gave him a wry smile as she stood. "I am in a tremendous hurry to arrive."

"It will be another day, yet," he reminded her as he rose in the smooth, graceful manner that Evie knew she'd never grow accustomed to.

"I know. At least we've clear weather," she replied with determined cheerfulness.

Perhaps, if she hadn't been quite so determined, she might have noticed the way McAlistair glanced darkly at the horizon or the way his lips moved to frame the words, "For now."

The sun of afternoon held none of the gentle warmth Evie had enjoyed that morning or the cheery light she'd barely noticed at noon. The afternoon sun was hot, harsh, and just as it had the day before, beat mercilessly down on her head and back.

She grimaced as a line of sweat trickled between her shoulder blades. She felt, and no doubt looked, positively gruesome. If only McAlistair would change direction for a few minutes so that she might roast a different part of—

She cut off her own line of thought.

Why the devil was the sun beating on her back? She twisted in the saddle to peer behind her, ignoring the shriek of protest from her sore muscles.

They were going east, she suddenly realized. They'd been going east nearly all day. Norfolk was not straight east. Stunned, she brought the horse to a stop.

"McAlistair?"

He'd been riding within speaking distance for a change and brought his own horse to a halt beside her. "Something the matter?"

"No. Yes. I have no idea," she decided.

A line formed in his brow. "Is it your leg?"

"No, I . . ." She shifted her weight. "Are we lost?"

"No."

She blew out a short breath of annoyance. Wasn't that just like a man? He wouldn't even consider the possibility he might be in the wrong, even when a great shiny orb in the sky indicated otherwise.

"You know where we are, then?" she asked.

"Not far from the village of Randswith."

Being completely lost herself, she had absolutely no idea if that was true. "The thing is, McAlistair . . . we're going east."

"Yes."

She opened her mouth, closed it. Oh, hell, what had she been thinking, following a man who likely hadn't left the Haldon grounds in nearly a decade?

"I . . ." She took a deep breath and tried for a gentle tone. "McAlistair, Norfolk is to the north, not the east. I mean, it is a *hair* to the east, certainly, but not a full day's worth of riding. We must be near Suffolk by now."

His eyes moved over the land as he spoke. "We'll be in Suffolk tomorrow."

"But the cottage is in Norfolk."

"Change of plans." He turned to study the subtle trail they had left through the tall grass.

"Change of plans?" She started a little. "What change of plans?"

"We're going to Suffolk."

A small bubble of laughter escaped her throat. "But *why?*"

He was quiet a moment, but rather than take immediate offense, as she might have two days ago, Evie waited patiently—relatively speaking—for him to speak. Silence following a question, she was beginning to realize, didn't necessarily indicate a refusal to answer. It didn't necessarily indicate he *would* answer either, but it seemed only fair to give the man a chance.

"We decided Suffolk would be best," he finally admitted.

Evie decided so little enlightenment had not been worth the wait. "We?"

"Whit, William, Mr. Hunter—"

"Before we left Haldon? You altered our destination *before?*"

"Yes. For the best."

"And no one thought to tell me?" If he answered with any variation of "for the best," she was going to kill him. Reach right over, grab his reins, and wrap them around his neck.

"We couldn't risk it."

She narrowed her eyes. That was dangerously close. "Risk what?

"You telling the staff where we were headed."

She jolted a little in the saddle, stung by the insult. "I can keep a secret."

His mouth hooked up at the corner. She wished she didn't find that quite so attractive.

"Did you?" he asked.

No, she'd told Lizzy, but she'd be damned if she'd admit to it. "No one asked me to."

He transferred his reins to one hand. "And if we had?"

"I am a Cole." She straightened her shoulders. "I always keep my word."

"I'll remember that."

She twisted her lips. "And I suppose I should remember you've no qualms about lying to me."

"Probably," he replied easily, which earned a small smile from her. "But in this case, I just didn't tell you."

"Lying by omission is still a lie."

"It was more a failure to correct a misunderstanding."

She laughed softly. "You've a clever tongue when you're of a mind to use it."

"It's been a great while since . . ." He trailed off and cocked his head just a little. "You're not angry."

"Of course not. Mine is vastly cleverer."

"For the uncorrected misunderstanding."

"Not particularly, no," she admitted. "At least, I'm not any angrier over this bit of misinformation than I am over the towering mountain of misinformation preceding it. I'd say my feelings on this fall somewhere between astonished and irritated." She sent him a hard look. "In the future, however, I would very much appreciate being informed of any changes in our itinerary."

He dipped his head in acknowledgment, which was as close to an apology as she expected to gain from the likes of McAlistair.

"Well then," she said, "if we're not headed to Mr. Hunter's cottage—"

"We are, just a different one."

She blinked at that. "How many does the man own?"

"A number."

"You don't say," she drawled. "Shall I take that to mean you don't know?"

"If you like."

She laughed again and urged her horse forward. It mattered very little to her where, exactly, they were going, as long as they arrived in a timely fashion. She desperately wanted a hot bath.

They rode for the next hour in much the same manner as they had earlier, with McAlistair prowling about and Evie left to her thoughts.

When a thick wall of gray clouds appeared on the horizon, those thoughts turned to rain. When the wall had moved to cover half the sky and block out the sun a mere twenty minutes later, she wondered if they were in for a storm.

"Ominous clouds," she murmured to herself before turning and repeating the same words to McAlistair as he rode up next to her.

He nodded. "We may need to stay in Randswith. Do you know anyone there?"

She smiled. "I am the niece of the dowager Lady Thurston. It's probable I've met someone from every city, town, and village in the country."

He dug through one of the bags attached to the saddle, pulled out a green woolen cape with hood, and handed it to her. "Here."

She took the unfamiliar garment and stared at it. "Where on earth did you get this?"

"Lady Thurston. Last-minute addition at Haldon."

"Where on earth did *she* get it? It isn't even remotely fashionable. I can't imagine why she would have it lying about." Her head snapped up to his. "Unless, of course, she had it made in advance. Because she'd planned on my having to use it. She *knew*—"

"Just put it on, Evie."

She almost reminded him of his agreement to listen to her concerns, before remembering she'd traded that right for a kiss. She sighed and pulled on the cloak. She couldn't regret her decision to lose the wager, even if the cape *was* a size too small across the chest—apparently, it *hadn't* been made for her—so that the material pulled uncomfortably across her shoulder blades as she closed the clasp under her chin. The kiss had been worth it.

She rolled her shoulders and grimaced at the way the rough wool scratched the back of her neck. She pulled the hood up and caught the strong odor of old trunk and . . .

She sniffed the inside of the hood and wrinkled her nose. What was that?

Pulling up a corner of the hem, she found a dark stain, and the odor got stronger. It couldn't be. It couldn't possibly . . .

She saw it then, caught in the inside seam, a small, dark pellet that could only be a mouse dropping. "Bloody hell." She struggled out of the ill-fitting garment. "I take it back. It wasn't worth it. I want a rematch."

McAlistair watched her tear off the garment. "Keep it on. A rematch of what?"

Thinking it best to ignore that last question, she held the cape out at arm's length and addressed the first. "I'll not keep it on. It's full of mouse droppings."

"I don't see any."

"Well, they're small, aren't they?" And full may have been something of an exaggeration. Still, one mouse dropping qualified as quite full enough, in her estimation.

"Shake it out, then," McAlistair advised.

She gave him a doleful look. "Above and beyond the fact that it doesn't fit and scratches horribly, there's a suspicious stain and an obvious smell. Somehow, I doubt shaking it out will alter the size and feel, nor disguise the signs that it has been, for goodness only knows how long, a home for rodents." She gave the cape a disgusted look. "I can't believe my aunt expected me to wear this. She could have at least had it washed out first."

"As I said, it was a last-minute addition. Shake it out and put it on."

She dropped her arm to her side with a sigh. "If I thought for a moment that our safety was dependent on my not being seen, I promise you I would—"

"There's your reputation as well."

Blast, he was right. She couldn't be seen at an inn with McAlistair. She'd be ruined. "Why don't we skip the inn and spend another night in the woods?" she suggested hopefully, even while her heart sank at the idea of forgoing a hot bath and decent meal. "We could find a quiet spot with a bit of cover and a stream. You can teach me to fish with my bare hands."

She rather liked the idea, now that she thought on it. She could make do with a cold bath. And without the fear of waking up in pain, another night spent under the stars, surrounded by the moonlight and the sounds of the forest, seemed an enjoyable prospect. Particularly with McAlistair beside her.

"It'll be lovely. The weather's cooled some, and—" She broke off when a fat raindrop hit her thigh. She scowled at it, then at the one that landed on her knee, her other knee, her wrist. "Bit of rain, that's all. Won't kill us. Might be nice, really, falling asleep to the sounds of the odd raindrop hitting the leaves."

The sky opened up, simply opened up and rained down a great wall of water. The noise was instantaneous, as was Evie's soaking—right down to the skin, as if someone had dumped a very large, very full bucket of water over her head.

McAlistair jerked his chin at the green cape, thick and dripping with water, and lifted his voice over the roar of rain. "It's washed. Put it on."

❈ Ten ❈

What little good had come from shaking out the cape was cancelled by the deluge of rain. Wet wool was never a pleasant thing to behold. Wet, ill-fitting, smelly wool moved right past unpleasant to utterly revolting.

Evie looked, felt, and no doubt smelled like a wet rodent. The inn's stable hand seemed to think so. After being subjected to her presence, the young boy had taken the horses and scurried off with such haste that Evie wondered if he feared she'd give pursuit.

"This is humiliating," she grumbled as they made their way under the eaves of the old building. With the rain and wind out of her eyes, she took stock of their shelter for the night.

Weathered wood, sagging roofline, and missing shutters all gave the distinct impression that whatever better days the inn might have seen were at least several decades past. At the sound of rhythmic squeaking above her, Evie stepped back and looked up to see the inn's shingle, dangling precariously from one chain.

"The Sow and Boar," she read aloud, squinting her eyes through the rain. That didn't bode well, did it?

"Why this one?" she asked McAlistair over the howling wind. "We passed a much nicer inn not five minutes ago."

"Nicer wants wedding bands. Keep your hands under the cape here," he suggested. "Just in case."

"Ah." She pulled her hands inside. "Right."

An inn catering to the well-heeled wasn't likely to sully

its reputation by allowing a man and woman who were not husband and wife to take a room. She and McAlistair might be tossed out on their respective ears if they tried it.

McAlistair tugged the hood farther over her face. "And keep quiet."

The first bolt of lightning lanced through the sky as they pushed through the heavy front door, and the chasing roll of thunder sounded as McAlistair closed the door behind them.

She was relieved to find the interior at least marginally more maintained than the exterior. The furnishings were as old and scarred as the floor beneath their feet—which, she couldn't help noticing, sloped heavily to the left—but someone seemed to have taken a broom and duster to them in the last year, and there was a not altogether unpleasant smell of candle wax and hot food in the air. Then again, a fresh pile of horse manure might seem an improvement at the moment.

She dearly wanted to get out of the wretched cape.

McAlistair procured a room with a minimum of fuss. Though the squat, balding man who introduced himself as the innkeeper made several poorly concealed attempts at sneaking a peak under her hood, he appeared more curious than concerned. And when that curiosity led him to lean just a bit closer, he received little more for the effort than a great waft of wet, stinking wool.

Nose wrinkled, he jerked back. "Top of the stairs, second door on the right. Fire going already to dry your things. Would . . . er . . . would the missus care for a hot bath?"

"Oh, *yes*—"

"A basin of water will do."

She scowled at McAlistair, for all the good it did her. The innkeeper wasn't the only one who couldn't see through her hood. Still, it made her feel a touch better to make a face at McAlistair's back as he led them upstairs.

The room was small and sparsely furnished, with only a table and two chairs, a changing screen, and a bed, but it was clean, dry, and came with a cheerful fire blazing in the hearth. She felt her spirits lifting.

She tore the cape off the moment the door closed and, fearing the odor might fill the whole room, decided to fold it into a corner rather than dry it in front of the fire.

"I should have liked that bath," she grumbled, then waved her hand dismissively before McAlistair could respond. "I know, we can't have staff coming and going." She grudgingly relinquished her daydream of hot water and soap and moved to warm herself in front of the fire. "Why didn't you ask for two rooms?"

McAlistair stripped off his overcoat. "Suspicious."

She wondered about the cleanliness of the floor, then considered whether she had the energy to drag a chair over from the table.

She took a seat on the floor. "You could have told him we were siblings."

"More suspicious."

"I can't see how."

He actually sighed a little, a fact she found both gratifying—gaining any sort of reaction from McAlistair was gratifying—and irritating. She didn't think it was too much to ask for him to explain his choice of actions.

"He knows we're lying, but assumes we're hiding a lovers' tryst. He's curious but otherwise unconcerned. Should we take separate rooms—"

"He'd have to assume we're lying for other reasons," she finished for him. "I suppose you're right."

He studied her a moment before pulling off his waistcoat

and tossing it in front of the fire. He hadn't bothered with a cravat that morning, and a smooth triangle of tanned skin was visible where his dry shirt opened at the chest. Evie found herself mesmerized by the sight. That skin was smooth and tan right down to the waist, she remembered. Feeling the beginnings of a blush, she tore her eyes and thoughts away from the memory of McAlistair's muscled chest.

"How is your leg?" he asked.

"I . . . fine, thank you."

His dark eyes searched her face. "Does it pain you?"

"I am a bit sore," she admitted, accepting that another conversation about her infernal leg couldn't be avoided. "But not unbearably so."

A line formed across his brow. "You're certain—"

"I'm quite fine, I assure you. A hot bath would have helped, but a decent night's sleep will no doubt be sufficient."

He nodded and reached for the leather tie holding his hair. "You'll want dinner first."

If it hadn't been for the mention of food, Evie was certain she would have sighed at the sight of McAlistair's thick hair falling forward to brush his shoulders, then sighed again when he swept it back and retied it. But even her peculiar fascination with McAlistair's locks couldn't compete with the promise of a real meal.

"Oh, yes, *please*," she breathed. "I know it's early, but—"

"I'll see to it."

Though she could have comfortably fallen asleep fully dressed right there on the floor, she gathered the energy to bend over and begin untying her boots. "Thank you."

"When I knock, stand behind the screen."

She straightened back up. "Behind the screen? Whatever for?"

"They have to bring in the tray."

"This is absurd—"

"The screen or the cape. Your choice."

She was too tired and too hungry to argue. "I'll take the screen."

Though she felt a fool, Evie moved to hide behind the wooden screen when the knock sounded at the door twenty minutes later. She debated for a moment as to whether a response was required, then shrugged and called for the group to enter.

A moderate commotion followed—furniture scraped, plates rattled. She heard something actually clang—which confused her—and someone muttered a mild oath. There had to be nearly half a dozen pairs of feet shuffling about, Evie realized, barely resisting the urge to peek. Why the devil would it take half a dozen people to haul up a dinner tray?

"Shall we put it behind the screen, sir?" someone asked in a strained voice.

"No. In front of the fire."

"And the screen, sir?" someone else asked. "Shall I move it?"

As she couldn't see properly, she could only assume McAlistair shook his head at the man. And why wouldn't he? Who ate behind a screen in a private room? She heard the distinct jingling of coins, the retreating shuffle of feet, and then the creak of the door before it closed.

"You can come out."

"It was hardly necessary for me to hide to begin with. What in the world was that—" She broke off as she stepped around the screen and saw a very small tub set before the fire. It was already filled almost half full of water hot enough to let off steam. A small stack of drying cloths and a fresh bar of soap sat beside it.

"A hot bath," she breathed, and turned to find McAlistair sitting at the small table now piled high with platters of food. "And a hot dinner."

He stood and moved to fold the screen and place it in front of the tub. "Better if it were one at a time, but this limited intrusions. Which do you want first?"

"First?" She looked from the tub to the table to the tub again. She felt almost lightheaded with anticipation. "I don't know."

"The bath, then," he suggested. "Before it grows cold."

"Yes . . . of course . . . um . . ." She eyed the food, unable to recall a time she'd felt so torn. "Perhaps . . ." A wonderful idea occurred to her. She lifted a lid off one of the platters to discover thick slices of lamb. Stabbing one piece onto the end of a fork, she lifted it to her mouth for a bite. "Both."

"Both? You want to eat in the tub?"

"Disgusting, isn't it?" Despite the fact that it was, she took her slice of lamb with her behind the screen. It took some doing, undressing with only one hand, but she succeeded after a time and soon slid into the warm water. The tub was small, and the lamb something less than skillfully prepared, but the combination after two days of hard riding was nothing short of wonderful. She groaned in pleasure.

She ought to feel uncomfortable, she mused, sitting naked in a tub not four feet from McAlistair with only a thin screen between them, but she just couldn't rouse the energy for it.

"This was a marvelous idea, McAlistair." She spoke around a mouthful of food. "And most thoughtful of you. Thank you very much."

There was a long pause before he answered. "You're welcome."

McAlistair stared at the screen. He couldn't pull his eyes away. He couldn't stop his imagination from dwelling on what was behind that thin barrier of wood—

Evie. Naked, and wet.

Through a tremendous act of will, he'd managed not to think of her undressing, concentrating instead on washing with the soap and basin of hot water he'd procured for himself. And he'd succeeded in ignoring that first soft splash of water when she'd slipped into the tub, studiously turning his attention to his meal.

But then she'd groaned—that low, soft sound of pleasure—and his mind had been wiped clean of everything but Evie.

Naked and wet.

It would be such an easy thing to stand up and walk around that screen.

She'd been so open, so willing, so responsive the night before. He'd have little trouble convincing her to let him join her now.

Because the idea was too tempting by half, he rose from the table quickly enough to scrape the chair legs against the floor. "You need something dry to wear."

The tub water swished, and he nearly groaned himself. He could just see how it would lap against her pale skin, and brush the edges of all that soft brown hair. She'd be smiling, gleaming—

"Beg your pardon?" she called out.

He actually had to clear his throat. He couldn't remember a time since he'd been a green boy that he'd actually had to clear his throat to speak around desire. "I'll be back soon."

But not, he decided, too soon.

Evie had scrubbed herself clean, dried herself off, and was trying to decide whether McAlistair's extended absence meant he hadn't been able to secure clean clothes and she should therefore reclaim her dirty ones, when he finally let himself back into the room.

She peeked around the screen, a large drying cloth wrapped tightly about her. "Where did you go?"

Keeping his eyes trained somewhere over her shoulder, he handed her a simple night rail and wrap. "To find you these. From the innkeeper's wife."

"Oh, thank heavens." She took the offered clothing. "You were gone a very long time."

"I waited in the hall." His tone was flat, but there was a hint of color to his cheeks.

Evie assumed it was from the heat of the room. "The hall? Whatever for?"

"To give you some privacy."

"Oh. That was very kind, I'm sure, but unnecessary. The screen was sufficient." She glanced at the table. "And now you've a cold meal and bath."

"The basin will do."

"But—"

"I ate some before I left."

"Oh, well, but still—"

"Get dressed, Evie."

She wondered at the gruff demand, before attributing it to exhaustion. Slipping behind the screen once more, she pulled on the night rail and wrap. They were a far cry from being a perfect fit—the sleeves ended well past her finger-tips, the hems of both dragged on the floor, and the wrap was wide enough to cover her twice over—but they were clean and soft, and she was grateful for them. She could cinch the wrap tight with the tie, and she could roll up the sleeves. The extra length, however, required her to bunch up the material and carry it over her arm.

McAlistair was sitting at the table when she emerged. He lifted an eyebrow at the spectacle she made. "You look as if you've been swallowed whole."

"Feel a bit like it, as well. It's lovely." She took a seat

across from him at the table, rubbing her sore leg a little without realizing it.

His eyes caught the movement. "Better?"

"Hmm? Oh, yes, much."

He nodded, and though she'd have been happy to do it for herself, he filled a plate for her. "Your injury's from a carriage accident?"

He asked the question casually, but it jarred her nonetheless. She wasn't used to probing questions about her leg or scar, casual or otherwise. "I . . . yes, it is."

"You needn't speak of it, if it bothers you."

It didn't bother her, exactly. Snide remarks or being treated like an invalid, *that* bothered her, but she would feel perfectly comfortable relating the story of the accident that caused those injuries . . . reasonably comfortable . . . probably. How was she to know? It had been ages since anyone had asked it of her.

"There's very little to tell, really," she began, taking the plate he offered. "We were returning from a birthday celebration at our neighbor's. It was dark, and the carriage veered off the road and slid into a tree."

"Veered off," he repeated. "Was it the weather?"

"No." She thought of her father's slurred voice, booming over her head as he whipped the horses to go faster, faster, and felt a hint of color rise to her cheeks. Perhaps there was a piece of the tale she was less than comfortable sharing. She reached for the teapot on the table. "Would you care for some?"

He shook his head. "Was the driver new? Unfamiliar with the road?"

She set the teapot down. "No."

"One doesn't just veer off—"

She twisted her fingers in her lap, then picked up the pot again and poured herself a cup. "He'd been drinking."

"I hope your father took a horsewhip to him." His face hardened as he spoke, and Evie had the passing thought that he was growing easier and easier to read.

With what she hoped was an air of nonchalance, she added two spoonfuls of sugar. "Difficult, as my father had been the one driving." There, she'd said it. "He was killed."

His expression softened instantly. "I'm sorry."

I'm not. The thought came unbidden, and though there was a moment's instinctive guilt that followed, Evie pushed it aside. She *wasn't* particularly sorry her father was dead; she was only sorry he hadn't been the sort of man she could grieve over. If that made her a terrible person, so be it.

She shrugged by way of answering McAlistair and poured a dollop of cream into her tea. "It was a long time ago."

And not nearly long enough, came the next unwelcome thought. Better he'd driven himself off the road years earlier.

"Do you miss him?"

"Not for a second." The spoon she'd been using to carefully stir her tea fell to the table with a clatter. "I don't know why I said that. I shouldn't have said that."

"Did you mean it?"

"I . . ." Her eyes fell on her cup. "I'm not even thirsty."

He nudged her plate with a finger. "Eat."

Hunger had disappeared as well. But the urge to talk, to tell the part of the story she'd kept from everyone save Lady Thurston, was overwhelming. She swallowed hard and bunched her hands in her lap. "He insisted on driving. He made such a fuss in the drive and likely embarrassed my mother. I remember he was fond of that—shaming her in front of others. One of the ways he kept her cowed." She frowned at the scarred table. "One of many. I shouldn't have said I didn't miss him." She swallowed hard. "But I meant it."

"Why should you miss him?" McAlistair asked. "Or lie and say you have?"

"He was my father."

"He was an ass." With that matter-of-fact pronouncement, McAlistair picked up his knife and fork and resumed eating.

"He—" She blinked, and then, to her astonishment, felt the corners of her mouth twitch with humor. "Yes, he was. That's exactly what he was. Nothing more than a habitually drunk ass."

He cut off a piece of lamb. "An inebriated ass."

Her smile bloomed. It felt wonderful to make light of it, of *him*—as if she were stealing away his significance. She couldn't imagine a worse fate for a bully. "An inebriated ass," she repeated as if testing the words. "Rather catchy, that. Pity we can't rework his grave marker."

"Who's to stop you?"

She laughed now, and reached for her fork. Hunger had returned. "I imagine my mother might. She visits his grave nearly every day, or so I've been told."

There was a pause before McAlistair asked, "How is it you were injured and she was not?"

"Luck, mostly, or lack of it. I was on the side closest to the tree."

He reached across the table and gently traced a thumb along her scar. "This?"

A shiver ran over her skin. She wanted to tilt her cheek into the palm of his warm hand. And she wanted to pull away and hide her face. "I . . . I'm not certain. It happened so fast. A sharp bit of splintered wood, I imagine, or a piece of metal from somewhere."

He drew his hand back. "And your leg?"

She resisted the urge to touch where the warmth of his

fingers still lingered. "My memory is fuzzy . . . I was trapped under part of the wreckage. It was already broken then, but not so badly, or quite so much, I think . . . There was a fire from the lanterns, and they had to pull me out without freeing it first. It made it worse."

He nodded in understanding, and to her relief, chose to steer the conversation to happier topics. They spent an hour or more discussing, among other things, the Rockefortes' son, Whit and Mirabelle's marriage, Kate's talent for all things musical. Once or twice, Evie made an attempt to inquire into McAlistair's past, but he either deftly avoided the question, gave one-word answers, or shrugged and changed the subject. Evie decided it was too lovely an interlude to push the matter and risk an argument. She simply enjoyed the relaxed—if slightly one-sided—conversation. She enjoyed the hearty meal as well, eating until she found she couldn't take another bite.

"Oh, goodness," she groaned, and pushed back a little from the table. "I can't recall ever ingesting quite so much in one sitting."

"Wasn't one sitting," McAlistair reminded her as he finished off the last of his own meal. "You had some in the tub."

"So much in so short a time, then," she said and then watched, a little stunned, as he began to stack the dishes neatly on the tray. The man certainly was tidy. She rose to help him. It wasn't until they'd finished and he reached for his overcoat that she grew confused.

"What are you doing?" she inquired.

"The tray needs to be returned."

"Of course it does." She gestured to the far wall. "There's a bell pull right there."

He shook his head and lifted the tray. "Faster this way."

"And doesn't require I hide behind the screen again," she guessed.

He nodded and headed for the door.

"But why your coat? Isn't the kitchen in the main building?"

"Probably."

She moved around him to open the door. "What of the tub, won't they come for that?"

"Tomorrow." He maneuvered his form to block any view of her from the hallway, and his voice took on an authoritative tone. "Get back inside. Lock the door behind me."

Whit and Alex often took that tone with her. It had ceased being effective years ago. She rolled her eyes at him.

McAlistair gave her a dark look as he stepped back into the hall. "This isn't a game, Evie."

"No, it's a very bad farce," she responded, and softly shut the door before he could argue.

❈ *Eleven* ❈

*M*cAlistair had been gone for ages.

Well, half an hour, anyway.

Much too long, to Evie's mind. She wandered to the window without any expectation of being able to see through the rain and dark. The yard was black, with only a few dim lights from the inn and the surrounding houses illuminating the perimeter.

If it hadn't been for the flash of lightning, she would

never have seen the solitary figure striding between the inn and the stable, and if that figure hadn't been glancing at her window at just the right moment, she would never have recognized McAlistair.

Baffled, she leaned forward and peered into the darkness, hoping to catch another glimpse, but he had disappeared into the night.

What the devil was he doing?

They'd only just gotten dry, hadn't they? Granted, his overcoat had done a better job of shedding the rain than her wool cloak, but he had still been soaked down to his waistcoat. And with his overcoat still damp, he was likely now to be soaked down to the bone.

He'd catch his death. If he wasn't struck by lightning first or felled by a falling tree branch or hit with flying debris from the crumbling inn or—

She was more than a little tempted to push the window open and call out to him—or, to be more accurate, in the general direction of where she'd last seen him—but she could well imagine what his reaction to that might be.

Well, no, she realized, she hadn't the faintest clue what his reaction might be. In fact, under other circumstances, she rather thought it might be worth drenching her head just to find out. But she intended to confront him over this nonsense when he returned, and it was only wise to begin that confrontation with her own behavior safely beyond reproach.

She resigned herself to scowling through the glass and waiting for his return. A return that seemed to take an inordinate amount of time. Frustrated, she looked for ways to occupy herself. She stoked the fire, brushed out her damp and dusty gown, and cleaned her teeth. She paced the space between the table and the window until her stiff muscles complained, then sat on the edge of the bed to glare at the door. And when fatigue made the soft mattress beneath her all too tempting, she rose and paced again. Was the man taking a bloody tour of the entire town?

She stopped to peer out the window for the dozenth time in the last ten minutes, and saw nothing in the flashes of lightning that punctuated the dark, nothing but an empty yard. McAlistair was nowhere to be seen.

She was nearly fuming, and even closer to throwing on her disgusting cape and heading out to search for him—she had a very nasty image of McAlistair trapped somewhere, neck deep in rising water—when he let himself into the room with a soft click of his key.

She opened her mouth, prepared to confront him, but snapped it shut when she saw the frighteningly intense expression on his face. With barely a glance at her, he closed and locked the door and strode straight past her to the window. He yanked the drapes shut.

"Don't stand in front of the window," he snapped.

"I . . . you're annoyed with *me?*"

"I want you to stay away from the window. I saw you from the yard—"

"Yes, and I saw you," she cut in, finding her footing again. "What the devil were you thinking, strolling about in a storm?"

The hard lines of anger drained from his face, and his mouth hooked up in a half smile. "I don't stroll."

She glared at him.

He shrugged out of his overcoat. "I was making a search of the grounds."

"And did you find anything? Besides great oceans of mud?"

He tossed his coat in front of the fire. "No."

"No," she repeated. "And do you know *why* you found nothing?"

He stripped off his waistcoat, revealing a mostly dry shirt. "Either he doesn't know where we are or he's holed up in the weather."

She didn't bother asking who "he" was; instead she threw up her hands in disgust. "For pity's sake, there is no conspiracy against my life. You found nothing, because there is nothing to find."

He didn't respond.

Evie felt frustration become a living, breathing thing crawling under her skin. She fisted her hands at her sides and made herself speak slowly and carefully. "One week ago, I overheard a conversation between Lady Thurston, Mrs. Summers, and Mr. Fletcher, a conversation that culminated in the decision to send me a threatening letter so that a gentleman of their choosing might have the opportunity to play knight-errant. This, all of this . . ." She struggled for the right word and tossed up her hands again when she couldn't find it. "This monstrous stupidity is nothing more, *nothing* more than an ill-designed, meddlesome, and arguably cracked attempt to see me wed."

"Yet you can't explain why Mrs. Summers sent you with me," he said softly.

"There are a dozen possible explanations," she countered, wracking her brain frantically to come up with at least one. "Perhaps it was merely for drama. Perhaps the man they've chosen will arrive at the cottage as a surprise and so it mattered not one jot with whom I rode off into the woods, so long as I was properly terrified." That made Mrs. Summers and the rest sound positively diabolical, she realized. "Terrified might not be the right word. Convinced might be more accurate."

"It might be, if you were right."

She waited for him to say more. He didn't. "You do realize that a mere 'you're wrong' is not a particularly compelling argument?"

He considered her for a moment. "I'm not compelled to argue with you."

She blew out a short breath. Now that he was back in the room, safe and relatively dry, the portion of her temper that had been fueled by worry—and she was beginning to think that comprised the majority share—was starting to fade. "I am not eager—"

"But perhaps it's unavoidable."

"Arguing?" She felt her lips twitch. "It would certainly seem so."

He stepped over to take one of the chairs from the table and set it in front of the fire. "Sit down, Evie."

She narrowed her eyes at him.

He stared back. "I can't imagine what you find offensive in that."

"I find taking orders offensive."

"Everyone takes orders from someone," he pointed out.

"Yes, but I don't take mine from you."

She thought perhaps his jaw tightened a little, but the movement was so brief, she couldn't say for certain. He gestured again to the chair. "Please, sit down."

"I—thank you."

A little wary at how easily she'd won that particular battle, she took her seat and waited for him to start the war.

McAlistair positioned the second chair facing Evie, not quite close enough to brush knees, which he would have found distracting, but close enough for a quick grab if she took it into her head to bolt. He didn't really expect it of her, but then Evie, he was fast discovering, had a knack for doing the unexpected.

And he wasn't certain how she would react to his questioning.

He sat down and resisted the urge to roll the tension out of his shoulders. "I need to know more of your work."

"My work?" she asked, jolting a little in obvious surprise.

McAlistair nodded, relieved it wasn't a jolt in the direction of the door. "I should have asked earlier."

"Why didn't you?"

"You were tired."

"I'm tired now," she pointed out.

"I wanted to . . ." He wracked his brain for the right words. "To give you time."

She blinked. "Time for what?"

"To become accustomed to the idea."

She looked utterly, hopelessly lost. "To the idea of telling you about my work? Fairly unlikely, as I hadn't a clue you were interested. Although—" She broke off as the light of realization dawned. "Accustomed to the idea that the threat, the danger, is real—*that's* what you mean, isn't it?"

He nodded.

"I don't understand. I told you I knew it to be a lie." Sudden disbelief dimmed the light on her face. "Surely, you didn't expect that simply because you said differently, I would—"

"Yes," he cut in. He didn't need his own mistake explained to him. "I did."

She gaped at him in the way one does when one is uncertain whether to be utterly appalled or terribly amused. "That is *remarkably* arrogant."

It wasn't arrogance. It was experience. "I have cause."

She sat back in her chair with a dramatic roll of her eyes. "Your sort always does."

You've never met my sort. Because he couldn't very well say that, he said nothing.

She waved her hand at him. "Well, then have at it. What do you want to know?"

He felt one eyebrow lift. "Just like that?"

"Certainly," she assured him. "I'm proud of what I do, and I so rarely have the opportunity to discuss it."

"Even with your friends?"

She pursed her lips. "From time to time, but I limit those conversations, and I speak only in generalities. I'd rather they weren't directly involved."

"Because you know it to be dangerous," he guessed, and watched as she shifted in her seat, recognizing the trap.

"Well, yes, there is that. But more . . . I don't think either of them is cut out for the work, really. I don't mean that to sound disparaging. It's . . . Well, honestly, can you picture Kate trying to go anywhere incognito?"

Whit's sister was renowned for her clumsiness. McAlistair imagined she'd get her veil caught in a door at the first opportunity. He didn't bother asking why Evie had kept things from Mirabelle. They both knew that until recently, Mirabelle had been busy fighting her own battles.

"Who knows what you do, in general or specifics?"

"Outside of family—and that includes the Rockefortes— only those of us on this little adventure, Mr. Fletcher, and Lizzy."

"That's all?"

"Yes."

Lizzy could be the key, he thought, but knew better than to disparage the woman in front of Evie. "What about those who work with you?"

"None of them know who I am. The vast majority of our conversations take place by mail, and most of us make use of pseudonyms. The few times I have met with others, I have kept my face hidden."

"Someone must know. How did you discover the group?

Who vouched for your legitimacy?" One didn't just stumble across an organization that relied on secrecy, and that organization wouldn't endanger itself by taking on a new member without a recommendation.

"Ah, yes." She bobbed her head. "Lady Penelope Cutler, a friend of my aunt's, and a great financial contributor to our group. Lady Thurston was aware of her work and arranged to introduce us when it became apparent we held similar interests."

"It was your aunt's idea?"

"Yes."

He nodded. That support and the work it allowed had no doubt been invaluable in restoring the confidence a heartless father had destroyed. "How long ago was that?"

"Oh . . ." She scrunched her face up in thought. "Six years ago, more or less. Lady Thurston made certain I had first experienced at least one London Season without distractions."

"And where is Lady Penelope now?"

"She passed. Four years ago."

"I'm sorry." He felt foolish saying the words. Just as he'd felt foolish and helpless when she'd spoken of her father. He wanted to offer her something more eloquent, more substantial, than "I'm sorry," and "he's an ass." But it had been years since he'd had to find any words, let alone the right words.

Evie shook her head. "It's all right. I didn't know her well."

He didn't allow the air in his lungs release with a sigh of relief. But he did change the subject. "What is it you do, specifically?"

"Well it differs by time, place, and necessity. I write letters to members of parliament and press, anonymously, of course. I keep track of—" She broke off and tilted her head at him. "I suppose you're interested only in the potentially dangerous bits."

It was all dangerous, he thought, but nodded rather than commenting. Better to hear the worst of it first.

"Right. I've been acting as a sort of liaison for women— occasionally women and their children—who wish to escape from an intolerable life."

"How?"

"Their trip—generally, though not always out of the country—is arranged beforehand, but there is always the risk that a woman might change her mind and return to her husband or father, or what have you, and confess all. As a precaution, she is given only enough information and funds to see her through one leg of her journey at a time. A member of the group meets with her at the end of each leg and provides the funds and information for the next. That is what I do."

His heart caught in his chest. "You meet with these women."

"Yes, but I keep my face hidden under a veil and stay only long enough to pass off the coin—"

"And no one in Benton has noticed a veiled woman haunting the coaching station?"

Her tone turned haughty. "Do give me a little credit, if you please. I've met a grand total of two women at the Benton coaching station in the last year."

"Two women?" That certainly narrowed the field as to who might be seeking revenge.

"At the Benton coaching station, yes. I also met two women at the bookseller's. One woman, sent by hired coach, on the side of a rarely used road. And three women in outlying villages. The year before was similar except that I used Maver's tavern instead of the bookseller's, didn't meet anyone on the road, and met only one woman at the station."

McAlistair frowned. Over several years, that was still a significant amount of time spent wandering around, wearing a veil. And nothing invited curiosity so much as a mysterious woman.

"Someone will notice eventually," he pointed out.

She made a face and, to his surprise, agreed with him. "I know. After next year, I'll have to give it up for a time. Work on something else or somewhere else. It was the same for London."

"You met women in London?" His palms went clammy at just the *idea* of Evie sneaking around London alone.

She didn't appear to notice his discomfort. "Oh, yes, and with far more frequency, but then, there are more women and more places to meet, aren't there? Still after a while, I thought it best to reduce the amount of time I was there."

A sensible decision, he was forced to admit. In fact, everything she'd told him so far struck him as being fairly sensible. And *that* struck him as infuriating. He didn't want her to be sensible. He wanted her to have been careless in some way. How else could he be angry with her for putting herself in danger? Never mind the fact that he admired her work; a small, selfish part of him wanted a reason to demand she stop.

And that small part of him was determined to have its way. "How is your mail delivered to you?"

Her brow furrowed a little at his sudden change of subject. "It is delivered to a small, unoccupied cottage at the far outskirts of Benton, where it is slipped under the door until I retrieve it. And before you ask, I am there no more than once a month."

"The cottage is in your name?"

"No, it belongs to a fictional widow by the name of Mrs. Eades. She lives with her sister in Wales. You'll have to ask

Lady Thurston, or perhaps Whit, how she managed to arrange for that." She paused to yawn. "I couldn't say."

McAlistair could have come up with a half dozen other questions for her, but knew now wasn't the time. Evie's eyes had gone from merely sleepy to red-rimmed, and her posture from defensive, to weary, to half asleep.

"We'll continue this later. It's time for bed."

"In a moment," she said, perking up a little in her seat. "I've a few questions for you as well."

Bloody hell. "It's late."

"It can't be much more than half past nine."

"It's been a long day."

"Hasn't it just." She pinned him with a hard look. "I answered your questions, McAlistair. It's only fair you answer mine."

"I'm not the one in danger." And he wasn't in the habit of playing fair.

She completely ignored that statement. "Why did you become a hermit?

"I was done being a soldier."

"Why did you become a soldier?"

He'd been unbearably angry. "I was good at it."

"You couldn't have known that until you joined." She scowled at him and slumped against the back of her chair once more. "You're not going to cooperate, are you?"

Since he knew she wouldn't care for the answer, he chose to say nothing at all.

Evie pressed her lips into a thin line, crossed her arms over her chest, and glared at him through narrowed eyes.

While he waited for the lecture that was sure to come, he let his eyes wander over her face—the high arch of her brows, the long sweep of her lashes, the soft sprinkle of freckles across her nose. The freckles were new, he realized, a result of riding without a bonnet. He should probably remedy that tomorrow. Or maybe not. He liked the look of them, nearly as much as he'd enjoyed seeing her soft brown hair tied in a loose braid down her back. If he found her a bonnet, she'd hide the braid and the freckles. Then again, if she hid the braid and freckles, maybe he would stop fantasizing about unraveling the first and trailing his lips along the second. Then again—

He blinked, cutting off his own line of thought. Why was it so quiet? Hadn't Evie been about to lecture him? He took in her cross-armed, narrowed-eyed posture. She hadn't moved a muscle in the last five minutes. And she hadn't said a thing.

Not a word. Not a syllable. Not a single solitary sound.

Holy hell, the chit was trying to stare him down.

Evie knew she didn't have a prayer of succeeding.

McAlistair had probably gone days, weeks, even months without speaking. Her record for silence, on the other hand, was directly correlated with the longest amount of time she'd ever spent asleep.

But she hadn't been able to come up with an alternative solution to his infuriating reticence. And fighting fire with fire had a certain expediency she appreciated. Pity it seemed to have so little effect on McAlistair.

He leaned back in his chair, appearing perfectly at ease and, unless she was entirely mistaken, a little pleased.

Her eyes narrowed further.

A corner of his mouth curved up.

The silence stretched out.

Woefully ill-equipped for such a contest, Evie tried fisting her hands, shifting her weight, and tapping her foot in an effort to alleviate her discomfiture. All to no avail. She was on the verge of surrender when, much to her surprise, he spoke.

"Are we to sit here the remainder of the night?"

It wasn't an admitted capitulation—likely as not, it was an act of mercy—but she'd take it. "That depends on you." Realizing that gave him more power than she had intended, she added a rather lame, "Somewhat."

"What is it you want, Evie?"

She uncrossed her arms. "To have my ideas, my concerns, and my questions taken seriously."

"I do take them seriously."

"Bollocks," she snapped, and refused to feel guilty for being vulgar. "You ask personal questions but refuse to answer any in return. You haven't listened to a thing I've said about this ruse—"

"I have. I don't agree with what I've heard, but I've listened."

She threw up her hands. "Well, how am I to tell? You won't speak."

"I'm speaking now," he pointed out.

"Yes, you are, but who's to say when you will again? I don't care to be at such a disadvantage, and your taciturn disposition combined with your insistence on my being forthcoming on every bit of information you deem of interest, most certainly puts me at a disadvantage."

He cocked his head, considering.

"Well?" she prompted.

"I'm trying to puzzle out how one can be simultaneously taciturn and insistent."

He had a point, but she was sure little good would come from admitting it, particularly as it wasn't the point *she* was trying to make. "That may be the longest sentence you've ever uttered in my presence."

"I suspect it is." He ran his knuckles across his jaw, keeping his eyes on her. "I am unaccustomed to conversation."

He wasn't just unaccustomed, she realized; he was uncomfortable. Guilt niggled at her conscience and had her fingers working into the folds of her wrap. "Yes, of course. And I am sorry to make such an issue of it, but we cannot keep on this way."

He nodded once. "I will attempt to be more vocal."

"Thank you." She relaxed her fingers and offered him a smile.

He didn't offer one in return. "In exchange, you will adhere to the safety precautions I set, without complaint."

"I . . . I'll adhere to them . . . but I reserve the right to complain."

"Fair enough," he agreed, and this time, his lips curved just a hair. He rose and held out a hand to help her up. "You need to sleep. We've a long day tomorrow."

Evie would have needed to sleep if they'd had nothing more grueling than a full day of napping planned for tomorrow. She couldn't remember ever being so exhausted. While McAlistair put out the candles, she crawled into bed, sighing at the exquisite feel of soft sheets and plump pillows. She was under the covers and her lids already drooping when he pulled off the extra blanket folded at her feet and tossed it on the floor.

She frowned at him. "What are you doing?"

"Going to bed."

It bothered her to think of him sleeping on the unforgiving wooden floor while she stretched out on an enormous feather mattress. It seemed terribly unfair and a little absurd, given that they'd slept side by side the night before.

"There's no reason for you to sleep on the floor when there's plenty of room on the bed."

"Floor will do." He grabbed a pillow and tossed it on the blanket.

"If it's the proximity that troubles you, I should like to point out that last night—"

"I know," he fairly growled.

She bit her lip, wary of his gruff tone, but unwilling to let the matter drop. "There are households where the entire family sleeps in one bed—if they're lucky enough to have one. The children, mother, father—"

"Mother and father. They're married."

"Usually. And tonight we are as well. Moreover, what if one of the maids were to come in?"

"The door is locked."

"Yes, but there are keys, aren't there? And it's customary for someone to come in the morning and light—"

"She'll knock first."

"But what if you don't wake, and—"

"I'll wake."

It was impossible to argue with that sort of arrogance. "What if . . . Couldn't you . . ." Her tired mind struggled to come up with another reason for him to take the bed.

McAlistair stepped closer to the bed, his voice turning gentle. "What is it, Evie? Are you frightened?"

She sent him a dry look. It may have been more convenient to tell him yes, she was very afraid, but she had her pride. "My greatest fear at the moment is that you'll wake up stiff, sore, and cranky. Cranky individuals make for unpleasant traveling companions."

"Yes, I know," he said wryly.

She smiled around a yawn. She'd deserved that small jab. And he deserved the truth, she decided. There wasn't a good reason for her to be dissembling. She wasn't certain as to why she was, except that admitting it bothered her felt too similar to admitting she cared, and that made her feel vulnerable.

She picked at a small tear in her blanket. "I . . . I don't care for the idea that you're to be down there on the hard floor whilst I've all this room up here."

"Trade?"

"No," she replied without a second's thought. "*I'm* not the one being stubborn."

His lips curled up in humor. "It honestly bothers you?"

She nodded again, but found it hard to meet his gaze. "It does, yes."

He didn't sigh, but he hesitated, which made Evie suspect he wanted to sigh. And that was very nearly the same thing. Despite his obvious misgivings, he scooped up the blanket and pillow and tossed them back on the bed.

"Roll over. Go to sleep."

She didn't care for the implication that perhaps she had planned on doing something *other* than going to sleep. Well, in all honesty, she wasn't *completely* averse to the idea of doing something else—kissing him again came to mind—but she hadn't *planned* on it. And no matter how much the idea of kissing McAlistair might appeal to her, at the moment, she was too exhausted to give any real thought to turning theory into reality.

She scooted over and turned her back without comment. The mattress dipped as he settled on the bed.

"Get some sleep," she heard him say from what sounded like the very far edge of the mattress. "We'll leave at first light."

She made a face into her pillow. Why did people always feel the need to leave at first light? "What's wrong with second or third?" she mumbled.

"Beg pardon?"

"Nothing. Good night, McAlistair."

She fell asleep without hearing his response.

* * *

McAlistair lay in bed, listening to the patter of rain and the last distant rolls of thunder. It was somewhere near four in the morning, he estimated, and he'd accumulated somewhere near three hours of sleep.

The creak of floorboards in the hall had woken him from a light doze. It had only been a late-arriving guest, but it had warranted investigation—as had the creak an hour before, and the sound of voices from the yard the hour before that.

He'd slept better the night before, surrounded by the comforting sounds of the woods. And with a little more distance between himself and Evie. Within minutes of falling asleep, she'd turned toward him and rolled over to his side of the bed. He hadn't had the heart to wake her, and he had no intention of moving to the other side of the bed, leaving her closer to the door. But it was damn hard trying to sleep with her legs brushing his, the scent of her hair on the pillow, and her sweet face just inches away. She was a sound sleeper, he noted. After that first migration to his side of the mattress, she hadn't moved except to wrap her arms around her pillow.

He'd noticed last night that she hugged in her sleep—only then it had been his waistcoat. He'd taken it off and slipped it under her head in the night. He'd even had to shift her a bit to untangle a curl of her hair from a button. But she hadn't woken, and she hadn't said a word about it in the morning.

Likely as not, she hadn't noticed, he thought with a small smile. The woman was hopeless before noon.

He hadn't expected that. He would have guessed—in fact, he *had* guessed—that morning was her favorite time of day. Morning fit her. It was soft and gentle, as she was. It had always reminded him of Evie.

There was nothing more pure, more promising than the first light of morning.

He suspected she wouldn't understand the comparison. He wondered if anyone else did or would. Her friends? Her family?

Her future husband?

He frowned at nothing in particular. What if she were right about the ruse? He didn't think it likely; there were too many holes in that theory. But what if? What if the events of the last two days were nothing more than a supremely idiotic way to see her matched? A hard burn flared in his stomach. Unsurprised by his violent reaction to the idea of Evie being attached to another man, he acknowledged the pain and set it aside.

If William and the rest had set this business up, and if, despite the ridiculousness of it all, Evie found a love that would make her happy, then so be it.

He'd congratulate her. Right after he gutted William, slowly, and with his dullest knife. Never mind that he didn't own a dull knife; he'd buy one just for the occasion. Something with a bit of rust on it.

He watched her sleep, knowing that after they reached the cottage, he'd never again have the opportunity.

Because she was never meant for him.

He lifted a finger and traced it a fraction of an inch above her cheek. He knew the pale ivory skin would feel soft and fragile—easily bruised with rough palms, easily soiled with dirty hands.

He drew his hand back.

No, she wasn't meant for him. And he wouldn't take her if she were.

A man didn't destroy what he loved.

He rolled to his back and stared at the cracks in the ceiling. A man could, however, buy a rusty knife and slice through the one responsible for giving that loved one away to someone else. And for playing him for a fool.

Even if it was only in his head.

Mollified by the thought, he closed his eyes, let his mind drift, and listened for the next creak in the hallway.

❈ Twelve ❈

*E*vie was having the most delicious and infuriating dream.

She was deep in the Haldon woods, seated on the soft forest floor, sharing a very heady kiss with McAlistair. It was a lush meeting of eager lips and heated breath that made her pulse race madly and her limbs feel heavy. Too heavy, in fact. She couldn't move them, couldn't lift her arms to touch McAlistair. She tried so hard, but . . .

"Evie."

McAlistair took her by the shoulders and shook her gently. It was, she decided, a devilishly hard way to kiss.

"Leggo."

"Evie, wake up."

"Leg . . ." Cautiously, she opened her eyes and found McAlistair leaning over her. They were at the inn, she realized, not in the woods. He was sitting on the edge of the bed, not next to her on the ground. And he wasn't trying to hold her; he was trying to rouse her.

She squeezed her eyes shut with a soft groan.

"Don't go back to sleep, Evie."

"I shan't." Probably. Much too groggy to feel embarrassed by her dream, she dragged two hands down her face and wondered just how awful she looked.

She felt McAlistair rise from the bed. "Do you want breakfast?"

"Chocolate," she nearly whimpered. "Please."

"I'll see if any is to be had in town."

Prying her eyes open, she glanced at the window. There wasn't the faintest hint of light peeping from behind the drapes. The only illumination in the room came from the glowing coals of the fire. "In town?"

"We need supplies. I won't be gone long."

He had his coat on before she found the energy to sit up and was out the door before she'd made a move to get off the bed.

The floor seemed so terribly far away.

She stretched her legs, then her back, hoping the movement would push aside the remnants of sleep. She found a little success and leveraged herself off the bed to shuffle to one of the chairs . . . where she sat and stared at the fireplace.

She was still staring at it, caught somewhere between asleep and awake, when McAlistair returned.

He crossed the room to hand her a steaming mug. "No chocolate, I'm afraid. Just tea."

"What?" She blinked at the mug. "Oh, right. Thank you."

"Not awake yet?"

She shook her head, breathed in the aroma of the tea and took a sip. It was strong and hot and it worked wonders to clear her head.

"Still dark yet," McAlistair commented.

Evie took another sip and felt another layer of grogginess slide away. "I noticed. How did you manage the tea and supplies?" She looked at him. "*Did* you manage supplies?"

"A few, already packed. I pounded on doors," he said,

and smiled a little at her sympathetic wince. "Just two, and I paid handsomely."

"And the tea?"

"Cook's up."

"Oh." He'd gone shopping, made tea, and packed supplies, all while she'd been sitting there. "How long have you been gone?"

"Little less than an hour. Thought you'd be ready when I returned."

An hour? She really had fallen asleep in the chair. "I move slowly in the morning."

"If you move quickly enough to dress before the sun rises, you can forgo the cape."

She downed the remainder of her tea and bolted for the screen.

To Evie's delight, the only sign of life at the inn as she and McAlistair made their way into the yard was the bang of pots in the kitchen and the muffled sound of voices from the stable. Both were easily avoided, the first by simply not going into the kitchen, and the second by waiting while McAlistair fetched the horses.

She shoved the cape in the saddlebag the moment McAlistair returned. She was going to bury the filthy thing at the very first opportunity. No doubt, it would be more satisfying—it would certainly be less work—to burn it, but heaven knew what sort of vapors the thing would give off.

For now, Evie was relieved just to have it out of sight and away from her nose.

The hour was much too early for her taste, and her aching body resisted both the climb into the saddle and the soft jolting as the horses moved forward into the street. But having escaped another encounter with the hideous cape was sufficient to warrant a measure of optimism for the coming day.

The storm had passed, leaving behind cool air and soft ground . . . well, soft once they left the confines of the soggy yard. The sun had yet to show itself, but a glow from the horizon had chased away the complete darkness of night. In the dim light, Evie could make out the gray shapes of shops and homes lining the street. A few windows flickered with candlelight, but for the most part, the town remained asleep.

With the inn nearer the edge of town than the center, it took no more than a quarter hour for houses to give way to farms, and soon those farms gave way to open fields of uncultivated land.

McAlistair led them off the road into one such field just as the sun broke over the horizon. With a wistful sigh, Evie twisted in her saddle for one last look at the road. It would be the last she saw of civilization for a while.

By midmorning, the weather had gone from cool to muggy. Heated by the sun and humid from the previous night's downpour, the air felt heavy and close, with the promise of becoming more uncomfortable as the day progressed.

Evie finished the apple McAlistair had tossed to her earlier—she was happy to say she'd only bobbled it once—and looked to the stream they'd been following since leaving town.

It wound through the land like a wide ribbon, twisting and curving, flowing in and out of view. She threw the apple core for the birds and watched as the stream disappeared into a narrow stand of trees that lined the water on either side. It would reappear, she knew, somewhere in the next mile or two.

And she'd be longing for a dip in it before the day was over.

She wondered if McAlistair would be agreeable to the

idea. It was impossible to know, as he'd made it impossible to carry on any sort of conversation. He'd spent no more than five minutes of the last five hours within speaking distance, and those only in ten-second increments. And during those brief interludes, his dark eyes seemed to be constantly scanning the horizon, peering at every rock or shrub large enough to cast a shadow, looking intently at every feature of the landscape, every mark in the dirt. Everything, it seemed to Evie, except her. Even when they'd stopped so she could rest her leg, McAlistair had left her to go prowling about. He rarely went out of sight and was almost never more than fifty yards away, but unless she cared to shout, conversation was once again out of the question.

She was giving serious thought to following him on his little excursions—just to see what he would do, really—when her horse stumbled suddenly, jostling Evie in the saddle. It took only a few steps for the mare to right herself again, but when she moved forward it was with an uneven gait.

"Well, look at us," Evie murmured, pulling the limping horse to a halt. "We're a matched set."

Chuckling a little at her silly joke, she swung her leg over and climbed down.

She'd barely righted her skirts before McAlistair had galloped to her side and dismounted. "Evie?"

"Thrown a shoe, I think," she informed him and bent down to gently coax the mare into lifting her front leg. The hoof was a little ragged where the nails had pulled loose, but it was nothing a good trimming couldn't remedy.

"No injury," McAlistair murmured, taking a quick peek over her shoulder.

"Mmm. Just a bit tender, aren't you?" she crooned to the mare, setting the hoof down. "I would be too, if I had to walk without one of my shoes. Not to worry, sweet . . ." Her voice trailed off. "I don't know her name."

"Sorry?"

She turned to look at McAlistair. "The horse's name. I've been riding her for days and haven't bothered to learn her name."

"That troubles you?"

"Yes, it seems . . ." She almost said it seemed rude, but feared he would laugh. "It seems as if I should know."

He nodded in quiet understanding and took the reins. "It's Rose."

"Rose?" She felt herself smile. "That's my middle name. Well, one of them."

His eyes shifted to something over her shoulder. "Is it?"

"Yes. The other is Elizabeth." She ran a hand down Rose's withers and nodded toward McAlistair's mount. "And what is his name?"

"I don't know. He's Hunter's."

"Oh." She shrugged, a little disappointed, and turned back to murmur to Rose. "What are we to do with you, then?"

"Replace the shoe," McAlistair suggested.

"Yes, thank you," she drawled with a half smile. "Where?"

"There's a village of sorts, not far." He tied the mare's reins to the gelding. "You'll need to hide your face.

"I am not, absolutely *not*, putting on that awful cloak—" She broke off when he pulled something dark and flowing from his saddlebag and handed it to her. "Oh."

It was a wool hooded cape as well, but it was a world apart from the ill-fitting green monstrosity. This one was rich brown, lightweight, soft, and clean.

She fingered the material. "Where did you get this?"

"Randswith. With the supplies."

"Oh, you should have said something." She reached into one of her own bags for her coin purse. "I owe you—"

"Keep your money."

She stopped her search to look at him. "But it's very fine. It must have cost—"

"Keep it."

She felt her brows go up at his stern tone. "It isn't proper for a lady to accept articles of clothing from a gentleman."

"Do you care?"

"Not particularly, not under the circumstances." And if it bothered him to take her money, she wasn't going to press the issue. Besides, it probably wasn't his money, was it? He was a hermit, or had been, and hermits weren't exactly known for their financial independence. Likely as not, Whit had given him funds before they'd left Haldon. She flung the cape over her shoulders. "I'll just say thank you, then. It was very thoughtful. And it feels like heaven, even without comparison to the last."

He gave a short nod, which she interpreted as "you're welcome," then swung up on his horse and held out his hand.

She stared at it. "Er . . ."

"Don't you need help?"

"Help?" She looked from his hand to his face. "With what?"

"Getting on the horse. Or were you planning on walking?"

She was, actually—or had been. It was simply what one did when one's horse came up lame. "You said it wasn't far."

"It's not, on horseback. Four miles."

"Oh." She let him pull her up behind him.

❈ Thirteen ❈

*E*vie found sharing a saddle with McAlistair a strange and wonderful experience. True, she felt a trifle insecure without the reins in her hands. And it bothered her a little that she wasn't able to see where they were going unless she leaned around him for a peek. But the sheer proximity to McAlistair's body lent an intimacy she found positively thrilling. Her knees bumped his legs, and her hands gripped the material of his coat at his hips. She'd considered wrapping her arms around his waist, but hadn't been able to work up the nerve. That would have put her snugly up against him, her front pressed firmly to his back, perhaps with her cheek against his shoulder. It was an appealing thought, really, and it was only a difference of inches from where she was now. But as they were traveling at a leisurely walk—eliminating safety as an excuse for her conduct—those inches marked the line between agreeably exciting and dangerously bold.

Bold wasn't such a terrible thing, but *dangerously* bold very well could be.

McAlistair turned his head to speak over his shoulder. "Nearly there."

She leaned around him and caught the faint outline of chimney smoke rising from beyond a distant roll in the land.

"Pull your hood up before we arrive," McAlistair ordered. "Keep your face hidden, and don't speak."

She sat back with a roll of her eyes. "Yes. Yes."

"I'll have your word on this, Evie."

"I won't give it," she replied in an easy tone.

He stopped the horse abruptly and shifted in the saddle to stare at her. As it was a look of surprise rather than his usual cool countenance, Evie decided not to take offense.

She shrugged. "Promises made without forethought are too easily broken."

"Very well."

To her own surprise, he turned back around without another word. And then, to her complete bafflement, he simply sat there, staring ahead, saying nothing, and moving not an inch.

"What are we doing?" she inquired after a moment.

"Waiting for you to think."

She ran her tongue across her teeth, fighting a smile. "And if, after serious consideration, I should still refuse to promise?"

"We'll wait for you to think again."

"That's what I thought." She laughed. She couldn't help it. "McAlistair, this is absurd."

He turned around again. "I'll have your word."

"I don't want to give it. There are too many variables, too many reasons I might need to break it."

"Such as?"

A reasonable question. *Blast.* "What if . . . what if I should see a crazed bull charging?"

"Is this a magical bull only you can see?"

"I . . ." What sort of question was that? "Well, it needn't be *magical*—"

"How else would I fail to notice a hundred-stone animal running straight for us?"

"A poor example," she conceded. "What if I should see a suspicious character lurking about in town, and—"

"Nudge me and point."

A reasonable solution. *Damn.* "Very well, what if . . . what if . . ."

McAlistair waited with an air of great patience while she wracked her brain for possibilities. To her frustration, she couldn't come up with a single situation that couldn't be resolved with a nudge and a point.

"Done thinking?" McAlistair asked after a time.

She scowled at him.

"Promise, Evie."

She couldn't see a way around it. Not unless she was content to spend the remainder of her life sitting on a horse with McAlistair in the middle of nowhere.

Not that she found sharing a horse with McAlistair unpleasant; it was the rest of her life in the middle of nowhere that—

"Evie."

"Fine." She heaved a sigh. "I promise."

"Not a word. Not a peep."

Although it amused her to hear McAlistair make use of the word "peep," amusement was overshadowed by the implied insult.

She raised her brows. "You would insist on my word in one breath and impugn its worth in the next?"

He inclined his head. "Point taken."

She sniffed rather regally. It was a bit much, but after losing the argument, she was inclined to make the most of what small victory she could claim.

McAlistair appeared singularly unimpressed. "Hop down."

She blinked at him. "Hop down?"

"You can't ride into town this way."

She glanced down at herself and knew he was right. Her skirt was up past her knees again. "I'd stopped noticing sometime yesterday," she said absently before looking to him. "Shall I walk?"

He shook his head and helped her off the horse. "Sidesaddle."

She peered up at him. "How am I to manage that?"

He scooted back a little and patted the saddle in front of him.

Evie felt her eyes grow round. His lap? He wanted her to ride in his lap?

"Um . . ."

"If you prefer, I can walk."

"No." She swallowed and reached out her hand. It wouldn't be fair to make the man walk the next two miles because she was feeling priggish all of a sudden. Hadn't she just been wishing for an excuse to be closer to him? "No, this is fine."

Rather than take her hand, he leaned down, turned her around, wrapped an arm around her, and lifted her into the saddle as if she weighed nothing at all.

Good heavens.

Evie had only a moment to marvel at his remarkable strength and balance before she found herself settled on the horse, half on the saddle and half on his legs. Then she simply marveled at how remarkably uncomfortable that position was.

She shifted in an attempt to escape the edge of the saddle digging into her leg. Shifted again to keep her feet from kicking the horse's shoulder. "This isn't at all how Kate's novels describe it."

"Beg your pardon?"

She squirmed a little to straighten out her skirts where they were bunched under her seat. "Kate. She has a penchant for torrid novels. They always describe sharing a saddle as a romantic and adventurous endeavor." She squirmed again. "Adventurous, I'll give them."

McAlistair wrapped his hands over her hips, lifted her up, shifted himself, and set her back down. This time she was settled against his chest and almost entirely on his lap.

"Better?"

She had to swallow past a dry throat. "Yes."

It *was* better. It was also suddenly every bit as romantic as Kate's novels had led her to believe.

Or perhaps romantic wasn't the right word. Perhaps *wicked* was.

She was, in a very real sense, *on top* of the man. The heat of him came through her gown to warm her skin. The smell of him, both familiar and exotic to her now, teased her nose, and she had the oddest urge to turn her face into his shirt and breathe him in. The taut muscles of his thighs shifted beneath her with the movement of the horse, making her heart race. He seemed to wrap himself around her as he shortened the reins, his broad shoulders looming over her. The hard expanse of his chest pressed into her side. And his arms, lean and strong, brushed against her breasts, sending a shiver of pleasure along her spine.

She felt embraced, surrounded, protected. And decidedly overheated.

"Not far, is it?" she asked in an attempt to break the spell. Her voice came out squeaky, but that couldn't be helped. She found it amazing she was able to speak at all.

"Not far," he replied gruffly.

Though she'd known the answer already, she nodded, stared resolutely ahead, and made a mental note to be more careful with what she wished for in the future.

The village consisted of no more than a half dozen huts very loosely grouped together around what she assumed was meant to be the town center, but was really little more than a large grassy field.

Evie tugged at the hood of her cape. "How did you know of this place?"

"Map. Keep your face hidden."

"It is hidden. This is on a map?"

"Mr. Hunter's map. No more talking."

As they had just reached the first hut, and because she had no intention of breaking her promise, Evie gave her hood another tug and fell silent.

The blacksmith's was easily located. The single-story, thatched-roof cottage sat at the end of a large dirt drive, a thick plume of smoke issuing from a workshop in back.

McAlistair brought the horses to a stop and dismounted before reaching up to grasp Evie around the waist and lifting her to the ground.

He leaned down to whisper, "How is your leg?"

Knowing full well he couldn't see her expression while her head was down, she raised her brows at the question. Did he expect her to break her promise so soon?

She shook her head at him.

Whether he took that to mean it wasn't bothering her or she wasn't going to answer, she couldn't say. He simply took her gently by the arm and led her to a small bench under the single tree in the yard.

"Stay here," he ordered as she took a seat. "I'll—"

"Trouble, sir?"

The pair turned their heads as the blacksmith came around the side of the cottage. Evie took a discreet peek from under her hood, careful to keep her features hidden. He was a broad man, thicker than he was tall, with wide arms and legs, and a barrel chest covered by a leather smock. His face was red, smashed flat like a bulldog's, and smeared with soot. If it hadn't been for his friendly smile, Evie might have found the man's appearance unsettling.

In a surprisingly graceful move, he bowed to McAlistair. "Mr. Thomas, at your service."

McAlistair returned the greeting and spoke in a hearty, even cheery voice entirely unlike his own. "Mr. Thomas, a pleasure. I am Mr. Black. My sister, Miss Black. On our way to visit our dear mother to the east. Bit of the gout, don't you know. Lord knows she'll be well by the time we make it, but you can't say no to your own mother, can you? Thought we'd make it in a day, but Lottie's—that is, Miss Black's—horse threw a shoe, not two miles back. Damned-est thing."

Mr. Thomas cocked his head at Evie. "All right, then, miss? Weren't hurt, were you?"

She wouldn't have been able to answer even if she hadn't made the promise to keep silent. Under the cover of her hood, she was gaping at McAlistair. Where the devil had this jolly idiot come from?

"A mite shy, my sister," McAlistair informed Mr. Thomas with a grin. "Right as rain, though. She'll be happy enough to sit a spell on the bench, if it's all the same to you."

"Sit as long as you like," Mr. Thomas told her kindly.

He turned to Rose, ran a gentle hand down her foreleg, and examined her hoof. "Nothing damaged," he pronounced, straightening. "Bring her along, then. We'll fix this lovely lady up." He looked to Evie again. "If you see my apprentice about—tall young man with a long nose—point him my way, would you, miss? Boy's forever disappearing when there's work to be had."

Evie nodded and watched as the pair disappeared around the side of the cottage, the blacksmith bemoaning his poor choice of apprentice all the way. "Whelp thinks he's still in London. Wants to spend his days drinking and chasing the lasses. Should've found a farmer's boy . . ."

His voice faded away, and Evie took the moment of solitude to tilt her face up in the futile hope of catching a breeze.

She snapped her gaze down again when the front door of the cottage opened with a slow creak of rusty hinges. As far as Evie was concerned, there was no sound reason to hide her face in this small village, but she had given her word, and she intended to keep it.

She waited for the newcomer to speak or make his way around back, but after a few moments of uncomfortable silence, Evie glanced up, pulling the bottom of her hood across her face.

Here was the missing apprentice, she realized. He was a young man, no more than twenty, tall, with muscles in his arms and the long nose the blacksmith had described.

Uncertain how to react to his disquieting stare, she used her free hand to point in the direction of the workshop.

The young man stepped forward and pressed a conspiratorial finger to his lips. "Old man looking for me, is he?"

Though she'd have preferred to ignore him now that she'd fulfilled her obligation to Mr. Thomas, there was nothing Evie could do but nod.

"Horse threw a shoe, did it?"

Evie nodded again and wondered why he was prolonging the conversation. He'd obviously been eavesdropping, and she was doing nothing to encourage his attention.

He stepped closer, throwing a wary glance around the side of the house. "Wager you've a nice face under that hood." He bent down a little as if trying to catch a peek. "Won't you give us a look, love?"

Evie could only assume the sickly grimace he produced was meant to be a charming smile. The close view of his sallow complexion and enormous yellow teeth nearly charmed a second viewing of her lunch. She shook her head.

"Bit shy?" He stepped closer. "I like a woman what knows how to keep her mouth closed."

A thousand cutting retorts flew to her lips, but aside from the fact that a confrontation with a stranger would likely exacerbate her stammer, there was also the damnable promise to McAlistair.

She stood and carefully edged her way around to the other side of the bench.

"What you playin' coy for? You're no more his sister than I am." He chuckled a little and loomed closer. "And you ain't on the road to Gretna Green. Only leaves one thing. Here now—" He reached into a pocket and pulled out a coin. "Just want a look, love. Maybe a taste." He held the coin out to her, his smile growing strained when she refused to take it. "That's good money, that is. Your fancy toff don't need know nothin' about it.

He waggled the coin at her. "Go on. Pull your hood back."

She shook her head again.

He shoved the coin back in his pocket with a hand that had begun to shake. "Likes a woman what knows to do as she's told even better than one what keeps her mouth shut. Pull your hood back."

He moved to circle the bench, and when she would have done the same to avoid him, he reached across and snagged her arm.

Promise or not, she might have yelled out at the feel of his bony fingers digging into her skin, but in a swift and agile move, he spun her around and yanked her back against him. He used one arm to pin her in place and the other to cover her mouth.

"No need for all this," he hissed when she squirmed. "No need. Only wanted a taste."

Her mind filled with fear and revulsion. The arm around her waist squeezed like a band of iron. The smell of smoke, sweat, and onions assaulted her nose, bringing on a wave of nausea.

She struggled, kicking at his shins, twisting an arm half free and throwing an elbow back into his stomach. But she hadn't the strength to break away, and there wasn't enough space between them for her blows to have any real power. Her efforts gained a single grunt from him and then a long, infuriating giggle.

"Cat still got your tongue?" he panted, pressing his fingers harder against her mouth. "I've somethin' better for it than that."

He moved to push off her hood with his chin.

She moved to bite his hand.

And then he was simply gone. In a single heartbeat, the hard fingers and rotten breath vanished.

Blinded by her hood, she whirled around and threw her hands up, expecting a blow or another grab.

"Evie? Are you hurt?"

McAlistair's voice cut through the panic. But with her own fingers trembling, it took several tries before she managed to pull the hood away from her eyes to find him standing four feet away, his arm locked around the apprentice's neck.

She hadn't heard him come from the workshop, hadn't even been aware of his presence as he pulled her assailant away. He'd just . . . appeared.

"Evie?"

She stared at him as her breathing evened, and her racing heart slowed. A strange sort of calm stole over her.

"*Evie.*"

She blinked slowly, finding her vision a little dim. It took a moment before she remembered his question. She shook her head at him.

"Certain?"

She nodded. Wasn't she certain? She felt fine . . . No, that wasn't quite true. She didn't feel fine, or calm, as she'd thought a moment ago. What she felt was oddly numb.

She watched, almost as if from a distance, as McAlistair turned his attention to his captive. The young man's face was turning red, his mouth gaping as he struggled to take in air around McAlistair's arm. He struggled once, only to have McAlistair briefly increase the pressure, cutting off his breath entirely. The man stilled, then gasped when the stingy amount of air returned.

"Apologize to the lady," McAlistair ordered.

She thought he sounded remarkably calm and wondered—rather stupidly, she would admit later—if he was experiencing the same sort of numbness that she felt.

But then she saw it—the cold fury in his eyes, the hard set of his jaw, and the taut coil of his muscles. He wasn't merely calm. He was *deadly* calm. His movements were smooth and precise, his voice soft and terrifyingly indifferent—as if he might snap the young man's neck at any second. Or not. It made very little difference to him.

This was no longer the McAlistair she had teased and flirted and argued with for days. This was the wild, dangerous man she'd almost forgotten was there under the clothes and manners of a gentleman. Here was the untamed hermit, the disciplined soldier, the lethal cat.

"Apologize." A knife appeared in McAlistair's hand. He ran it down the apprentice's cheek until the tip of it pressed into the underside of his jaw.

The young man strained his neck back to avoid the blade. "But she's only a bit o' muslin!"

Evie saw McAlistair shift and felt her stomach drop to her toes. She stepped forward, intent on pulling him away.

His name formed on her lips, but one bone-chilling look from McAlistair had her swallowing the words and stopping in her tracks. There was such violence in his eyes that she felt a shiver of fear along her spine and guilty relief when he turned his attention back to the apprentice.

"You'll use that black tongue to form an apology," McAlistair said softly. He brought the knife up to the man's gasping mouth and poised it between his lips in a vicious mockery of a kiss. "Or I'll cut it out of your head."

"Sorry! I'm sorry!"

McAlistair looked to her, but it took several seconds for her to realize he was waiting for her to accept or refuse the apology. She nodded frantically.

She let out a slow breath as McAlistair put his knife away. It was done, then. It was over. They could leave and—

"What's all this? Let the boy go."

The relief Evie had just begun to feel drained away at the appearance of the burly Mr. Thomas. He'd seemed large to her before, when the matter was only a business transaction, but now, with his friendly smile replaced by a glower, and his enormous hands curled into fists, he looked a veritable giant.

He'll tear McAlistair in two.

She braced herself, for what she didn't know—to run, to pull McAlistair away, to pull the blacksmith away

McAlistair threw a hard glance at Mr. Thomas.

"You'll stay out of this," he said, very much like a man who didn't merely expect to be obeyed but knew without question that he would be.

Mr. Thomas didn't appear inclined to disabuse him of that notion. He stopped in his tracks. "What's the boy done?"

"Accosted the lady."

To her surprise, the blacksmith looked first to her for confirmation. Her nod elicited a string of desperate denials from the apprentice.

"I weren't doing nothin'! They lie! They're liars! She—" He had no choice but to cut off his words when McAlistair once again tightened his hold.

"Let the boy go," Mr. Thomas said. "I'll see to him."

McAlistair seemed to consider it.

"Your horses are ready," Mr. Thomas added. "And if you hold him much longer, you'll kill him." He rubbed the side of his jaw and his gaze turned speculative. "Don't think I could stop the likes of you, if you've a mind to murder." He dropped his hand. "But I'm a law-abiding man. Damn if I won't turn you in after the fact."

McAlistair waited a heartbeat more before releasing his captive. The apprentice dropped to his knees in the dirt yard, holding his throat and breathing in ragged gasps.

He was still there gasping, with a very unsympathetic-looking Mr. Thomas standing over him, when Evie and McAlistair mounted their horses and left.

❈ Fourteen ❈

They rode in silence, skirting the same wide stream they'd followed most of the morning. The birds were still singing, the sun still bright, and the gentle beat of horse hooves on the soft ground provided a familiar and somehow reassuring rhythm. But it wasn't the same.

McAlistair had asked Evie once more if she were un-harmed, as he'd helped her to mount her horse. She'd said yes, and neither had spoken another word in the twenty minutes since.

Evie was vaguely aware of him keeping close to her and of the concerned glances he sent her way, but most of her concentration was focused inward.

She was shaking. Letting go of the reins with one hand, she watched as her fingers trembled. Only part of the reaction was caused by a lingering fear and disgust of the attacker, and perhaps some of it was shock at what she had seen in McAlistair's eyes. But the majority of it stemmed from anger.

She gripped the reins again and gritted her teeth in impotent fury. There was nothing she could have done, or very nearly nothing, to save herself from the apprentice.

True, she'd learned the best ways to fend off an overly ardent suitor—a quick knee to the groin, she had been informed, would usually do the trick. But she hadn't been in a position to try that tactic at the blacksmith's. And even if she could have maneuvered to the proper angle, what if she had missed, or he had moved, or it wasn't as effective as she'd been told?

The sobering truth was, she very likely would not have escaped if McAlistair hadn't come along. She wasn't big enough, she wasn't strong enough, and she quite obviously didn't know how.

The incident left her feeling small and weak . . . and increasingly furious.

How dare he?

How dare any man? What did it matter if she *were* a mistress? She'd made it patently obvious she wanted nothing to do with him or his coin. He had no right to ignore that, to push her resistance aside as if it meant nothing. As if *she* meant nothing.

But he had.

Because he was a man, she was a woman, and he could. Because she'd let him.

"To hell with that," she heard herself mutter. "To bloody hell with that."

Without signaling to McAlistair, she drew her horse to a stop, and twisted in the saddle to dig through the bags.

So intent was she on her mission that she didn't notice McAlistair had drawn his horse up alongside until he spoke.

"What are you looking for?"

She pulled out the gun Mrs. Summers had given her. "*This.*"

"Put it away."

"Oh, I will. *After* I shoot him."

He reached over and grabbed the reins of her horse. "Now."

"No. Let go. I'm going back."

He swung off his horse, keeping a hold of her reins. Evie had no opportunity to ask what he was doing before he reached up and lifted her down from the horse.

As soon as her feet were on the ground, she shoved at him. Not hard and more with mindless frustration than an intention to harm. "I have had more than enough of being pushed about for one day," she snapped.

"I know. Give me the gun, Evie." His voice was filled with understanding, and the grip he retained on her waist was both implacable and impossibly gentle.

She wanted to brain him with the butt of the gun.

Sympathy and kindness were the very last things she wanted at present. They ate away at her fury, and that fury was the one thing standing between her and the unbearable feeling of helplessness.

"It's not your gun." Now she was just being juvenile, but that too was preferable to the alternative.

"I know," he said softly.

"Mrs. Summers gave it to me to use as I saw fit." And she could very clearly see herself shooting the loathsome apprentice precisely where it would give the man the most pain for the longest amount of time.

"You wouldn't let me hurt him."

"He didn't come after *you*, did he?" She heard her voice crack, and it frightened her. A bubble formed in her throat, and tears welled and burned in her eyes. She shoved the gun at him. "Here, then. Take it."

"I'm sorry, Evie."

She didn't answer. She couldn't. Without another word, she pulled away, spun around, and stalked off in the direction of the stream. Her body itched to run, to get as far away as fast as possible, but there was so little dignity to be had in running—particularly when one was burdened with a weak leg—and she was in desperate need of what little dignity she could muster.

McAlistair fought the urge to chase after Evie. It didn't seem right to let her go off, hurting and alone. He scowled as her form disappeared into the shade of trees that bordered the stream, but aside from leading the horses near enough that he could easily hear her call out if she needed him, he made no other move to follow. She wanted solitude, and he could give her that—give her a few minutes to storm off the worst of her temper and pull herself together.

Bloody hell, he hardly knew what to say to her, or what to do for her. He had no experience with this sort of thing. He'd grown up with brothers. He'd lived as a soldier, an assassin, and a hermit. What did he know of comforting women?

Frustrated, he shoved her gun back into the pouch behind her saddle. He needed a few minutes as well—to calm the animal still pacing inside, to bank the fury that still pounded in his blood.

He'd wanted to snap the apprentice in two.

His arms had itched to squeeze the man's neck tighter. The hand holding the knife had ached to push deeper.

He'd wanted vengeance, and eight years ago, he would have taken it. One slice of the knife or twist of the neck, and that would have been it.

But he wasn't the same man he'd been eight years earlier.

He'd killed for vengeance once. He knew better than most what little consolation it brought.

And then there'd been Evie, staring at him with those wide, frightened eyes. He couldn't very well slice the bastard open with her watching, could he?

She'd already been through enough.

He looked toward the stream and decided Evie had had enough solitude.

He couldn't tolerate the thought of her standing there alone—hurt, afraid, and angry. Maybe he didn't know what to say, but he could at least be nearby if she needed him.

He wondered if he should force her to talk to him. It seemed the sort of thing to make her feel better. Evie was inordinately fond of talking.

He tied the horses and picked his way toward the water.

Would she be weeping? He felt his hands grow clammy. *Please, God, don't let her be weeping.*

He could make conversation, stilted perhaps, but he knew the basics. He hadn't the faintest idea of what to do with a crying woman.

To his immense relief, he found her sitting at the very edge of the stream, her arms wrapped around her knees, and her perfectly dry eyes fixed on the water.

He sat next to her and struggled to find something to

say—anything that might erase the glum frustration etched on her face.

"Feel any better?" The question was, to his regret, the very best he could come up with.

She gave the smallest of shrugs. "A little. I threw rocks at the water."

He looked to the stream. It was narrow here, the water flowing deep and fast. He imagined a good-sized rock would produce a respectable splash. "That can help."

"And I kicked a tree."

"Also beneficial."

"I don't like it," she said, her voice sounding heartbreakingly fragile. "I don't like the way it made me feel."

He wanted to take her in his arms. He wanted to rub at the pain in his chest. He wanted to go back to the blacksmith's and kill the apprentice. Feeling awkward and helpless, he reached out to gently stroke her back.

"Angry?" he asked, hoping beyond hope that talking really would make her feel better.

"Well, yes, but . . ." She swallowed hard, and he felt her lean, just a little, into his touch, ". . . but mostly weak . . . and helpless."

He led his hand slide up to her neck to gently knead knotted muscles. "You were fighting."

She sighed quietly at the comforting pressure of his fingers. "I wasn't winning."

"You might have, if you'd gotten that bite in."

She turned to look at him for the first time, resting her cheek on her knee. "You saw that?"

"You missed him by an inch—and only because I'd pulled him away."

She smiled, just a little, and only for a second, but he'd seen it. It made him feel positively heroic.

"Still . . ." she said softly, and looked back to the stream, "I want him to suffer. I want him to pay."

"You'd rather I had cut out his tongue," he guessed.

"No." She unwrapped her arms to pick up a smooth pebble. "I'd rather I had done it."

"A compromise then," he offered, letting his hand fall away. "I'll hold him down. You cut out his tongue."

The smile returned, a hair wider this time. "He could still die from infection."

"He's a blacksmith's apprentice. Ample opportunity to cauterize his own wound."

The smile was joined by a small laugh. "What an image."

"Satisfying, isn't it?"

"Yes." She toyed with the stone in her hand, staring at it thoughtfully. "Would you do that?"

"Hold him down for you?"

She nodded.

"With pleasure." He couldn't help himself; he reached over to tuck a lock of hair behind her ear. He left his fingers there, toying with the softness of her tresses. "If it would make you feel better."

He didn't think it would, but if it was what she needed . . .

She blew out a short breath and tossed the rock into the water. "It would make me sick, likely as not."

The first time always does, he thought, and, disgusted with himself, dropped his hand.

Evie didn't seem to notice his discomfort. "I suppose an act of revenge loses something if one tosses one's crumpets in the midst of it."

He smiled because he knew she needed it. "Depends on where the crumpets are tossed. Aim for his shoes and you have insult added to injury."

She laughed in earnest this time. "There's an idea."

"Now are you feeling better?"

"A little." She blew out a short breath. "Better than when I kicked the tree." She brushed her hands on her skirts. "I suppose we need to go."

"We'll stay as long as you like."

She shook her head and stood. "I'd just as soon get as far away from this as possible."

In truth, Evie felt more than marginally better. It couldn't be said that she felt entirely well, but the red haze of anger had passed—most of it after she'd thrown the rocks and kicked the tree—and the fear and frustration had been blunted by the simple act of talking and laughing. She had McAlistair to thank for that.

She glanced at him as they made their way back through the trees to where the horses were tied. Comfort in the form of laughter wasn't something she would have expected from him. To be honest, comfort in *any* form wasn't something she would have expected of him.

Apparently, he wasn't quite the man she'd thought him to be—which reminded her . . .

"Why were you different?" she asked him as they skirted a large tree. "When we first arrived at the blacksmith's, I mean. You changed your voice and your behavior." She laughed a little at the memory. "You sounded like a London dandy."

He actually winced, which she very much enjoyed witnessing. "I wanted him to recall a London dandy, should anyone ask after us."

"You were yourself at the inn," she pointed out. "What if someone should ask after us there?"

"Our meeting with the innkeeper was short, and he is accustomed to dealing with strangers. We wouldn't have stood out to him."

She nodded, following his line of reasoning. "But the arrival of visitors must be an unusual event for Mr. Thomas. He'll remember us."

And not, she thought, in the way McAlistair had intended. As there was nothing to be done about it now, she pushed the matter aside, mounted her horse, and followed McAlistair east.

With each mile that passed, she felt a little more like herself. She wouldn't have cared to admit it aloud, but it helped that McAlistair chose to ride at her side. She already felt a trifle foolish for her outburst—digging out her gun, *honestly*—and if McAlistair had chosen to gallop about in his usual manner, she would again be left to question whether he was avoiding her, and to wonder why.

But McAlistair seemed content with her company. And, if not content, at least willing to scan the countryside in long sweeping glances from his place beside her.

As a conversationalist, he was . . . well, not a *dead* loss, not exactly. It could safely be said, however, that he would never be considered one of the great orators of the *ton*. But what he lacked as an active contributor, he made up for as a passive participant. As Evie rambled from topic to topic— and after the stressful events of that morning and two days of riding in silence, she couldn't seem to keep herself from rambling—McAlistair nodded, commented, and even asked the occasional question. In short, he listened.

And not in the way that Whit, and even Alex, sometimes listened when manners and familial loyalty dictated they feign interest in a topic they cared very little about. Just the other week, she'd seen Whit listen to Lady Thurston discuss Kate's upcoming Season in just that way—the glazed eyes, the tapping finger, the covert glances of longing at the nearest exit.

No, McAlistair paid attention—as if he cared, as if what

she said and what she thought were important. It was just what she needed after being made to feel small and helpless.

She spoke of her friends and family, of her work and her hobbies. She was so engaged in the exchange—she really didn't know what else to call it—that it took her several minutes to realize he'd led them onto a narrow road.

She lapsed into silence. Until now, McAlistair had taken pains to keep them away from all signs of civilization whenever possible.

The road was little more than two long ruts separated by a line of tall grass. Still it was, by definition, a road, and she was surprised to be on it. She was even more surprised when they came upon a small hunting box settled back in a stand of trees. The lack of chimney smoke and the shuttered windows indicated it was unoccupied, but how could McAlistair possibly have known?

"Do you know this place?" she asked.

"Belongs to Mr. Hunter."

"Oh." She eyed the building thoughtfully. "Why would Mr. Hunter have a box here and a cottage only a few hours away?"

"How far is Haldon from your London townhouse?"

"Not far at all," she admitted. "They're for two very different purposes."

"This is a hunting box. The other's a coastal cottage."

"One can't hunt on the coast?"

"One fishes on the coast."

"Yes, but . . ." She trailed off, shaking her head. What did it matter if Mr. Hunter owned half the buildings in England?

McAlistair led them around the side of the house, passing a half wall in need of repair and a small garden long since gone to seed.

"Doesn't look as if he's been here recently," Evie commented.

"He's never been here. He just owns it."

"Why would anyone purchase a hunting box and never visit?"

"Have you been to every property owned by your family?"

She hadn't the foggiest idea how many properties Whit owned. "I can say, with complete confidence, that I have never failed to visit a property I personally own."

"*Do* you own any property?"

"Not a square inch."

He smiled at her and led them along a small trail through the stand of trees at the back of the house. It opened immediately onto a large pond surrounded by tall reeds and rimmed green with algae. A short, boatless dock jutted out from the muddy shore.

McAlistair turned to her. "Are you hungry?"

"I could eat." Her stomach was a little jittery yet, but it was well past noon, and she'd had only the tea and apple from that morning.

"Lunch, then."

They spread a blanket out on the soft ground a little way from the shore and dined on bread, cheese, and fruit. McAlistair had brought more than enough, and Evie found her appetite satisfied before finishing half the portion he'd given her.

Her eyes and mind turned toward the pond. With its green, murky water, it was less appealing than the clear bubbling stream they'd been following, but it would do for a quick, cooling soak of the feet . . . or hands. An intriguing idea came to her.

"McAlistair?"

He made some sort of masculine grunting noise to indicate he was listening, but didn't look up from his meal.

"Do you suppose that dock is sound?"

He spared it a brief glance. "Looks it."

"Are there fish in the pond, do you think?"

"Fair bet."

"Can you fish with your hands from a pond?"

This time he looked up and smiled at her. "Harder, but I imagine so. You want me to teach you."

"If we haven't time, I understand—"

"We've time." He finished the last of his apple, stood, and crumbled the remainder of the bread in his hand. "Not likely to catch anything this time of day, not in a pond, but I can show you the basics."

She bounded up. "Excellent."

"You're very interested in this," he commented.

She shrugged and followed him toward the dock. "I'm interested in anything that lends itself to self-sufficiency."

"You'd like to be self-sufficient?"

"I should like to know I could be."

He glanced at her. "Why?"

"Well, there's a freedom to it, isn't there? I imagine you experienced it as a hermit. Your existence relied only upon yourself."

"It also relied on your family allowing me to stay."

"You managed to go years without being seen by almost anyone. You could have kept hidden from Whit and Lady Thurston."

"Perhaps." He reached the dock first and put a hand out to hold her back while he tested its safety with his own weight. "Sturdy," he declared after walking to the end and back.

Though she didn't need it for the six-inch step up, she

accepted the assistance he offered and followed him onto the dock. "Is that why you came, why you're helping me?"

"Because Mr. Hunter has a sturdy dock?"

She made a face at him. "Because you feel indebted to my family."

He stopped to look at her. "I *am* indebted to your family," he said quietly.

Well, it wasn't the answer she'd most like to have heard, but she couldn't fault him for his honesty, or sincerity.

"But I would have come," he added. "With or without the debt."

That was much better. "Oh?"

She rolled her eyes when he did nothing more than give that lopsided smile. "There you go again, rattling on and on. You're quite determined to talk my ear off, aren't you?"

"Does it matter why I came? You don't believe in the purpose."

It did matter, more than she cared to think about, and because of that, she steered the conversation into more comfortable territory. "Would you rather I believed wholeheartedly and spent the trip being hysterical?"

"No." He gave her a curious look. "Would you be?"

"No." At least, she hoped not, but having never been in such a situation, it was impossible to say for certain.

He turned to the water, looking from one side of the dock to the other as if searching for the perfect spot. "What would you do differently?" he asked casually.

"If there really was a madman determined to do me in?" She shrugged. "I hadn't thought about it, really. I'd certainly have argued against Mrs. Summers coming along."

"Why?"

"Because it would be ridiculous—endangering herself to guard my virtue." She blew a loose lock of hair from her face. "Given our current situation, it *was* ridiculous, ruse or not."

"But you'd have left Haldon willingly?"

"Of course. Why would I stay and risk the people I love?"

"If there is a madman, Christian, Mr. Hunter, and I are also at risk," he pointed out.

When he turned to look at her, she gifted him with a sweet smile. "Yes, but I barely know the three of you."

"Point taken."

She laughed and turned to look out thoughtfully across at the water as he crouched down to peer over the edge of the dock. "I don't know what I'd have done, to be honest. Probably, I'd have kept the letter to myself and found a way to leave Haldon."

"Handle things on your own?"

"Why should anyone else suffer?"

"They'd suffer a great deal if something happened to you. You're not invincible, Evie."

"No one is."

"Some individuals are more fragile than others."

She rocked back on her heels to glare at his back. "Are you calling me fragile?"

"No. I'd say you were more delicate." He brushed his fingers along the water.

"Delicate," she repeated slowly. "Really."

Evie figured it was a testament to how long McAlistair had been secluded from members of the opposite sex that he didn't show the slightest reaction to her annoyed tone. Not so much as a wince.

"There's a gentleness to you," he said absently. He stood up and narrowed his eyes thoughtfully at the water below his feet. "It's too deep here."

Gentle and delicate. Though she wouldn't have gone so

far as to call herself rough and indestructible, she rather thought she at least merited strong or, heaven forbid, clever.

"I do believe you've a mistaken impression of me."

He spared a look over his shoulder, one infuriatingly condescending look. "I don't think so. You're a lady, through and through. You're . . . good," he decided.

"Good." What a dreadfully bland description.

He returned his attention to the pond. "Hmm, and a bit naive with it. Dock might not work."

"Naive?" There was nothing bland about naive. It was thoroughly insulting.

"A bit. It's tied up with the delicacy, I suppose. Far shore looks promising."

Gentle, delicate, good, and *naive?*

Well, every good woman had her limits.

❈ *Fifteen* ❈

*E*ven in the years to come, Evie would never be able to look back at what happened next without laughing and wondering what in the world had possessed her to do something so childish, so petty, so *ill-advised* as pitch the dark and dangerous James McAlistair into a dirty pond.

But that's exactly what she did. She just reached out, planted the flat of her hand against his back, and gave one mighty shove to send him toppling headfirst into the green, slimy water.

Despite not knowing exactly *why* she'd done it—aside from feeling rather put out over being called naive—Evie was certain, even then, that she'd never regret it. Not for a single minute.

He went in with a loud splash, and for a split second he disappeared beneath the murky water. Then he broke free of the surface. He didn't come up gasping or swearing or any of the things she rather suspected she'd be doing if she'd been tossed into the water. He rose smoothly, almost gracefully. Then he just stood there, staring at her.

Aside from his less-than-ideal reaction, Evie thought it priceless, absolutely priceless, to see the extraordinarily unflappable McAlistair standing chest deep in a pond, sopping wet from head to toe. Water ran in steady rivulets from his dark hair. A long strip of plant matter draped his shoulder. Something black and gooey marred his right cheek. Still staring at her, his dark eyes slitted, he wiped it away slowly with the back of his hand.

"Care to rethink your opinion of me?" she asked sweetly, and wisely began to quickly back away toward the shore.

"Come here, Evie."

She swallowed down a laugh and took the last step off the dock. "Would you add simpleminded to your list of compliments?"

He didn't answer. Instead, he kept his gazed fixed on hers and began an unhurried but determined walk toward the shore—toward *her*.

She danced farther away from the water's edge as the first bubble of laughter slipped out. "You've no right to anger, you know. You insulted me."

"I said you were delicate." He reached the muddy beach.

She pointed an accusing finger at him. "Exactly."

He came at her in long, deliberate strides. She yelped, dropped her hand, and made a somewhat belated dash for it.

She didn't get far.

He caught her from behind. Wrapping his arms around her, he pulled her back and up against his chest, lifting her off her feet. Then he headed toward the water.

"No! Stop!" She squirmed and kicked, but protests were rarely taken seriously when laughter was involved, and she was laughing so hard she could barely get the words out.

He walked to the end of the dock and let her feet dangle over the edge. "Can you swim?"

She hesitated before answering. "No."

"Liar."

He grinned and stepped off the dock.

There was just sufficient time to either scream or take a deep breath. She took the breath.

Then she was underwater. It wasn't quite cold enough to hit her as a shock, but it was a very near thing, and when he brought them back up to the surface, she was gasping, laughing, and swearing.

"You bloody fool! I cannot believe—! *Cannot* believe you—"

She cut off, astonished, as she realized her laughter wasn't the only one sounding across the water.

McAlistair's was, as well.

He was laughing. And it was no mere chuckle either. It was a loud, rolling, straight from the belly sort of sound that stunned her far more than her sudden immersion in the pond.

"You're laughing," she said softly.

Because he *stopped* laughing at her comment, she added, "I rather like it . . . even if it does sound like two boards being struck together."

His laughter didn't return, but he did grin at her. She smiled in return and wondered which of them would make the first move to draw away. It wouldn't be her, she decided. She liked the feel of his strong arms around her waist, his broad shoulders under her hands, and the sensation of being held up so easily, as if she were weightless. She liked it very much.

He let go with one arm, but kept the other holding her weight. "You've a bit of . . ." He chuckled and wiped a smear of algae from her shoulder.

She looked at it a moment, then threw her head back and laughed. "You've a bit of . . ." She wiped her finger across his algae-covered coat and held it up. "Everywhere."

He glanced down at himself. "I do seem to have taken the worst of it."

"No more than what you deserved."

"For being shoved into a pond?"

"For speaking of me in a manner that required shoving." She sniffed primly. "And for enacting an unjustified revenge."

"Unjustified, was it?"

"And ungentlemanly," she pointed out.

"Never said I was a gentleman."

"You rarely say anything," she teased.

"You speak enough for the both of us."

"And now I'm a babbling ninny. Name-calling is no way to begin an apology, you know."

"Evie?"

"Yes?"

"Hold your breath."

"Hold my—?" She saw the glint in his eye just in time to gulp in air before he dunked her.

When she came up, spluttering and splashing, he was already halfway to shore.

"You're deuced lucky I *can* swim," she called out after him, pushing aside sopping hanks of hair.

"Not really," he called over his shoulder. "Water's no more than four feet deep."

Which put it halfway up her neck when her feet hit the muddy bottom.

And when her feet sank into the muck, it put it nearly to her chin.

"Oh, ick."

Thinking it might be better to swim rather than walk her way out of the pond, she tried pushing off the bottom, which only served to push her toes deeper into the pond floor.

Attempting to kick free, she discovered, only served to create enough space for mud to slide, thick and heavy, into her boots.

"Oh, damn."

Disgusted, she twisted, jerked, paddled, and yanked, and accomplished absolutely nothing beyond further churning up the already murky water.

"Um, McAlistair?" She looked to him, and found him calmly watching her from the shore.

"Having a bit of trouble?" he inquired.

"Yes, I . . ." She trailed off, noticing for the first time that his tone was condescending, his hands were gripped behind his back in the manner of a man patiently waiting, and he was grinning like an utter loon. He *knew*. "You *knew* the bottom was muddy."

"I might have noticed."

"You knew I'd be stuck."

"I might have considered the possibility."

"You . . . I . . ." A thousand ugly names and a thousand more dire threats occurred to her, but not one of them would sound anything short of ridiculous coming from a head floating in the water. She tilted her face back to avoid getting water up her nose, then sniffed with all the haughtiness and dignity she could rally, which was really none at all.

"Are you going to help me, or not?"

"Wouldn't you prefer to be self-sufficient?"

She glowered at him. Likely the impression wasn't any more impressive than the name-calling and threats, but it made her feel a tad better.

She sniffed again, because that too made her feel better. "Very well."

Unable to think of any other way, she took a deep breath, closed her eyes, and dunked herself back under.

It was impossible to see through the murk, but vision wasn't necessary for what Evie had in mind. She intended to undo her boots and slip out of them with the hope that without her weight pushing them down, she could pull them from the mud. She ran the very real risk of losing track of them once she was free, which was the *only* reason she'd asked for help initially, but it was a gamble she was now willing to take. Better she go barefoot for the rest of the day than suffer McAlistair's condescension.

It was no easy feat to unknot wet laces, but she managed to loosen the first before needing to come up for air. Straightening, she broke the surface and took another deep breath. She heard McAlistair call her name, but she ignored him and went back under.

It took three successive rounds of dunking herself, but eventually she succeeded in slipping out of one boot and pulling it free from the mud. She broke the surface for the fourth time with a triumphant, "Aha!" And came within an inch of smacking McAlistair in the chin with her boot—would have, in fact, if he hadn't caught her wrist at the last second.

"What the devil are you doing?" he demanded.

She blinked water out of her eyes. "I should have thought that fairly obvious. I'm taking off my boots."

He took the boot with his free hand. "You looked as if you were drowning."

"In four feet of water?" she scoffed. "I'm not quite that short. Although it would have served you right, abandoning me to the mire, as you did. Now, if you'll excuse me, I have another boot—No!" She held her hand out when he reached for her. "I can do this myself."

"You've made your point." He pushed aside her hand, wrapped an arm under her shoulders and hauled her up against him.

There was nothing else for Evie to do but slip her arms around his neck and grin at him. "And what point was that?" she inquired, eager to draw out her victory.

He hooked his other arm under her knees and carried her toward the shore. "That you've a clever mind."

Not quite the same as admitting she was self-sufficient, but she'd take it. At any rate, she wasn't capable of forming a coherent argument at present, not with his arms around her again.

Would he kiss her? she wondered as they neared the bank.

Did she want him to?

She studied his handsome face—the full lips that were too often serious, the hard jaw that was too often clenched, and those wonderful dark eyes that were quite obviously avoiding her.

He'd said she wasn't meant for him, and—despite the fact that she'd told him she was meant for whoever she was meant for—Evie had always believed that, in truth, she hadn't been meant for anyone. She was, and thought she'd always prefer to be, a woman of independence.

But she wasn't so certain of that now. How could she be, when a mere touch, sometimes no more than a single look from the man, sent her heart racing?

How could she be after she had heard him laugh? The sound of it, that wondrous joyful sound, had unlocked something in her heart. And knowing she'd been the cause of that laughter—even if indirectly—had given her more pleasure than she would have ever imagined possible.

She wanted him to laugh for her again. She wanted him to look at her in the way that made her skin tingle. She wanted him to touch. She wanted *him*.

No, she wasn't at all certain she hadn't been meant for someone.

And yes, she very much wanted him to kiss her.

Just in case he was considering the possibility, she wrapped her arms a little tighter around his neck, drawing their faces closer. His hair tickled her fingers and she had a strong urge to reach up and undo the tie that restrained it. It was wet now, turning the normally rich brown to nearly black. It looked rather dashing, really, like a pirate from one of Kate's novels. She wondered again what it would feel like to run her hands through it. And wondered if it was strange that she couldn't stop wondering.

Her fingers twitched of their own accord. It was the smallest of movements, just a brushing along the skin of his neck, but McAlistair clearly felt it. His gaze snapped to hers and for a moment she was certain, absolutely certain, she saw her own desire reflected in his eyes.

Surely, he would kiss her.

Without looking away, he set her down, letting her feet slowly slide to the muddy shore. It seemed only a single heartbeat passed while she stood in his arms, caught in his gaze, every nerve in her body dancing.

Suddenly, his jaw tightened, and his eyes snapped away. She thought perhaps he shuddered once, but it may well have been her and then he let her go.

"I'll pack our things. Put your boot back on." With that staggeringly unromantic comment, he handed her the boot, turned away, and headed for the blanket.

He wasn't going to kiss her.

Because he couldn't see her with his back turned, she indulged herself and mimed tossing the boot at his head.

I'll pack our things? Put your boot back on? Of all the wonderful, tender things he might have said or done in that moment, *that* was the very best he could do?

Hurt warred with irritation. It was only natural she found the irritation easier to swallow. She walked to the grass, sat down, and shoved her foot into the soggy boot.

She didn't need tender, romantic moments from the likes of James McAlistair, she fumed. She certainly didn't need him to kiss her. She'd been caught up in another fantastical moment, that was all. And hadn't she berated herself once already for being too fanciful where he was concerned?

Apparently, she'd been in need of a reminder.

She scowled at his back and decided his hair didn't look dashing in the least. It just looked wet. Maybe even a little mucky.

She returned her attention to the laces on her boots.

Running her hands through mucky hair didn't sound at all appealing, now that she thought on it. Likely as not, she'd get her fingers caught in a snarl.

The image of that, of getting her hand hopelessly snagged in his hair, was just absurd enough to make her smile.

"Mood passing?" McAlistair asked in an offhand manner.

She glanced at him, and found him watching her. Her instinct was to sniff primly and turn away, but she pushed it aside. He hadn't actually done something to merit her anger. It wasn't required that he find her attractive, after all. And who could blame him for not, she thought with a rueful look at her muddy gown. She must look an absolute fright.

Also, she'd sniffed (primly, haughtily, or otherwise) at least three times in the last half hour. A fourth would probably be overdoing it.

She concentrated on wringing the water out of her hair. "I'm not in a mood," she said carefully, and hoped he believed it.

He raised one brow, but refrained from comment.

She shrugged at the expectant look. "Just a trifle tired. And unquestionably damp. How much farther is the cottage?"

"Another three hours, give or take." He picked up the folded blanket. "We should be on our way."

She wrung water from her skirts. "But we're wet."

"We were wet yesterday."

"For less than an hour. You said it was three yet to the cottage." She looked at the horses. "It hardly seems fair, to weigh them down unnecessarily."

"It's water, not rock," he pointed out, packing the blanket into one of the saddlebags. "I suspect they'll manage."

"I don't know that I will." The chafing alone—

"If you'd rather wait a bit, we can."

She opened her mouth to agree, then shut it again, realizing that doing so meant sitting next to McAlistair, feeling embarrassed—and embarrassingly needy—for the next half hour. It would be unbearably awkward.

"I . . ." She struggled to come up with a creative alternative. "I think . . . I think I'd like a small walk."

"A walk," he repeated, and really, who could blame him? As creative alternatives went, it was undeniably lame.

"Just," she waved her hand a little at the edge of the pond, "up and down a little. The movement will help dry out my gown." It seemed a reasonable assumption, at any rate.

McAlistair gave a minuscule shrug—which annoyed her to no end—and took a seat on the ground. "Suit yourself."

❋ Sixteen ❋

As Evie began her little stroll along the edge of the pond, McAlistair let out a long, quiet breath.

He was not quite as unaffected as he would have led Evie to believe. In truth, his heart and mind were racing—*had been* racing, since the moment he'd surfaced from the pond, a struggling Evie in his arms, and heard the sound of his own laughter.

He couldn't remember the last time he had laughed. He honestly couldn't recall when he had stopped finding joy in his life. It had been well before he'd arrived at Haldon, he knew that much. He could remember, clearly, pretending to laugh years ago at clubs and dinners, but that had been a means to an end.

For too long, everything he did and said had been a means to someone's end, literally, which was, of course, the very reason he'd stopped laughing.

He looked to Evie and found her carefully nudging something brown and mushy-looking with her toe. Rotted wood, he imagined, or a glob of beached pondweed. She was no doubt disgusted and no doubt too curious to turn away. He smiled at the picture she made, walking along the bank in the sun—wet, bedraggled, and beautiful.

He'd smiled a great deal these last two days, more than he generally did in a year—a very good year. But he hadn't realized how close he'd come to being happy until he'd laughed. The sound of it had stunned him. The idea of it still amazed him.

She'd made him laugh. She'd made him forget his shadowy past, his ambiguous future, and simply enjoy the pleasure of holding a dripping, sputtering, laughing woman in his arms.

He'd enjoyed it far too much.

He'd nearly kissed her when they had reached the bank. She'd been so close, so soft, so damnably tempting, he'd imagined indulging in more than just a kiss. He'd imagined laying her down, where the water lapped the edge of land, and peeling off her wet clothes to discover the soft curves he'd dreamed of a thousand times. He'd ached to taste, feel, and touch, to cover her soft form with his own, and forget himself completely.

Forget who he was, where they were, and what was after them.

A selfish act and a foolish mistake—that's what it would have been. Bad enough he should overlook the danger she was in for a few moments in the pond, much worse that he'd remembered and still been tempted to overlook it for another hour or two.

Though it had nearly destroyed him, he'd set Evie aside and turned away.

She hadn't been too pleased with his decision. Perhaps he was a little out of practice when it came to reading the moods of women—he certainly hadn't seen that little dip in the pond coming—but he knew desire when he saw it, and he knew wounded pride and disappointment when they were staring him in the face.

He rolled his shoulders. It stung him to injure Evie's feelings, but it couldn't be helped. She was an innocent. She hardly knew what she asked for, surely didn't realize of whom she was asking it. She knew too little, and perhaps he knew too much.

What he'd done was for the best. And she was the resilient

sort—she wouldn't let a few uncomfortable minutes sour her mood for long. By the time she was done with her little walk, she'd be smiling again. By the time they were on the horses, she'd be chattering.

In a few short hours, they would reach the cottage and she'd have Mrs. Summers to keep her company. As the only two women in the house, they would likely seclude themselves away to . . . well, he hadn't the foggiest—to do whatever it was ladies did when they secluded themselves away.

It was possible he'd only see her for meals, or perhaps passing in the hall. The thought of no longer having her completely to himself tore at his heart, but not nearly as much as knowing he would one day be little more to her than a memory of passing adventure and flirtation. And that tore less than knowing that anything else would be a terrible mistake.

McAlistair was right on one score. Evie was smiling by the time she deemed her gown dry enough—and adequately brushed free of pondweed—to endure a long ride in the saddle. She wouldn't have described herself as happy, and she hadn't suddenly forgotten that McAlistair had chosen not to kiss her. It was simply that, in Evie's opinion, smiling was the most advantageous of the limited options available to her.

Feigning a pleasant mood was the most expedient way to hide her injured vanity. Reason told her that if McAlistair found her unattractive, he wouldn't have already kissed her twice. But reason and vanity often existed independently of each other, and while she accepted and generally refused to dwell on the matter of her flawed countenance, it was impossible to wholly ignore the ugly scar that marred her face and the leg that was more often hindrance than help. It was similarly impossible to keep from wondering if McAlistair had kissed her not because he found her attractive, but because he pitied her.

That idea, however irrational, wounded deeply. And because it did, she searched out other excuses for his behavior.

Perhaps McAlistair had failed to kiss her for no other reason than that he hadn't realized kissing had *clearly* been in order. He'd been a hermit a very long time, after all, and he'd already made it apparent he was rather out of practice when it came to reading the moods of others. Hadn't she tossed him in the pond for that very reason? True, he'd noticed she was put out before her walk, but temper was easier to see than desire. Anger was an emotion recognized from earliest childhood.

It was a much simpler matter to smile as they rode away from the pond, once Evie took into consideration McAlistair's lack of exposure to . . . well, *anyone* in recent years.

Chatting, however, was beyond her. She felt better, even reconciled, but not cheerful. They spent the next hour in silence, with McAlistair once again dashing off this way and that—not that he *looked* dashing, he was merely engaged in the act of dashing—and Evie watching the scenery.

They followed the same meandering stream until it joined a small river, and then followed the river until it emptied into a small cove of salt water. Beyond the cove, Evie could see the more turbulent waters of the North Sea and its long beaches of golden sand.

It was a picturesque scene—the pristine shore, the bright flashes of amber light from the setting sun reflecting off the waves. She stopped her horse, turned her face into the soft breeze coming off the water, and breathed in the sea air.

McAlistair rode up beside her. "Something the matter?"

She shook her head. "It's lovely."

"It's lovely from the cottage as well."

"Is that a hint for me to move?" she asked with a laugh.

"Merely a reminder the cottage isn't far."

"I see." She nudged her horse forward and wondered if he was eager to be rid of her.

Rather than ride off ahead, as she expected, McAlistair pulled his horse up alongside hers. "Will you confront Mrs. Summers when we arrive?" he asked.

She bit her lip. Distracted by thoughts of McAlistair, she'd neglected to give the matter serious consideration. "I suppose . . . I suppose that depends."

"On?"

"You."

"Ah." His mouth curved. "You want me to keep your suspicions to myself."

"It's fact, and that's a very odd way of putting it, when one thinks about it. But yes, I prefer that you keep what I know about the ruse—"

"Theorize."

"Fine, theorize," she agreed. She wasn't in a position to argue at the moment. "Will you keep quiet?"

He nodded once. "If you like."

"You'll give me your word?"

"Yes."

"Why?" she asked, wary of his quick agreement.

"Because you asked it of me." He caught her gaze. "You can ask anything of me, Evie."

What an interesting thing to say. And what a remarkably effective balm on her injured feelings. She tilted her head at him. "Would you *do* anything for me?"

"No." The corner of his mouth hooked up, even as his eyes remained guarded. "But you can ask."

She laughed. "Very well, I am asking you not to mention what I told you about the matchmaking."

"Done."

"Thank you."

They rode in silence for a few moments, before something else occurred to her.

"McAlistair?"

"Hmm?"

She shifted in her saddle, wishing very much she possessed even a fraction of Kate's talent for beguiling the male of the species. "Would it . . . would it be too much to ask that you also keep the unfortunate incident at the blacksmith's to yourself?"

"Completely to myself or just from Mrs. Summers?"

"Either will do."

"I suppose I can manage it."

She let out a quiet breath of air. *Excellent.* "And you needn't mention the business with the adder."

"Needn't I?"

She pretended not to hear the amusement in his voice. "Or that my leg gave me trouble."

"I see."

"Or—"

"What *can* I tell Mrs. Summers?"

She gave him a hopeful smile. "That aside from a spot of wet weather, we had a lovely yet uneventful trip?"

"Are you in the habit of lying to your friend?"

Because he asked in a tone that was academic rather than accusatory, Evie found it difficult to take offense. As she found it even more difficult to actually answer the question, she adopted a curious tone of her own instead.

"Are you in the habit of passing judgment?"

"No." He smiled oddly, as if laughing at himself. "It's an entirely new experience for me."

"Well, being a pawn in someone else's game is a new experience for me." She fiddled a little with the reins. "Divulging all to Mrs. Summers would only serve to upset her. She'd be horrified to learn their ruse put me in any real danger."

"You'd lie to spare her feelings, then?"

"You do sound unconvinced," she muttered.

"I am."

"I assure you, I am quite willing to engage in some minor dissembling in order to avoid discomforting Mrs. Summers."

He said nothing for several long seconds, which was ample time for her conscience to weigh on her. In a bid to relieve it, she lifted her arm as if to rub at her cheek and mumbled into her hand.

"And to avoid the certainty of a lecture."

"Beg pardon?"

"Nothing," she chirped. She'd said it, hadn't she? No need to repeat herself.

"Something about a lecture?"

Damn it, the man's hearing was too good by half. Resigned, she slumped in the saddle. "Mrs. Summers has a tendency to lecture."

"You didn't do anything wrong."

"No, but there will have been something I could have done better or something I can learn from in the experience or something I should think upon." The possibilities were limitless. "It would be a worrier's lecture."

"I see. Isn't your acquaintance with Mrs. Summers relatively new?"

It was. She'd met Mrs. Summers only two years ago, when she'd become friends with Sophie Everton, now the Duchess of Rockeforte. But the older woman had become rather like an honorary aunt as quickly as Sophie had become an honorary sister. Evie wasn't certain McAlistair would understand such a rapid attachment, so she merely shrugged and said, "It's the governess in her. I don't think she can help it."

❊ *Seventeen* ❊

Evie's first impression of Mr. Hunter's cottage was that it was no cottage at all. Two stories and dormered attic of stone and wood sat in a field not a hundred yards from the shore. It was much smaller than Haldon Hall, certainly, and gave the appearance of being taller than it was wide, but Evie suspected it held at least a half dozen bedchambers, with more room for staff in the attic. Though it was not what she had expected, it had a sturdy, substantial look that was both reassuring and, in its own way, rather charming.

They rode up to the front of the building just as the sun dipped below the horizon. Evie dismounted just in time to see Mrs. Summers dispense with decorum and come running out the door in a swirl of green skirts.

She was quick for a woman of advancing years. Evie had no more than righted her gown and handed the reins to McAlistair before finding herself enveloped in a surprisingly fierce hug. "You're here," Mrs. Summers cried. "I was so terribly worried, but here both of you are, safe and sound. Christian saw you coming and . . . why are you damp?" She drew back and held Evie at arm's length. "Is it raining to the west?" She cast an accusing glare at McAlistair. "Did you make her ride in the rain?"

Evie laughed, shaking her head. "The skies were clear all day. It's a very long story."

"It is one I should like to hear."

McAlistair mumbled a comment about seeing to the horses.

"You will find Mr. Hunter in the stables," Mrs. Summers said to his retreating back. "And Christian in the kitchen." She turned back to Evie. "You are well, aren't you? And Mr. McAlistair?"

"Yes, perfectly. And you?"

"I am much better now that you have arrived." She sighed happily and patted Evie's cheek. "You must be quite done in."

"Rather," Evie admitted, taking Mrs. Summers's hand and leading her toward the house, "but the journey wasn't entirely terrible. After a bath and change of clothes, I might go so far as call it . . . memorable. It's not often one has an adventure such as this."

Mrs. Summers eyed her with suspicion. "You enjoyed yourself?"

Realizing it was too late to feign distress, Evie mentally winced and hoped she might be able to pull off bravery with a hint of indignation. "Better that I should have been miserable?"

"Best that you be sensibly alarmed."

Evie stepped in front of Mrs. Summers to the front door, and used the opportunity to discreetly roll her eyes. "I assure you, there is little about this business I do not find alarming."

The attempt to marry her off, sending her into the woods with a man who was not her husband, the encounter with the blacksmith's apprentice, not to mention the adder—it was all exceedingly alarming.

And then there was McAlistair. Evie rather thought her feelings toward him qualified as alarming as well.

"I am relieved to hear it," Mrs. Summers replied.

It took Evie a moment to realize Mrs. Summers was referring to being alarmed, and not to Evie's growing attachment to the Hermit of Haldon Hall. The momentary confusion left her flustered, and she strove to change the subject.

She waved her hand about. "This is a lovely cottage . . . er . . . house."

The interior removed any doubt that it was, in fact, a house and not a cottage. Where she had expected comfortably worn and rustic furnishings, she found instead furniture and décor that still had all the hallmarks of being new and expensive. Peeking into the parlor, Evie noticed there wasn't so much as a snag in the gold upholstery, a stain on the dark green carpet, or a wrinkle in the lush red drapes.

The room was a testament to wealth, she mused, eyeing the ornate marble mantel and the elaborate crystal chandelier she thought was somewhat out of place in a coastal parlor.

"Are all the rooms like this?"

"Most," Mrs. Summers replied. "Though some of the bedrooms are slightly less ostentatious."

Evie looked down and slid a toe across the wood floor of the front hall. The thin layer of dust she found there was absent from the furniture. She suspected the latter had been covered with dust cloths before their arrival.

"Is there staff here?" she inquired.

Mrs. Summers followed her gaze to the gleaming wood of a side table. "No. We uncovered the furniture ourselves when we arrived."

Evie envisioned the sophisticated Mr. Hunter engaging

in mundane domestic chores. She was rather sorry she had missed it.

On the way to Evie's bedroom, Mrs. Summers offered something of an abbreviated tour of their temporary residence. Though it was no great estate, it was fitted out to resemble one, and before they were even halfway to her room, Evie found herself appreciating, even approving of Mr. Hunter's house. It was so delightfully unapologetic in its splendor. And it fit its master perfectly. He too had come from humble beginnings and could now lay claim to the very finest life had to offer.

They stopped to peek into a small library where luxury had taken the form of comfort rather than opulence. There were plush rugs, plusher chairs, and a window seat so thickly cushioned, Evie imagined that climbing in and out of it would be something of a challenge.

"This is a lovely room," she sighed.

"Isn't it?" Mrs. Summers agreed before leaning down to whisper softly, "Have a care with the window seat. It's rather complicated to maneuver."

Evie laughed softly. "Did you become stuck?" What a delightful picture.

"Very nearly called out for help," Mrs. Summers admitted. "The seat, like everything else in the house, was clearly designed to be used by a man."

Though her damp gown weighed nearly as heavily on her as exhaustion, Evie was too charmed by the room to resist wandering to the window. She drew her hand across the dark green cushions. "I suppose you're right. Was it difficult for you, traveling with just the gentlemen for company?"

"Not in the least. They were most attentive."

Evie glanced out the window toward the sea beyond. She could hear the rhythmic wash of waves hitting the beach, but the water was barely visible in the rapidly dimming light.

"What happened after McAlistair and I left?"

"We untangled the horses and then imposed on a very nice man passing in his cart. He took us into the nearest village. From there, we sent a letter to Haldon and proceeded on horseback in a very roundabout way to the cottage."

Evie turned from the window. "How do you know you weren't followed?"

"How do you?"

"McAlistair and I traveled almost exclusively off the road."

"As did we."

"Oh." Evie tried to picture Mrs. Summers traversing the countryside on horseback and sleeping under the stars, and just couldn't do it. "What of our things on the carriage?"

Mrs. Summers gave a pained expression. "I'm afraid the majority of it was returned to Haldon. We brought only what we could carry."

"Returned?" Oh, bloody hell. There were things in her trunks she needed, absolutely needed. "But I carried nothing of my own. I haven't so much as a clean change of clothes. I can't possibly—"

"You needn't worry, dear. Our departure was not so rushed as yours. I was able to pack a number of your things."

"Which things?"

"Three gowns, a night rail—"

"Oh, bless you." She was more than eager for a change of clothes.

"Also several undergarments," Mrs. Summers continued, "a brush and pins, and your ledger."

Evie exhaled an audible side of relief. "My ledger. Thank heavens."

Mrs. Summers motioned for Evie to follow her from the room. "I thought you might like to have it with you."

Evie was a little upset at not having thought to bring it along herself. She stretched up in the doorway to give Mrs. Summers a peck on the cheek. "Thank you for thinking of it. I promised the ladies I'd have a new budget drawn up by the end of the month." And while the information in the ledger was anonymous, and therefore unlikely to be dangerous, the idea of it being made public was nonetheless unnerving.

Mrs. Summers waved away the gratitude and led Evie to her bedroom, a spacious chamber decorated in soft blues and yellows.

"You'll find your gowns already put away," Mrs. Summers told her. "I imagine you are eager to be out of that one."

"You've no idea." Evie plucked at her skirts. "I'll need to wash it out. I doubt a simple brushing will do." She blew out a tired breath, realizing suddenly that if she wanted a hot bath, she'd need to go back downstairs and fetch the supplies herself. "We shall certainly be fending for ourselves for a time, won't we?"

"I am afraid so." Mrs. Summers pressed her lips into a line. "And there has been some disagreement over the distribution of responsibilities."

Evie stifled a yawn. "What sort of disagreement?"

Mrs. Summers sniffed. "The gentlemen were laboring under the impression that I could cook."

"I see." Well, no, she didn't, really. "Can't you?"

"No." Mrs. Summers sent her a skeptical look. "Can you?"

"I . . . I can manage some of the basics. Toast, for example, and eggs. I can make sandwiches." She scrambled for something else, something a bit more impressive. "I assisted Cook in baking a cake once."

"And how old were you at the time, dear?"

She'd been eleven, if memory served. "That's not at issue. Surely you haven't roused the staff every time you've had a mind for a snack, or early meal, or—"

"Certainly not. I am capable of waiting until it is convenient for everyone, or assuaging my hunger with a bit of bread and cheese."

"Ah. Well, what responsibilities would you prefer?"

"I am to make tea, see to the linens, and otherwise keep the cottage tidy."

"That seems reasonable." She was wary of asking her next question. "What am I to do?"

"You are to clean up after meals."

Evie winced. "I should rather try my hand at cooking."

"You may take that up with Christian, if you like. He's been given that task at present. As men seem to have a natural aversion to using the stove, I suspect he would be more than welcome to cede the responsibility to you." Mrs. Summers glanced at the door and lowered her voice. "It might be best if he did. Breakfast this morning consisted of one part egg, six parts salt, and an appalling amount of butter." She pressed a hand to her stomach. "I am still recuperating."

"Did Mr. Hunter comment on it?"

Mrs. Summers brow furrowed in a perplexed expression. "No. He ate quite heartily, actually. They both did. And spent the whole of the meal discussing animal husbandry . . . I'm so very glad you're here, dear."

"I am as well, though *here* turned out to be someplace altogether different from what I was expecting."

"Oh." Mrs. Summers's hands fluttered up to toy with the lace at her bodice. "Yes. Hmm."

"You *knew*," Evie accused.

"Yes, well . . . hmm."

"And didn't tell me."

Mrs. Summers dropped her hands. "It was for the best."

"You know very well I can, and will, keep a secret."

"When it is important to you, yes."

"When it is *asked* of me," Evie corrected with a bit of heat.

Mrs. Summers put up her hands in a sign of defeat. "You are quite right. It was wrong of me to doubt your word. I apologize for it and for not informing you of the change of plans."

Evie couldn't stand against such sincere regret. She stepped up to give Mrs. Summers another peck on the cheek. "I'm not truly angry with you. It's only that fatigue has made me cross. Please don't trouble yourself." An idea occurred to her. She smiled hopefully. "Although . . . if you were to assist me in fetching the tub from downstairs, I might see my way clear to forgetting the incident entirely."

Half an hour later, Evie had her bath. But rather than change into a fresh gown when she'd finished, she chose the comfort of her night rail instead. She'd have a brief nap and be up for dinner . . . or so she thought.

The moment her head hit the pillow, she fell into a deep, dreamless sleep. She never heard the knock on her door signal it was time for dinner, didn't so much as stir when Mrs. Summers peeked in on her. She slept for sixteen straight hours.

❊ Eighteen ❊

Evie woke the next morning feeling refreshed and energetic. She stretched languorously before rolling out of bed and pulling back the drapes to let in the bright sun. Mornings, she decided, weren't nearly so dreadful when they began at quarter after eleven. Throwing open the window, she breathed in the warm salt air and watched a pair of gulls battle over a bit of something in the sand.

"What a lovely day," she murmured. Eager to begin it, she dressed quickly in a soft white muslin day gown with a subtly embroidered hem and flattering neckline. And after several minutes of frustration, she managed to pin her hair up in a style approaching—but not quite arriving at—fashionable.

She made a face in the vanity mirror. With McAlistair in the house, it would have been nice to look her very best, particularly since the man had been seeing her at her very worst for the last two days.

Accepting that there was nothing to be done about it, she turned from the mirror and crossed the room to open her door. She found Mrs. Summers on the other side, her hand raised to knock.

"Ah. I was just coming to check on you. How are you feeling?"

"Very well, thank you." Which was obviously more than could be said for Mrs. Summers. The woman looked positively green. "Is everything all right, Mrs. Summers?"

The older woman brought an unsteady hand to her stomach. "Everything but my constitution. Breakfast was worse today than it was yesterday. I believe Christian saved you a plate . . . I suggest you claim a desire for toast, dry."

Evie winced sympathetically. "I will, thank you. What of dinner last night?"

"I had fruit and cheese. It seemed a wise choice. You will speak to the man about taking over the cooking, won't you, dear?"

"I can't promise he will agree or that you'll notice a marked improvement if he does, but yes, I'll speak to him." She glanced down the hallway and asked in what she hoped was a casual tone, "Where are the others?"

"Mr. Hunter is giving Mr. McAlistair a tour of the house and grounds. I would offer to provide you with the same," Mrs. Summers swallowed loudly, "but I am afraid I must lie down for a bit."

"No need to trouble yourself. I can explore the house on my own well enough."

"Oh, thank goodness," Mrs. Summers very nearly groaned, then promptly shuffled into the room next door.

Evie spent what little remained of the morning investigating her new surroundings. Though she found Christian in the kitchen, she chose to postpone speaking to him about the cooking. She barely knew the man, really. Suppose he was temperamental, or sensitive? What if he should take her desire to cook as a personal insult?

When lunch turned out to be what Evie suspected was the remains of breakfast reheated, her concern for Christian's sensibilities was promptly replaced by concern for her health. Mrs. Summers—who'd had the sense to remain in her room with another meal of cheese and fruit—had been right. Every bite of egg tasted like a great forkful of butter. It was ghastly.

She pushed the offending food around on the plate in an effort to disguise her lack of interest in eating.

"Do you often c-come to the shore?" she asked Mr. Hunter, stifling a grimace at the return of her stammer. She was not yet as comfortable around Mr. Hunter and Christian as she was with Mrs. Summers and McAlistair.

Mr. Hunter swallowed a mouthful of food. Mrs. Summers was right on that score as well; neither he, nor Christian, nor McAlistair seemed to have the least bit of trouble eating the butter-soaked meal. "Not as often as I would like."

"And what d-do you do for amusement whilst in residence?"

"Very little, to be honest. I generally come with a staff and spend my hours reading, sailing, or—"

"Sailing?" Her interest was immediately engaged. "You've a boat?"

"Several. It's something you enjoy, I take it?"

"I haven't the foggiest," she admitted. "I've n-never been on the sea."

"Never?" The question was echoed by both Christian and McAlistair.

"Not once. The opportunity hasn't arisen often, and—" And when it had, she'd been strongly discouraged from taking advantage of it. The family physician had insisted that the combination of rough water and her weak leg posed a risk to her safety. Utter nonsense. It was *her* leg, and she knew her capabilities better than anyone else. "Circumstances arose to make my p-participation impossible," she finished and looked hopefully at Mr. Hunter. "But I should dearly love to try now."

Mr. Hunter picked up his glass and smiled. "Certainly. McAlistair can take you out."

McAlistair raised a single eyebrow at Mr. Hunter. "I suppose I could."

It wasn't quite the enthusiastic offer a woman might hope

for, but since it was *an* offer, Evie chose not to quibble. "Today? Can we go—"

"Tomorrow," McAlistair cut in. "I've things to do first."

"What things?"

"This and that."

When he failed to elaborate, she rolled her eyes. "Oh, that's fine, then."

It earned a chuckle from Mr. Hunter. "I believe McAlistair means to ride into Charplins, the nearest village."

"I see." She wanted to ask if she could go along, but knew too well what the answer would be. "Is it far?"

"The round trip takes several hours," Mr. Hunter supplied.

"So long?" She couldn't imagine climbing back into a saddle for hours so soon after their arrival. She turned to McAlistair. "Surely you needn't go today. Couldn't you take a day to rest?"

"No. The town has an inn."

"Many towns do."

"Inns are the center of information in a town," Christian said, lifting his attention from his enormous plate of food for the first time.

"Oh." She looked to McAlistair, wondering why he hadn't given her the explanation, why he was offering almost nothing to the conversation.

And then it came to her. He'd grown silent for the same reason she'd begun stuttering . . . because there were others in the room.

She didn't think it was shyness, as it was for her. It was caution. The man was careful in a way she didn't understand. He was deliberate in everything—what he said, how he moved, in the company he kept. She wondered if he was being careful of himself or of everyone else.

He'd become much less careful around her, she realized.

The change had simply been so gradual over the past few days, she'd hardly noticed the vast difference until now.

Wary of destroying a progress she'd only just discovered, she made no further attempt to draw McAlistair into conversation. Not that she was given much opportunity. With the business of sailing settled, the conversation soon moved to the topic of steam power, of which Evie knew absolutely nothing. After ten minutes of listening to Christian and Mr. Hunter debate the future of such an unlikely resource, Evie made her excuses, gathered up a batch of dishes, and with a stifled groan, reluctantly brought them to the kitchen for washing.

It was going to require a mountain of soap to remove all that butter.

❋ *Nineteen* ❋

*B*loody hell, he was sore.

McAlistair stood inside the front door of the house and indulged in a brief acknowledgment of his various aches and pains. The majority centered on his lower body, and all of them were attributable to too many hours in the saddle.

He rolled his shoulders, stretched his back a little, then peeled off his gloves. Aching or not, saddle-sore or not, the trip into town had been necessary. It hadn't netted him any new information, but it had been fruitful nonetheless.

According to the proprietor of Charplins's sole inn and tavern, McAlistair and Christian were the only newcomers to cross his threshold in the last four days. For a reasonable fee—reasonable by the innkeeper's reckoning, substantial by anyone else's—he would be more than happy to send word to Mr. Hunter's should any travelers arrive.

McAlistair had handed over the money—along with a word of caution against failing to own up to the bargain—and that had been the end of his business at the inn. After a ride through town to familiarize themselves with the streets, he and Christian had ridden back to the Mr. Hunter's.

They'd carefully scouted the area along the way—assessing routes, vantage points, and hiding places—but they discovered nothing out of the ordinary. Either their enemy hadn't followed them to Suffolk, or he'd found shelter elsewhere. There was little else to do now but watch and wait.

It scraped at his nerves, this waiting. A man of action, he longed to hunt Evie's adversary down himself, and though he'd not admit it aloud, it grated not to be included in the chase. But far more unappealing was the idea of leaving Evie's safety in someone else's hands.

Pulling absently at his cravat, McAlistair made his way down the hall. He stopped at the open doorway of the library, a slight movement catching his eye.

Evie sat at a small writing desk, her back to the window, a stream of late-afternoon light falling over her hair, infusing the soft brown with strands of bronze. His heart tripped. It always did at the first sight of her. Unaware of his presence, she slowly brushed the end of her pen back and forth along her bottom lip. He found the act adorable . . . and painfully erotic.

He forced his eyes downward, only to have them catch on the bodice of her gown when she leaned forward to scribble. His mind was instantly wiped clean of every other thought. There was only the creamy expanse of forbidden flesh, the soft swell of generous breasts, and the beguiling hint of the deep valley between. He imagined exploring that valley with his tongue, slowly, thoroughly. He saw himself filling his hands, his mouth, his heart. He saw himself filling *her*.

Swallowing a groan, he squeezed his eyes shut, gritted his teeth, and breathed raggedly through his nose until he regained some semblance of control. When he had, he lifted his lids and studiously kept his gaze on the desk.

Evie appeared to be writing in a ledger, but it was difficult to tell from the doorway. And what would the woman be doing with a ledger, at any rate? Curious, he crossed the room silently and peeked over her shoulder.

It was a ledger. "What are you doing?"

She started, dropping her pen and nearly coming out of the chair. "Good heavens!"

"Sorry, did I startle you?" He knew it was a stupid question even before he'd finished asking.

Laughing softly, she rubbed a hand against her chest as if willing her heartbeat to return to normal. "Of course you startled me. You move like a cat."

"Old habit."

She tilted her head. "What sort of habit is that for a hermit to have? Did you catch rabbits with your bare hands as well?"

"Routinely," he lied, in part to make her smile, and in part to avoid the first question.

She tapped her finger absently on the desk. "You returned from your trip very quickly."

"I've been gone for hours."

"Have you?" Her eyes darted to the clock on the mantel. "Five o'clock already? That can't possibly be right."

"It is," he assured her, a little disappointed that the time he'd been gone had simply flown by for her.

Her brow furrowed. "I wanted to finish this before dinner. I was nearly done."

"You've time. Christian hasn't begun—"

She shook her head. "I traded responsibilities with him before you left today. I'm to cook tonight."

"You've time," he repeated and gestured at the desk. "What are you doing?"

"Oh." She looked back to her work. "I'm balancing the accounts of the group I work with."

"You keep a ledger for that?"

"Certainly. It takes a considerable amount of money to relocate a woman and possibly children, and that money needs to be accounted for and budgeted."

He considered that. "Where does the money come from?"

"Here and there. Private and anonymous donations, mostly."

"How much of it is yours?"

She shrugged and reached for her pen. "What I can afford to give."

He imagined that translated to be a great deal. Leaning over her, he watched as she turned the page of her ledger, looked at a long column of numbers, and put the total at the bottom without so much as a crease in her brow for the effort.

"That's bloody amazing."

She stopped to look at him. "Did you just swear, McAlistair?"

He bloody well had. He motioned at the ledger. "How do you do it so quickly?"

"I don't know, really. I've always been good with numbers."

Good, he decided, was not an adequate description. He'd met men who had spent all their lives training in the mathematics. Not one of them could add and subtract an entire page in a ledger with such speed. "Why—"

Mr. Hunter's voice sounded from the doorway. "Ah! McAlistair. Anything of interest to report?"

McAlistair shook his head, unaccountably annoyed with the intrusion.

"I assumed as much," Mr. Hunter responded, before turning his attention to Evie. "Mrs. Summers has informed me you're a formidable chess player, Miss Cole. Might I interest you in a game?"

"I can't, I'm afraid," Evie replied with an apologetic smile. "I've a ham to prepare m-momentarily. I've traded duties with Christian."

"Another time, then."

"Of course." She tapped her pen against the desk. "Are you an accomplished player?"

"There's none better." He flashed a devilish smile at her, then wisely disappeared before she could argue.

The silly maneuver left Evie laughing, and McAlistair equal parts pleased and irritated. He loved to hear her laugh. He appreciated less that it was Mr. Hunter who had charmed the delight out of her.

He ignored the irrational urge to cross his arms over his chest. "You enjoy playing games of strategy?" Why hadn't he known that?

"I enjoy *winning* games of strategy," she clarified with a smile.

"Mr. Hunter appears confident."

"Hubris." She waved her hand dismissively. "The downfall of all great men."

Now he had the irrational urge to construct—and share with Evie—a list of all the very good reasons Mr. Hunter was not to be considered a great man. He wouldn't have done it—probably—but he was relieved to have the temptation removed by Evie shutting her ledger and changing the subject.

"I suppose I'll have to finish this another time." She rose and winced a little, stiff from sitting in a hard chair for hours. "Perhaps I'll work up the nerve to try the window seat. I was going to, you know, but then I had this awful vision of becoming stuck and—"

"Why should you become stuck?"

She gestured at the window. "Well, look at it."

He studied the seat. "Seems a normal sort of window seat to me."

"The cushions are ten feet thick." She rolled her eyes when he lifted a brow at the exaggeration. "Two feet, anyway. Thick enough that a person under six feet of height runs the risk of sinking into those cushions and remaining trapped there until someone comes along to retrieve her."

"Stay off the cushions, then."

"They look terribly comfortable."

He felt his lips twitch at the sound of her wistful sigh. "I could attach a rope to the wall. You'd be able pull yourself out."

She laughed, for *him*, and his tension eased away.

"I'm not sure if that would be more, or less, humiliating than having to call for help, but I'll take your offer into consideration." She sighed and turned to scoop up her ledger. "I really ought to be starting on dinner. Should anyone have need of me, I'll be in the kitchen."

Though it was difficult to say for certain, he thought she might have added something to that statement as she turned to leave. Something along the lines of, "heaven help us."

Mrs. Summers hesitated outside the kitchen, experiencing a slight crisis of conscience.

She had very nearly harassed Evie into cooking. True, Evie had been the first to suggest trading duties with Christian, but Mrs. Summers was forced to admit she had taken the idea and run away with it. The poor girl had been left with very little choice but to follow through—and only one day after what must have been a frightening and arduous journey.

That Evie *should* follow through was not up for debate. Mrs. Summers simply could not stomach another meal of butter-drenched eggs or cheese and fruit. She could, however, offer assistance if it were needed. Not with the actual preparation of the meal, of course—she wouldn't know where to begin—but she could be on hand if, just for example, a fire were to start.

She stepped forward toward the doorway, then stepped back again. The trouble with offering assistance was that one never knew if the recipient might take offense. Few people cared to have their limitations pointed out to them, and those with additional limitations, like Evie and Christian, seemed to care for it even less.

Mrs. Summers squared her shoulders. Until she was certain Evie's limitations did not extend to cutlery and open flame, she was going to keep an eye on the girl . . . discreetly.

She walked into the kitchen and found Evie slicing potatoes next to the sink. No bleeding fingers, she noted with relief, and a quick glance at the stove showed no excessive smoke or towering flames.

Evie glanced up from her work. "Good evening, Mrs. Summers."

"Good evening, dear. Have you everything you need?"

"I've more than enough," Evie assured her with a smile and returned her attention to the potatoes. "We've sufficient provisions to outlast a year's siege."

As she'd helped in unloading the cart Mr. Hunter had taken into town that first afternoon, Mrs. Summers knew all too well that the kitchen was fully stocked. It seemed wise not to mention as much to Evie. Instead, she took a turn about the room, inspecting the various accoutrements required for preparing a meal for five.

There was a small ham on the center table. Mrs. Summers frowned at it. The poor child hadn't put so much as a clove in. Well, perhaps she wasn't much help in the kitchen, but she certainly knew that ham required a dash of mustard and a few cloves. While Evie's back was turned, Mrs. Summers discreetly sought out both from the larder. She quickly rubbed the first into the side of the meat, and snuck a few of the latter into the underside of the ham.

She wiped her hands off on a rag before addressing Evie. "You seem to be getting on well enough."

"What?" Evie turned from the counter and blinked a few times. "Oh, Mrs. Summers, you'd grown so quiet, I thought you'd left."

"Just acquainting myself with the kitchen." She made a show of opening several cupboards.

"Are you looking for something in particular?"

"No, but under the circumstances, I think it wise that every person in residence becomes familiar with each of the rooms in the house."

Evie ran her tongue over her teeth. "Are you afraid someone might be hiding in the larder?"

As the larder no longer held space enough to hide so much as a small dog, Mrs. Summers merely raised an eyebrow and peered down the length of her nose. She'd long ago learned that look was effective in silencing saucy children. "The situation does not warrant sarcasm, Evie Cole."

As Mrs. Summers expected, Evie became instantly contrite. "You're right. I apologize."

Mrs. Summers nodded primly and let the matter drop. It seemed only fair since the whole business with the cupboards had been for show. "Well, you seem to have everything quite in hand here. I shall let you return to your work."

She took another glance at the stove before making her exit. There might not be smoke coming from it now, but that could change in a quarter hour's time. Perhaps she'd send Christian down for a more informed opinion of the situation. The man was a dreadful cook, but he had managed to avoid burning down the house, and that accomplishment was not to be understated.

Christian didn't hesitate outside the kitchen. Heartily sick of being anywhere near the kitchen, he meant to get the bothersome business of checking on Evie over and done with. He wouldn't have agreed to it at all—surely the girl could manage a simple meal without injuring herself—but Mrs. Summers had insisted. And it was an easier thing to agree than to argue with such a formidable woman.

He found Evie occupied with chopping carrots and adding them to a fine pile of sliced potatoes. "Evening, Christian."

"Evening, lass." With less sensitivity than Mrs. Summers would have appreciated, he walked straight to the stove. "You've a fine flame started."

"Oh, good." She spared him a brief glance and smile. "I suppose I'll need more wood soon, if I'm to c-cook an entire ham."

"Plenty in the back. I'll bring it in for you."

"You needn't—"

"I've nothing else to do at present," he assured her. He couldn't have the lass hauling wood, for pity's sake.

"Oh, well, thank you." She gave him another smile, and returned to her carrots.

As he moved to leave, Christian's eyes fell on the ham.

He frowned at it a moment, then at Evie's back, then at the ham again. Women were forever underseasoning meat, he thought, and Evie looked to be no exception. There wasn't a clove in sight, and Lord knew she'd skimp on the pepper. Bad enough they should cook his eggs without the proper amount of butter, but a man had a right to meat with a bit of flavor to it. With another glance to be certain Evie wasn't looking, he made a quick trip to the larder for pepper, cloves . . . and a nice dusting of ground mustard wouldn't go amiss either.

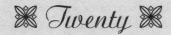

❋ *Twenty* ❋

*D*ear, sweet heaven, what had she done?

Swearing, Evie grabbed a pair of rags and retrieved the ham from the stove. It wasn't done yet. It couldn't possibly be. She'd only put it on an hour ago.

Why, then, did it smell so pungent? She set the ham on a platter and went to throw open the back door and all of the windows. The whole of the kitchen reeked quite badly of—she walked to the ham and bent down to sniff—of cloves, for starters.

Had she put too many in? She looked over the small black sticks poking out from the meat and thought it looked to be very near the same amount that one generally saw in a ham.

Was it the pepper she'd added, or the mustard?

Maybe it was just the meat. It *had* seemed rather grainy when she'd put the cloves in, but she'd assumed that was a normal variant of the ham.

Wary, she cut a small piece from the top, where the meat was thoroughly cooked, and sampled.

And promptly spat it out into a rag.

"Euhhhh." She scrubbed at her tongue with her fingers, rinsed her mouth out with water, ate a large piece of bread, and otherwise tried everything she could think of to rid herself of the overwhelming bite of . . . of whatever horrible biting thing was on the ham. It took a considerable amount of doing, but eventually she was able to swallow again without fear of retching.

While her tongue continued to tingle and burn, she stood in the center of the kitchen with her hands on her hips and glowered at the atrocity that was dinner. "Well, *damn.*"

"Trouble?"

She didn't bother wincing at the sound of McAlistair's voice in the doorway, or pointing out that he had once again snuck up on her. Instead, she gestured angrily at the ham. "It's ruined. I've ruined it."

"The ham?" He moved to stand next to her. "Smells a bit strong, but I'm sure it's fine."

She blew out a long, annoyed breath and let her arms fall. "No, it's not. It's ghastly. Completely inedible."

"You're overreacting."

There it was again, that infuriatingly gentle, placating tone.

"Do you think so? Really?" Eyes narrowed and determined, she sawed off a piece of meat, stabbed it with a fork, and held it out to him. "Why don't you give it a try?"

One eyebrow winged up. "Another dare, Evie?"

"If you like."

"And what if I should meet the challenge?"

"I promise to arrange for you a very tasteful funeral. No man can eat that and live."

"I want you to admit that I was right, and you were over-reacting."

She shrugged. "Very well."

"And I want you to inform Mrs. Summers of your suspicions."

"About the matchmaking scheme, do you mean?" She shrugged again and leaned a hip against the table. "Certainly, but two prizes require two challenges." She smiled wickedly. "You have to chew a minimum of four times before swallowing."

The smallest hint of unease clouded his dark eyes. "You're very sure of yourself."

"Oh, yes. Yes, I am."

"So am I. What is your boon should I fail?"

She spoke without thinking and asked for the one thing she hadn't been able to get out of her mind. "A kiss. On my terms."

His face darkened. "No. Choose something else."

"Why?" The sting of his quick rejection added a cool edge to her voice. "What difference could it possibly make what I choose? I'm overreacting, remember?"

There was a pause before he spoke. "And so you are." He took the fork and gave her a hard look. "Are you certain you want to do this? I'll hold you to the bargain."

"I do not require threats to keep my word," she reminded him. "I'll speak to Mrs. Summers, directly after sending for the undertaker."

His retort was to pop the ham into his mouth.

The previous day, Evie had been certain, absolutely certain, that nothing could *ever* surpass the sight of McAlistair drenched in pond water.

Never before had being wrong been quite so satisfying.

The very second the ham hit his tongue his expression

went from smug and confident to comically horrified. His jaw hardened. His eyes watered. He made an unpleasant noise in the back of his throat.

He failed to manage even one chew of the meat before he rushed to a basin and spit it out.

Evie watched, delighted, as he searched out fresh water to rinse his mouth.

"It's a bloody spice rack," he rasped after the third rinse.

She barely heard him over the sound of her own laughter. "It's worse," she managed to sputter. "It's *infinitely* worse."

He straightened and grabbed a strip of cloth to wipe his mouth. "What the devil did you do to it?"

She wiped her own watering eyes. "I've no idea. But words cannot express what a gratifying spectacle that was."

He sent her a scowl, then sent one to the ham.

Evie took pity and poured him a glass of watered beer from a nearby carafe. "This should help."

She watched as he downed the glass in greedy swallows and waited until he was almost—but not quite—done before adding, "And I should hate to have a second taste of that ham when I kiss you."

She had no idea what possessed her say it—probably the same inexplicable impulse that had compelled her to dump him into the pond two days ago or the itch that had demanded she chose a kiss for her boon. Whatever the reason, she wasn't the least bit sorry she had. It was always rewarding to obtain unguarded reactions from the stoic McAlistair.

And his reaction to her statement was most decidedly unguarded. He made some sort of choking noise and though he managed not to spray the liquid at her—which was, in hindsight, a possibility she should have taken into consideration—he did do quite a lot of coughing.

She made sympathetic noises, the sincerity of which were

no doubt thrown into question by her expression of glee. "Oh dear, would more beer help?"

He set the glass down with a satisfying amount of force. "No. Thank you." He gave her one very hard look and then, to her complete astonishment, said, "Let's have done with this."

"Did . . ." She blinked rapidly for a moment while she struggled to add sound to the workings of her mouth. "Did you just say, 'have done with this'?"

He gave a curt nod.

And she gave serious consideration to feeding him the remainder of the ham. It was very tempting, but aside from the fact that she wasn't physically capable of force-feeding a grown man, she was still clinging to the small, fragile hope that she had misunderstood him in some way. She *must* have misunderstood him, because . . . well, honestly—

Have done with this?

"For the purpose of clarification," she said carefully, "are you referring to our bargain?"

"Yes."

So much for misunderstanding. Temper, disbelief, and hurt battled inside her. Alarmed by a sudden press of hot tears at the backs of her eyes, she reached for her temper and latched on. "Need I remind you that you made an identical bargain only days ago?"

"I remember."

Swamped by her own emotions, she failed to see the way his jaw tightened and his hands curled into fists at his side.

"But why?" she demanded. "If you find the experience so disagreeable—"

"I don't find it disagreeable."

She opened her mouth, closed it, and fought the urge to pull her hair, or his. "I don't *understand* you."

* * *

McAlistair frowned at the flushed woman before him.

He wasn't handling this well.

But what did she expect of him? To be overjoyed at the prospect of further torment? For pity's sake, he couldn't stand within ten feet of her without imagining what it would be like to drag her to the nearest flat surface—he'd eyed the center table twice already—and ease the ache he'd lived with for eight bloody years.

Couldn't she see what she did to him? Didn't she know how much harder it was to resist temptation once he had his hands on her?

He took in her baffled and hurt expression. Apparently, she did not.

"It's not me," he said. "It's men."

Unsurprisingly, that statement did not clear things up. "I . . . what?"

"You don't understand men."

She spluttered a bit before responding. "I've no trouble at all understanding Whit and Alex."

"They're family."

"And a familial connection alters gender?"

"No, it's different."

"Not so very different." She crossed her arms over her chest, a defensive posture that pressed the soft mounds of her breasts up another tantalizing inch. He dragged his eyes to her face and watched as she caught her plump bottom lip with her small, white teeth.

It was too much. The need that had been clawing painfully under his skin like a wild animal tore free.

He took a step toward her and gained a wicked satisfaction at the way her eyes widened and her breath hitched. "They don't want to kiss you," he growled.

Her arms fell to her sides. "Well, no, not—"

He took another step and had her retreating.

Oh, he liked that. He liked the unfamiliar power in having the upper hand. For once, *for once*, she could be the one to back away. "They don't think about it, every bloody second of the day."

"I . . . I should hope not."

He stalked her mercilessly. "They don't imagine what it would be like to have you alone, like this. Like the night in the woods. At the inn."

She stopped backing away and swallowed hard. "Why should you only imagine it?" she whispered unsteadily. "You know I want to kiss you."

He swallowed a groan and reached up slowly to rub the pad of his thumb across her bottom lip. "A man's imagination extends beyond kissing."

"You don't want to kiss me because you'd rather do . . . something else?"

He nearly laughed. "Something else" was certainly one way of putting it. "Everything" would be his way.

"It's not an either-or proposition. The first is a step to the rest. Beginning makes it difficult to stop."

Finally, *finally*, the light of comprehension dawned. "Oh, do you—"

He didn't give her the opportunity to ask any more questions. "But since you began it—"

He took that last step to close the space between them and hauled her into his arms. He shouldn't. He knew he shouldn't.

He simply couldn't stop himself.

Evie's hands flew up to his chest. "It's to be my way. You agreed—"

He lowered his head slowly. "I lied."

"But—"

"I'm not a Cole, Evie. I never said my word was good."

Her mouth dropped open, just in time for him to cover it with his own.

Thoughts of what he should and should not do evaporated the very second their lips touched. In all honesty, those thoughts had begun a rapid disintegration the moment she'd offered the bargain and had disappeared almost entirely when she'd crossed her arms over her chest, but *now*—Now he could feel the warmth of her, the hard hammer of her heart, the delicate flutter of her hands.

He gave in to the fantasy he'd had since he'd seen her toying with the pen in the library and nipped at her bottom lip. She gasped, trembled, and reached up to twine her arms around his neck. The soft weight of her breasts pushed deliciously against his chest.

He speared his fingers into her hair and with a tug forced her head back farther, deepening the kiss, demanding she give over control.

Later, he would think it a pity he had lost his own.

He didn't take her mouth in gentle seduction. There were no careful tastes or lingering sighs. Driven by the need he'd kept chained for too long, he simply held her still, and feasted. His lips moved over hers in hungry demand, his tongue sweeping inside the warm haven of her mouth, seeking out the flavor he craved. She was delicious, addictive, intoxicating.

He turned to trap her between the table and his body. The hand at her back slid over and up, molding her waist, her rib cage, and finally reaching her breasts.

He rubbed his thumb across a fabric-covered nipple and swallowed her soft whimper.

He heard his own growl. It wasn't enough. It would never be enough.

He was dimly aware of hiking her up to sit on the table, of roughly spreading her legs so he could stand between them. He was *almost* conscious of his fingers seeking out the buttons at the back of her dress.

He'd just found them when the floorboards creaked loudly overhead—a stark reminder of where they were.

He broke away, panting, *hurting*.

"Bloody hell." Struggling to regain control, he braced his hands against the table on either side of her. "Bloody, buggering hell."

He'd almost done it. He'd almost taken her on the kitchen table.

He hooked his hands under her arms to pluck her from the table and set her on her feet.

"No more dares, Evie," he snarled, and turned to stride from the room.

With the exception of the hand that reached out to grip the table, Evie didn't move for several long minutes. She wanted to. She had the almost irresistible urge to chase after McAlistair, but aside from knowing it would do her no good (not while there were others in the house), she also found it impossible to put one foot in front of the other. Her legs, along with her heart, mind, and almost every other part of her, had turned to mush. She rather wondered how she managed to stand at all.

She blew out a long, long breath. So *that* was what kissing McAlistair—*really* kissing McAlistair—was like. It wasn't the soft meeting of lips they'd shared in the past. He hadn't held her at arm's length, hadn't been gentle or careful. She wasn't entirely certain he'd even been in control.

And wasn't that just lovely?

Her lips spread into a slow smile. Mr. James McAlistair

had lost control. Not completely, she admitted, and apparently not quite so thoroughly as she—*he* obviously had the full use of his legs—but just enough for her to know that it could happen. And that she wanted it to happen again. And again. There was no reason it shouldn't, she thought as her smile grew into a grin. After all, he'd said, "no more dares," *not* "no more kissing."

It was only a matter of maneuvering him into an interlude without the use of wagers or challenges. She gave a passing thought to trying her hand at seduction before deciding that, like fainting on cue, it was probably best left to those with a bit of practice. Perhaps on the boat tomorrow, she could—

"Have everything you need, Miss Cole?"

She started at the sound of Mr. Hunter's voice. Heavens, she'd been so lost in her woolgathering, she hadn't even heard him enter the room. "I . . . yes. Yes, I'm fine."

"Excellent."

She expected him to leave, content with that reassurance, but he continued to stare at her with an odd look on his face. Suddenly uncomfortable, she lifted a hand to her hair . . . and found great sections it falling out of her pins.

Oh, dear.

"I . . . er . . ." Her lips felt strange as she tried to form an explanation, and she realized they would be red and swollen. Bloody hell, she must look a mess. "I . . . I was . . ."

Mr. Hunter smiled pleasantly, as if he saw not a thing amiss. "Looks as if you're earning your keep."

She felt her eyes go round. "Earning m-my keep?" Did he mean to imply—?

"Cooking," he offered helpfully and gestured at the ham. "Dinner."

"Dinner? Oh! Yes. Right." She'd quite forgotten.

"It smells . . . interesting."

"Ahh . . ."

"I'll just leave you to it."

As she seemed unable to form any comment of value, she kept her mouth closed and offered what she hoped would pass for a friendly smile.

She kept that smile in place until he disappeared through the door, and she kept still and silent until his footsteps disappeared down the hall. Only when she was certain she wouldn't be seen or overheard did she indulge in a long groan.

Oh, that had been *mortifying*.

And it was only the start of her humiliations for the evening. There was still the ham and dinner to contend with.

Both would have to wait, however, until she made a quick trip to her room.

❋ *Twenty-one* ❋

*A*fter her righting her appearance, Evie returned to the kitchen with the intent of cutting out the middle, perhaps less seasoned, part of the ham and cooking it in slices. Combined with the carrots and potatoes, she thought she might still be able to cobble out something edible.

Unfortunately, the final product proved more cobbled than edible.

Evie thought it was a testament to her friends' loyalty that they each took several bites—Mrs. Summers even managed a strained smile during the first mouthful—before admitting defeat.

"I'm sorry, dear, but this meat is something less than appetizing."

All things considered, Evie felt that statement was exceedingly diplomatic. "I know. I'm sorry. I had a spot of trouble with the seasoning."

"I'm not finding a thing wrong with it," Christian announced and polished off his last piece. "If you're not wanting yours, Mrs. Summers . . ."

"Here you are," Mrs. Summers chimed in quickly.

While Mrs. Summers and Mr. Hunter passed their shares to Christian across the table, Evie shot a covert glance at McAlistair. For all her bravado after he'd left her in the kitchen, she'd found herself unable to meet his gaze in the dining room. Her body still hummed everywhere he'd touched her and in a few places he hadn't. She was certain the prickly need she felt for him was evident in her eyes, along with the stinging heat of embarrassment. Perhaps McAlistair hadn't been the first man she'd ever kissed, but he had certainly been the first man to kiss her like *that*.

Feeling the beginnings of a blush, she looked at him only long enough to discern that he didn't appear to be suffering from any lingering aftereffects of the kiss, the insufferable cad. He wasn't blushing or shifting about in his chair or sneaking peeks through lowered lashes—all of which she'd been guilty of in the last quarter hour. He was sitting still as a statue, his gaze—and she could only assume his thoughts—fixed firmly on his plate.

At the sight of his indifference, Evie felt her heart crack just a little.

Then he looked up, caught her eye, and smiled. And she felt that crack widen, until she thought her heart might split in two . . . for him.

No one should have to smile like that, was all she could think. No one should *ever* have to smile like that.

There was no pleasure in the small, nearly imperceptible curve of his lips. There was nothing that spoke of amusement, or subtle teasing, or even the simple delight to be had in a shared secret. She searched his dark eyes, hoping to find a spark of joy, but she found only apology, and a sorrow she didn't understand.

She wanted to stand up and go to him. She ached to put her arms around him and press her lips to his . . . and demand he tell her why he hurt.

Instead, she smiled back.

Setting aside the pain in her chest, she offered a smile infused with every ounce of laughter and affection and forgiveness that she could muster. Never mind that she hadn't any idea what she was forgiving him for—if he needed it, he'd have it.

His lips curved a little higher.

Her smile grew into a grin.

And then, to her vast relief, some of the dark clouds lifted from his eyes.

Better, she thought. So much better.

"Does that sit well with you, Miss Cole?"

Evie barely refrained from jerking at Mr. Hunter's question. She snapped her eyes away from McAlistair. Oh dear, what had the others been speaking of? "Er . . . yes?"

"Excellent. You can assist Mrs. Summers and Christian in their duties as needed. McAlistair can take over the preparation of meals."

McAlistair raised a single brow at the assumption, then shrugged. "I can cook."

When the meal—such as it was—was completed, Evie took herself off to the library, Mrs. Summers retired to her room with her needlework, and the gentlemen headed to the study with their brandy. Evie found the last highly amusing. She'd always considered the business of brandy in the study a ritual reserved for formal dinners and house parties.

But if this was a house party, it was quite the oddest one she had ever attended.

Smiling to herself, she stepped into the library, gave the window seat an assessing look—perhaps tomorrow—and began to hunt for a book that might catch her imagination. As she was an avid reader with a broad range of interests, it was generally a task completed in a matter of minutes. But she soon discovered that Mr. Hunter had inexplicably filled his shelves almost exclusively with books dedicated to the businesses of trade and farming.

Eventually, she managed to find a small section of philosophy and chose several tomes from there. It wasn't a topic that usually captured her interest, but it was preferable to a detailed history of the various breeds of English cattle.

With her selection tucked comfortably under her arm, she headed for her room, planning to retire early so she might start her day of sailing before noon.

She barely spared a thought to the murmur of masculine voices drifting from the study . . . until she heard her name mentioned.

Evie paused at the entrance. The door to the study was ajar, leaving an inch or two of space, and she could see—with a bit a maneuvering that required her to set down her books—McAlistair, Christian, and Mr. Hunter seated around a small, ornate table in the corner.

"As no one appears willing to bring it up, I suppose the duty falls to me." Mr. Hunter swirled the brandy in his snifter. "Perhaps we should consider drawing the culprit, or culprits, out of hiding."

"With what?" Christian asked.

Mr. Hunter looked up pointedly to the ceiling, which also happened to be the floor to Evie's bedroom. "Bait."

McAlistair fairly snarled. "No."

"Merely exploring all the avenues available to us. It doesn't sit well with me, this sitting about, doing nothing, whilst Alex and Whit see to business." Mr. Hunter scowled down at his glass. "I feel like a wife."

"It's sensitive, you are," Christian said with a grin. "On account of that pretty face. Would you be wanting someone to take care of that problem for you?"

"I'd *have* to be a woman to lose a fight to the likes of you," Mr. Hunter said with a snide smile of his own. "An old blind, deaf, senile, bedridden, armless—"

"If we're done?" McAlistair pinned Mr. Hunter with a cold look. "We brought Evie here to keep her hidden, to keep her safe—"

"Evie, now, is it?"

McAlistair ignored that. "I'll not put her in danger, or frighten her—"

"What she doesn't know won't frighten her."

McAlistair rose from the table and spoke with chilling finality. "Evie stays hidden. She stays safe. And if you think to maneuver things otherwise"—he pulled out his knife, calm as you please, and stuck the blade of it into the wooden table—"that pretty face won't be the only reason people mistake you for a woman."

Mr. Hunter rose to lean across the table, his palms flat against the wood. "That a threat, McAlistair?"

McAlistair mirrored Mr. Hunter's position, so that the two were nearly nose to nose. "If need be."

Evie couldn't listen to another word.

"Enough! That is quite enough. There is no need for this." She pushed open the door, stepped into the room and planted her hands on her hips. "Bickering and fighting like children. You should be ashamed of yourselves."

She jabbed a finger at Mr. Hunter. "You—wanting to use me as bait without my knowledge or consent. That is *contemptible.*" She whirled to McAlistair before Mr. Hunter could even open his mouth in response. "You—threatening a man in his own home, sticking knives in furniture. That sort of behavior is unacceptable. And you—" She spun to Christian, who had the audacity to lean back in his chair and smile at her.

"What have I done, lass?"

Very little, Evie was forced to admit, but since she'd already jabbed her finger in his direction she'd have to think of something. "You're enjoying yourself. It's unseemly."

Christian coughed into his fist, but she could still see the smile playing on his lips. "Well, now, Miss Cole, I'm thinking 'enjoying' might be the wrong—"

"Oh, don't bother." More annoyed than hurt—and perhaps a little anxious to make an exit before someone thought to comment on her eavesdropping—Evie gave them all one more disdainful look before turning toward the door.

Mr. Hunter was in front of her, blocking her escape, before she could reach for the handle. "A moment if you would, please, Miss Cole."

"I can't imagine why I should," she said with a haughty lift of her brow. Of all those in the room, Mr. Hunter's behavior had been the most unsettling.

Bait, indeed.

He stepped back and dipped into a very low bow. "Nor can I, but I should like the chance to apologize. Our behavior was indeed inexcusable. Mine in particular. I sincerely beg your forgiveness. I can only plead the strain of the journey and the frustration of being so far removed from the efforts of capturing our enemy."

She surprised herself by snorting. "I don't believe the first half of that statement for a second. But it was a very nice apology all the same," she relented. And she'd no doubt the second half was the absolute truth. "Apology accepted."

Mr. Hunter threw a hard glance at the other two men in the room. Christian stood and bowed. "Begging your pardon, Miss Cole."

McAlistair, on the other hand, merely dipped his head in acknowledgment.

Evie might have taken offense at that, if she hadn't come to know him well enough in the past few days to recognize the silent apology.

"I suppose we have all been under considerable strain," she said carefully. "Perhaps a bit of distraction will serve us well. I look forward to sailing tomorrow," she told McAlistair. "And to besting you at chess," she teased Mr. Hunter. "Christian, I'm told you are a remarkable shot. Perhaps you could find the time to indulge me with a lesson?"

Christian's face seemed to light up at the prospect. "Aye, lass. It'd be a pleasure."

"Excellent. Well . . ." She found herself with nothing else to say, and now that her temper had settled, she felt her discomfort at being the center of attention begin to seep in. She'd be stammering again in a moment. "Well, good night, gentlemen."

McAlistair watched Evie turn and leave. After a moment's hesitation, he moved to follow, intent on offering in private the apology for which he'd been unable to find the words in front of the others. He made it into the hall before Mr. Hunter's voice called him back.

"McAlistair."

He shot a glance over his shoulder and found Mr. Hunter grinning at him.

"You owe me a new table."

Though Evie wouldn't have recognized it as such, this too was an apology. McAlistair returned in kind. "Be grateful it wasn't your pretty face."

To conclude the touching moment, Mr. Hunter made a vulgar gesture with his hand and followed it with a bit of advice. "She's satisfied with how this ended, McAlistair. It might be wise to let well enough alone."

McAlistair grunted by way of answer. It wasn't until he was halfway up the stairs and heard Evie close her door that he realized Mr. Hunter was right. Evie was content with the apologies offered. If not, her door would have shut not with the soft click he heard, but with a resounding bang. He remembered well the slam he had earned that first day at Haldon. It had echoed through half the house.

No pretty speech required of him, then. He reached her door and paused, torn between jumping at the reprieve her forgiving nature had already granted, and forgoing it in favor of giving her the apology she deserved . . . preferably one as eloquent as Mr. Hunter's.

In the end, he turned away without knocking. He had no business troubling her with his conscience and even less trying to compete with Mr. Hunter.

Evie wasn't his to fight for. And if it came down to a war of words, he couldn't hope to best Mr. Hunter. The man had a gilded tongue. The bastard.

❋ *Twenty-two* ❋

For the first time in her life, Evie greeted the early morning sun with a smile. The tension of the previous evening was forgotten in her enthusiasm for the adventure to come. Today she was going sailing.

She washed and dressed with more speed than she would

have imagined possible before nine in the morning (particularly without help), and left her bedroom with a spring in her step, intending to pound on every door in the house until she found McAlistair.

As it happened, not so much as a single rap was required. McAlistair stepped out from the room across the hall just as she was closing her door. Before she'd had a chance to so much as open her mouth, Mr. Hunter emerged from the room to her left—at the exact same time Mrs. Summers exited the room on her right.

She looked from one to the next to the other. She'd been neatly surrounded. "Should I surrender?"

"Surrender what, dear?"

Because there was nothing she could do about the silliness and because it didn't really concern her—except in that it was, in fact, tremendously silly—she shook her head, stifled a laugh, and reached up to plant a kiss on Mrs. Summers' cheek.

Then she badgered McAlistair into leaving the house with her before he, or anyone else, could remember he'd been appointed the new cook.

In Evie's admittedly layman's opinion, it was a perfect day for sailing. The sun was out, the sea appeared calm, and a lovely breeze was coming off the water.

Rather than heading to the dock farther down the shore, McAlistair took her to a very small boat sitting on the sandy beach. It was covered by a canvas tarp strapped down with rope, but a few inches of wood showed at the bottom. Wood, Evie couldn't help noticing, that was weathered, worn, scraped, and gouged.

McAlistair briefly but thoroughly scanned the shoreline and patch of woods at the side of the lawn—just as he had before they'd left the back of the house—and then crouched to untie the rope.

Confused, she frowned at him. "What are you doing?"

He glanced up. "I thought you wanted to go out on Mr. Hunter's boat."

"I did. I do. That hardly explains what you're doing with—"

She broke off as he pulled back the tarp to reveal what one might consider—if one wasn't at all finicky about the subject—a bow and stern—separated by no more than eight feet—two small benches, a pair of oars, and very little else.

"*That's* Mr. Hunter's boat?"

McAlistair pulled out the oars and handed them to her to hold. "One of them."

"But it hasn't any sails." She wasn't entirely certain it had a bottom.

"Never said I'd take you sailing. Said I'd take you on a boat."

"Yes, but that's a rowboat. I thought—"

"The larger boats take a crew."

"Oh." In all fairness, she couldn't fault him for that, and really, common sense should have told her as much. But it was rather disappointing. She'd been looking forward to the chance to try out her sea legs. By the looks of the tiny boat before them, that particular experiment would have to wait. Just the simple act of standing up would likely capsize them.

She noticed several patches in the wood. "Is it seaworthy?"

He looped the loose rope and tossed it aside. "We'll find out soon enough."

"That's not at all reassuring."

"Thinking of changing your mind? We could go back inside, play cards or—"

"No." Good heavens, no. She detested cards. "I'm sure it's perfectly safe. Probably. Why else would Mr. Hunter keep it?"

McAlistair shrugged, which again did very little to reassure her.

She tapped her toes against the bottom. "It looks as if it might leak."

Actually, it rather looked as if it might take on gallons of water at a time, but she preferred the appearance of caution over cowardice. "Should we take something along just in case it does take on water? A pail perhaps?" *Or a lifeboat?*

"We'll be fine." He gathered up the tarp and set it with the rope. "And it's *she*, not *it*."

She felt her brows rise. "You can't be serious."

"All boats are *she*."

"No matter how small?" And pathetic?

"Yes."

She pursed her lips thoughtfully. "So, if it floats—and to be honest, I have my doubts where this boat is concerned—one refers to the vessel as a female."

"Yes." He pushed the boat into the water. "As long as it was made by man."

"Who else would make it?"

"I meant you can't grab a floating log and decide to name it *Santa Maria the Second*."

She thought about that. "What of rafts, then? They're no more than a few logs tied together with a bit of rope. Does that still count?"

He gave her a blank look. "Get in the boat, Evie."

"I'll take that to mean you don't know."

She stepped in and eyed the closest bench warily. It would be humiliating indeed if she were to end up with splinters in her backside. But as McAlistair was watching and waiting, there was nothing else to be done but bunch her skirts up a bit and take a seat.

"Comfortable?" he asked, tilting the boat some as he stepped in and took his seat.

There was already an inch of cold water in the bottom, seeping through her half boots. "Quite. You?"

He nodded and used an oar to push them off the beach.

Evie's heart gave a small leap of excitement as she felt the bottom of the boat scrape away from the shore.

This was nothing like rowing about on a lake. The water there was always still, always placid. Rowing with any strength and skill would send a boat gliding over the lake in a seamless line.

But here on the sea, there was endless movement. Gentle waves rolled up to lick at the wood and send their little boat rocking. And rather than cutting smoothly through the water, the boat seemed to struggle through each wave, the oars battling against the tide that would push them back to shore.

Evie estimated that it took them almost thirty minutes to make it a full ninety yards from the beach. From there, McAlistair turned the boat and began a course parallel to the shore.

Though just that morning she had imagined sailing off into deep waters, Evie was forced to admit that, given the condition of their little boat, staying within sight of land was a wise decision. She didn't fancy a half-mile swim back to shore.

"What do you make of your first trip to the sea?" McAlistair asked after a time.

"Oh, I've been to the sea before," she explained. "I've even been in it—well, my feet have—I've just never been *on* the sea before."

"Ah. Well, what do you make of being on the sea?"

She studied his appearance, noting the fine sheen of sweat that had appeared on his brow and forearms. "It appears to take a considerable amount of work."

"Takes some," he agreed.

"May I give it a go?"

He gave her a dubious look.

"I've rowed a boat before, McAlistair. We've a pair of them on the pond at Haldon."

"I know," he replied, but made no move to hand over the oars.

She tilted her head at him. "Are you afraid of how it might look, letting yourself be rowed about by a woman?"

He thought about it. "Yes."

"Male vanity," she muttered. "I should have known you hadn't gone uninfected."

"I believe you mean unaffected."

"No, I really don't." She made a shooing motion with her hand. "Move over, then. I promise not to tell a soul."

"I don't think so."

"Then I promise to tell every soul who will listen that I rowed the whole of the day at your insistence."

An eyebrow arched up. "You would lie to get your way?"

"I'd have to, now, wouldn't I? I just promised." She smirked and waved her hand at him again.

Though she was certain he knew her threat had been made in jest, McAlistair nonetheless acquiesced. He set down the oars and stood to take hold of her waist to help her balance. He pulled her close as they shuffled past each other, and the heat of his hands and the nearness of his form sent a shiver of pleasure along her skin.

If she hadn't been afraid of tipping them both out of the boat, she might have drawn the moment out.

Stifling a sigh of longing, she took her seat, waited for him to do the same, then began a leisurely row up the coast. Leisurely in pace, if not in effort. Forcing the oars through the churning waters was far more difficult than McAlistair had made it look, and it hadn't looked particularly easy to start. Her arms began aching within minutes. It would be well worth the struggle, she told herself, to be able to say she had not only been rowed about on the sea, but that she'd rowed *herself* about on the sea.

Enjoying herself and her idea, she smiled despite the strain. And despite the patronizing look on McAlistair's face.

"Do you expect me to give up so soon?" she asked, leaning back into the next stroke.

"Not for a few minutes yet."

"O, ye of little faith."

He smiled and made a show of stretching out his legs before him, as if settling in for a show. "Think you can row us back to shore?"

"Certainly, I could." She wouldn't make it halfway. "But I'm not ready to go back. We've only just come out."

"Nearing two hours now," he informed her. "And the longer you wait, the less energy you'll have for the trip."

"I'll rest a bit before the attempt."

"It won't—"

"If we stay out here long enough, you won't have to cook lunch."

He stopped arguing.

They spent the whole morning in the little boat, rowing up and down the shore, trading seats whenever one grew tired. Well, whenever Evie grew tired—McAlistair seemed never to run out of energy. Away from the others, he once again became the less reticent man he'd been on their trip. He spoke a little of his family, and she was surprised to learn he had kept in contact with them during his time as a hermit, with Whit bringing mail to and from the woods. She discovered he'd had a fear of storms as a very small child, and a revolting—in Evie's opinion—fascination with insects as an older boy. He even hinted at his time as a soldier, but as he did so only with prodding and seemed to grow quiet afterward, Evie didn't push the subject. She dearly wished to know everything about him, but she needn't learn it all today. Today was for pleasure—for sun and smiles and laughter. She managed to draw the latter out of him. Only because she accidentally dropped an oar in the water and in her eagerness to retrieve it nearly fell overboard herself, but it was still laughter, and it warmed her heart no less than the first time she had heard it.

They stayed out for another half hour after that, before McAlistair insisted on rowing back to shore. It was well past noon, and they couldn't remain in their little boat forever, he maintained. A shame, to Evie's mind. She found she liked being on the water.

She found she liked having McAlistair as captive company even more.

But there was no arguing with him, and all too soon he had escorted her up the back lawn and into the house, where they parted ways. He headed for the kitchen, the poor devil, while she dragged herself to her room. Her arms ached terribly, but a hot soak would likely ease the worst of it.

She imagined hauling up the tub and water.

Perhaps she'd just curl up in the comfortable-looking chair by the window and read for a bit.

Then perhaps she would see about visiting McAlistair in the kitchen.

She fell asleep in her chair and woke several hours later to a stiff neck and a loud rapping, followed by the creak of her bedroom door.

"Evie?" Mrs. Summers stuck her head into the room. "Evie, it is time for dinner."

"Dinner?" She blinked the sleep from her eyes and turned to the window. "But it's light out yet."

"Yes, well, Mr. McAlistair appears to be accustomed to eating at an earlier hour."

"He is?" He was? Bloody hell, why hadn't she learned *that* today? "But I—" . . . *wanted to* not *dare him into kissing me again*. She snapped her mouth shut.

"Would you prefer a plate set aside for later?" Mrs. Summers inquired.

Evie shook her head, and stood. "No, thank you. I am rather hungry." Just not quite as hungry as she was disappointed. "I'll be down momentarily."

By the time Evie had shaken out the more unsightly wrinkles from her dress, pinned her hair back up, and made her way to the dining room, dinner had already been served and a plate fixed and waiting for her. The meat looked to be some sort of fowl, but it was impossible to ask McAlistair which sort, as he was notably absent from the room.

"Won't Mr. McAlistair be joining us?" she asked Mrs. Summers as she took her seat.

"He will. He has gone to the kitchen for the rolls."

"Oh, I'm not terribly late, then."

Christian smiled at her. "Not late at all. We've only just sat down."

"I'm relieved to hear it." She scooped up a forkful of peas to her mouth, hesitated, and glanced about the table. Only just sat down? They hadn't yet begun eating?

Considering the last few meals prepared at the cottage, perhaps it would be best if she let someone else brave the first bite. Not that she hadn't faith in McAlistair's ability as a cook—she did. She'd eaten what he'd prepared in the woods, after all, and suffered no ill effects. But then, he hadn't had access to spices or butter, had he? A person could do a great deal of harm to a meal with injudicious applications of spices and butter.

She looked to Mrs. Summers, who, unfortunately,

seemed to have come to the same conclusion. Her fork was raised no more than an inch above her plate, and her gaze was fixed squarely on Evie.

Evie's gaze jumped to Christian, who was poking at his food while simultaneously stealing glances in her direction, and Mr. Hunter hadn't bothered picking up a utensil at all. He sat watching her, a slightly amused smile on his face.

Bloody hell, they were all waiting for her.

She set the fork down. "Perhaps we should wait for McAlistair."

"Does seem rude to begin without him," Mrs. Summers was quick to agree, almost as quick as she was to set down her own fork.

They sat in uncomfortable silence, made more awkward by McAlistair's return with the rolls. Apparently unaware, or merely unconcerned, with the unnatural stillness in the room, he set down the rolls, took his seat and proceeded to eat.

When he showed no immediate signs of illness, Evie sampled a piece of the fowl.

It tasted like . . . tasted like . . . she stopped chewing. It didn't taste like anything but meat. It hardly tasted like anything at all. There was no flavor to it. Not a hint. Not even a suggestion of a hint. It was as bland as the meat he'd cooked in the woods.

Granted, that was preferable to the meat she'd cooked last night, but couldn't he have added something? Anything? Fish and snake cooked in the woods on a cross-country journey could at least claim to be flavored with adventure. Even *that* was something.

She looked to the others at the table and found Mrs. Summers frowning thoughtfully at her plate, Mr. Hunter looking expectantly at McAlistair, and Christian, not surprisingly, halfway through his meal.

McAlistair glanced up from his plate and must have noticed that only he and Christian were eating, because he asked, "Something the matter?"

Evie and Mrs. Summers shook their heads in unison, while Christian grunted and shoveled in another mouthful.

Mr. Hunter threw his head back and roared with laughter. "Devil take it, man, what did you do to it?"

Unoffended, McAlistair scooped up another bite. "Nothing."

"Exactly." Mr. Hunter stabbed a finger at him. "There's not a thing on this, is there? Not a pinch of salt, a dash of thyme, even a grain of pepper. You said you could cook."

McAlistair smiled a little around his mouthful. "It's cooked."

"Insofar as it's not raw, yes."

"Oh, dear," Mrs. Summers murmured. "This won't do."

"I could give it another go," Evie offered, eager to take the focus off of McAlistair's failure. "Something simpler—"

"*No.*"

The rejection may have stung a bit less if it hadn't been uttered, loudly, by everyone at the table. She sniffed and set down her fork. "Very well, has anyone a better idea?"

McAlistair calmly cut off another piece of meat. "Mr. Hunter's turn."

She saw it then, the sly amusement in his eyes. She'd known he found their reaction to his meal to be amusing, but it was the quick flash of smug victory that told her it was *sly* amusement, which was an entirely different animal. He'd expected, even planned for his meal to be a failure.

Delighted with the trick, with him, she picked up her napkin to hide her smile.

Mrs. Summers cleared her throat delicately. "Can you cook *well*, Mr. Hunter?"

Mr. Hunter kept his eyes narrowed on McAlistair. "It appears we'll find out."

❊ *Twenty-three* ❊

*U*nlike Evie's offering from the night before, McAlistair's meal was easily salvaged by a quick trip to the kitchen for salt and pepper. Evie wouldn't have gone so far as to call the end result savory, but it was edible, even by the standards of Mrs. Summers, who after days of barely eating, managed to clear more than half her plate.

After a spot of confusion over whose responsibility it now was to see to the dishes—settled by Christian's entertaining, and ultimately ill-fated (for him) suggestion of drawing straws—Evie accepted Mr. Hunter's offer of a game of chess. She rather hoped McAlistair would join them in the library, but he declined, citing a need to see to the horses.

Evie stifled a pang of disappointment. It was a perfectly valid excuse, she told herself, and feeding and watering a handful of horses was hardly a chore that required an entire evening to accomplish. Surely, McAlistair would join them eventually. In the meantime, she had Mr. Hunter to keep her company. Generally, Evie didn't relish the company of men she barely knew, particularly uncommonly handsome men like Mr. Hunter. Though she knew it to be irrational, she couldn't help but look at such a man and be reminded that while she was looking at near physical perfection . . . he was not.

But to her delight, she found Mr. Hunter to be—if one was willing to set aside the fact that he'd suggested she be used as bait—a man rather easy to grow comfortable with. He was exceedingly charming, and though there was a glibness and polish to him she didn't entirely trust, she found her stammering easing in the face of his good humor and friendly manner.

To her further enjoyment, she discovered his assessment of his chess skills hadn't been entirely off the mark. She wasn't yet willing to acknowledge his claim to being the very best, but she would grant, and appreciate, that he was a challenging opponent. Further to recommend him was his obvious appreciation of her own skills.

On the last of occasion of playing one of Kate's admirers, Evie's opponent had made a flustered—not to mention transparent—excuse to quit the game when it became obvious he would lose. Women, apparently, were not supposed to be accomplished at games of strategy.

Mr. Hunter, on the other hand, seemed not to mind the possibility—the very real possibility—of defeat.

He frowned thoughtfully when she took one of his bishops. "Does all your family enjoy chess?"

She watched him put his other bishop into a more secure position. "Yes, though Kate and I are the most evenly matched."

"And how is Lady Kate?" he inquired.

Evie was careful not to smile at the topic she was most interested in discussing with Mr. Hunter. "She was quite well the last I sp-spoke with her."

"And her maid . . . Lizzy, isn't it?" He waited for her nod before continuing. "How is it she was at Haldon rather than with her mistress?"

She pushed one of her pawns forward. "Lizzy is my lady's maid as well as Kate's."

"That's unusual, isn't it?"

It was more unusual that he should ask after a lady's maid at all, but Evie couldn't see the benefit of mentioning it. "For women of our rank, you mean?"

"I suppose I do."

"And I suppose it is," she replied. "Lady Thurston attempted to p-persuade us at one time to take on another young woman, but neither of us was willing to give up Lizzy for someone new."

He brought out his queen. "She's very good at what she does, then."

Evie thought about that. "Not particularly," she decided, and smiled at his surprised expression. "But we love her dearly."

"And Lady Kate? Does she feel the same?"

"Very much so." She chose her next words carefully. "I'm surprised you've not asked her for yourself."

"I would, if she'd sit still long enough for me to attempt conversation." He tapped his finger on the table idly. "She seems to be in a hurry every time we meet."

In a great hurry, Evie knew, to distance herself from a man who flustered her. Evie didn't doubt for a second that Mr. Hunter was aware of Kate's reaction to him, or that he took some pleasure from it. She'd watched the interplay between the two more than once, and she hadn't missed the amused gleam in his eyes. Nor had she missed the desire.

"Are you in love with my cousin?" She shouldn't have asked, or at least should have found a way to ask with a modicum of tact, but the words were out of her mouth before she'd realized she meant to say them.

Mr. Hunter didn't so much as bat an eyelash. "Whit? That would certainly be ill-advised."

Evie laughed with a mixture of humor and relief that he hadn't derided her for her rudeness. "Yes, it would. Mirabelle would have your head."

"The countess is too generous a soul for that and too confident in Whit's affection. She'd pity me, and I can't abide being pitied." He gave her a sorrowful expression. "Do say you'll keep my desperate secret?"

"The Coles never make a promise they can't keep." She fingered the top of a bishop before changing her mind and pushing forward another pawn. "I was referring to Kate."

"Were you really? Imagine that."

"Are you going to answer the question?"

He looked directly at her. "I am not in love with Lady Kate."

She studied his face, expecting to detect some sign of discomfort, an indication that he was hiding something, but his expression gave nothing away.

"You may be just a g-good liar," she said.

"I take offense to that. I am an exceptional liar." He waited until she stopped laughing to continue. "But as it happens, I speak the truth at present. I don't believe in love. Not the sort you're referring to."

"Have you ever believed in love?"

"Perhaps, when I was boy. Then again, I also believed that if I found a comb on the ground and bent to pick it up, the mermaids would come to spirit me away." He smiled at her bewildered look. "An old Irish myth. My grandmother was an O'Henry."

"Oh. Did you dismiss the idea of love when you dismissed the idea of mermaids? Or is there a story behind your reluctance to believe? Did someone break your heart?"

"Of course. But not romantically."

She opened her mouth to respond with a clever quip, but thought better of it. Heartbreak under those circumstances could have originated from anywhere—a family member, a friend. For all that she knew, he could have lost a child.

"I am sorry to hear it," she said instead.

He smiled and used his rook to take her pawn. "The heart is merely a piece of the body, and it heals like any other."

It scarred like any other, too. She thought of McAlistair's sad smile and resisted the urge to touch the line on her cheek.

McAlistair watched Evie and Mr. Hunter from the darkened hall. There was nothing particularly remarkable about the scene—nothing untoward in the time or setting, nor in the behavior of the people involved. There was nothing at all to justify the tight ball of fury that had settled in his chest.

Though he had little experience with the emotion, he knew it to be jealousy. Nothing else could possibly explain the irrational anger, the longing, the sense of impotence. *Not for you,* he reminded himself, and curled his hands into fists.

She's not for you.

Even as he imagined using those fists on Mr. Hunter's grinning face, he turned and walked away.

❈ *Twenty-four* ❈

*E*vie greeted the next morning with considerably less enthusiasm than she had the previous day. A quick peek through the drapes told her it was raining, which meant there was no chance of cajoling McAlistair into another row on the sea. A late start to the day meant she'd missed breakfast, which Mrs. Summers was kind enough to inform her had been exceptional. And the news that Mr. Hunter and Christian were engrossed in a card game in the study while McAlistair was out searching the grounds meant there was little else to do but accept Mrs. Summers's suggestion of needlework in the parlor.

It was, Evie decided, a perfectly stupid way to spend the day.

"Did you enjoy your chess match with Mr. Hunter, dear?"

"Hmm?" Evie glanced up from the knot of thread she was trying, and failing, to untie. "Oh, yes. He's a charming man and a skilled player, though not as skilled as he would lead me to believe."

"You won the match?"

"Well, no. We've not finished it yet, but I will win." She studied Mrs. Summers. "I hadn't realized you'd come into the room. I thought you had retired for the night."

"I came down for a spot of warm milk. I peeked in briefly."

"Oh." Had she peeked in when they'd been discussing Kate? Evie couldn't imagine Mrs. Summers would approve of such a conversation.

"You seemed . . . preoccupied." In an uncharacteristic show of nerves, Mrs. Summers set down her sewing. Picked it back up again. Set it down once more. "You find him charming?"

Ah, so here it was at last. Evie weighed her answer carefully. "I find many people charming. Present company included."

"Oh, well, thank you, dear. But . . . do you . . ." Mrs. Summers cleared her throat delicately, and to Evie's great surprise, reached forward to clasp her hands, a very pained expression on her face. "You have not developed a *tendre* for the man, have you?"

"No," Evie said, startled into honesty. "I have not."

"Oh, thank goodness." Mrs. Summers let out a shaky breath and straightened once more in her chair. "I had feared . . . well, I had thought . . . it would have been disastrous."

Because they had chosen someone else, Evie realized. "Disastrous seems a rather strong word. Why—"

"He is not meant for you."

Heavens, was the woman going to admit all? "Oh? And whom am I meant for?"

"I am sure I do not know," Mrs. Summers said primly, dashing Evie's hope of a confession. "But it is not Mr. Hunter."

"You don't approve of him?"

"Certainly I do." She picked up her sewing once again. "His interest lies with Lady Kate."

It was several seconds before Evie found her voice. "You *know* of that?"

"Well, I'm not blind, am I?" Mrs. Summers huffed. "Why is it the very young assume only they can recognize these things? One would think they might be capable of recognizing experience just as well, and—"

"I beg your pardon," Evie cut in, and wisely bit the inside of her cheek to keep from smiling. "I don't know what I was thinking, when you've a beau of your own."

Mrs. Summers looked as if she might say something disapproving, but then her lips twitched and her eyes lit up with pleasure. "I have, haven't I?" She gave a lustful, and therefore most un-Mrs.-Summers-like, sigh. "I must say, it is quite a thing to find oneself in love at my age."

"You're in love with Mr. Fletcher?"

"I rather think I might be." She sighed again and with a dreamy expression—also most unlike her—returned to her needlework.

Evie had seen that sort of wistful, far-off expression on Kate before and knew quite well that she'd been summarily dismissed from Mrs. Summers's thoughts.

Not bothering to hide her smile now, Evie set down her own work and murmured a desire for something to drink. She didn't take offense when Mrs. Summers failed to respond; she simply slipped quietly out of the parlor and, upon discovering the rain had eased, quietly out the front door as well.

A brisk stroll was just what she needed to sort out her thoughts—or, perhaps more accurately, to sort through her confusion. Working her way around the house, she headed for the beach, barely noticing the fine mist that still clung to the air.

If Mr. Hunter was not her would-be rescuer, who the devil was? And what the devil was taking him so long? It was her third day at the cottage—how long did her matchmakers think to keep her sitting about, waiting?

And how would she feel when he arrived? It would mean making clear, once and for all, that she was not to be swept off her feet. It would mean returning to Haldon. It would mean parting ways with McAlistair.

She stopped next to a stand of rocks on the edge of the shore and looked out across the water.

The last time she and McAlistair had kissed and parted ways, she had neither seen nor heard from him again for months. Would it be the same?

Did it matter so very much if it was?

It did matter. She knew even before she'd asked the question that it mattered a great deal. For pity's sake, she'd been disappointed merely because he'd been out of the house that morning. What would she do with a lifetime of mornings without him?

Her heart sank at the mere thought.

And then it froze when a shot rang out. The sharp sound sliced through the wet air, and something ricocheted off the rock behind her, sending up a fine mist of dust. Instinctively, she dropped to her knees and scurried behind the rocks.

Stunned, her first thought was that some idiot had come out to hunt in the woods next to the house and she'd walked between that idiot and his target. But even before she'd finished that thought, another occurred to her. There shouldn't be a soul for miles, other than those in the house. And she was wearing an ivory gown and standing next to a dark rock. Unless the shooter was blind as well as stupid, it would have been nearly impossible to overlook her presence. Realization crept in like frost, chilling her to the core.

Someone had shot *at* her.

She glanced up quickly to determine how much protection was provided by the rocks. Enough, she thought. She hoped. Enough as long as she stayed low to the ground. The image of herself, helpless and crouching like a cornered animal, flashed through her mind and was firmly pushed aside. The rocks would keep her safe . . . unless the shooter moved. Her gaze shifted to the left, then the right . . . just in time to glimpse the dark form of a man before he dove on top of her, shoving her to the ground.

Panic raced through her, with fury chasing close behind. She shoved herself to one side, using the rock for leverage, and threw her fist out at the same time. It was an awkward movement, but she would have landed the jab on the man's chin, if McAlistair hadn't been quick enough to intercept her fist.

"It's me. It's all right." McAlistair released her arm to hurriedly run his hands over her, frantically checking for injuries. "Evie, are you hurt? Are you hurt anywhere?"

She shook her head.

His eyes tracked over her. "You're certain?"

"Yes, I . . . yes." She was too stunned yet to notice the shudder that ran through him. She swallowed hard. "Someone shot at me."

"Your gun," he said tersely.

"What?"

"Your gun, where is it?"

What the devil was he talking about? "I don't have a gun."

He swore and nudged her back onto her stomach. Crouching over her protectively, he half pushed, half dragged her closer to the nearest rock. "Keep your head down."

It was sound, if needless, advice—did he think she was going to pop up and demand an explanation? With blood pounding loudly in her ears, she watched as McAlistair aimed a gun over the top of the rock.

"How fast can you run?" he asked without looking at her.

"Not very, usually." But then she'd never had someone shooting at her either. She almost asked if they should wait for Christian or Mr. Hunter to come from the house—surely, they had heard the shot—but she swallowed the suggestion at the last moment. She didn't want someone else to make himself a target on her behalf.

McAlistair narrowed his eyes and squeezed off a shot. The resulting blast echoed off the rocks and set her ears ringing—she barely heard the succinct curse from McAlistair that followed.

"He's gone."

She heard that. "He is?" She gathered the courage to raise her head and peer around the edge of the boulder. "You're certain?"

He stood, looked around, then hauled her to her feet by way of answering. "He had a horse."

"You saw him?" she asked as he took her hand and started toward the house at such a clipped pace she had to run or risk being dragged. "Who was it? Why—"

"I only saw the horse and his back. I don't know who it was. Why the devil didn't you bring the gun Mrs. Summers gave you?"

Oh, *that* gun. "Because I'm not in the habit of strolling about with firearms." She threw her free hand up as he pushed through the back door and hauled her into the kitchen. "For pity's sake, where would I even put it?"

They ran nearly headfirst into Christian, Mr. Hunter, and Mrs. Summers. All three, Evie noticed, were carrying weapons and looked quite prepared to use them . . . even Mrs. Summers, whose implement of choice appeared to be some sort of wooden club.

Oh, hell. Oh, bloody hell. Had she been so very wrong? A carriage accident was one thing, but guns and . . . whatever that was Mrs. Summers held . . . were quite another.

"Evie!" Mrs. Summers set aside her weapon to throw her arms around Evie. "We heard shots. Are you hurt?"

"No . . . I . . . ." Feeling dazed, Evie extended the hug to the point of clinging. "No, I'm unharmed."

"Oh, thank heavens." Mrs. Summers whipped her head toward McAlistair, obviously checking for injury even as she asked, "Where is he?"

"Gone," he answered, but he didn't look at Mrs. Summers. His eyes, dark and unblinking, remained focused on Evie. "Horseback."

"We can track him," Mr. Hunter said, shoving his pistol

into a coat pocket and heading toward the door. "The rain will make it easy."

McAlistair shook his head. "He's gone to the road."

Mr. Hunter swore.

"The road?" Evie pulled away from Mrs. Summers. "Isn't it easier to find someone on a road?

"Not unless you're already looking at them," Christian explained. "Can't distinguish one set of hoofprints from another on a road. He'll follow it a bit, no doubt, then head off before reaching town."

"Oh," she murmured, quite at a loss for anything more intelligent to say.

Christian ran a hand through his hair. "Where was he shooting from?"

And still McAlistair didn't take his eyes off of Evie. "Woods. West side."

"And where were—?"

"Evie was at the rocks. I was leaving the house."

Mrs. Summers gave Evie a hard look. "You were walking about *alone?*"

She *hadn't* been alone, apparently, but she knew that wasn't what Mrs. Summers meant.

"I thought it was safe," she mumbled instead. "I've been out on the beach before—"

"Not alone."

"Chastising her now won't help," McAlistair said quietly.

Evie was torn between gratitude for his defense and embarrassment at the use of the word "chastise." She felt like a naughty five-year-old. A five-year-old of less-than-average intelligence. "If I'd thought, even for a moment, there might be a l-lunatic hiding in the woods waiting to shoot at me, I certainly would not have gone. I'm n-not an idiot. I'm not—" She broke off when her voice cracked. She wasn't angry with Mrs. Summers; she was frightened and ridden with guilt. And furious with herself for *twice* having been caught in a dangerous situation without her gun. She crossed her arms across her waist, gripping her elbows in an effort to stem her trembling.

Mrs. Summers patted Evie's arm gently. "We'll speak of this later. After we have both settled."

"We'll be needing to send word to Haldon," Christian commented. "I'll ride into town. Could be someone will have seen a lone traveler come before me as well."

Mr. Hunter nodded as Christian left. "McAlistair and I will search the grounds."

McAlistair didn't move. His gaze remained steadfastly on Evie. "He's gone."

"Can't hurt to double check." When McAlistair still failed to move, Mr. Hunter took him by the arm, nearly dragging him away. "You can take the grounds closest to the house," Evie heard him say, "in case the women have need of us. I'll search past the cove and to the north . . ."

Mr. Hunter's voice faded to an unintelligible murmur as he led McAlistair off in one direction and Mrs. Summers, taking Evie's arm, led Evie off in another.

❀ *Twenty-five* ❀

$\mathcal{M}$cAlistair searched the grounds closest to the house, and he searched the house itself, checking and rechecking the locks on the doors and windows. He knew full well there was nothing wrong with them. Just as he knew full well that anyone determined to get inside would find a way.

But he needed *something* to do while Mrs. Summers settled Evie in her room.

It seemed to take a prodigious amount of time.

In truth, it may have been no more than half an hour, but it felt like an eternity passed before Mrs. Summers slipped out through Evie's door and headed to her own. And another eternity before a soft snore emanated from Mrs. Summers's room.

He considered what he knew regarding the lady and her naps, and estimated he'd have at least two hours.

What he meant to do in those hours, he hadn't decided. He only knew he needed to spend them with Evie.

Unwilling to knock and risk the chance of being turned away, McAlistair pushed open Evie's door. Decisively at first, then cautiously when it occurred to him she might be sleeping—or changing.

She was standing by the window, but *not*, he noted, directly in front of it. She stood a good four feet back from the glass. A good, safe distance that kept her hidden from anyone who might be looking from the ground.

She was afraid now. It occurred to him that he might have been mistaken in his efforts to convince her that the threat was real. He hated that she'd been made to feel afraid. Better he had kept a closer eye on things, caught the bastard, and *then* convinced her.

She turned as he stepped into the room. "Did you find him? Did you—?"

"No. We will." He shut the door behind him. "How are you?"

"Aside from embarrassed, I'm perfectly well." She walked over to fiddle with a piece of paper on a desk. "Mrs. Summers isn't feeling quite the thing after all the excitement. She's gone to lie down."

"I know."

"Oh. Well. I . . ." She cleared her throat before continuing in a soft voice. "I owe you an apology. You were right, it would seem, about the ruse. You must be—"

"I don't care."

"Oh. Right." Her eyes darted away from his. "Of course. You've every call to be angry. I—"

"That's not what I meant." He didn't bloody care who'd been right and who had been wrong. "That's not what matters. I'm not angry with you, I . . ." He drew a hand through his hair. "I thought you'd been shot. I thought . . ."

He wasn't surprised to see her mouth fall open a little at his lack of composure. "I'm fine," she said carefully. "Honestly. I've little more than a few scratches to show for the incident."

"You were lucky." He hadn't realized quite how lucky until he'd returned to the spot where she'd been standing and found the bullet mark in the rock less than a foot away. The bullet had missed her by inches. Mere *inches*.

He'd noticed her absence too late. She was already at the rocks by the time he'd left the house, and when the first shot rang out, he'd still been a solid fifty yards away. It felt like fifty miles, and might just as well have been, for all the good he could do her from that distance—close enough to see the largest flecks of rock go flying, but too far away to protect her.

He'd never run so fast in his life, and never felt so slow. His legs had felt impossibly heavy and his heart and lungs had begun laboring before he'd taken the first step.

He'd been certain he was going to lose her, terrified the bullet had cut through her before hitting the rock.

It nearly had. Bloody hell, it nearly had.

"I need . . . I . . ." He strode forward and wrapped his arms around her. She came willingly into the embrace, sliding her arms around his waist and pressing her face against his chest. She was warm, soft, and alive, and he took some measure of comfort from the beat of her heart and the rise and fall of her chest.

But it wasn't enough. She was alive, yes. She was unhurt, yes. But both only by sheerest margin of luck.

"You nearly . . . you could have . . ." He pulled back to cup her face in his hands. "I have to," he whispered, lowering his head to hers. "I have to."

The kiss, like each before, was unique.

He kissed her with the desperation of a man who had nearly lost what he loved most, and with the aching tenderness of a man terrified to harm. He kissed her with the desire to make up for every soft word he'd wanted to offer, but hadn't been able to find. He kissed her with passion and need, affection, and reverence. And he kissed her as if his very life depended on the next whispered breath, the next ragged sigh, the next trembling moan.

She offered all of those and more—a quiet breath when he shifted to trail soft kisses down the side of her neck, a quick gasp when he gently nipped her shoulder with his teeth, a soft hum of pleasure when his hands moved to form her curves.

He was lost in a fog of fear and pleasure. He knew at some point he unfastened the buttons on her gown and slipped off her dress. He was almost certain it was she, and not he, who stripped him down to his shirtsleeves. And he was vaguely aware of lifting her in his arms and placing her gently on the bed. The removal of his boots was something he would never be able to recall clearly in the future, but he would always remember bunching the hem of her chemise and slowly, ever so slowly, dragging it up to reveal the heated skin beneath.

It was his every fantasy come to life.

Every desire he'd thought hopeless, every dream he'd thought unattainable, was given to him in that moment, and he relished it, even as his fear urged him to hurry.

Take more. Take all.

Take while you can.

He yanked it back, chained it down, and allowed himself the pleasure of savoring.

He let his hands explore without hurry and his mouth wander without direction. His fingers brushed the tender spot behind her knee. His lips trailed up the inside of her thigh to the ivory skin of her belly. He lingered over the generous flair of her hips, the subtle tuck of her waist, the soft weight of her breasts.

Evie's hands moved over him with more eagerness than skill, and he reveled in that as well. The sensation of her small fingers undoing the buttons on his shirt and the heat of her palms against his chest sent his blood roaring.

He waited until he was certain she was absorbed in pleasure before removing his breeches and covering her body with his.

"Evie. Evie, look at me now." He caught her face in his hands, pressed a soft kiss to her brow and clung to his last shred of control. "We can stop. I will stop. If you ask it of me—"

"Don't stop."

He was a bastard for waiting so long to offer her a chance to back away. A bastard twice over for taking her at her word and going forward. He couldn't find it in himself to be sorry for either. He was bloody *tired* of fighting against what he wanted most.

His hand moved down to cup the back of her knee. Gently, he hooked her leg over his hip.

There would be pain. He knew there was no way to avoid it entirely, but he tried his best anyway—entering her in small, careful strokes, searching her face for any sign of discomfort. He couldn't find any. Evie arched and moaned, wrapped her other leg over him, and gripped his shoulders hard enough to dig her nails into the skin.

He relished in the sight of her lost to her desire and cringed when he reached her maidenhood.

"I'm sorry," he whispered. He pushed through with a hard press of his hips to bury himself inside.

He heard his own long groan of bliss.

And Evie's sharp yelp of discomfort. Her lids flew open. "Bloody hell."

Her chocolate eyes, which had been glazed with pleasure only a moment ago, widened, cleared, and—unless he was much mistaken—took on the sharp edge of annoyance.

He wondered if she would start swearing. He worried she might cuff him.

"I'm sorry." He lowered his head to take her mouth in a long, lingering kiss. He ran his hands over her, seeking out the places that had made her moan and writhe earlier. "Sweetheart, I'm sorry. No, lie still. Just wait . . . wait."

He set about seducing her all over again. The process was both a delight and a torture. He wanted to move. He *needed* to. But he didn't, not until her eyes once again clouded over. Not until he was certain she could feel, if not all, at least some of the ecstasy he knew.

When he was certain she did, when she began to arch beneath him in wordless demand, he allowed himself to pull out and slide back. He set an excruciatingly slow rhythm, both in consideration of Evie and for his own self-ish desire to draw the moment out.

Evie wasn't having it. She struggled to pull him closer, struggled to grasp what he was holding out of reach. Her breathing grew more labored, her struggles more frantic.

"Please."

He gave in to her demands, increasing the pace, driving deep. He listened and watched and filed away in his memory every exquisite heartbeat of Evie Cole reaching for rapture in his arms. When she found it, when she shuddered beneath him, he pressed his face against her neck and took his own.

Evie had never before experienced such an incongruent mix of emotions. She felt elated, anxious, vulnerable, replete, and a host of other things she couldn't hope to name.

She wanted to dive under the covers to hide, almost as much as she wanted to bound out of bed and dance about, but not *quite* as much as she wanted to close her eyes and immediately give in to the sleep tugging at her weighted body.

McAlistair shifted, rolling onto his back and gently tucking her against his side. He pulled the edge of the counterpane and wrapped it over her. "Are you all right, Evie?" She nodded against his shoulder as a thousand questions raced through her mind.

Had she done the right thing?

Had she done the thing *right?*

The first question would require a more sedate frame of mind to figure through. As for the second . . . she looked up at McAlistair. He had one arm bent behind his head, one hand trailing soft brushes up and down her spine, and the single most serene expression she'd ever seen on his face.

At a guess, she'd done *something* right.

Emboldened by the modesty the counterpane allowed, she let her hand reach up to touch the white jagged scar on his chest she'd noticed earlier. The man had a frightful number of scars on his body, and it occurred to her that she hadn't any idea how he'd received even one of them. Frowning a little, she traced the white edges of the skin.

"How did this happen?"

McAlistair felt laughter tickle the back of his throat. Evie would, of course, want to talk. Rather than respond, he drew a hand down her hair, hoping to lull her into the sleep she needed.

"I know very little of your life before you came to Haldon," she prompted.

His hand stilled. "It's important to you? My past?"

Let her say no. *Please* let her—

"Yes."

Damn.

"It's part of who you are," she whispered.

"No. I am a different man than I was eight years ago."

"All right, then it is a part of what made you that man." She lifted her head to look at him, a crease appearing across her brow. "You don't want to tell me."

He bloody well didn't, but though he could stand against her displeasure, he was no match for the disappointment he saw in her eyes.

He cleared his throat. "I left home at fourteen." This, at least, he could try to tell her.

"For school?"

He shook his head. "Just left." He pulled her closer. He wanted—needed—to have his arms about her as he told the story. "My mother had fallen in love, again. Mr. Carville. Young, wealthy, and demanding of her time."

"Was he unkind to you?"

"No, he wasn't the sort to intentionally wound a child." Not intentionally. "But they were in love, and . . . selfish with it."

"I'm sorry. What happened?"

"He took my mother to the Continent and sent us, the children, to live at one of his country estates."

She lifted a hand to brush at a lock of his hair. "Were you not treated well there?"

"Yes and no. We had a roof over our heads, clothes on our backs. There was a skeletal staff on hand. Some of them were . . . not unkind." Cowed, but not unkind.

"Some?"

"Our care was overseen by the estate manager and his wife, Mr. and Mrs. Burnett." Even saying the name aloud turned his stomach. "They didn't care for the intrusion."

Or perhaps they had. Perhaps they had enjoyed it very much. They'd been mad enough for that.

"They hired and dismissed tutors and governess on whims. Complained they were too lax in discipline. They wanted their house—they saw it as theirs—to be well ordered, spotless, and silent.

"That's not possible with seven children."

"Just six of us at the time, but no, it wasn't possible." Absently, he fingered the scar she'd asked about. "Punishment was severe."

Her breath caught. "That's from—"

"Horsewhip," he supplied. "Mrs. Burnett liked to grab whatever was handy. At the time of my infraction, I'd been in the stable." The corner of his mouth hooked up. "Devil's own temper, that woman."

"How can you jest about this?"

Because short bursts of temper could be outlasted. Blows could be dodged, or endured for those first few moments when the pain was sharp and new, and then ignored when it dulled.

"Mr. Burnett's brand of punishment was worse." It had been cold, extensive, and inescapable.

"Worse than a horsewhip?"

He spoke before the resolve to do so left him. "He used the bottom shelf of a small linen closet."

"Used it . . ." Evie's voice weakened into a trembling whisper. "Used it for what?"

He waited as the memory of those dark times brought on echoes of fear and pain. Waited until those echoes dimmed. "There was just enough room to lie on your side and tuck your knees up to your chin." Just barely enough room.

He'd fought those first few times, but Mr. Barnett had been a giant of a man, or so it had seemed to a boy of thirteen. After a while, he'd given up trying to best him physically and clung to what little pride could be found in marching to the closet, flinging open the door, and climbing inside of his own accord. As if he hadn't cared. As if it hadn't mattered to him one jot. As if pretending indifference was, in itself, an act of defiance.

"How long?" Evie's voice was filled with horror. "How long did he keep you in there?"

"It varied. Minutes, hours, days."

"Days!" She shot up. "He kept you . . . were you given food, water—?"

She broke off when he shook his head. Reaching up, he once again tucked her head back on his shoulder. It was easier to talk, to tell her of it, without seeing his pain reflected in her eyes.

"He could have killed you," she whispered. "You could have died."

The thought had occurred to him at the time. Every time. "I know."

And that thought—of dying in a small closet, huddled like an animal, had driven him nearly insane. He had a hazy memory of shouting once, of giving up his pride and calling out for help when the thirst and the pain of being unable to move had become unbearable.

No one had come. No one had answered.

Neither seen nor heard.

That had been Mr. Burnett's rule.

"Couldn't you write to your mother for help?" Evie asked gently.

He shook his head. "Tried. Got caught."

"I'm so sorry." She stroked a hand across his chest. "I'm glad you ran away."

"I didn't, initially. I had my brothers to consider."

"He hurt them as well?"

"Rarely." Not when McAlistair had been there to take the blame. "He preferred using me as an example. It was . . . effective in gaining their cooperation."

"Why you?"

He gave a small shrug. "I was oldest, the most resistant."

"How did it stop?"

"I had a growth spurt. Shot up inches in a matter of months." He hadn't realized it. He'd thought it was just his fear making the closet smaller and smaller. "One day, I just wouldn't fit on the shelf." He felt his lips curve in cold humor. "The man tried damn near everything to wedge me in, nothing worked. When I stood again, I noticed for the first time that I was looking at him eye to eye."

Mr. Burnett had noticed it too. McAlistair remembered seeing that spark of horror come into the older man's eyes and his hand coming up to strike him down again. "He wanted to try a new closet. I refused. We fought."

Mr. Burnett had still been stronger, but the difference in their sizes was no longer so great that he'd been able to grab and keep hold of his quarry. And in the months since they'd last grappled, McAlistair had had ample practice of how best to elude capture and hits, thanks to Mrs. Burnett. But in the end he'd still been just a boy.

"He might have overpowered me, but . . ." He paused

and glanced at the top of Evie's head, wondering how she would take the next part of the story. "I grabbed a vase and hit him with it."

"Hard?" she asked.

"Hard enough to render him unconscious."

"Excellent." It was impossible to miss the grim pleasure in her voice. "Did it kill him?"

"No." Not that time, he added silently. "But it gave me time to tie him up, steal a large amount of money from his desk, and see my brothers safely out of the house."

"What of the staff? Of Mrs. Burnett?"

"Mrs. Burnett was visiting a neighbor. The staff thought nothing of our walking to the stables. Only one of the grooms knew. I paid him a small fortune to help saddle the horses, then turn a blind eye."

"You ran away with five brothers in tow?"

He almost laughed at that memory. "I did, and what a nightmare it was." Charles had been no more than four. "But we had funds enough to see us through—"

"Where? Where did you go?"

"To the Scottish border. We stayed with Mrs. Seager, my brothers' retired nanny, until Mr. Carville and my mother could be found."

He hadn't been certain they would return, and he'd been terrified they would, only to send the children back to the Burnetts. He hadn't known Mr. Carville then, but he'd known his mother well enough. When she loved a man, she loved with a blind and dangerous devotion.

"What did they do, when they returned?" Evie asked.

"Sent men out to search for the Burnetts, who'd disappeared after my brothers and I had run off. Mr. Carville apologized." McAlistair frowned thoughtfully. Apology wasn't quite the word. The man had been swamped with remorse. He'd been appalled by what had happened and determined to see it was never repeated. McAlistair believed him, but had been too angry, too battered still, to forgive. "I ran away. I was angry."

"And became a soldier? At fourteen?"

"No, I went to London, worked at whatever came to hand."

"What sorts of things came to hand?"

He fought back a chuckle. She was so bloody *persistent*. "Another time, sweetheart. I have to go." He ran his hand down her back once more, kissed her gently on the forehead, and rose from the bed.

Evie sat up, taking the counterpane with her. She stifled a sigh as McAlistair began to dress, but she didn't argue for him to stay. She knew the others would return soon. Just as she knew that when they did, it would be over. This golden afternoon would end and, over time, it would be nothing more than a memory, stored along with the memories of all her other firsts. The first time she'd seen McAlistair, the first time they'd kissed in the woods. The first time she'd felt his hands on her skin. The first time she'd heard his deep rumble of laughter.

Only it wouldn't be just a string of firsts for her, she realized. It would be a list of lasts and onlys as well. The first, last, and only day she and McAlistair had stood chest deep in pond water and laughed. The first, last, and only day they had made love. Her chest tightened painfully. She didn't want that. She didn't want just one of anything with McAlistair.

She felt McAlistair's hand on her hair and realized she'd been staring at her lap for the last five minutes. "What is it, Evie?"

She made herself lift her head and smile. "Nothing. I'm trying to find the energy to stand." It wasn't a complete fabrication. She was exhausted, and it would be lovely to lose her worries in sleep for an hour or two.

"Lie back down," McAlistair suggested. "Rest."

"I should like that." She gave him a wry smile. "But I can well imagine what Mrs. Summers' reaction would be were she to find me napping without any clothes on."

McAlistair frowned and glanced around the room until his eyes landed on the armoire. Without a word, he retrieved her night rail. She accepted it with a murmured thanks and, after a bit of maneuvering, succeeded in pulling it over her head without dropping the counterpane.

She ignored the amused expression on his face. "I suppose . . . I suppose I shall see you at dinner."

He stared at her a moment, then reached down to cup her face with his hands. "And after," he murmured before taking her mouth in long, thorough kiss.

Evie felt her heart lighten even as her blood warmed.

After. He'd come to her again. It wasn't to be just an "only."

She was smiling a bit stupidly when he drew away.

"Lie back down," he urged. "Sleep."

Seeing no reason she shouldn't, Evie did as he suggested. She was nearly asleep when something occurred to her. She opened blurry eyes to find McAlistair reaching for the door.

"McAlistair?"

He turned back. "What is it?"

"Did they ever find the Burnetts?"

"No. They didn't."

Had she not been so tired, she might have remarked on his hesitation. Instead, she closed her eyes and slept.

McAlistair stood at the door a few minutes longer, watching the steady rise and fall of Evie's chest and contemplating the tightness in his own.

There was no regret in his heart for what they'd done. He refused to allow his own shame to taint the most beautiful gift he'd ever received.

What troubled him now was how he cared for that gift. He'd lied to Evie. Only minutes after taking her innocence, after sharing a piece of his past only his family knew, he'd stood four feet away and lied to her.

He'd done it out of instinct—to protect her and himself— but that didn't alter the fact that it had been a lie, or that one day, one day soon if there was to be any chance of forgiveness, he would have to tell her the truth.

The men Mr. Carville had sent never found Mr. Burnett. But he had.

❋ *Twenty-six* ❋

Evie woke smiling into her pillow. She'd dreamt of McAlistair: of his rare smile and elusive laugh and of the glorious two hours they'd spent together in her bed. She rolled to her back and stretched luxuriously. The aches and soreness of her body were another welcome reminder of how she'd passed the afternoon and how she hoped to pass the night.

There remained the question, of course, of how she would spend her nights in the days and weeks to come. Eventually, she would have to leave the cottage. And then what? Would that be the end of the affair? It was better than the "only" she'd worried over earlier, but was it what she wanted?

She sat up and stared thoughtfully at the dim light piercing through the drapes. Did it matter, really, what she wanted? Openly becoming McAlistair's mistress was out of the question, as was hoping she might hide a long-term liaison from her family. The only avenue left was marriage.

She was taken aback by the flicker of excitement that thought elicited.

She'd never cared for the concept of marriage.

To relinquish control over one's life to another human being was a terrifying prospect, and a path she believed too many women took out of necessity rather than choice. There was a shameful lack of opportunities for women to earn their way in the world . . . as few as there were ways for her to be with the man she desired without first promising to love, honor, and obey.

She grimaced at the mere thought of promising to obey.

Did she desire him so very much?

She sighed heavily, and as she sighed, caught sight of herself in the mirror over the vanity. Little could have stunned her more than what she saw reflected back. She looked exactly, *exactly*—right down to the wistful eyes—as Mrs. Summers had when she'd been contemplating her love for Mr. Fletcher.

"A coincidence," she heard herself murmur. "Only a coincidence, or a trick of the light, or . . ."

Oh, damn and blast, she was in love with McAlistair.

How could she hope to deny it? She thought of him constantly, wanted him outrageously. She wished him back the moment he left a room, and wished him closer the moment he came in. She hurt for the frightened boy he'd been, and was endlessly fascinated by the powerful man he'd become.

She'd gone to bed with him.

She was considering marriage, for sweet pity's sake . . .

well, she was considering the *possibility* of being *amenable* to the *idea* of marriage, but still—*marriage*.

"Oh, damn."

"Evie?"

The sound of Mrs. Summers's voice and a rap at the door had Evie jumping up out of bed with a nervous start and carefully erasing all signs of wistfulness from her expression. "Come in."

Mrs. Summers appeared, looking slightly refreshed from her nap, but still pinched about the nose and mouth.

Oh, dear. Evie sent her an overly bright smile.

Mrs. Summers didn't return the gesture. "Have you recovered from your scare?"

Evie wasn't certain it was possible to ever be fully recovered from such a scare, but she felt the need to reassure her friend. "Quite, thank you. And you? Are you feeling at all better?"

"In some regards," Mrs. Summers replied.

"I . . . you're angry with me."

"I am, rather," Mrs. Summers admitted with a short sigh. "And I should like to discuss what happened today." She folded her hands in front of her primly, sighed again, and said, "It has appeared to me, from the very start, that you have not fully grasped the seriousness of this situation, Evie. I attributed your poise to bravery and a confidence in your family's ability to see you safe. But after today—"

"I am confident in my family," Evie cut in, taken aback.

"And you are a very brave young woman," Mrs. Summers agreed. "But the extent of your assuredness leaves me troubled, and this carelessness strikes me as most unusual. I should like an explanation."

Evie shifted her feet and repressed the urge to wince. An explanation *to* Mrs. Summers would no doubt result in a lecture *from* Mrs. Summers. An unpleasant prospect, to be sure, but there was no avoiding it.

Evie cleared her throat. "Perhaps we should sit."

"Very well." Mrs. Summers moved to the nearest chair and lowered herself to perch on the very edge of the seat, her back ramrod straight and her narrow shoulders tense.

The stiff—well, stiffer than usual—posture made Evie nervous. But it was the *look* that worried her most. The raised brows, the tight lips, and the sad eyes all added to the impression of a woman bearing up under the strain of receiving a confession that would most assuredly break her heart.

Evie took a seat across from her. "I . . ." She bounded up again. "Should I fetch us some tea? It would only take a minute."

"Thank you, no."

She regained her seat slowly. "Are you comfortable?" She certainly didn't look it. "Perhaps we should move—"

"I am quite content with this room and this chair."

"Oh. Right. Good . . . But perhaps—"

"Get on with it, Evie."

"Right. Well." Because she needed to do something, Evie straightened her own shoulders and blew out a long breath. "A fortnight ago, or thereabout, I . . . I overheard a conversation in the library between you, Lady Thurston, and Mr. Fletcher."

Mrs. Summers raised one brow even higher. "Overheard? How?"

"Oh, just . . ." She waved her hand about. "By chance. That's not really relevant at present." Not if she could help it. "What *is* relevant is the topic of that discussion. You were plotting a scenario in which I was to find a husband. Or, to be more accurate, in which you were to find a husband for me. A scenario that very much resembles the one we are in now." Except for the shooting bit, of course. And the riding through the woods with McAlistair bit. And possibly the fact that she was in a secluded location with three gentlemen who were not, for a variety of reasons, the most likely of matches.

Bloody hell, she was an idiot.

She fiddled with the cuff of her sleeve. "I was under the impression the threat, this entire trip, was nothing more than a matchmaking scheme."

"A matchmaking—?" Mrs. Summers broke off and closed her eyes. "Oh, good Lord, William's plan."

Evie nodded. "He spoke of sending a threatening letter, and not long after, I received one. I thought I would play along, in the interest of settling this idea of marriage once and for all. I'll admit I was a bit confused when it was decided I should leave Haldon, and I was a little put out when the carriage—"

"The carriage." Mrs. Summers' eyes snapped open. "You think so little of me? Of all of us?"

"Little of you? Of course not—"

"Yet you would believe us capable of cruelly engineering a carriage accident simply to trick you? After what you had been through as a child?"

"I—" She hadn't thought of that, not once. "It didn't occur to me. I . . . I'm not afraid of carriages. I've never been afraid of them."

"That is not the point."

"Well, it was *a* point," Evie argued, "and an important one. If I had a fear of being in a carriage accident, then engineering one *would* have been a cruel trick. One I would have known you are incapable of. As it is—"

"As it is . . . you would accuse us of being deceivers and actresses and—"

"You weren't involved then, in Sophie and Alex's meeting? Or the business with Whit and Mirabelle?"

Mrs. Summers hesitated before answering. "I had nothing to do with Whit and Mirabelle's matching."

"But you had everything to do with Sophie and Alex . . ."

"We have gone off topic."

"Seems on topic to me." And she rather liked it. She didn't much care for being on the defensive end of a disagreement. "And I *did* hear you conspiring with Lady Thurston and Mr. Fletcher to find me a husband. As well as Mr. Fletcher conspiring to send me a threatening letter. For heaven's sake, what are the odds of a fabricated threat and a legitimate one being simultaneously considered?"

"I grant you, they are slim."

"Exactly. What was I—"

"However," Mrs. Summers cut in, "the coincidence would not have saved your life, had your assailant been a better shot."

Evie winced. "No, it would not have."

Mrs. Summers sighed. "I do not condone eavesdropping, Evie. However, if one is going to indulge, one ought to make an effort to do it properly—or at least thoroughly. Clearly, you were not privy to the whole conversation."

"Apparently not," Evie muttered.

"Lady Thurston and I took immediate opposition to Mr. Fletcher's tactics. You were to be introduced to the gentleman through one of the members of your group."

"How?" Evie asked with a small start. "None of the women know who I am. I certainly don't know who any of them are."

"Lady Thurston and I do."

"You . . . How . . . Why . . ."

"Did you really think your aunt would not only allow,

but encourage your participation in an organization with which she was not familiar? Lady Penelope, I was informed, gave a detailed accounting of the group's members."

"Lady Penelope knew who all the members were? And she *told?*"

"Yes, on both accounts. She knew because she was responsible for the organization's conception. Even a secret organization requires a founder and leader, and one cannot lead without being fully aware of who is following."

"No," Evie replied thoughtfully. "I suppose not."

"And she told because she trusted your aunt and it was a prerequisite for your participation."

"Oh. Well." That made sense, and using her work as a means to finding her a match was quite clever, actually. She'd have been interested—academically, at least—in any man who actively took up the cause.

Mrs. Summers tilted her head at her. "Who on earth did you think we'd chosen for you? You've nothing in common with any of the gentlemen in residence."

"I . . ." . . . have more than enough in common with McAlistair, she wanted to say, but now wasn't the time. She wasn't sure that time would ever arrive. "That puzzle did give me some trouble, I'll admit. Who was I to meet?"

"Sir Reginald Napertin."

She went still, blinked, and wracked her brain. All for naught. "Who the devil is Reginald Napertin?"

Mrs. Summers tutted at Evie's language. "*Sir* Reginald Napertin is a very nice gentleman recently returned from the Continent. He was knighted as an officer for his service to the Crown."

"A war hero?"

"He was injured saving his commanding officer and several of his subordinates. He nearly lost his leg."

Evie tried to picture herself on the arm of such a man and

found she could only envision the three-legged races of which she'd been fond as a girl. "Between the two of us, we'd have managed a whole set of legs."

"That is not amusing."

It certainly was, particularly when paired with the vision of the two of them riding Rose without her shoe, but Evie had long ago realized that those who loved her were sometimes even more sensitive about her infirmity than she was. "If he's the sort to take offense at it, then I suspect we wouldn't have suited."

"I never said he would take offense. I said it was not amusing. At any rate, you may discover the sort of man he is when the rest of this dreadful business is dealt with."

Evie opened her mouth, then closed it. There was no sense in arguing.

"Well," Mrs. Summers said with a bracing breath, "I am most relieved to have that misunderstanding cleared up. No doubt the others will be similarly reassured when you explain—"

"The others?" Explain? To Christian, and Mr. Hunter? "Couldn't we just—"

"No. They have done a great deal on your behalf and are likely wondering not only why their efforts to keep you safe were nearly undone by your own carelessness, but if it is likely to happen again."

"But the secrets I'd have to reveal wouldn't only be my own." And even if they were, she'd have undergone every torture known to man before she had a conversation with Christian and Mr. Hunter similar to one she was having with Mrs. Summers.

They were discussing matchmaking, for heaven's sake.

"Certainly an apology is in order," she continued. "And I mean to offer one, but an explanation would—"

Mrs. Summers waved her hand. "An apology will suffice."

She stood and brushed her skirts. "I believe Christian returned with food from the inn. I shall see the table set."

Evie turned to frown at the drapes drawn over the windows. "Dinner. I hadn't realized it was so late."

"You needed the sleep," Mrs. Summers said. "We both did." She leaned down to bestow a gentle pat on Evie's shoulder. "I am glad you were not harmed today."

Evie took her hand and gave it a squeeze. "Thank you . . . Oh, wait—" She held fast to Mrs. Summers's hand when the older woman would have pulled away. "What in the world had you planned on doing with that club?"

"Club?"

"Downstairs, in the kitchen, you were carrying—"

"Ah, the broken broom handle." Mrs. Summers frowned thoughtfully. "I am sure I have no idea." She waved the idea away with a hand. "Come eat and make your apologies. You will feel better for both."

"I will," Evie replied, laughing softly. "I'll be down shortly."

In Evie's opinion, "shortly" was rather like the word "mild." It could mean anything, really.

For her, it meant a half hour of dressing, pinning her hair, pacing, and otherwise building up her nerve for the apology that was to come. When she thought she might have managed enough of the last, she made her way downstairs to find the others just starting their meal.

She demurred when the gentlemen would have risen, and took her seat with a mumbled greeting. For some reason, she found it impossible to meet McAlistair's eyes. Part of that was a fear of somehow giving away their shared secret, but most of it, she conceded, was a fear of McAlistair somehow discovering her own private thoughts.

She'd only just realized that she loved him. She needed to sort out how she felt about that before facing how *he* felt about that.

Evie picked up her fork and concentrated so very hard on her plate that she likely wouldn't have noticed Mrs. Summers's pointed look if it hadn't been preceded by a loud clearing of the lady's throat.

She set her fork down, berating herself for a coward. Swallowing past a lump of guilt and embarrassment, she addressed Mr. Hunter and Christian.

"I owe you, all of you, an apology. I should n-not have gone out alone. My decision to do so was based on . . . on . . . well, it hardly matters," she mumbled, unable to think of a way to defend herself without explaining all. "It w-was careless of me, and I apologize."

To her amazement, Mr. Hunter accepted her apology with a quick, almost disinterested nod while Christian merely shrugged.

"Don't fret on it, lass," he replied in an offhand manner.

Knowing it was expected of her, she looked to McAlistair.

"Nothing to forgive," he said softly.

"You should know," Christian added before she'd had a chance to respond, "a letter to Haldon's been sent, and we've checked the grounds. He's not on them."

"Oh. Good."

"Well, what is to be done now?" Mrs. Summers inquired. "Are we to stay? The point, I thought, was to remove Evie from danger."

And that, it seemed, was that. No need for a drawn-out and mortifying confession, Evie realized. She sat back in her chair, equal parts relieved and guilty for having gotten off so easily.

"Not entirely," Mr. Hunter replied by way of answering

Mrs. Summers. "The point was also to take her someplace easier to guard."

"And to keep others safe," Evie pointed out. She hadn't been serious the first time she'd made that argument—hadn't seen any reason to be—but she was bloody well serious now.

"There's no reason for Evie to leave now," McAlistair said.

If she hadn't instinctively turned at the sound of his gravelly voice, Evie would have missed the quiet look of understanding he shared with Christian and Mr. Hunter.

"What do you mean by 'now'?" she asked.

"Just that, lass," Christian offered. "There's no point in leaving just now. We can keep you safe—"

"I'm not an idiot, Christian. That wasn't the sort of now McAlistair meant."

"It's not a word with multiple definitions, dear," Mrs. Summers said.

She looked to McAlistair. "The attacker's appearance here changed something else. What is it?"

He hesitated before answering. "We know where to look now. We can find him."

Evie's throat went dry. She'd become bait after all. "In town, you mean?"

"And the surrounding area."

"There must be hundreds of people. How can you possibly hope to find him?"

Mr. Hunter answered. "It helps that McAlistair caught a glimpse of the bas . . . er . . . blighter."

"You said you saw only his back and his horse," Evie said to McAlistair. And, if logic followed, the back of his horse. Did they hope to identify a man by the rear view of his horse?

"It's something," Mr. Hunter muttered.

She chose not to comment.

Mrs. Summers set down her fork. "Well, until such time as this man is apprehended, I think it would be best if a guard was taken up. It would hardly do to have the man sneaking inside whilst the lot of us slept."

"Agreed," all three men said at once.

"And I shall be sharing Evie's room for the remainder of—"

"My room?" she heard herself spluttering. "But . . . I . . . surely—"

"I would feel the better for it."

"Yes, of course, but . . . I . . ." She risked a glance at McAlistair, but his face revealed nothing. Then again, what could he possibly say? *Not to worry? I'll see she's not alone?* Evie stifled a sigh of disappointment. "I'm sure that will be fine."

"Excellent. Now, as for the other precautions to be taken . . ."

Evie listened as a long list of rules was set out before her. Drapes were to be kept closed, doors were to be kept locked, she was not to go outside.

Though they stung, Evie had no trouble agreeing to every dictate. She adored her freedom and she adored being outdoors, but neither quite so much as she adored being alive.

Common sense aside, she was relieved when the exhaustive catalog of safety measures came to an end. And she was grateful for Mr. Hunter's offer to continue their chess match in the library while Christian went on guard and McAlistair saw to the horses. She didn't relish the idea of accepting Mrs. Summers's suggestion of more needlework or the notion of returning to her room with a book.

Someone had tried to kill her. Someone had *been* trying to kill her, and all the while she'd thought it a grand joke, a silly charade. Now that she believed it, she'd become not a houseguest, but a prisoner in someone else's home.

And—as if that wasn't quite enough to make one's head spin—she'd just spent two heavenly hours in bed with McAlistair . . . the man she'd recently discovered she loved. And she'd just lost the opportunity to do so again.

How was she to concentrate on even stitches and Greek philosophers after that?

She needed an activity that interested her if she hoped to take her mind off the day's events.

While Mrs. Summers took up her needlework in a seat by the fire, Evie and Mr. Hunter matched skill—and even wit, as Evie grew more comfortable—until the late hours of the night. But an engaging game and Mr. Hunter's charm alone could not keep her thoughts of McAlistair at bay.

She wondered how long it would take for him to return, and once he had, she wondered why he sat in the corner, scowling and holding a book he clearly was not reading. When he set the book aside and excused himself from the room a half hour later, she wondered where he'd gone. And when Christian came in and informed them that McAlistair had asked to take the first guard that night, she wondered if he were in danger, or . . .

"Check."

Evie blinked. "Beg your pardon?"

"Check," Mr. Hunter repeated. "Your king? A game of chess? Recall something of either?"

"I . . . oh." Evie glanced at the board and winced. "I'm sorry, I was distracted."

"Yes, I noticed." He reached over to pat her hand gently. He'd done that more than once tonight, she realized. She must look as miserable as she felt.

"I suppose I must seem a mess," she mumbled.

"No, you seem understandably preoccupied."

"And tired." Mrs. Summers set aside her needlework and rose from her chair. "It is late, and you could do with a bit of sleep."

Evie poked, a bit petulantly, at the rook she'd *meant* to push another space over. *Blast.*

"It will be here tomorrow," Mr. Hunter said in a sympathetic voice. "You can wait until then for defeat."

It was just the sort of swaggering comment she was coming to expect from him, and just the thing she needed to hear.

She left the room smiling.

❁ *Twenty-seven* ❁

$\mathcal{I}$t was a perfectly lovely day to be on the coast.

The sun was shining, the temperature was mild, and a soft salty breeze was coming off the sea.

Anyone who cared to look about would find very little lacking in the picturesque scene. Anyone, that is, but a man in a temper.

"Damn, bloody sand." McAlistair shook out his boots at the back door. If he didn't, Mrs. Summers would comment on the trail he left. And he wasn't interested in having an argument with Mrs. Summers this morning. It was Evie he wanted to argue with this morning.

He'd been waiting, patiently almost, since last night for a chance to speak with her alone. Now, finally, Christian was patrolling the grounds and Mr. Hunter was asleep after taking over for McAlistair in the small hours of the morning.

That left only Mrs. Summers to contend with. McAlistair considered his options as he put his boots back on and dug out his key. Perhaps the direct approach would work.

Mrs. Summers, I should like a moment of privacy with Miss Cole.

That was allowed, wasn't it? Evie had been left alone to play chess with Mr. Hunter.

And she'd been alone with him for two days, so what would a few minutes in a parlor or library matter?

He was scowling as he pushed through the door, locked it behind him, and went in search of Evie. Allowed or not, he was taking those minutes.

Flirt with Mr. Hunter, would she?

McAlistair took the back steps two at a time. Maybe he shouldn't have put his hands on her, but it was too late to take that back. It was much too late for her to change her mind. And if Evie thought otherwise, she was sadly mistaken.

She belonged to him now.

Perhaps not forever, perhaps for only as long as it took to make her safe, but for now, for today, she was his. And *only* his.

Sharing, to McAlistair's mind, had always been overrated. Any man with six brothers could attest to that.

After a brief and irritating search, he found her in the library, alone, and curled up—nearly swallowed, really—in the cushions of the window seat, with a book against her knees.

The gentle light from a spray of candles illuminated the room and cast a gold glow over her frame. A few warm brown tendrils of hair had slipped from their pins to fall in soft curls down her back. She'd grow annoyed by them eventually and shove them back in. For now, she appeared content, comfortable, lost in whatever world her book had opened for her.

She looked so beautiful.

How many times would he have to look at her before that instant of wonder he felt when she first came into view finally dimmed?

Because the answer to that sat like a weight on his heart— it hadn't dimmed in eight years of looking at her—he cleared his throat loudly to break the moment.

She glanced up and offered a shy smile. "Good morning."

"You shouldn't be sitting in front of the window."

Her brow furrowed a little at his rough tone. "The drapes are closed. And I had to try it at least once." She closed her book and made an awkward attempt to swing her legs over the edge of the seat cushion. She succeeded in tangling her skirts and nearly rapping her head against the wall, but very little else.

Eager to get to the topic at hand, and not one to bother himself with the finer points— or any points, really—of tact, he asked, "What is Mr. Hunter to you?"

"Hmm?" She didn't look up from where she was—he could only assume—attempting to scoot her weight to the edge of the cushions. "I believe he's still abed."

He stepped forward and plucked her off the cushions and set her on her feet with more force than finesse.

"Heavens." She stepped away to right her hopelessly twisted gown. "What's gotten into you?"

"You. Mr. Hunter."

She blinked at that. "Well, which is it?"

"Both."

The beginnings of temper flashed in her eyes. "I see, and what is it we've done?"

"That's the question I asked you."

She titled her head at him. "You want me to tell you what we've done to irritate you?"

"I want you to tell me if you've done something I should be irritated about."

"As you're quite obviously irritated already, I would say we have." She gave her gown one final tug. "Now then, if you're done asking silly questions, I'd like to finish my book."

"I'm not done." And he damn well wasn't silly. Assassins, former or otherwise, were categorically incapable of being silly. "What's between you and Mr. Hunter?"

Her eyes widened slightly, the temper flashed in her eyes, and then her face hardened into a cold mask. "At the moment, there are several walls and the space of roughly thirty yards between Mr. Hunter and myself."

"Don't play games, Evie." He felt his hands ball into fists. "I watched you last night."

"Watched me *what*, precisely?"

"Flirt."

Flirt?

Evie didn't mind jealousy from McAlistair. In fact, she quite liked the idea—it was a first for her, after all. She did not, however, care for the accusation that her behavior had been the cause. She'd much prefer a general sort of jealously—the kind she'd seen Whit and Alex exhibit when another gentleman glanced too long in their wives' directions. That was rather sweet.

This was rather insulting.

"Do you think I hopped from your bed to his?" she asked in a cool, soft voice.

"I . . ." He had the grace to grimace a little. "No. No, I don't."

That was something, anyway. "Do you think me *capable* of—"

"No."

"Then I fail to see why you're angry with me."

A muscle worked in his jaw. "He's a rake."

She gestured impatiently at the door. "Well, go lecture him, then."

He scowled—or continued to scowl, to be precise—and then clasped his hands behind his back in a supremely dignified sort of way that reminded her of Whit.

"I don't like that he touched you," he said.

Her heart softened at the reluctant embarrassment in his voice. "That he patted my hand, do you mean?"

"Was there something else?"

"No," she quickly assured him. "It was only a consolatory gesture, McAlistair. He was being kind."

"He was being . . ."

He trailed off, and she saw the uncertainty, the frustration . . . Wasn't that marvelous? she thought suddenly. Oh, not that he was unhappy, of course, or at least not *entirely*—he did look rather adorable at the moment—but that she could actually *tell* that he was unhappy. He'd grown more at ease with expressing his emotions, and she more adept understanding them.

"Would it help," she asked softly, "if I were to tell you that my interest in Mr. Hunter stems from *his* interest in Kate?"

He considered that. "It might . . . Does it?"

"Yes." When he said nothing, merely grunted in a non-committal, perhaps-I'll-give-it-some-thought sort of way, she gathered her courage and stepped closer. "I was disappointed when you left the room."

Again, the grunt.

She reached up to finger one of the buttons on his waistcoat. "I nearly paid for the distraction with my king."

His lips twitched. "Did you?"

"Mm-hm." Her eyes caught on his mouth. She did so

dearly love the way he expressed himself with that mouth—
the half smiles, the subtle frowns, the heated kisses. She
stepped closer, until she was pressed against him. Slowly,
she stood on tiptoe, letting her breasts brush his chest. "I do
believe you owe me a—"

He hauled her into his arms and sealed his mouth over
hers. Evie let herself fall into the excitement of the kiss, allowed herself to revel in the feel and taste of him. But she
knew it couldn't last.

"Mrs. Summers," she breathed when he broke the kiss to
trail his lips down the side of her neck.

"What?"

"She's in the parlor." Directly down the hall. "She could
come in."

He stilled, swore, and stepped away.

They stood there, breathless, staring at each other with
pounding hearts.

Suddenly, McAlistair grinned. "It was my turn to clean
the dishes this morning."

"Er . . . I see."

"Haven't got 'round to it yet."

"Oh, I see." And this time, she really did. "Would you
care for a bit of help?"

"Wouldn't mind."

She fought a bubble of laughter the entire way to the
kitchen, but gave up the fight the moment they were inside.
"This is outrageous."

McAlistair's answer was to back her against the wall and
begin where they'd left off in the library.

Her skin heated, her heart melted, and all thought spun
away.

Until a vaguely familiar and wholly unexpected male
voice said, "Well, isn't this a naughty bit of business?"

McAlistair swung around, throwing an arm up to keep

Evie from stepping out from the protection of his body. He needn't have bothered; she'd frozen in shock at the sound of the voice.

"Ah, ah, ah," it drawled from somewhere in front of McAlistair. "Keep your hands where I can see them, McAlistair. There we are. Now step away from the girl."

McAlistair didn't move.

"Step away, or I'll blow a hole through the both of you. I've heard a shot to the gut is Hell's own way to go. Would you like that for her?"

McAlistair's fury was palpable. He was standing perfectly still, just as he'd been at the blacksmith's, but the muscles of his back were bunched and strained. Tremors too small to be seen rippled along his skin. She could feel them through his waistcoat, where her hands rested beneath his shoulders.

She wanted to tell him it would be all right, almost as much as she wanted him to tell her the same—he was in a better position to know, after all.

Slowly, McAlistair stepped aside, giving Evie her first look at their assailant. His clothes bore the unsightly wrinkles and dust of travel and his usually tidy blond hair stuck out from his head in great tufts, but there was no denying, or mistaking, the handsome Byronlike features of John Herbert, the footman from Haldon Hall. Lizzy had pointed them out ad nauseam.

Her mind whirled with questions, but before she could open her mouth to speak, he turned cold blue eyes on her. "Miss Cole, if you would be so kind as to move a bit to your left?"

Moving left required she step in front of a small hutch against the wall. And that meant moving a step nearer to Herbert. "I . . ."

"Do as he says, Evie," McAlistair said softly.

Yes, well, that was rather easy for *him* to say. Battling every natural instinct to move away from the dueling pistol pointed at her, she stepped closer to Herbert. And saw the butt of a second pistol protruding from his coat pocket.

"Not too close, my dear, just enough to make McAlistair think twice about reaching for that gun in his pocket. Excellent. Now then . . ."

He turned his full attention to McAlistair and grinned— an excited, almost giddy show of teeth that twisted his handsome features into a gruesome mask. "So, there he is, the very devil himself. Oh, I've dreamt of this moment. Imagined everything I would do. Everything I would say. But now that it's come, I find I'm quite overwhelmed." He rubbed his free hand against his thigh. "Let me see, let me see, where was I to begin? Ah, yes . . . Do you have any idea, any idea *at all*, how difficult a thing it is to find you?"

When McAlistair said nothing, Herbert looked him over as if he were studying a rare and fascinating specimen under glass. "How did you manage it? Even when we were in the same bloody house, I couldn't find you. Just that glimpse before you left and I . . . You don't know who I am, do you?"

McAlistair shook his head once, his eyes never leaving the crazed footman.

"She does." Herbert turned that wide, maniacal smile at Evie, and her blood ran cold as ice. "Don't you, girl? Tell him."

"John Herbert." Her voice came out soft and wavering. "He's a f-footman at Haldon."

He waved the gun at her, the smile disappearing in a heartbeat. "It is Mr. Herbert. *Mister*. There was a time I could have bought and sold you twice over."

Gone were the politely modulated tones he had used at

Haldon. Even more than his words, the hard edge of Herbert's voice portrayed a raw and deep-seated hatred.

Her hands flew up, palms out. Fear shot through her, but only a small part of it was for herself. "I beg your pardon. I d-didn't know."

"No. No, you didn't. You couldn't." He cocked his head at her, his tone turning conversational. "And do you know *why* you couldn't have known?"

Evie shook her head.

Herbert grinned again and this time spun to aim the gun at McAlistair. "He does."

McAlistair didn't move, didn't so much as bat an eyelash. Evie ruthlessly shoved down the urge to step forward and speak, to draw John Herbert's attention back to her. She'd do it without a second thought if she knew for certain he wouldn't just shoot both of them. Two dueling pistols. Two shots. He could manage it if he were quick.

Herbert's grin morphed into an angry sneer. Keeping his eyes on McAlistair, he swung his arm around to point the gun at Evie. "You've thirty seconds, you bastard. Thirty seconds to remember Mr. John Herbert before I blow her brains—"

"He was an agent for the war department," McAlistair said, cutting him off.

"He was more than just an agent," Herbert snapped. "He was a man of power and wealth and rank. He was courageous and bold. He was brilliant. The sort of man a common criminal like you couldn't hope to begin to understand."

"He was your father," McAlistair guessed.

"He was a *hero*. He sacrificed his time, his money, the happiness of his own family, again and again, in service to the Crown. And how did the Crown repay him?" When

McAlistair didn't answer, Herbert swung the gun at him again. "Tell her how the Crown repaid him!"

"He was killed. Ten years ago."

"Nine! It was nine years!" Herbert laughed suddenly, a razor-sharp sound that tore from his throat. "Have there been so many, McAlistair, that you so easily lose track?"

"It was a long time ago."

"It was bloody yesterday." Herbert stopped laughing, sighed, and closed his eyes. It was just for a moment, but that moment had Evie tensing, itching to reach out and snag the gun in his hand, knock him down before he could reach for the second. Failing that last part, she could at least be certain he only had the one gun. Just the one bullet. And if he was battling her, there was no doubt he wouldn't waste it on McAlistair.

She flicked her gaze to McAlistair and saw the slight but decisive shake of his head. It was an order. *Don't.* She might have ignored it, but for his eyes. He stared at her, unblinking, his dark gaze holding a thousand terrors. They didn't demand. They begged.

Though it cost her, she stood where she was and watched Herbert once again raise his lids.

"It was yesterday to me. I can still hear him whispering to my mother in the dark. He knew you were coming. He wasn't afraid of you," Herbert was quick to insist. "But he feared for my mother and me."

"I never killed an innocent."

"My father was innocent," Herbert snapped. "An innocent man who made a mistake."

"He made a choice. That choice netted him a substantial amount of money. And cost the lives of half a dozen good men."

"He made a *mistake.* How was he to know what the information was to be used for?"

"He knew."

"Did you ask him?" Herbert demanded. "Did you give him a chance to explain before you slit his throat? Did you?"

McAlistair shook his head.

"Well, then," Herbert's mouth curled up in a sneer, "it would appear I am the better man."

Slit his throat? Evie looked from one man to the other. Had Herbert's father been a soldier for the French? Had he met McAlistair on a battlefield? That would make sense, but how would he have known it was to happen? Why would he fear for his wife and child? "I don't understand—"

"You'll speak when spoken to," Herbert snapped without looking at her. "I've things to say to McAlistair." He took a deep breath, as if steadying himself. "I spent years looking for you. Years hunting down every damn McAlistair I could find." He laughed suddenly. "Would've bloody helped to learn earlier you spell it differently than most. Do you know how *cold* it is in Scotland? Sogging lot of McAlistairs there too. I was tempted to kill a few on the off chance they might be related. But then, I'd have been no better than you, would I? No worse, but no better."

McAlistair said nothing.

Herbert shrugged. "But even the most obscure rumors eventually reach that godforsaken country. I left the moment I heard of the mysterious McAlistair, Hermit of Haldon Hall. I assume a man like you found eating insects and picking vermin quite a step up in life?" He chuckled a little at the jab before continuing. "And *still*, even after taking a position at Haldon, I couldn't find you. It didn't help matters," he snapped suddenly, swiveling his head to glare at Evie, "to have so little time off."

"I . . ." Was she expected to say something? "I'm terribly sorry?"

Herbert snorted and turned back to McAlistair. "By the time I discovered your little cabin, you were gone. *Gone.*" He groaned and laughed at the same time. "Have you any idea how *aggravating* that was? To search so long, to come so close?" He shook his head as if dismissing the memory. "Luring you into the open remained the only avenue left to me. And you, my dear," he said with a quick, almost appreciative glance at Evie. "You provided me with the perfect means. All it took was one glimpse of the veiled lady creeping back into her room in the dead of night to spark my interest and a quick peek in your little desk to discover what you were about."

Evie's stomach twisted. Her ledger, her drafts of letters to newspapers and government officials. Yes, it would have been easy to figure out what she was doing by picking the lock on her desk.

"You used her," McAlistair growled.

"Speaking again, are we?" Herbert jeered. He shrugged. "As I said, it was the only avenue left to me. The staff could talk of little else but how you'd come out of hiding to help Lord Thurston save his pretty wife. How brave. How daring. How romantic." He smirked. "How very convenient for me. One threat and you came running to Haldon. One shot at Miss Cole and you came running to the beach. It was indulgent of me, I know, but I needed to see you fear, just once see you fear the way my father did."

"She's an innocent."

The sneer returned, colored by a hint of amusement. "Doubtful, given what I just walked in on. Now, as enjoyable as this interlude is—and it is *immensely* enjoyable—I fear it's time for its inevitable conclusion. Your friend outside will realize the trail he's following is a false one sooner or later. McAlistair, if you've a final word—"

"You sabotaged the carriage," Evie said quickly. She

knew she risked bringing on his wrath, but she had to do something, and since Herbert had taken every opportunity to brag, stalling him with a question seemed the best way to purchase time.

Herbert waved his hand about in false modesty. "A simple enough thing. Hadn't expected you to run off to Suffolk, mind you, or for you to push forward so quickly after your little accident. But I had a bit of luck breaking into Thurston's desk. Needed coin for the trip, you know, and what should I find but these lovely dears," he waggled one gun and patted the other, "and a letter from Mrs. Summers detailing the accident and mentioning your progress to Suffolk. I left that very hour. It being my half day off, I imagine I made it all the way to Cambridgeshire before I was missed. Now then, no more questions, I'm afraid. I'm quite out of time."

He lifted the gun and took square aim at McAlistair.

Terrified, desperate, and unable to think of another question, Evie did the only thing that came to mind.

She fainted.

Much to Evie's dismay, it quickly became apparent that executing a proper swoon really *was* something a person ought to practice a time or two before attempting in public.

It was also best left to those with a soft chair or large settee at their disposal.

She hit her knee against the table leg on the way down, bent her knees in what had to have been an obvious ploy to soften her fall, and had she not thrown out her arm at the last second, would have cracked her head soundly against the wood floor.

Fortunately, form, grace, even believability, had not been Evie's ultimate goals. She wanted a distraction, and *that* she accomplished quite well.

Herbert laughed, and from slitted lids, Evie saw his feet turn toward her.

Then he swore, and there was a flash of tangled arms and legs as McAlistair lunged into Herbert, sending them both crashing to the ground.

She scrambled up to her hands and knees, and heard herself cry out in terror when the gun went off. But the bullet flew wide, shattering a glass platter on a shelf behind McAlistair.

The struggle lasted only a moment, just long enough for Evie to crawl over and snatch the pistol that had fallen from Herbert's pocket and gone skittering across the floor. And just long enough for McAlistair to land one hard punch to Herbert's jaw, rendering her newly obtained weapon unnecessary.

Herbert was out cold.

She remained where she was, shivering and panting, while hideous visions of McAlistair dying before her eyes danced through her head.

Not dead, she told herself firmly, raking her eyes over his crouching form.

He's not dead.

"You're all right," she heard herself whisper raggedly. "You're all right."

"Are you hurt?" McAlistair demanded.

Her lungs felt too small, her knee throbbed like the very devil, and her heart was pounding hard enough to qualify as torture. She shook her head, tossed the gun aside, and scrambled over to throw herself around him.

She was shaking uncontrollably and knew her attempts to bring him near were awkward and clumsy. She didn't care. She couldn't help it. Burying her head in his shoulder, she grasped at his back, his shoulders, his waist.

McAlistair crooned in her ear, "Shh. Easy, sweetheart. You're safe. You're safe now."

She struggled against him. He wasn't close enough. She couldn't bring him close enough. And he wasn't helping. He'd only put one arm around her shoulders in a half embrace.

"Hold me," she pleaded.

A low groan rumbled through his chest. *"Evie."*

"Hold—"

"Sweetheart. My arm."

She unwound herself from him in a trice, her eyes jumping to his left arm. He was holding it protectively at his side, and blood had begun to seep through his upper sleeve, turning the green fabric a horrifying dark brown.

Fear, thick black waves of it, swamped her. He was bleeding. He'd been shot. He could die.

"No," she heard herself say. "No, it hit the platter."

"Caught me first. But it's—"

She wasn't listening. She flew to her feet, the pain of her knee forgotten, and snatched a clean rag from the table. Dropping down beside him, she pressed it to his wound. Tears gathered and fell as the white cloth turned crimson.

"I need more rags."

"Evie, sweetheart. It's only a scratch. I'll be all—"

"It's not a scratch," she choked out on a hiccup. In her mind, it was an enormous gaping wound, and it was bleeding rivers of blood. "You need to lie down. You need a physician. You need—"

"Bleeding's slowed."

She blinked, hiccupped again, and looked at the cloth. He was right; the flow of blood had diminished.

Letting out a tremulous breath, she dashed tears away with the back of her hand. "You still need a physician."

"Right now I need some rope for Herbert."

Sniffling, Evie drew back a little to look down at the still-unconscious footman. She noticed for the first time that her knee was wedged solidly into Herbert's side.

Good.

"There should be some rope or twine about." McAlistair said. "I need you to find it."

"Yes, yes, of course." The quicker Herbert was tied up, the quicker she could find help.

Before she had the chance to stand, Mr. Hunter came charging into the room, half dressed and wielding a gun. Mrs. Summers followed directly behind him, a large silver candlestick at the ready. She took one look at the scene before her and, tossing the candlestick aside, dropped to her knees beside Evie. "Evie! Are you hurt? Are you—"

"No. McAlistair."

McAlistair shook his head at Mr. Hunter's and Mrs. Summers's concerned glances. "Just a scratch. Bleeding's nearly stopped."

"It's not a bloody scratch," Evie berated. But there was no edge to her tone. Relief had taken it away. It *wasn't* a mere a scratch—the man wouldn't move his arm, for pity's sake—but it no longer looked to be life-threatening, either. "It needs to be seen to."

"Mr. Hunter can look at it, after we've taken care of Herbert."

"Who the blazes is Herbert?" Mr. Hunter demanded.

"John Herbert." Evie accepted Mrs. Summers's assistance in standing. "A footman at Haldon. He . . . I . . ."

"Herbert's grievance was with me," McAlistair told the group. "Mr. Hunter, get me some rope. Mrs. Summers, take Evie upstairs."

Mrs. Summers slipped an arm around her shoulder and coaxed her toward the door. "Come along, dear."

"But—"

"Pour a bit of brandy in her," Mr. Hunter suggested.

"I don't need brandy. I—" I need McAlistair, she thought.

But her protests went ignored and in short order she found herself bustled out of the room.

❋ *Twenty-eight* ❋

*W*ith his arm aching like the devil, McAlistair paced the hallway outside the library. It was an unusual behavior for him, pacing, and one he found fairly lowering. He wasn't in the habit of indulging in nervous movement. But though he had tried, he couldn't seem to sit still. The inner calm he'd relied on for years had abandoned him, leaving him a bundle of nerves and energy.

Not wholly unexpected, he supposed, when a man was working through the details of a marriage proposal.

But still irritating.

And absurd. He hadn't a thing to be nervous about. His plan was sound, his reasoning infallible. Evie would marry him.

He had come to the decision only minutes earlier, while he, Christian, and Mr. Hunter had draped a bound and newly conscious Herbert over the back of a horse. The man had ranted and raved, promising one revenge after another. That was only to be expected, and McAlistair might have simply ignored the noise if Herbert had limited his threats to him. But the footman had had quite a lot to say about Evie as well . . . until Christian had stuffed a gag in his mouth, anyway.

McAlistair stopped pacing just long enough to drag a hand down his face.

It was *his* fault. The threatening letter, the carriage accident, the attempt on Evie's life—all of it was because of him. Evie had been no more than a pawn in a man's quest for vengeance. Bloody hell, if it hadn't been for him, she would have spent the week safely at Haldon, comfortably going about doing . . . whatever it was she did at Haldon.

Scowling, McAlistair walked to the door to stare at it without seeing.

It was exactly what Evie *did* do when she wasn't embroiled in someone else's vengeful scheme that had propelled him to decide on marriage. The woman didn't spend her days balancing ledgers and rowing out on the lake. She spent at least some of her time thumbing her nose at violent men. True, at the moment she did so in secret, but how long would she be content with that? How long before someone else broke into her writing desk?

She was rash by nature and too overconfident by half.

He remembered, yet again, that horrible moment when he had been certain she would throw herself in front of Herbert's gun. She never would have reached him in time to keep him from firing. She simply wasn't fast enough. The act would have killed her. And yet she would have tried.

He'd never felt so sick, so horrified, so utterly helpless as he had in that moment. Not even when he'd heard the shot on the beach or seen her fighting the blacksmith's apprentice or disappearing beneath the water of the pond, or . . .

Bloody hell, the woman was in perpetual peril—half of it of her own doing.

And between the danger he'd put her in and the danger *she* courted, Evie's future safety looked fairly bleak.

Well, he could do something about that.

He could protect her. He *would* protect her. From herself and from whatever ghosts from his past sought to punish him through her. But to do so, he needed to be close to her, not hidden away in a remote cabin. And being close required marriage. There was nothing else for it.

She might not be amenable to the idea of becoming his wife—and he, admittedly, was no longer amenable to the idea of her becoming someone else's wife—but she could be made to see reason. Or he could drag her in front of a vicar, kicking and swearing. Either way, he wasn't letting her out of his sight again.

Resolute, he pushed his way through the library door.

Evie stood next to the fireplace, a blanket wrapped around her shoulders and Mrs. Summers at her side.

"I want a moment with Evie, alone."

Mrs. Summers merely winged up one brow. "Do you, indeed?"

"Please," McAlistair added begrudgingly.

Mrs. Summers pursed her lips but nodded. "I shall be just down the hall."

He waited impatiently for Mrs. Summers to leave. When she finally did, he stepped to Evie, and wrapping his strong arm around her, pressed his face to her neck and simply breathed her in.

Evie burrowed into him. "Your arm? You're all right?"

"I'll be fine." He set aside nerves and anger, and let himself savor the feel of Evie, safe and warm against him. He ran his hand up her back, into her hair, down her shoulders. "Mr. Hunter bandaged it for me. He and Christian have taken Herbert to the magistrate in Charplins."

She nodded, her cheek brushing against his chest. "It's over then."

No, not over, he thought, pulling away. Not quite yet.

★ ★ ★

Evie started a little at McAlistair's sudden withdrawal.

"Is something the matter?" she asked hesitantly, pulling the blanket closer around her.

His answer was to give her a hard, penetrating glare, then turning to pace the length of the room.

"Are . . . Are you angry with me?"

"Yes. No." He stopped pacing. "Yes."

"Well, if you're certain," she said unsteadily, hoping to tease him out of his mood.

He stepped closer to her and pinned her with one very unamused stare. "You were going to step in front of that gun."

"Hardly necessary, as he was already aiming at me a good deal of the—"

"You know bloody well that's not what I mean!"

Evie's felt her eyes turn to saucers at McAlistair's bellow. She watched, torn between feeling awful and fascinated, as he stormed to one end of the room and stormed back. He muttered, ran a hand through his hair once, twice, *three* times, until the majority of his dark locks slipped free from their tie and fell across his face—a face that held none of the cool assurance to which she was so accustomed. There were deep furrows across his brow, a muscle working in his jaw, and his lips—when they weren't muttering—were peeled back in something akin to a snarl.

Misery lost to fascination, and to relief that he should show so much vigor so soon after being shot. Good Lord, the man was *furious*. She hadn't expected that, hadn't even once considered the possibility that he was capable of such a temper.

Oddly enough, the knowledge that he was, and that he lost that temper because she'd thought to place herself in danger, made her feel stronger, even calm.

He stopped and stabbed a finger at her. "You were going to try for the gun. When his eyes closed. You were going to try."

"Yes." Remembering, she felt her stomach roll in a queasy circle. Perhaps not entirely calm, she amended, perhaps just better.

"What the bloody hell were you thinking?"

"That I was closer."

The snarl grew more pronounced.

"Well, I was." Really, what did the man expect her to say?

He jabbed a finger at her. "You're rash, impetuous, hard-headed, and reckless."

She pursed her lips, thought about that, and decided she preferred the description over gentle, delicate, and naive. "I can live with that. Although——"

"You'll marry me."

"——I don't . . ." She immediately forgot what she was about to say. "I'm sorry, what was that?"

"You'll marry me."

Suspicion bloomed alongside hope. "Will I? Will I, really?"

"Unless you care to live in sin?" he inquired in a derisive tone.

"Not particularly."

"Then we marry. I can't protect you if we're in separate houses, and you need looking after."

Hope and suspicion were swallowed by absolute shock. *"Looking after?"*

"Yes, you——"

"That wasn't a request for clarification," she snapped. "It was a statement of disbelief." Accompanied by a healthy dose of insult. "I most certainly do not need looking after. Furthermore——"

"Your connection to me is no longer secret. That in itself puts you in a precarious situation. In addition, you work for a dangerous cause. You visit the worst slums of London." He jabbed his finger at her yet again. "There will be no more of that. You can find other ways of helping those women."

She tossed her blanket aside. "How dare—"

"You sneak out of your home to sleep alone in the woods. You kiss strange men in those woods—"

"Man," she corrected. "One man. *You.*"

"You thought to wrestle a gun from a lunatic."

"I didn't *want* to. And you *did*—"

"You gave your innocence to a near stranger."

"A hermit, a soldier, and the man I love, you arrogant, heartless *arse.*"

He visually started at that, and for a moment, it looked as if he might relent, but then he shook his head, as if shaking off her words. "You're being foolish—"

"Don't! Don't you dare tell me what I'm being. What I am. *Who* I am. I've had enough of that from you. More than enough."

"Evie—"

She didn't wait for the remainder of his sentence, couldn't think of any reason she should. With tears of anger burning her eyes, she left the parlor at a run, intent on making it safely to her room, where she could fall apart in private.

He called for her again, at the bottom of the stairs just as she reached the top. But she didn't turn around.

And he didn't come after her.

McAlistair watched her go.

That hadn't gone quite as he had planned.

He took hold of the banister and climbed the first step

with the intention of following her. They'd have this out. She would listen until—

He winced when the door slammed hard enough to rattle his teeth.

Perhaps he'd wait until she'd settled, he decided, and stepped back down again.

She'd come around. She just needed time. He could give her that while they were at the cottage, and on the return trip to Haldon. Safety wasn't such a concern at present, not with Herbert gone, and with Evie miles away from the work that put her in danger.

It would be best if he let her be for now—gave her the opportunity to see the sense in what he'd said.

And give himself the opportunity to come to grips with what she had said.

The man I love.

Holy hell.

He spun on his heel and headed straight to the study. From there, he headed directly to the sideboard. He rarely drank. In fact, he could count on one hand the number of times he'd indulged in the last eight years. Nearly all of them, he realized grimly as he poured himself a finger of brandy, had occurred in the last week.

The man I love.

He added more to the glass.

She couldn't mean it. She couldn't possibly love a man who'd been nothing to her only months, possibly only weeks, ago. A man whose sins had put her life at risk. That had been his initial, albeit in part irrational, reaction—she didn't *know* all his sins, did she?—the moment the words left her mouth, followed shortly thereafter by the single most brilliant pang of joy he had ever known.

Evie wouldn't say the words unless she meant them. It wasn't in her nature to lie. Well, yes, he amended, it was in her nature to lie, but not about *that*. He was sure of it. She wasn't the sort to make a sport of something so important.

She *loved* him. Despite his reticence, despite his less-than-auspicious origins, despite all common sense, really, she loved him.

The man I love. Her voice echoed in his head. *You arrogant, heartless arse.*

He downed the glass in one long swallow.

If she bloody well loved him, she could bloody well marry him. What could be more natural?

Admittedly, a woman in love might have hoped for a proposal with a bit more romance. But how the devil was he to have known she was in love?

She complained of *his* reticence. He snorted—actually snorted—and considered pouring another glass. She hadn't said a word about love. Not a single word.

If she had, he might have broached the idea of marriage a little differently. He might have tried to appeal to her heart rather than her head.

She would just have to live with it, he decided in another burst of temper. In fact, she should be thrilled for it. What was wrong with having appealed to her head—to her sense of reason—as he would have a man's? Isn't that what she'd harped on about in the past? Women not being respected for their minds?

It damn well was.

He slammed the glass down on the counter and strode from the room.

He was going to his bedroom. Then he was going to pack his things for tomorrow's journey back to Haldon. Then he was going to wait.

Evie could bloody well come to him.

★ ★ ★

Evie could not recall a time in her life when she'd ever indulged in such a fit of violent temper. It could be assumed that she'd had her moments as a small child, but as an adult, she preferred the simplicity of a few choice curses followed by a short period of brooding. Nothing too dramatic.

But right now, right at this very moment, she wanted to break something. Pick it up, dash it against the wall, and watch it shatter into a million little shards. Then she wanted to do it again. She wanted to scream, to lash out, to destroy something.

She stood in the middle of her room, seething with a rage that could find no outlet. Making a loud fuss would only bring members of the house rushing to see what was the matter.

And there was nothing in the room she could break, because nothing in the damn room belonged to her. She dearly wished there was something in it that belonged to McAlistair. Something expensive and fragile. Like her heart.

Frustrated beyond measure, she stalked to the bed, picked up a pillow, and hurled it against the wall. The soft and wholly unsatisfying thump it made only served to infuriate her further.

"Argh."

After a moment's hesitation, she picked up another pillow and tossed it as well. It was, she decided, marginally better than nothing.

"Need keeping, do I?" she fumed between gritted teeth. *"Keeping?"* She tossed the next pillow. "Like a child, or a *pet?"*

She hurled the last. "Bloody *keeping?"*

She couldn't believe, quite simply could not wrap her head around the fact that he'd had the gall to use such a monstrously insulting phrase. There was little else the man could have said that would have infuriated her so effectively . . . or cut her more deeply.

She felt the sting of that wound now, as the worst of her temper began to ease in small increments.

With a sound that was half growl and half sob, she sat heavily on the edge of the bed.

Hadn't he come to know her *at all?*

Didn't he love her even a little?

The sting grew into a heavy ache in her chest. She pressed at it with the heel of her hand, as if she could rub it away as McAlistair had rubbed away the pain in her leg.

Exhausted and heartbroken, she crawled on top of the bed, curled into a ball, and wished she had a pillow to cry on.

❈ *Twenty-nine* ❈

*E*vie slipped into a fitful sleep and woke to the late-afternoon light barely seeping through the wool curtains.

She could open those now, she thought dully, and rose stiffly from the bed.

After letting in the meager light, she straightened her appearance, replaced the pillows on the bed, and then, finding herself with nothing left to do, sat back down.

She felt drained to her very core, completely hollowed out . . . except for her head, which felt stuffy . . . and her neck, which had a substantial kink in it . . . and her knee, which still throbbed from its encounter with the kitchen table. But the *rest* of her felt empty, as if someone had reached inside and torn out her heart.

It was almost amazing, she thought without feeling the

least bit amazed, how one could be numb and yet hurt unbearably at the same time.

It was similarly odd that one could feel ill and hungry at the same time. But then, she'd had very little to eat all day, and while her appetite might occasionally suffer some from nerves and anger, it was never quelled for long. She hadn't gained her curvy figure by skipping meals.

Resigned to filling her grumbling stomach, she headed downstairs, careful to keep an eye out for McAlistair. She wasn't ready yet to see him, let alone speak with him—not while she was surrounded by what she assumed was expensive artwork and knew to be fragile vases.

She was careful to keep her foray into the kitchen brief. The room held unpleasant memories now, too fresh to linger over food choices. She grabbed an apple—a convenient and inexpensive projectile, should she run into McAlistair—and headed back upstairs.

She was at the foot of the main staircase when the front door swung open with a crash.

Heart in her throat, Evie spun around to see the Duchess of Rockeforte come stumbling in. Short of breath, wearing a wrinkled and dusty traveling gown, and with her dark hair escaping in large sections from her bonnet, she looked positively wild.

Evie gaped at her. *"Sophie?"*

Sophie ran forward to throw her arms around her. "Evie. You're safe."

"Yes, I—" She returned the embrace. "What are you doing here? Has something happened?" A horrible thought occurred to her. Mirabelle, Whit's wife, was expecting. "Mirabelle. The baby. Has something happened to—"

"No. No." Sophie drew back, but gripped Evie's shoulders. "It's John Herbert," she panted. "The footman from Haldon."

"John Herbert?" Alternately relieved, baffled, and alarmed, Evie shook her head. "I don't understand. Did he escape?"

"Escape?" Sophie blinked. "From Haldon?"

"Haldon? What? No, from Christian and Mr. Hunter."

"Christian? Mr. Hunter?" Sophie dropped her hands. "We're a set of parrots. What are you talking about?"

"John Herbert. He was here this morning. Christian and Mr. Hunter have taken him to the local magistrate. What are you talking about?"

"Absolutely nothing of relevance, apparently." Sophie laughed suddenly. "We'd come to inform you of John Herbert's treachery."

"We?"

"I came with Alex, Whit, and Kate." Blowing out a long breath, and looking calmer for it, Sophie searched out a chair next to the hall side table and sat down heavily. "We came as soon as Herbert's absence was noticed."

"Oh." Evie still felt utterly lost. "Well, that was very . . . er . . . loyal of you. I'm surprised Alex allowed it."

"He didn't." Sophie shrugged. "I came anyway."

"Ah." She looked in the direction of the still-open door. "Where is he? And the others?"

"A minute or two back." She stretched out her legs with a grimace. "We raced the last two miles. Well, Kate and I did. Alex and Whit were checking their map and left somewhat unawares."

"You left them *behind?*"

"Unfortunately, they gave chase soon enough," Sophie replied. "They've been the worst of traveling companions. Arguing for the first half of the journey and lecturing for the second."

Evie looked warily at the front door again, expecting a storming pair of men at any moment. "I suppose Whit is no more pleased with Kate at present than Alex is with you."

"They are a mite put out," Sophie admitted, without, Evie noticed, the slightest hint of regret. "As is Lady—"

Sophie broke off as Lady Kate Cole entered through the front door, looking much as Sophie had only a minute before, her pale blonde hair mostly loose from its pins, and her wide blue eyes bright with worry.

"Evie! You're all right!"

"I'm perfectly well," Evie insisted, even as Kate flew into her arms.

Keeping a tight hold on her friend, Kate threw a look over her shoulder at Sophie. An easy maneuver, as Kate was several inches taller than Evie. "Did you tell her? Does she know about John—"

"She knows," Sophie cut in. "She knew already."

Kate drew back, a line appearing across her brow. "What? How?"

Sophie untied the ribbons of her bonnet. "Mr. Herbert made an appearance several hours ago and was subsequently apprehended."

Unless Evie was much mistaken, Kate's shoulders slumped a little. "It's done then? It's over?"

"You needn't sound disappointed," Evie pointed out.

"I'm not, I , . ." Kate drew back and made a face. "Well, yes, I am. Just a little. I rather fancied the idea of riding to your rescue."

"The effort is noted and appreciated," Evie drawled.

Kate snorted, but her eyes danced with humor. "I missed Miss Willory's birthday celebration for this."

Evie smirked. Miss Willory was one of Kate's least favorite people. One of her own, as well. "I am so terribly sorry."

"And my mother is *supremely* irritated with me."

"You disobeyed Lady Thurston by coming?" The very idea was bewildering. "Kate—"

"No lectures, I beg you. I've had my fill."

"You'll make room for more," a cool voice said from the front door.

Whit entered, looking travel-worn and more than just "a mite put out," as Sophie had phrased it. He shut the door carefully behind him, sent one cold, hard look at Kate and Sophie that promised retribution of a most grievous nature, and then stepped forward to place a kiss on Evie's cheek.

"Evie, you're well?"

She'd never been so miserable. "Perfectly."

Whit nodded and pulled off his gloves. "Fetch the others, if you would. I'm sure Kate and Sophie have taken it upon themselves to inform you of our news."

"It *is* why we came," Sophie pointed out.

"And it hardly matters now, at any rate," Kate added. "It's over. We've come too late."

Evie rolled her eyes at the overly dramatic statement.

Whit went still. "Too late? Herbert was here?"

"This morning," Evie confirmed, and wondered if she would have to explain yet again when Alex arrived. "Christian and Mr. Hunter have taken him—"

Whit swore viciously even as concern, and just a hint of fear, crossed his face. He cupped her chin in his hand, his eyes searching. "You're not hurt? He didn't hurt you?"

"I'm perfectly well," she repeated. "We all are."

He looked at her a moment longer before dropping his hand and enveloping her in a hard embrace. "I'm sorry I wasn't here," he said hoarsely.

Touched, as she always was by his unfailing loyalty, she blinked back tears and returned the embrace. "I'm quite well, Whit, honestly. You can't be everywhere at once."

"I should have been here. It is my responsibility to see to the safety of my family." He looked around her to glare at Kate. "Though some would do their best to make that task impossible."

Kate sent Evie an exaggerated look of sympathy. "Pay him no mind. It's not your fault John Herbert is a lunatic."

Whit let go of Evie to jab a finger at Kate. He opened his mouth to deliver what would no doubt be a blistering response, but the sound of the front door once again swinging open cut him off.

Alex, the Duke of Rockeforte, marched in. In the past, Evie had thought Alex's tousled coffee-colored locks gave him a somewhat boyish air. That thought didn't occur to her at present. Just now, he looked to her to be very much a grown duke—a tall, dark, and furious duke. "Whose bloody idea was it to race?"

Sophie smiled brightly at her husband. "It was a joint decision."

"It sure as hell wasn't a group one," he growled.

"Well, it couldn't have been," Sophie argued reasonably. "You'd have said no."

"You're damn right I would have," Alex snapped and either didn't hear, or chose to ignore, Sophie's mumblings about the annoyance of poor losers. Instead, he turned to Evie and looked her over. "You're well?"

Evie managed, barely, to swallow a groan. "I'm entirely unharmed and John Herbert is on his way to the magistrate."

"He's been caught?" His face brightened as he stepped forward to plant a kiss on Evie's cheek. "Excellent. How?"

"He made an appearance this morning. Perhaps we should wait until Christian and Mr. Hunter return for a full recounting. I'm certain you have questions for them as well."

Alex and Whit nodded.

"If that's settled," Sophie commented, "I should like to find Mrs. Summers. Perhaps—"

"The issue of your impromptu race has not been settled," Alex interrupted in a cool tone. "It was reckless. You could have been injured."

"Can we have this lecture somewhere with more seating?" Kate inquired. "Sophie has the only chair in the hall."

Whit glared at his sister. "You'd be a sight more uncomfortable if you'd taken a spill from your horse."

"I have *never* fallen from a horse," Kate said with some indignation. Several pairs of brows rose at that statement. "I have never fallen from a *moving* horse," she clarified with a sniff. "I may be clumsy, but I am hardly a danger to myself, generally."

"Kate is a fine horsewoman," Sophie said loyally. "We both are, and we have engaged in a number of races in the past without mishap." Her eyes briefly jumped to Kate. "Significant mishap," she amended.

"Racing across familiar terrain is not—"

Alex broke off at the sound of Mrs. Summers's voice coming from farther down the hall. "Good heavens. What is all this?"

Evie poked her head around Whit's shoulders. "We've visitors."

A round of greetings followed, and then another when Christian arrived. It was a great mass of noise and movement, as bows and handshakes and embraces were exchanged. Sophie held on to Mrs. Summers for an extended period of time, Kate answered questions on the progression of their journey, and Evie sidled up next to Whit to whisper in his ear.

"Handle your wife and sister, can you?" she asked, reminding him of his pronouncement the morning she'd left Haldon.

"Mirabelle's not here, is she?" Whit pointed out.

Evie doubted Mirabelle had been foolish enough to consider riding cross-country in her condition. "I'm sure convincing her to stay was a great trial."

Whit pretended not to hear her. "Where's Mr. Hunter?" he asked Christian.

Christian jerked his head toward that back of the house. "Cleaning a bit of dirt from his boots. I expect we arrived from the north not three minutes after you came from the east."

"Two minutes for the ladies," Sophie corrected.

Alex narrowed his eyes. "What if Herbert had been here? What if something had happened to both of us? Where would that have left our son?"

Sophie stood and stretched out the kinks in her back. "I imagine you should have thought of that before insisting you come along."

When a low growl emitted from Alex's throat, Mrs. Summers stepped between them. "Would anyone care for a spot of tea in the parlor?"

The answer to that question was delayed by the sudden appearance of McAlistair.

And just as Evie had feared, the sight of him turned her inside out. She felt her fingernails dig into the apple she'd almost forgotten she was holding, and she might very well have winged it at his handsome head if others hadn't been present. Because the temptation still remained, she turned her attention to Sophie and Kate, who, unfortunately, had their attention turned to McAlistair.

Sophie dipped in a quick curtsy upon their introduction. Kate, on the other hand, had lived with the legend of the hermit McAlistair for a third of her life without having ever seen him. She indulged in a moment of gaping and then a long and obvious perusal of his person.

"The Hermit of Haldon Hall," she breathed, fascination evident in every syllable. "I could scarcely believe it when Mirabelle told me you were real."

"I've been telling you for nearly a decade," Whit pointed out.

"Yes, but you're my brother," she said dismissively.

"And?"

"Brothers lie." She ignored Whit's grumbling and offered McAlistair a sunny smile. "I am delighted to finally make your acquaintance."

Eventually, tea was prepared and consumed in the parlor, and the story of John Herbert's plan for revenge summarized and discussed. Though there were still questions Evie would have liked to ask McAlistair about some of the things Herbert had said, she found she wasn't quite interested *enough* to speak to McAlistair directly. Not yet.

She answered the questions of others instead, drank her tea and ate her apple, and then excused herself from the early dinner Mrs. Summers suggested, pleading nerves after the trying day.

In retrospect, it hadn't been a very clever excuse for her exit. No one who knew her well was likely to believe she'd succumbed to a fit of nerves, and so she wasn't terribly surprised when a knock sounded at her door an hour later.

Though she knew it to be foolish, a small part of her couldn't help but hope, just for a moment, that it might be McAlistair.

It was Kate, holding a plate of cold meat and cheese. The early dinner, Evie surmised.

Without bothering to wait for an invitation, Kate swept past Evie into the room, took a seat on the bed, and shoved the plate at Evie. "Sit, eat, and tell me what's happened."

Left with no other choice, Evie took the plate, but set it on the nearby desk. "You know what happened. John Herbert—"

"Oh, devil take John Herbert. What's the matter with you?"

"A run-in with a murderer isn't enough?"

"He didn't murder anyone—"

"That we know of."

"From the sound of it, a man like that would have bragged. And that's beside the point. You don't suffer from *nerves.*" Kate accented the last with a roll of her eyes.

"Well, I might. I—" Evie gave up the fight and sat down heavily next to Kate on the bed. "Oh, all right. It's McAlistair."

"What about him?"

"I'm in love with him." Oh, it hurt just to say.

Kate's face expressed shock for a moment before it brightened. She gave one long, dramatic sigh. "Oh, that's lovely."

"It certainly is not."

"Is so," Kate countered in the silly way only sisters can manage. "I should dearly love to fall in love with someone."

"You were in love with Lord Martin not three years ago," Evie reminded her. "And look what that got you."

"It got me my first kiss," Kate countered. "And I rather doubt I was in love with him. In retrospect, I believe I merely had a long-standing *tendre* for him."

Evie couldn't think of anything else to say but, "You told me he kissed like a fish drowning on land."

"He does, or did, which is why I no longer have a *tendre* for him." She scooted a little closer. "Have you kissed McAlistair?"

And a great deal more. "Yes."

"And?"

Sophie's appearance at the door kept Evie from responding.

"What's all this?" Sophie asked.

"Evie's in love with McAlistair."

"Kate!"

"Well, you are, and you would have told her."

True and true. "You could have given me the opportunity to do so for myself."

Completely unrepentant, Kate leaned over to deliver a kind pat to her knee. "I'll leave it to you to tell Mirabelle."

"Thank you so much."

Sophie sat down on the other side of Evie with a dreamy sigh. "Hmm. McAlistair. He's a fine one to look at, isn't he? All that dark and broody . . ." She waved her hand about. ". . . what have you."

That statement was met with wide-eyed silence. Sophie blinked at her friends. "What?"

"You're married," Kate said. "Happily married."

Sophie studied the gold band on her finger. "Oddly enough, it hasn't struck me blind as of yet." When the other women only continued to stare—Kate in a fascinated sort of way, and Evie with a slightly suspicious scowl—Sophie laughed and dropped her hand. "A happily married woman can appreciate a handsome man without being attracted to him. I suppose you'll discover that for yourself soon enough," she added to Evie.

Though her scowl remained in place, suspicion was replaced by misery and frustration. "Not if things continue to progress as they have been," she grumbled. "He told me . . . he told me I need *keeping.*"

The pouring of outrage that followed went a very long way toward soothing Evie's pride. She suspected some of the outrage was a direct result of—and perhaps targeted at—Whit and Alex's own brand of keeping for the last two days, but a shared indignation only added to the sense of camaraderie.

The three spent the next hour sharing Evie's tray of food and condemning all men for their monstrous arrogance.

It was most satisfying.

And it was most disappointing when Kate announced it was time for her to seek an early bed. Evie couldn't imagine trying to sleep at present, and she certainly didn't care for the idea of sitting up alone without the laughter of her friends to distract her from the ache in her heart.

But she couldn't ask Kate to stay. Not when she'd ridden all this way only to learn she'd be turning around and riding all the way back the next day.

"I suppose you must be exhausted," Evie commented to Sophie when Kate had gone.

"Rather. But I wished to discuss something with you before I find my own bed." She cleared her throat and gave Evie a hard look. "I was downstairs in the parlor with Mrs. Summers just now, and she told me the single most unbelievably, outrageously, ridiculous thing."

"Oh, dear."

"Matchmaking, Evie?" Sophie huffed out a breath. "Honestly."

"Well, it's not as far-fetched as all that."

"It's more. However did you come up with such an implausible theory?"

"Implaus—" She gaped, simply gaped. "I heard them, with my own ears, discussing the death-bed promise to Rockeforte, the threatening letter they would send, my intended rescuer—"

"The promise?" Sophie started at little. "You know of it? All of it?"

"Yes . . . well, nearly all."

"Oh." She blinked rapidly for a moment. "And you heard them plotting to send you a letter like the one you received, and a gentleman to rescue—"

"Yes."

"Oh," Sophie repeated and turned narrowed eyes in the general direction of the parlor. "She neglected to mention that bit."

It wasn't a *bit;* it was the whole bloody thing. "What *did* she tell you?"

Sophie had the grace to wince. "Only that you'd taken it into your head that the whole affair was nothing more than a ruse to see you matched. She never quite got around to mentioning why."

"You could have asked."

"Yes, well." Sophie fidgeted a little. "Questioning her doesn't come naturally to me."

"You're a duchess," Evie pointed out.

"But she was my governess. Also, she gets that look. You must know the one I mean. With the haughty brows and . . ." Sophie titled her chin up and stared down at Evie. "Not quite an accurate impression, I'll grant you. I haven't the nose for it. But—"

"I know the one you mean," Evie admitted with a small laugh. "Lady Thurston has a similar expression."

"Doesn't she just? Though Kate seems to be less affected by it of late." She dismissed that last thought with a shake of her head. "I *am* sorry for the hasty judgment, Evie."

"No harm done." She slipped an arm over Sophie's shoulders for a brief hug. "Although, if you were to explain why a deathbed promise to Rockeforte required I make a trip to the altar, it would go a very long way to appeasing my indignation."

Sophie laughed and scooted back on the bed to rest comfortably against the headboard. "It's a simple enough, if ridiculous, matter. William Fletcher promised—or was tricked into promising, to hear him tell it—into seeing that each of you found love."

"Each of—"

"Alex, Mirabelle, Whit, yourself, and Kate. The story goes, he considered all of you the children of his heart."

"Did he?" With nothing else to occupy her hands, Evie found herself picking idly at the bedspread. "I barely knew the man."

"Hardly follows that he shouldn't have known you."

"Yes, I suppose, but . . . it seems so odd, really. I . . ." She trailed off, uncertain what to say.

"You would have been a small girl when he died, correct? Only just come from your mother's home?"

Evie nodded.

"I should think that a child's perception is very different from an adult's." Sophie tilted her head. "Do you love Henry?"

"Your son? Of course, how can you ask—?"

"For the purpose of illustration. What if you were not to see him again for twenty years? Would you love him still?"

"With all my heart."

"And yet he might have no idea who you are," Sophie said softly.

"I . . . that's true. Dreadfully maudlin but true." She picked at the bedspread a moment longer. "He loved me."

"Like a father."

"A father." It was a tremendous revelation that a man, a good man, had loved her as a daughter. Loved her well enough that he had thought of her, of her happiness, on his very deathbed. Suddenly, the matchmaking ruse seemed not at all silly. Rather, it seemed a priceless gift.

"Whit has told me he was the best of men," she said quietly.

"Alex tells me he was the best of fathers."

It would seem that he had been.

The return journey to Haldon might have been an enjoyable experience for Evie. The weather remained fine, she had a comfortable carriage from Charplins to ride in, and Kate, Sophie, and Mrs. Summers to keep her company. But despite these luxuries, Evie was hard-pressed to find any real pleasure in the journey.

She exchanged no more than a few words in passing with McAlistair for the entire trip. She asked after his wound. He assured her it didn't trouble him. She offered a seat in the carriage should he tire, but he declined. He rode beside the carriage, was distantly polite during their stops, and took meals in his room at the inn.

It was maddening to have him so near but not be able to speak to him or touch him or shove him off his horse.

Bloody "keeping."

She waited for him to apologize. Waited for him to admit he was wrong and make amends.

She waited for him to give her some sign that he respected her, that he trusted her, that he *loved* her.

But in the end, he simply left her on the front steps of Haldon, surrounded by her friends and family and staff.

He bowed just once. "If you need me, Whit knows where to find me."

Then he remounted his horse and rode away.

❊ Thirty ❊

 𝒮he would come today.

Hands clasped behind his back, jaw set, and a line of worry etched across his brow, McAlistair stared out the front window of what might *loosely* be called his front parlor and told himself what he had been telling himself for the last four days.

Evie would come today.

He was certain of it. Why else would he have cleaned the cabin from top to bottom? Why else would he have furnished it with an actual bed and settee and dishes? She would want those things. She would need them while they lived in the cabin and waited for their new house to be built.

Wouldn't she?

"Bloody hell."

He spun away from the window, tired of looking out at the narrow drive and seeing only trees and dirt. He couldn't stand the wait anymore. He couldn't stand the *silence*.

She had ruined that for him, he thought darkly. She had taken away the pleasure of solitude. It had been a refuge for him. It had been peaceful and restorative.

Now it seemed only empty.

He took up pacing the small room in a show of nerves that had recently become routine rather than exceptional.

He needed to hear her voice, damn it. He needed to see her smile, hear her laugh, taste her lips. He needed to touch her, to breathe her in . . .

It would be lemons and mint. He bit back a groan at that recurring thought. Now that she was back at Haldon with her own things, she would once again smell and taste of lemons and mint.

The idea of it was driving him mad. He'd woken up every damn night since returning, certain he could smell that intoxicating combination. And every damn time he had lain awake afterward wondering about her, worrying over her, missing her.

Was she safe? Was she happy? Did she miss him? Or had William and the others introduced her to some arrogant, pinched-faced dandy who played chess nightly and read poetry with an affected lisp?

"To hell with that." He stormed over to the front door, yanked his overcoat off a hook on the wall, and strode outside. "To bloody hell with that."

He could play chess, damn it. Maybe not as well as Mr. Hunter, but he could play. He could read poetry too, if that's what she needed. He could . . . well, no, he wasn't going to fake a lisp. But he could damn well do everything else.

Anything else, if it meant she'd come back to him . . . even find the words to admit he'd been wrong. That he'd acted out of fear. That he wanted her as his wife for every reason but the one he'd hurled at her. That he'd been a coward.

The ride to Haldon took no more than ten minutes, but that was long enough for McAlistair to lash down his temper and come up with a plan.

He would do things right this time. Nothing would be left to chance. Evie would have no reason to turn him away again . . . unless she no longer loved him.

Refusing to dwell on that fear, he left Rose in the stable and, desiring privacy for the first part of his plan, once again let himself in a side door of Haldon without being seen.

He wasn't surprised to find Whit in his study, the door open, and his head bent over a stack of papers. When it came to running his estates, the man was as predictable as clockwork.

"I want to talk to you."

Whit started in his chair. "Devil take it, man. Can't you learn to knock?"

"Yes."

Whit snorted and set down his pen. He gestured toward a chair in front of the desk. "You might as well have a seat. Care for a drink?"

"Yes. No." Damn it, he'd never had trouble making up his mind before. "Yes."

Whit eyed him speculatively—as well he might—but said nothing as he retrieved two glasses of brandy. He handed McAlistair one and resumed his seat. "Right then, what's on your mind?"

"I've come to ask after Evie." He'd come to ask *for* Evie, but he figured a man was allowed a bit of nerves in a moment such as this.

"Evie?" Whit set his drink down, a furrow appearing in his brow. "Chit's been moping about the house for days."

Pleasure warred with worry and guilt. "She happen to tell you why?"

"The girl won't tell me anything other than that, as a member of the male species, I deserve to be slowly roasted on a thick spit over an open flame. I'd say that safely rules out any lingering distress from her trip to the coast. In fact, I'd venture to assume there's a gentleman involved except, well, Evie's *never* had a particularly high opinion of men. And she's been with the lot of you for the last week."

McAlistair steeled himself for the worst and met Whit's eyes. "Yes. She has."

Whit was too astute to miss what was *not* being said. His

expression went from baffled to black in the space of a heartbeat. "Do I need to call you out?"

"Your choice. I want to take her as my wife."

"That's not what I asked you." Whit rose from his chair. "Did you touch her?"

"Evie is a woman grown."

"She is my cousin, unmarried, and under my care," Whit snapped.

"And what was Mirabelle?"

Whit's lips compressed into a thin line. McAlistair could practically hear the internal debate between defending his wife's honor and retaining his own by telling the truth. It had to be hell on a man like Whit.

Apparently deciding that discretion really was the better part of valor, Whit sat back down, but his expression remained hard. "The fact that I may or may not be guilty of a similar transgression does not absolve you of—"

"I'm in love with her."

It was a moment before Whit responded, and when he did, it was with a much softer and much more worried expression. "I see."

"I've been in love with her for years."

"You hardly knew her until just recently."

"I know," McAlistair replied with just a hint of wryness. "But I loved her."

"I see," Whit repeated. "And has she made her feelings known to you?"

"Yes. No." *Damn* it. "In part."

"That sounds something less than promising."

"She said she loved me."

Whit's expression brightened. "Well, then—"

"Then referred to me as an arrogant, heartless arse."

"Ah." Whit's lips curved up in a knowing smile. "Does

create something of a problem. Any particular reason she's put out with you?"

"I spoke of marriage."

"Again, less than promising."

"When I say 'spoke,' I mean 'demanded.'"

"You demanded marriage?"

"More or less." He shoved aside the urge to wince. "Mostly more."

"Placing demands on Evie is the most likely way to ensure the least amount of cooperation. Demanding marriage from Evie is doubly—"

"I'm aware of it," McAlistair cut in. "What I need to know is if I have leave to make things right with her."

"Leave?"

The urge to wince now required a harder shove. "I am asking for permission to court your cousin."

"But not to marry her?" Whit asked in a cool tone.

"I'd like to do things in the proper order this time."

"Bit bloody late for that. The proper order now is marriage. And you'll offer it, properly, as you put it, today."

"She deserves a courtship—" He cut himself off as the meaning behind Whit's words filtered through the rising temper. "You really want us to marry."

"Have I left that in doubt?"

"I was uncertain you would agree to the match."

"Why wouldn't I? You love her and will treat her well, there seems to exist the possibility she loves you in return, and—" Whit's expression caught somewhere between sympathetic and amused—"to be honest, I can't make any promises where her treatment of you is concerned. I suspect she'll drive you half mad at least once a week."

A small bloom of hope settled in his chest. He tried not to let it grow. "You know what I've been."

Whit nodded once. "Yes, and I know what you are now."

"It could hurt your family, to have your cousin attached to the Hermit of Haldon Hall."

"I don't think so. You're not the first man from a good family to become a hermit."

"Name one," McAlistair dared.

"Mr. John Harris." Whit sat back in his chair. "He has spent the better part of the last century in a cave after his parents refused to allow him to marry the woman he loved. Brought his manservant along, if I'm not mistaken."

"You made that up."

Whit shook his head.

"His manservant." The hope grew until it manifested in a smile. "Really?"

"Mr. Harris was good enough to give him his own cave."

"I'll be damned."

"Not if you convince Evie to marry you," Whit said darkly. "Otherwise, yes."

Still smiling, McAlistair nodded and rose from his chair.

"You should speak to my mother about this," Whit added. "She's in the parlor."

McAlistair felt a moment of raw panic. "Lady Thurston? You want me to confess all to Lady Thurston?"

Whit made a face. "I would consider it a personal favor if you were to refrain from confessing all to my mother. She's not one for the vapors, but that conversation just might do it." He picked up a pen from his desk and tapped it thoughtfully. "I think she would find it touching if you sought her approval of the match."

"Of course." He should have thought of that himself.

Whit stopped tapping the pen to give him a pointed look. "I think Evie would as well."

"Yes, of—" He broke off, again, and for the first time in days, actually grinned. "That's good. That's brilliant."

Because she was a woman, Lady Thurston's agreement was not considered necessary. In fact, in the eyes of society, her opinion need not be sought at all. It was just the sort of inequality Evie despised. And knowing McAlistair had given Lady Thurston the respect afforded any senior male member of a family might be just the thing to soften Evie's heart.

He would have paid that respect, anyway—at least, he would have once Whit pointed it out—but there was no reason not to enjoy the added benefit of impressing the woman he loved.

He turned to leave again, only to be stopped short of the door.

"McAlistair?"

"What?" He was in a hurry to leave.

"If you can't convince Evie to have you, I won't call you out."

"Yes, fine."

"But I will make your life a living hell."

"I . . . fair enough."

Though the idea of speaking to Lady Thurston was, in fact, brilliant, the execution of that idea was a trifle harder to appreciate. The conversation was distinctly uncomfortable. Fortunately, it was also decidedly brief. After a moment of well-hidden, but nonetheless perceivable surprise and pleasure, she settled into the business of finances and prospects. They were topics he had ready answers for. He had ample money saved from his days in the war department. Mr. Hunter had handled his investments successfully. He planned to take Evie to his cottage while he built a modest home not far from Haldon.

She adamantly refused to hear of Evie living in the hunting cabin, but relented on her position that the two of them reside at Haldon until their new home was built. She even smiled when they reached a compromise—McAlistair would let and build a house near Benton. But her smile dimmed a little when next she spoke.

"I shall be frank, Mr. McAlistair. You are not what I would have chosen for my niece."

He kept his gaze steady and unapologetic. "Yes, I know."

"I had someone a bit . . . softer in mind. An academic or a poet."

"I understand." He didn't really. Bloody hell, a soft-spoken, nose-in-a-book, milquetoast for Evie? She'd run roughshod over him in a fortnight and leave both of them miserable. It seemed wiser, however, to say he understood than to say anything that began with "bloody hell."

Lady Thurston sighed. "That choice, I think, would have been a mistake."

It bloody well would have been.

She tilted her head at him. "Do you love her?"

"I've been in love with her for nearly eight years," he admitted.

"Eight?" Lady Thurston gaped at him. He wouldn't have thought her the sort of woman who gaped, but there it was. "Eight years? And you are only now getting around to doing something about it?"

"Apparently."

"Well, for heaven's sake." She rose from her chair. "I shall fetch her from her room immediately. Eight years," she breathed again as she headed toward the door. "Honestly."

He waited for Evie with something approximating patience for twenty minutes.

Twenty excruciatingly long minutes of pacing the parlor, eyeing the decanter of brandy, picking up and studying feminine little bits and pieces in which he hadn't the slightest interest.

Would Evie want to fill their home with such things?

"Do you have a fondness for rosebud vases, Mr. McAlistair?"

He set the vase down and turned slowly.

There she was. And there was that sweet pang he felt every time he saw her.

She was so heart-wrenchingly beautiful . . . and she looked so terrifyingly resolved. He could see it in the stiff posture of her small frame and the way she kept her chocolate eyes shuttered—she'd given up on him.

"Have I come too late, Evie?"

Please, God, don't let it be too late.

Only a slight widening of the eyes told him the question had taken her aback. "Too late for what?"

"For you."

She twisted her lips and stepped into the room. "Is this another demand of marriage?"

"No." He forced a breath into a chest gone tight. "It is a request to court."

He had the small pleasure of seeing her stop in her tracks. "To court?"

"If you would allow it," he answered with a nod. "I have obtained your cousin's approval and your aunt's."

"Lady Thurston?" She sat down heavily on the settee. "You asked Lady Thurston's permission to court me?"

"Yes. If you—" He swallowed hard. "If you could find it in yourself to forgive me for my earlier . . . stupidity."

Very well, it wasn't the most eloquent of speeches, but it was effective. Her expression softened—just a little about the eyes and mouth, but it was enough to give him hope.

"McAlistair—"

She cut off when he held up his hand to plead for silence. "Before you make a decision, any decision, you should be aware of who I am. Who I was."

"Who you were?"

He nodded and placed his hands behind his back where she couldn't see them curl into tight fists. "You have asked me of my past, of my days as a soldier."

"Yes," she said with a small, careful nod.

"I . . . I was not a soldier, not in the traditional sense." He cleared his throat. "I was responsible for discharging certain individuals whose immediate and silent removal was vital for the safety of our country."

"You . . ." Her face scrunched up as she deciphered that convoluted—and well-rehearsed—bit of information. "You killed people?"

He could barely hear himself speak over the hard pounding of his heart. The truth now, he told himself, she deserved the truth. "I was an assassin."

Her hand flew to her chest. "An . . . You . . . I don't know what to say to that."

He wanted to go to her. He had an almost painful urge to wrap his arms around her, to bind her to him long enough for the chance to explain, to plead his case. But he feared her resistance, her rejection, as strongly as he desired her touch. So he settled for walking to the door, turning the key in the lock, and dropping the key in his pocket.

She watched him with an eyebrow cocked. "Why would you do that?"

He walked back to stand before her and thought his words through before speaking.

"I have tried to keep you at arm's length for this very reason. I warned you that I was not meant for you. You refused to listen."

"If you were so very certain of it, why did you . . ." Two spots of pink rose high on her cheeks. "Why did we—"

"I am only a man. We made love because I wanted you, beyond reason. I proposed . . . because I love you."

Her shock was evident, and painful to see—why hadn't he had the courage to tell her before now?—but he pushed forward before she could speak—or perhaps it would be more accurate to say he stumbled forward. It was so damnably hard to find to find the right words.

"I . . . I never thought you could . . ." No, that wasn't right. It hadn't been a resistance on her part. "I thought perhaps you shouldn't . . ." No, pointing out why she *shouldn't* was a terrible idea. He blew out a frustrated breath and tried again. "I was resigned, almost, to not having you. But you . . . you changed things. You gave me . . . things." Oh, bloody hell. "You made me laugh. You gave me hope. And love."

He looked down at his hand, flexed his fingers. "It is one thing to . . . to not reach for what you desire. It is another to let what you have . . . what you *love*, go without a fight." His gaze came up to settle resolutely on hers. "I'll not let you go without a fight. You'll listen to what I have to say." Suddenly remembering that his high-handed tactics were in part responsible for his current groveling, he added a belated, and somewhat anticlimactic, "Please."

It was clear by her serene expression that sometime during his spectacularly dreadful speech, Evie had gotten over her shock. She stared at him in silence for a moment, then cocked her head to the side, and asked, "Do you know what I find troublesome?"

Did the woman want a list?

She didn't wait for his response. "That you should claim to love a woman in whom you have so little faith."

He started at the accusation. "I have every faith—"

"Then why insult me?" she demanded. "Why imply the love I've offered you is so weak, so fickle, that I would toss it and you aside because of a murky time in your past? And without even allowing you a word in defense?"

It was a trifle more than "murky," as she so delicately put it, and he had no defense to speak of, but McAlistair knew better than to argue against himself. "My apologies."

"Accepted." She held out her hand expectantly.

Though it cost him to do so, he fished the key out of his pocket and handed it to her. He watched, a little baffled, as she simply palmed the key.

"Aren't you going to unlock the door?" he asked.

"No, I want to finish this."

"What happened to trust and—"

"I'm not the one in the habit of hiding away."

He might have been annoyed at the sentiment if he hadn't seen the corners of her lips twitch. She was teasing him.

He took a seat next to her and took her hand to press a kiss into her palm. "I don't deserve what I intend to keep."

She smiled a little and closed her hand as if to keep the kiss. "Whether or not you have me and whether or not you're deserving is still up for debate. I believe you were telling me what sort of soldier you were."

He nodded and sat back, but he kept hold of her hand.

"I worked for William Fletcher, for the War Department. I accepted missions to . . . to . . ."

"Assassinate," she prompted.

He nodded. "Yes, but only those whose actions endangered the lives of our own men—spies and traitors. Those who couldn't be brought to trial because of their rank, or because they were not British, or because of information they would reveal."

"John Herbert's father?"

"A prominent member of the War Department," he said. "He sold a list of agent names to the French. Several of those agents paid for his betrayal with their lives. I didn't kill at random, Evie, or for money. I was paid, I wouldn't have you think otherwise, but I didn't kill for money. I believed in what I was doing."

"I see." Evie stared at their joined hands. The idea of executing a man without a trial troubled her deeply. The fact that every soldier who fired a shot on a battlefield did essentially the same thing was cold comfort.

"War is a dark and ugly business," she murmured.

"It is, yes." He gripped her hand tighter. "And it is easy . . . too easy, for a young man to grow comfortable in that darkness. After a time, it is easy to forget it is another life taken."

"Is that why you stopped?" she asked, looking up. "Why you wouldn't tell me of this?"

There was a long pause before he said, "I failed in a mission. I killed the wrong man."

Her heart contracted painfully in her chest. "You . . ."

"That surprises you."

"I . . . yes," she admitted. "It shouldn't, I suppose. You're only human, after all, and humans make mistakes. But when that mistake results in the death of an innocent man—"

"It wasn't a mistake," he corrected, his voice growing cold. "Not in the sense you mean. And he wasn't innocent."

"I don't understand."

He nodded, but it was a moment more before he spoke. "You asked earlier if the Burnetts had ever been found."

She shook her head, clearly confused by the jump in topic. "You said no."

"I lied."

McAlistair steeled himself against the hurt in Evie eyes. The truth, he reminded himself. All of it.

"I found him. In the very house of a man I'd been sent to silence. He was living under an assumed name and working, of all things, as a tutor."

She made a sound of disgust.

Perversely, he found comfort in her reaction. "My target was having a house party—"

"You were going to sneak in and kill a man during a house party?"

"No, I wanted a lay of the building—the rooms, where the staff slept, that sort of thing. I charmed an invitation."

Later he would sneak in and kill him.

"It was night. The guests were drinking champagne in the ballroom." Bought, he remembered, at the cost of four good lives. "I checked on the children, saw they were asleep, the governess next, and then the tutor." His jaw clenched. "He was awake still, at his desk, his door open." The sickness and anger had boiled up in him and spilled over. "He hadn't seen me. I could have walked away, come back, and completed my mission."

"But you didn't."

"No. I didn't." He thought of the sleeping children. And he remembered that hard, dark shelf. "I killed him. I compromised the mission for personal revenge and walked away."

She was quiet for a long moment. "I don't suppose I want to know how."

He'd slit his throat in one long, clean slice. "No."

"Are you sorry for it?"

"Not as sorry as I should be."

"You condemn yourself for this," she said softly. "Do you look for me to condemn you, as well?"

"I—"

"Because I'll not. I'll not offer condemnation for doing what you thought was right." She lifted a hand to his face. "I love you. The man you are today and the man I think you will be in time to come. I can't offer anything but that."

It was enough. It was more than enough. It was his every dream come true. "You'll not regret this. I swear to you—"

"A moment, if you please." She held up her hand. "There is still the matter of my needing *keeping*."

He winced. "I apologized for that."

"In a roundabout sort of way," she allowed. "And I accept that apology. But how am I to know it won't happen again? How—"

He'd known she would ask. "When do you next go to meet a woman in Benton?"

She started at that non sequitur. "What? Why?"

"I would prefer . . . I would *much* prefer you allow me to be a part of what you do. But . . ." He steeled himself for what he was about to offer. "If you ask it of me, I will give you my word that I will not follow, defend, or assist you in any way."

She pursed her lips thoughtfully. "You told me once before that I wasn't to trust your word."

He hadn't a sound argument against that, but he tried to find one anyway. "I wanted to push—"

"That will have to change once you're a member of the Cole family."

"Beg your pardon?"

"Coles keep their words. As my husband, you will be expected to—"

She cut off when he laughed and stepped forward to sweep her off the settee and into his arms.

"Your wound," she gasped.

"It's fine." He hadn't thought of it in days. "You're in earnest? You'll marry me?"

"Are *you* in earnest? Do you love me? Because—"

"I've loved you for eight years."

"—that's all I needed to . . . *Eight?*"

"I've loved you since the first time I heard you laugh."

"Oh . . . well . . ." She gave a perfunctory smile. "That's nice."

His mouth quirked with amusement. "But?"

"It's nothing. It's only . . . it's only that . . . I wouldn't have minded if you'd fallen in love at the first sight of me . . . fallen in love with the way I look."

"Ah, well, I didn't." He bent his head slowly to hers. "I fell into lust."

Her mouth curved into a smile right before he took it in a long, lingering kiss.

There it was, lemons and mint. He followed the taste of it across her jaw.

Her voice sounded tremulously in his ear. "McAlistair?"

He caught the lobe of her ear between his teeth, making her gasp. "Hmm?"

"I . . ." She sighed heavily as he trailed hot kisses down the side of her neck. "I . . . the wedding. About the wedding . . ." She sighed again. "The vows."

He brushed his lips across her collarbone. "Yes?"

"I'll promise to always love you. And—" His tongue darted out to taste the hollow at the base of her neck. "Oh, my."

"Always love me," he prompted.

"Yes, and . . . and always honor you."

"Mm-hm."

"And obey you on those occasions when I am in agreement with—"

Evie broke off at the hard puff of breath against her neck. McAlistair's shoulders began to shake with suppressed laughter. "Evie. Sweetheart." He lifted his head and took her face in his hands. "It would be my great misfortune to be saddled with a gentle, delicate, naive wife. Just give me the promise of love."

She grinned, lifted her hands to frame his face in turn, and pressed her lips to his. "You have it."

SHIRL HENKE

The Cheyenne Seer

Since childhood the amber-eyed, red prairie wolf has filled Fawn's dreams. After being educated in the white world, she returns to the Cheyenne to guide them with her medicine dreams.

The Red Wolf

With his cunning and his Colt, Jack Dillon has become a feared lawman. But he faces his toughest job ever when he agrees to protect Fawn and her people from the scum trying to steal their land.

The Grand Design

When Fawn meets the amber-eyed, russet-haired Irishman, she is both infuriated by his cocky self-confidence and irresistibly drawn to his charismatic charm. He is the wolf totem of her dreams who holds the key to unlocking her visionary powers. Together they can save her people, if only he chooses to love the...

CHOSEN WOMAN

ISBN 13: 978-0-8439-6248-2